Mayhem and Mischief Most Foul

Mayhem and Mischief Most Foul

By
Scharlie R. Martin

iUniverse, Inc.
New York   Bloomington

Mayhem and Mischief Most Foul

iUniverse books may be ordered through booksellers or by contacting:

iUniverse
1663 Liberty Drive
Bloomington, IN 47403
www.iuniverse.com
1-800-Authors (1-800-288-4677)

Because of the dynamic nature of the Internet, any Web addresses or links contained in this book may have changed since publication and may no longer be valid. The views expressed in this work are solely those of the author and do not necessarily reflect the views of the publisher, and the publisher hereby disclaims any responsibility for them.

ISBN: 978-1-4401-4369-4 (sc)
ISBN: 978-1-4401-4370-0 (ebook)

Printed in the United States of America

iUniverse rev. date: 6/18/2009

This book is dedicated to all those children who start their lives full of exuberant promise and hope and for reasons totally beyond their control don't get to finish the adventure—one in particular, Marsh Lincoln will remain forever an enigma for me.

Prologue

When I was in the first grade, my parents moved us from a rented farm in Iowa to a farm they purchased in Minnesota. There were several things about our new home that were memorable. First of all, it was on the Crow Wing River and the fishing was good. One day in particular that I remember going fishing was the day President Truman announced the United States was dropping atomic bombs on Japan. I was so busy watching and waiting for the sky to turn into a great ball of fire that day I didn't pay enough attention to my bobber to catch any fish. Some time during that time frame I also remember sneaking off behind some bushes on the edge of the school playgrounds to play kissing games with a sweet little girl whose name I can't seem to remember.

I mention those two things because the major premise of this book is that we never know what kind of surprises life holds in store for us. We are all, each in our own way, greatly impacted by the memorable things that happen to us not only in our early years but throughout our lives, whether they be sweet or traumatic. Well, I didn't grow up to become a mad sex fiend or a mad bomber either, for that matter—but maybe that was just the *luck of the draw*.

Russell's Story

The reflection of the full moon lay on the water like a golden flapjack on a china plate; the syrupy ripple of the water's surface an infinitesimal whisper against the sides of the pool. The edges of the pool framed the image like the warm glow of a Terry Redlin print. In another time and another place and there might have been romance in the air—but not tonight. Tonight there was murder in the air.

Somewhere, a street or two away, a dog barked. Judging by the yapping tone, a small dog, one that would as soon sink its needle teeth into the back of your ankle as let you pick it up. Fortunately, the barking was probably an ordinary part of the cacophony of the evening. Otherwise Bud might have picked up his head, cocked an ear, raised a wrinkled Basenji brow, and started barking.

Russell thought about that for a moment. Not that Bud's barking would be a big deal. A couple of soft "Woof … woofs," not much more. He wasn't so much worried about that as he was about what those "Woof … woofs" might start with the other dogs in the neighborhood. That could be disaster.

Surveying the backyard moonscape, Russell sensed rather than saw that Bud was probably laying somewhere near the backdoor with his head resting on his forepaws, like always, ready to spring into action at a moment's notice. Bud was a good watchdog. He wasn't much worried about Bud's watchdog capabilities either.

Even at such a great distance from home, in this strange new place, Russell knew there was that old familiarity between them that would always be there between dog and master. If not for that, there'd be hell to pay. If he had been an intruding stranger, Bud wouldn't start barking. No, Basenjis don't exactly bark. Bud would start yodeling then, like some fool coyote revved up on locoweed, the way he always did when he heard a fire engine or police car siren. There'd be hell to pay then and Russell's world would come crashing down around him like a house of cards.

But that wasn't happening. Instead of calamity, there was this perfect silence. The city lights of Jacksonville forming an insulating bubble over Russell, dimming the stars; his thoughts blanking out the sounds of the city like earplugs, making him feel engulfed but strangely at ease. It was like being in a gigantic, accommodating cocoon the way Luisa's garage intersected with her house and the six-foot board fence, which jogged off at a right angle separating Luisa's yard from the neighbors'. There was just enough space between the gatepost and the fence so he could see perfectly the spot he needed to see. He was completely hidden in the shadows of the neighbor's scraggy pine tree with the moon providing just enough of a spotlight to illuminate the important part of the evening's stage with enough light to do what he needed to do.

Russell smiled a sinister smile at the irony of it. "Smoking is going to kill you," he'd told Maria once. He suspected that'd had a lot to do with her reasons for leaving him. He'd somehow managed to quit smoking his pipe *cold turkey* with complete ease. Whereas she'd spent weeks running around with a stupid looking fake cigarette hanging out of her mouth like some macho cowboy—until she'd finally declared victory.

The victory had been short lived. She'd come to visit him one week while he was doing temp work in Chicago. After a few days, he'd realized that she was going to the bathroom after every meal. It didn't take long to figure out what that was about and, sure enough, he'd found the cigarettes tucked away under the bathroom sink. Russell had thought the whole thing pretty silly. Apparently Maria had had a different view.

A car honked in the distance and Bud gave out a little "Woof" allowing Russell to quickly locate Bud's shadowy form between the chaise lounges at the end of the Luisa's pool near the backdoor. *Perfect!* It was good to know exactly where Bud was.

All things considered, it was a miracle the dog was still alive. The poor thing had had so many fatty tumors the vet had recommended he be put down. But Maria's mother loved the dog, so Maria had no qualms about laying out a thousand dollars to fix him. If Maria had cared that much about their relationship, the evening might not be going down the way it was.

At that point, Russell could have and definitely should have just stepped back out of the shadows and walked away down the street—but he was not thinking very clearly at that moment. In fact, he wasn't really thinking at all. If he had been, he would have been somewhere else entirely.

As it was, Russell didn't have long to wait. He was

barely secure in his position when he heard the soft squeak of the screen door hinge on Luisa's backdoor. He drew in a deep breath and held it. There was a momentary flash of light as Maria stepped out the backdoor. Bud raised his head for a few seconds and then let it sink back to rest on his paws as Maria lit her cigarette and blew a smoke ring, which Russell couldn't see but knew was there. It's what she always did.

Russell didn't rush the moment. It would not do to hurry. He knew he had to give his eyes a few seconds to adjust after the flashes of light from the door and the cigarette. Years ago he had stayed out after dark plowing on the Miller Creek bottom. His parents had yelled at him because the tractor didn't have lights. Something about the night air seemed to give the tractor extra power. It was contagious. "I could see fine," he'd told his parents, still reveling in the feeling of power. "The moon was real bright." Now, in the moonlight once again, that old feeling of power returned.

For just a second, Russell let his mind flash forward, wondering if Maria's sister Luisa would scream as loudly afterwards as she had that time the stupid cat tried to walk on the suspended ceiling and fell into the bed she was using in their basement. *Served Luisa right. Snotty little bitch!*

Dismissing the thought, he raised the bow and sucked in another deep breath. *At such a short distance, it would be almost impossible to miss.*

That was another thing. Maria was the one who'd set up a bale of straw in the backyard and taken up bow shooting—served her right, thinking she always had to out do every man she came in contact with.

Russell wasn't sure, but he thought he heard the bow give out a small groan as he pulled back on the arrow. The release was a gentle "whooshing" sigh.

Bud's reaction was perfect. The thud of the arrow brought Bud to his feet with a puzzled frown that Russell could only feel rather than see. As Maria toppled backwards, Bud moved quickly toward her, his head cocked dramatically to one side as he tried to figure out what was going on. *Was this a new kind of game?*

The biggest thing now was not to panic. Russell held his breath again for a long minute and tried to assess sounds around him. *Was there anything different?* Back home there would be the country sounds of frogs and crickets and what not hammering away at the silence of the night. But here in the big city it was mostly the drone of cars and honking horns.

Good, Bud's former master thought, satisfied that his world wasn't going to come crashing down around him. He slipped one end of the bow under his jacket and pulled his jacket against his body to make the bow less visible, then stepped back out of the shadows and started toward his car. *Hopefully, the damned dog wouldn't start licking up the blood.*

...

"Wouldn't it be nice," Captain Dugan of the Florida Highway Patrol suggested, smiling at young Lyle Peterson, the patrol officer who had taken the report, "if people would stick around long enough to be a witness?"

"Be different," Peterson nodded, returning his Captain's smile.

"People don't realize," Captain Dugan continued,

"how difficult policing these interstate freeways can be … it's bam, bam, thank you ma'm and the perp's gone. These motorcycle guys are probably three states away by now."

It was a bit of an exaggeration but Peterson knew exactly what Captain Dugan was talking about. He raised his patrolman's hat and ran his puffy hand over the blond stubble of his crewcut. For a young couple to go to sleep in an open convertible in front of a rest stop on a major U. S. freeway was certainly asking for trouble. Then, for the woman to just leave her purse lying out in the open. Pretty damned tempting for some one coasting by on a motorcycle. If it hadn't been for the lady coming out of the bathroom at just the right moment to let them know what had happened, the woman probably wouldn't even have missed her purse until she was halfway home—and there would be no witnesses at all.

Not that the witness was much help. By the time these young people woke up enough to absorb what the lady was telling them and found a phone to call the highway patrol, the thieves were long gone. The witness had also claimed there was a guy in a blue Escort parked next to the convertible, but he took off before she'd thought to get his license plate number. Not that it mattered. Thousands of people a day passed through these rest stops. The odds that this guy in the Escort had seen anything and would be willing to talk about it were pretty small. Even if he did see anything, he probably wouldn't want to get involved.

Who could blame him? He could be five hundred … maybe even a thousand miles or more from home with business of his own to attend to. Being a good citizen in

Scharlie R. Martin

your own neighborhood was one thing, carrying it out on a nationwide basis quite another. Of course, they could put out an "all points" bulletin. But why bother. There were plenty of older, light blue two-door Escorts on the road yet, and without a plate number....

"Didn't see a thing," the guy would just claim.

...

Patrolman Peterson was right about that—Russell wasn't about to claim he'd seen anything. He wasn't about to claim he'd even been in the area. In fact, it would be best if no one even knew he was in Florida.

The entire trip was pure impulse, although Russell had been thinking about it for quite some time. The day before yesterday he had driven from his home in north central Minnesota to Menomonie, Wisconsin for his weekly corporate tax class. The class ran from 1:00 to 5:00 O'clock in the afternoon. By 5:28 p.m., Russell was gobbling down a burger as he barreled down Interstate 94 heading towards Eau Claire, Wisconsin and points beyond. Twenty-four hours later he found himself in Jacksonville, Florida with just a few catnaps at rest stops.

Which was how he became a crime witness shortly before graduating to *perp*.

Now, all Russell had to do was *get the hell out of dodge before the nasty old sheriff could track him down!* Except now, just minutes after his descent into lunacy, he had this horrible nagging feeling he wasn't quite finished—that there was something else he desperately needed to do to deflect suspicion away from his obvious candidacy as "the *perp*" in the eyes of the police. They always zeroed in on ex-husbands, or in his case, the soon to be ex-

9

husband. Only now, feelings of regret were beginning to overshadow his impulsive actions.

His choice of weapon had certainly been impulsive.

Most of the people Russell knew, including Maria, unless they knew his full life story, would never suspect he even knew how to shoot a bow. He had Vietnam and Green Beret Sgt. Vincent Ortega to thank for that. And after all this time, no one was ever going to connect an ex-Air Force supply sergeant with an Army Green Beret, who was probably dead by now anyway. Bringing in bow and arrows for Ortega to use on night raids had seemed like a good idea at the time. And practicing on his own had helped Russell wile away some long *in-country* afternoons. No one would ever suspect he had been in training to kill someone with a bow and arrow or otherwise … not even Russell.

The actual reality of what he'd just done still had not registered. For one thing, he hadn't had more than a couple of half-hour catnaps and a few pitiful hours of fitful sleep in the past sixty plus hours—and it was hard to call any of that real sleep. For another, the Escort did not have air conditioning and with the coastal heat and humidity he was feeling a lot like a cooked goose. And then there was the traffic.

Jacksonville was a maddening city. It seemed like the traffic never let up and everything had to be funneled over the bridges. He'd never been in a city with so many damned bridges. It was one thing he'd never expected about Florida—the strange intracoastal waterways winding their way along the coastline like meandering rivers. Didn't seem to make any geographic sense.

Crossing the Dames Point Bridge over the St. Johns

River (he could never remember the official name of the bridge—something to do with Napoleon) with its big inverted cable arches always made him think of McDonald's golden arches and it made him hungry. It seemed crazy, but somehow he was pretty sure it was Luisa's love of this bridge that had helped her persuade Maria to pack up and move to Florida with her.

Russell resisted the urge to get something to eat, crossed the bridge and wound his way north, not paying too much attention to where he was going. He wasn't even sure exactly what he was looking for. Intuitively, he knew he had to do something to take some of the focus off Maria. With just one corpse, the police would be after her ex- ... or soon to be ex-husband like blue-tick hounds after a coon. Except now, since she would no longer be able to sign the papers, the divorce wasn't going to happen. *Now, he'd be the unlucky widower instead of a 60 year-old divorced man. And killer!*

The thought had very little impact. That was the one thing that he and lots of other guys had brought home with them from Vietnam—a passiveness about death. In midst of modern warfare it was sometimes difficult to tell whether you had ever actually killed another human being or not. Especially bomber pilots. They were so far removed from the action that it did not become a personal thing, just a job you did.

And that's the way Russell viewed what he was doing now—just a job.

He continued driving north, letting his mind wander back over the events that had brought him to this strange, fateful place. Back before Maria's sudden announcement that she was leaving him, they had driven to Dallas to

11

visit his son, Paul, and then on to New Orleans and along the coast, then cross-country to Jacksonville to see Luisa's new house with her swimming pool and smug attitude. Divorcing Ron had seemed to Russell like a really childish, bitchy thing for Luisa to do. Especially, when it meant leaving a teenage son and daughter behind.

Poor Ron ... finally thinks he has it made, moving back to North Dakota with his huge golden parachute retirement settlement only to be told by Luisa, "No—I'm moving to Florida and I want half the money."

But then, who ever said Luisa was anything but a self-centered bitch. She certainly was a big baby. She must have considered talking her mother into leaving Pedro quite a *coup d'état*. Not that Pedro was such a great guy, but he wasn't that bad either. Apparently, the sanctity of marriage meant very little to Luisa ... or Maria either, for that matter.

It suddenly occurred to Russell that Luisa was the one he should have shot—but then, she didn't smoke. *Whatever that had to do with anything?*

When he and Maria had take Kalina to visit Chen and Pedro in Puerto Rico that time, it had seemed like her mother and step-father's marriage could have coasted through old age without a hiccup. True, Maria's mother did have some knee problems and stairs to deal with, and Pedro did seem to need his daily quota of whiskey. But they seemed happy enough. *What gave Luisa the right to butt in? What gave her the right to play God?*

Russell really hated Luisa for a lot of things. Like having to give up his stall in their garage that winter so Luisa could put her car in. He hadn't known it then, but he realized now, that her working for Maria that tax season and staying with them during the week had just been a trial run for her eventual divorcing of Ron. He'd always thought good Catholics didn't divorce, but it didn't seem to matter to her. Being the one calling the shots, queen of the hill so to speak, was the important thing.

That Luisa should live and Maria had to die might have seemed odd if Russell had spent very much time thinking about it. The way it was, it kind of made sense. He had to live without Maria because of Luisa, so she could damned well live without Maria because of him. He wasn't sure where Chen fit into the equation.

He also wasn't sure why he was driving north either. The streets seemed to get more congested and less like what he was looking for as he drove, even though he didn't know what that was. On impulse, he drove around one block and headed back toward the Dames Point Bridge.

After crossing back over the bridge, he meandered his way toward the ocean. He wasn't sure why, but he felt that was where he'd find what he was looking for, even though he wasn't sure yet what that was. He would know it when he saw it—and he was right. When he spotted the shadowy figure of an apparently middle-aged man walking his dog, a Beagle, he cut the headlights, coasted the Escort over to the curb about thirty yards or so behind the man. He got out of the car, took the bow and one arrow out of the trunk, and moved up the slight rise separating the street from the beach and tried to catch up to the man without giving himself away.

Looking out at the silvery white caps sloshing over the beach Russell was instantly transported back to another time when he and Wilson and some other guys had driven Wilson's stupid Chevy station wagon from Keesler Air

Force Base out to Jacksonville. He'd fallen asleep in the back and Wilson thought it was pretty damned funny to drive out on the beach and then wake him. Being a farm boy from central Minnesota who'd never seen the ocean before, it was like waking up in another world.

It wasn't much different now. Russell needed to make this a really good shot. He damned sure didn't want to hit the dog—and he didn't want to hit any vital organs on the man either. Maybe just a grazing shot in the fleshy part of the guy's thigh. Even that was a mean thing to do to a total strange.

But it was part of the job.

He took a moment to assess the evening breeze coming in off the ocean. *Something like that could screw up a shot if you weren't careful.* By now, the distance between them had decreased to about twenty yards, and the guy was walking very slowly, giving the dog a chance to find that perfect spot. The light wasn't so good now either, partly because of the spacing of the streetlights, but mostly because the moon was now fighting an onslaught of wispy clouds. The gentle rhythm of the surf sloshing in on the beach and running back out seemed to whisper, " Do it! Do it."

Russell sucked in a deep breath, held it, took aim and let the arrow fly.

The arrow's flight glistened silvery in the moonlight instead of the reddish gold of the tracer bullets they'd fired over his head in basic training.

Afterwards, Russell wasn't sure whether the man had even made sound when the arrow struck him, or whether the emotional strain of the evening's events had put his head in just that right place where one wouldn't hear a sound even if there had been one. *Does a tree make a sound if there's no one in the forest to hear it fall?*

All Russell could remember about the event afterwards was that the man had gone down, and the dog hadn't reacted at all. He felt rather methodical as he put the bow back in the trunk with the remaining four arrows, got back into the Escort, and drove away. He did not turn on his headlights until he was a good two blocks away.

...

Maybe it's time to get something to eat, Russell decided, pulling into a parking spot back at the motel.

He probably should have gone somewhere else, but it was after ten and a lot of the fast food places were already closed for the evening. It didn't really matter, except he didn't want people remembering him for any reason. Fortunately, the motel was pretty big and had its own bar and restaurant. Nobody seemed to be paying much attention.

Part way through his spaghetti Russell noticed a Hispanic woman come in with a little girl of about six. The girl was wearing a skimpy little blue dress with buttons and white lace up the middle of the front. The skirt was so short it hardly covered the puffy white panties her skinny legs were sticking out of. Obviously the mother hadn't instructed her about lady-like behavior the way she was bouncing around on the seat flashing her crotch.

Damned fool, Russell chastised himself, angered by the stirrings he felt, *it's not bad enough you've takin' up killin' ... now you're becomin' a damned pervert!*

Chapter 2

To Russell's surprise he slept the sleep of the dead. Obviously, the impact of his actions hadn't really sunk in. Either that, or Maria had been right in leaving him. His brain was so riddled with pain it no longer functioned. He didn't feel anything any more—neither pleasure nor pain—just a dull, aching emptiness.

He checked out of the motel at a little after seven the next morning, not bothering about breakfast. He didn't want people having any extra reasons for remembering him. In retrospect, he really wished he'd had the foresight to leave the city the night before. The motel was just off Highway 202, a few blocks from the intersection of Interstate 1 and only minutes from Luisa's house. *How dumb was that?*

He didn't bother looking for a newspaper either, but he wasn't sure why.

The most likely reason for not looking for a newspaper was because he wasn't ready for the truth just yet. Like some advanced star-ship engine, he was still running on impulse. Instead of driving north on Interstate 1 and getting *"the hell out of Dodge,"* as he should, he meandered around awhile, then finally took 295 across the St. Johns River and picked up Interstate 10. It seemed like a really *stupid* way of running a criminal activity—spur of the moment that way, without any obvious rhyme or reason.

Take the bow, for instance. *How weird was that?*

Yesterday morning he'd gotten out of bed with the single intention of just proving that Maria had moved to Jacksonville to start a new tax business—one that didn't involve H & R Block franchise royalties or controlling franchise directors. He had spent the better part of a near sleepless night scouring various maps and phone books trying to locate the "Quick Return" tax business that had supposedly just opened somewhere in Jacksonville. Unfortunately, the advertising paper that had come in the mail with an article on this so-called "new business" was still back home on his kitchen table.

So much for planning!

Not knowing what else to do, he had driven over to Crosby Lane toward Luisa's house. He drove past in one direction, then turned around and drove back, parking a few houses down the street so he could see what Maria did when she came out. He'd expected her to come out get in her car and drive north towards Barnes Road. Hopefully, he would be able to follow her to the new business, confront her there, and thereby persuade her to stop trying to make a killing on their divorce the way Luisa had on hers.

It didn't work out that way. Instead, Maria came out with Luisa. They got into Luisa's car and, to his dismay, drove straight towards him.

For a second, his heart just stopped.

Russell had no idea what he would have done if they had spotted him. Fortunately, he had been studying the map just seconds before they came towards him and he was able to quickly shield himself. Besides, in the quick glance that he got, Luisa was running her mouth, like she always did, and had her head turned toward Maria. That meant, of course, that Maria's head was turned toward Luisa and that she might have caught a glimpse of him before he got the map up, but even if she had, she wouldn't have been looking for him and therefore probably nothing registered.

Even if she had seen him and said something to somebody, unless it was Luisa, what would it matter?

One thing certain, the close call had brought Russell's blood to a boil. Suddenly, he knew exactly how that creep on the motorcycle must have felt that day when their eyes met just before the guy copped that girl's purse at the rest stop. *What a rush!* He knew the guy was going to grab the purse even though Russell was watching, and he also knew instantly the guy knew he wasn't going to do anything about it.

One minute he was watching Luisa's car in his rearview mirror as it disappeared around the corner at the end of her street, the next he was in a panic trying to get turned around and catch up to her without giving his presence away. By the time he'd gotten turned around and made it around the corner, Luisa and Maria were long gone.

Not knowing what else to do Russell had driven around for awhile, in ever widening circles, hoping to spot Luisa's car or the so-called new tax business. *Pretty smart, huh?* But Jacksonville was too big. When that didn't work, he just drove at random until mid-afternoon, when he found himself in some old woman's garage.

"How much for the bow and arrow?" he's asked, the sound of his own voice bringing him out of his reverie.

That he would stop at a garage sale was pure whim.

Out of all the improbable things he might have done, that was the most improbable. It certainly wasn't something he would have done at home. Garage sales were something that women did. That he would buy a used bow and six target arrows was even more improbable. In the first place, the bow had seemed so completely out of place amidst the ancient TV trays, old-fashioned clothes, canning jars, and junk that he almost didn't even ask about it.

The woman was just a stick with a hair-netted gray bun for hair, leathery wrinkled skin, and flower-print housedress. "My grandson's," she'd said, offering an explanation for the out-of-place bow even though he'd asked for none. "How about $10?"

In the first place, that was a hell of a bargain. Secondly, the woman seemed to have some compelling need for him to buy the bow. Maybe because he was a man and probably the only one she'd seen in the hot afternoon sun. Or maybe it had something to do with the grandson. Whatever the reason, he hadn't bothered to ask.

The plan to actually use the bow and arrows on Maria hadn't started percolating until much later in the afternoon.

By the time the sun went down his mind was mush but the plan was firmly fixed in place. The only way Luisa could experience the pain he was feeling was for him to do to her exactly what she had done to him. That he should do it with a bow and arrow seemed the perfect irony, considering Maria's competitive nature.

And now it was done!

Or was it? As Russell drove west on Interstate 10 towards Lake City he toyed briefly with the idea of going back and doing Luisa—but that would be stupid. *Maybe he should just do a drive-by … see how many police cars were buzzing around Luisa's house.* On the other hand, if he put the hammer down and high-tailed it for home, he'd probably be home before anyone even realized he'd been gone for several days—and that would be good. With no special person in his life these days, it was hard to tell if he was going to need an alibi. He could probably stay away for a month and not be missed.

As he drove, Russell's mind kept turning back to the guy on the Honda Goldwing who had swiped the girl's purse. If he had to make a guess, he was pretty sure it was the kind of thing this guy did all the time. Who knows, he probably made his living that way. Just come tooling in real quiet like, grab some lady's purse, and "*Zap!*" you're gone. It made the interstate seem like those silly air tubes at the bank—just stick in the little carrier, close the door, and "*Zap!*" you're out of there.

It would be real nice if he could just get home that way.

By the time Russell stopped for breakfast at Lake City, a new plan involving the "snatch and flee" concept was beginning to form in his mind. All he really had to do was continue across Florida snapping off an arrow or two here and there … leaving a false trail. The police would think they had some interstate *Robin Hood* nut on their hands and be completely stymied.

Of course, he would have to be very careful. He really didn't want to kill anyone else—just finish the job he'd started.

Lake City was unlike any town he had ever experienced before. He left Interstate 10 at U. S. Highway 441 expecting to find a restaurant. Instead, he found only a Days Inn Motel and some pretty beat up old houses half hidden among the pine, shrubs, and moss-covered live oak as he drove south toward the downtown section in search of a place to eat. Toward the center of town, judging by the town-square, he spotted a place called Ruppert's Bakery & Café. The streets were quite narrow with a few diagonal parking-spaces carved out along the sidewalk. Not quite like anything he'd ever seen before.

Ruppert's was even more bizarre. The entire southwest corner of the place seemed to be devoted to bakery equipment, ovens, and coolers. There was a glass case with baked goods and cash register along the south wall toward the front. Along the north wall there was a counter with stools that looked like it had once been a soda fountain. The rest of the room was filled with a mish-mash of round and square tables, some with white lace table clothes and others with brown and green flowered oilcloths. There was a black Baldwin upright piano against the back of the bakery equipment and the word "PRESCRIPTION" across the top of the back wall as if the place had once been a drugstore. The eight or nine ceiling fans were more than enough to fly the place right out of time.

Russell ordered the breakfast special and coffee and tried not to look at the waitress who seemed to want to engage him in conversation with her "How y'all doin' today?" While he waited for his food he let his mind drift back over some of the events (like the trip to Puerto Rico) that had led to his current predicament.

...

"Aren't we going to bed pretty soon?" Russell had asked that first night in Fajardo, surprised that Maria was still going strong after 10:00 O'clock in the evening.

They had taken the 10-mile ferry trip to Vieques Island that day so Maria could fill Russell and Kalina in on the family connection there. Despite the fact that the U. S. Navy controlled most of the Island and used it for bombing practice, her stepbrother Manny had run some cattle there. They had toured the island in a family friend's car and then climbed on foot to the old fort overlooking the harbor. Normally, the climb alone would have been enough to put Maria down for the duration.

"You go ahead," Maria had replied. "Kalina won't get a chance to spend much time with Mother and Manny so I'm gonna stay up a bit."

At that point, Russell had felt sort of pot committed. If he had opted to say, "No, I'll stay up with you," there was the implication that he didn't trust her—which he didn't even though he had no reason not to. There was just something about the way Manny looked at Maria. Russell knew they had lived under the same roof while Maria was in college. *Who knew what a college girl would let an older stepbrother get away with?*

Not wanting to seem paranoid, he'd said "Okay," gave her a peck on the cheek and climbed the stairs to the third floor of the "bed and breakfast" Pedro and Chen ran. Maria's mother and stepfather were both beyond retirement age, but hung onto the place anyway.

Waiting for Maria to come up, Russell had let his mind flow back over the events that had brought them to Puerto Rico.

It had all started with Maria doing a lot of moping around on holidays. He and Maria were both on their second marriage, but there was nothing obvious about that that would explain Maria's obvious depression around holidays—especially at Christmas time. He'd finally badgered her into telling him the truth … that she'd had a child before her first marriage and had given it up for adoption.

Some time later, the beautiful Kalina had come into their life.

Kalina had already graduated from high school and was working as a cook when Catholic Charities contacted her and let her know that her birth mother was interested in meeting her. Everything else had just followed naturally.

There was that first meeting in Minneapolis filled with apprehension and curiosity, then the eventual meeting with Kalina's biological father, and finally the trip to Puerto Rico to learn what kind of stock her mother came from. Kalina's curiosity was certainly understandable. *Who wouldn't be curious about their biological heritage?* Especially someone with Kalina's brown skin, dark hair and eyes and so-called lily-white parents—who turned out to be lovely people. The mother was a nurse. The father some kind of salesman.

Up to that point, everything would have been fine—except that Russell had heard the sound of the door to the bedroom across the hall opening and closing. *Kalina must have gone to bed,* Russell decided. He lay there for a long time, expecting either Kalina to go down again or Maria to come up to bed.

Neither ever did….

As he lay there, Russell found himself reviewing what he knew about his new wife. Of course, by then they'd been married for over five years, but he still considered her new. There were lots of things about her past that he was still struggling to understand, like her never ever telling her father that she'd gotten pregnant and had given her baby up for adoption. That would never happen in Russell's family. But with a Catholic father like Maria's, maybe it wasn't so hard to understand.

Luis Munoz was kind of an arrogant prick who thought he could have any woman he wanted. He'd been married to Maria's mother three times before she finally took after him with a butcher knife. Luis was an educated man from a well-to-do family of doctors, lawyers, and engineers. His biggest problem, other than not being able to keep his hands off the ladies, seemed to be that he'd had daughters instead of sons. And that seemed to be the major driving force behind most of Maria's actions.

When Maria finally came up to bed, hours later, Russell was a stone about to start an avalanche.

"If you're trying not to wake me," he'd said softly, "I think you're pretty much wasting your time."

"Oh," she murmured.

"You get Kalina all caught up on family history?" he'd asked.

"Russell, please—"

"What?"

"It's late … I'm tired."

He had waited a moment before speaking. "If you're so tired … I thought you would have come to bed earlier—like Kalina did."

It was a challenge they really didn't need at just that moment.

"Dr. Diego came by … if you must know," Maria snapped back.

"Who's Dr. Diego?"

"An old family friend."

"Oh," He'd felt a little sheepish and had turned toward her to put his arm across her breasts. When he tried to kiss her she was stiff as a poker. He should have turned back on his other side then and gone to sleep, but her resistance angered him. He'd never forced his intentions on her at any point in their relationship, but on this night he couldn't seem to stop. *What was she doing down there all this time? Was everything all innocent the way she claimed?* Normally, he knew Pedro and Chen went to bed with the chickens, but if a family friend showed up and gave Pedro an excuse to drink more whiskey—

He'd moved his body against hers and cupped her right breast in his left hand.

"What are you doing?" she'd snapped, angering him even more.

"Give you three guesses," he'd tried to joke.

She had not been amused. "I told you I was tired!"

"And I'm horny," he had insisted, the thought of "sloppy seconds" with his own wife egging him on. *Would a man ever be able to tell?*

Chapter 3

Russell was still dwelling on the concept of "sloppy seconds" thirty-five minutes later when Highway Patrolman Lyle Peterson fired a short siren burst at him and pulled him over on his way back to Interstate 10. A quick glance in his rearview mirror brought Russell's heart up into his throat. *Had he forgotten to tip the waitress? Or was she pissed because he hadn't fallen for her "y'all" drawl trying to drag him into long conversations—maybe get him to tell her what he was doing in Lake City?*

Or maybe it was the convenience store? After eating he had stopped at a convenience store to buy a newspaper. *Did something happen in that store that would get the cops after him?* The jig couldn't be up already. True, he hadn't bothered to check the newspaper he'd bought yet, but still— His mind flashed quickly back to the convenience store. The clerk had been one of those two-ton types you automatically assume only took sponge baths because she couldn't get her fat butt through a bathroom door—at least that's the way she'd smelled.

That's what he'd thought at the time. Now he wasn't so sure.

A black kid of about ten (a boy, he'd thought) had called the woman "Mama Jo." Surely a woman who went by the moniker of "Mama Jo" wouldn't be so offensive as to go around smelling of stale sweat. Then it occurred to him that perhaps he might be the offender. He was getting so paranoid about his situation anything was possible. And he'd definitely been sweating like a pig lately. He couldn't even remember whether he had bothered to shower that morning. *Maybe Mama Jo took one whiff and called the fuzz—*

The sudden rap of knuckles on the driver's side window brought Russell crashing back to reality.

"I-is something wrong, Officer?" Russell stammered, rolling the window down

"Hope I didn't startle you," Peterson said, with an easy smile. "Looked like you were pretty far away."

"No … just wondering what I did wrong."

Looking up at a highway patrolman through a car window can be completely unsettling, especially if you're guilty *as hell* and trying not to show it. Russell tried to focus on the patrolman without appearing overly nervous. Mostly, he just wished his car was one of those bank air tube carriers and he could just "*Zap!*" it the hell out of there.

"Nothing," Peterson said, "I just need to ask you a couple of questions."

"W-what's that?" Russell said, hoping he wasn't about to break out in a cold sweat.

"We had an incident over on the Interstate a couple of days ago." Peterson continued. "Didn't happen to be out that way, did you?"

"N-no," Russell lied, thinking frantically. "I mean, I was … but that was more than a week ago. I've been down in Daytona Beach on vacation. Why?"

"A witness reported a car like yours in the area—thought you might have seen something."

"Nope, no … at least not that I know of."

For a moment, Peterson looked like he wasn't buying Russell's lies and Russell began to worry he might want to search his car. The incriminating bow and four arrows were still in the trunk. Even if the officer knew nothing about Maria or the guy on the beach, the bow would be enough to cause closer scrutiny. Something Russell wasn't anxious to bring down on himself.

"What happened?" he asked, breaking the silence deadlock.

Peterson shrugged. "A little petty larceny … we get that all the time."

Russell nodded and tried to smile.

"You have a good day, Sir," Peterson said, turning to head back toward his patrol car. "Enjoy your vacation."

"Thanks!" Russell answered. He watched in the rearview mirror until Peterson had climbed back into his patrol car and driven away. For just a second, he let his eyes wander over his own image in the mirror half expecting his hair to be at least several shades grayer than it was before.

Obviously, the nice officer had been talking about the purse-snatching incident he'd witnessed and was probably well aware that he was lying, but what could he do?

Russell sat there for much longer than should have been prudent for someone in his precarious position, his mind out of control like a World War I fighter plane in a tailspin, smoke pouring out as he spiraled into oblivion. A quick dash for home might keep people from noticing they hadn't seen him in a while. On the other hand, a trail of arrows across Florida could have the police looking for a ghost. Actually, the only thing he wanted to do at that moment was chuck the damned bow and "get the hell out of Dodge." Only, to do that it seemed like he needed the cover of darkness and a good spot to dump the bow.

Of course, he could do his dumping on the way back to Minnesota and probably get away with it. But by the time it got dark he'd probably be up past Atlanta and if they started looking in that direction— He suddenly realized he was falling into the same trap he always fell into when it came to making what he called "executive decisions." He was worrying everything to death before he ever got to any real facts. He didn't know for sure whether he was a killer and a widower, or a double killer, or what. The thought that he might have killed an innocent man didn't sit too well with him. The smart thing to do would be to go back to the convenience store—better yet, another store in the area—and buy a map of the area. That way he could find a place to park where people wouldn't bother him while he looked through the newspaper to find out exactly how much damage he had inflicted the night before.

As he drove around the outskirts of Lake City looking for another convenience store, he got to thinking that what he needed for getting rid of the bow would be some nice secluded swamp. There had to be lots of swamps in Florida, but the only one that came to mind that he knew by name was the Everglades and that was way the hell down at the bottom of the state. He could leave a trail of arrows going down there, and then dump the bow—but that would eat up a lot of time.

To his dismay, he wound up back at the same convenience store where Mama Jo was still riding "herd" over the pop and pretzels and fish bait. He almost missed that last part. As he was pretending to select another newspaper he suddenly realized the store sold fish bait. That meant there had to be water close by.

He grabbed a couple of papers and asked Mama Jo, "Do you have any local maps?"

"What kinda maps?" She gave him a look that left little doubt that she wasn't anxious to get up from the stool or whatever it was that was hidden under the skirt of her dress—a dress that some people would have kidded must have been made by some tent and awning outfit. It reminded him of Mrs. Kunkel back home.

"Oh, you know … local fishing spots, stuff like that."

No sooner were the words out of his mouth than Russell realized he was going to have to buy some bait to keep her from thinking much about him. Not that buying some bait would be such a big deal. Not if it meant his anonymity was safe. If people fished around here, no one would pay too much attention to a fisherman.

"Over by the cooler," Mama Jo told him, turning her attention back to the romance magazine she was reading.

He wound up buying nearly twenty dollars worth of stuff including newspapers, a couple of maps, a container of night crawlers, one of minnows, and some junk food—Ding Dongs and silly stuff like that. Not normally a nervous muncher, Russell was surprised that he was thinking about food again so soon after eating breakfast. Maybe that was Mama Jo's problem—she was a master criminal. If he wasn't careful, Russell realized ruefully, he could easily wind up weighing as much as she did.

He decided to drive back toward the downtown section and try to find a parking spot among the host of cars already parked in the public-square to study the maps. One car among many wouldn't stand out too much and those that did see him wouldn't pay much attention, if he didn't stay too long.

It became quickly apparent glancing at the maps that he had a couple of choices that could be considered on the way home. To begin with, the Okefenokee Swamp spilled across the Georgia-Florida border and was an easy drive that was definitely on the way home. There was also the Suwannee River, of Stephen Foster fame, just north of the interstate. In fact, the Stephen Foster State Folk Culture Center was just north of White Springs only a few minutes drive away. Maybe he could find a fishing spot there where he could read his papers and dump the bow and arrows as well.

But first, he decided he should go to a hardware store and buy a roll of duct tape. *Nothing like duct tape for tying up loose ends.*

...

When Russell came out of the hardware store his mind was still on the Suwannee River up in the White Springs area, wondering whether he would find a fishing spot there or not. So he didn't immediately focus in on the scene that unfolded before him in parking lot at the side of the store. In many ways, it was like that time his Father had gotten his arm caught in the baler. One second Russell was driving the tractor on the rake, wondering why his father was laying on the apron of the baler, one leg waving up and down in the air. The next he was on the ground running. Only in this case he was running toward his car to follow the van as it whipped out of the parking lot and sped away. The closed-loop image of what he'd seen playing over and over in his mind as he ran:

At first, just the blurred image out of the corner of his eye of a white girl of about ten with blonde pigtails, a white blouse and blue jeans riding a bicycle across the parking lot. A middle-aged black man in a metallic blue T-shirt and ragged jeans put out his arms to stop her, as if she was going to hit him. And finally, the girl's stunned eyes as the man dragged her a few feet across the parking lot and shoved her into a beat up old van.

The whole scene seemed surreal.

Fortunately, the van's hasty departure was in the same direction as Russell's car was pointing. And, since he was parallel parked against the curb, it was a simple matter to swing out and follow without attracting the van driver's attention.

Chapter 4

The van's initial rapid acceleration quickly settled back to a steady 23 miles per hour. In a world where everyone but the littlest of little old ladies drives at least 5 miles per hour over the speed limit, that in and of itself was highly suspicious. And the black guy driving the van was anything but a little old lady.

Russell couldn't believe what was happening. He had initially been scanning the area outside the hardware store as he walked towards his car just to make sure that no one was paying any special attention to him—something he'd been doing a lot of lately. His eyes had passed quickly over the scene in the parking lot without anything registering.

A snapshot in time: a middle-aged black man in ragged jeans, metallic blue T-shirt, and tennis shoes stopping and then jostling a pigtailed white girl towards an old Dodge van the same color as his T-shirt. The parking lot was fairly wide so it took a good dozen steps to traverse the distance—plenty of time to take everything in. The girl hadn't seemed scared exactly, just puzzled. It was the man's grip on her upper arm that clinched the deal.

Even at a distance of forty feet or so, Russell thought he could discern discoloration as might be evidenced by a vise-like grip. Did he actually see that, or was his mind filling in the gaps. He was experienced enough to know that the mind can do some pretty funny things when pressed.

In that split second that the gravity of the situation actually registered, Russell had started to turn back and head toward the parking lot, but his mind did a quick projection forward and he knew instantly he would be too late—probably get run over before he got there. It was a good thing he saw it that way because the guy came out of the parking lot accelerating as if the devil himself was on his tail. But only for about that first half a block—by the time Russell had started the Escort and had pulled out, there were two cars between them and the guy had settled into a slow, easy cruise.

Smart!

The van looked as if someone had picked it up and polished it so hard that the paint had worn through, but it didn't seem to be rusty. Puzzling, because in a place so close to the ocean there had to be salt in the air. In Minnesota and Wisconsin road salt caused cars to rust out. In coastal states such as Florida salt in the air had the same effect—unless the guy was from somewhere inland.

Russell tried to get closer to get a better look at the van's license plate, but every time he could almost make it out, the guy would turn into another side street without signaling. That made the situation tricky. Either the guy was the worst driver in the world, or he was trying to figure out whether he was being followed, or maybe driving with one hand while holding the girl with the other. Fortunately for Russell the area was flat and open enough to easily keep track of the van from a pretty good distance.

For Russell, it would have made sense for the van to be heading for the interstate. To his surprise, that wasn't the case. After a lot of twisting and turning and doubling back the van pulled off the street in what was becoming a familiar neighborhood and parked under a huge tree with a lot of Spanish moss or whatever hanging down. The convenience store Russell had already been to twice that day was less than a block away.

It was basically a quiet neighborhood. Most of the houses were older single story bungalow types with screened porches and carports. The houses weren't very close together and most were set back from the street quite a ways. The street had been paved once, but it had been so long ago it was hard to tell.

At first, Russell didn't even see the house the van was parked in front of. The various shrubs, bushes, and vines surrounding it were so over-grown it was all but invisible. One shutter hung at a forty-five degree angle, obscuring part of the window and a patch of tar- paper where the siding was gone. The screened porch was reddish-brown with rust. The house certainly didn't look lived in.

Which might explain why the guy wasn't getting out of the van.

Russell was parked a good three houses away, but he had a pretty good view of the passenger door of the van. When the guy didn't get out right away he started worrying that maybe he'd missed him somehow—or that he was reading the situation completely wrong.

What if the guy was raping the girl in the van at that very moment?

What if the guy had a knife or a gun?

The longer Russell waited, the more questions and

doubts poured through his mind. *What was he doing here, anyway?* Firing an arrow into your ex-wife's unsuspecting body from blackness of the night was a whole lot different ballgame than confronting a younger, virile black man without a weapon.

Strangely, Russell never thought of his actions or, as in this case, his lack of action as being a cowardly thing. The *hero* or *coward* thing didn't enter into it at all.

He was about to move his car to get a better view when the black guy suddenly appeared from the driver's side of the van. He opened the passenger door, but then stood there for the longest time.

At first, it was hard to tell what was going on. Then Russell realized the guy was helping the girl out of the van, but doing it in such a way that no one could tell much from a distance. He lifted the girl out of the van backwards and made her stand on top of his feet. Then, holding both her wrists with one hand, he backed up a couple of steps, slammed the van door and walked toward the house.

Unless you were actually looking for it, no one would have ever seen the girl. The guy kept his back toward the street the whole time.

Instead of using the door on the screened porch, the odd couple disappeared through an opening in the shrubbery.

For a moment Russell panicked. Part of his mind wanted to fire up the Escort and get "the hell out of Dodge," like always. Something made him stay. Suddenly he was remembering an image of the girl's discarded bicycle in a heap in the parking lot. This had to be a kidnapping—with potential rape and murder as a possible outcome. And there wasn't a soul to do anything about it except him.

It was one thing to "Doink" your ex-wife with an arrow in the dark of night—if she had it coming. Quite another to ignore the plight of an innocent, young girl in the hands of some damned sex-pervert. Russell would have to be some sort of heartless monster not to want to help this girl. That's when he suddenly remembered the bow and arrows in his trunk. He slipped quickly out of the car, popped the trunk and looked around to see if anyone was looking.

The coast seemed to be clear so he grabbed the bow and the remaining four arrows and walked quickly along the front edge of the ragged lawns. This was definitely not the newest part of town. When he got directly behind the van he ran quickly past it and looked for the opening in the shrubbery. If he hadn't seen the guy disappear he never would have been able to find the opening.

As Russell made his way along the side of the house he wondered briefly if he needed to be worrying about snakes. Obviously no one had lived in the house in a very long time. The windows were so dirty that you wouldn't be able to see much through them even if the shades had not been drawn. Russell had serious doubts that his villain had any idea he was about to be busted.

Russell's intuition would prove to be 100% correct.

There was an enclosed back porch, but it was not screened. In fact, the only window in it was boarded up. Russell had to use the light from the back door to get orientated, then reach back with an arrow and push the outside door closed as best he could. For a moment, he wasn't sure what to do with the extra arrows, then it occurred to him that the elastic band of his sock would make a suitable quiver to keep the arrows handy. When he was ready, he pushed what had to be the kitchen door open with a notched arrow and brought the bow up to bear on the black hulk standing in front of the girl. The light was dim, but Russell could see the girl had been placed on the edge of a beat-up table. A beam of light from the still slightly open outer door shot over Russell's shoulder, illuminating the tears streaming down the girl's terrified face. Her jeans and panties lay in a crumpled heap on the floor beside the table.

At that point, time did a sort of *implosion* thing.

Russell took the scene in for a split second and then realized the black hulk was turning towards him. "Hold it!" he ordered sharply, realizing he was silhouetted in the doorway.

"Aaagh!" the guy let out a startled yell and jumped about a mile.

The guy's yell startled Russell so he inadvertently let the arrow fly. It stuck in the wall with a thud. *Thank God for that! It was more convincing that way. Showed he meant business.*

Russell quickly grabbed one of his remaining three arrows from his sock-quiver, notched it, and brought it quickly to bear on the shadowy hulk in front of him.

"I wouldn't move again, if I were you," he said menacingly.

"What chew want, mistuh?" the guy demanded as if Russell was the one in the wrong, like raping under-aged girls was expected of him. He was turned partly toward Russell trying to peer through the shadows, one hand still clutching his privates.

"Seems like you should be picking on someone more your size," Russell suggested.

The "perp" made no reply.

The girl's face was still illuminated by the shaft of sunlight coming from over Russell's shoulder, golden dust motes dancing in the space between them. "You okay, honey?" Russell asked, directing his voice past the black hulk. In addition to the tears streaming down the girl's cheeks, her lower jaw was trembling as if she was sitting in a tub of ice water.

"Y-yes," she sobbed shakily.

"Tell you what, honey," Russell continued. "You get dressed … then go up the street." He paused to make sure she was following what he wanted her to do. "There's a convenience store up on the corner. You run up there and tell Mama Jo to call the police. You tell her that this creep was trying to molest you."

The girl looked at the black man as if waiting for permission.

"Can you do that?" Russell prodded.

She hesitated another moment. "Yes," she said, pushing herself off the table and starting to dress.

"I expect you better go out the door here behind me," Russell offered, when she picked up her shoes.

She didn't bother to put them on and Russell didn't blame her. The sooner she was out of there, the better. "Run like the wind," he told her as she slipped past him.

That was a big mistake.

Russell's attention was momentarily diverted as he turned slightly to make sure the girl got out the back door okay. That was all the opportunity the would-be-rapist needed. Letting out a mighty roar and he literally sprang at Russell, sending him crashing back against the side of the porch with such force that he momentarily lost control of the second arrow, which shot up and stuck harmlessly in the kitchen ceiling.

Thinking Russell was stunned, the *perp* tried to push past him to stop the girl—but Russell wasn't about to let that happen.

There wasn't enough time or space to bring up a third arrow, and besides, the bow had gone flying. Russell grabbed the guy and tried to throw him back into the kitchen, but the guy was much younger and stronger and they wound up wrestling in the tiny porch. The last thing Russell remembered after the short struggle before his head was smashed into *oblivion* was the view of the second arrow sticking in the kitchen ceiling.

Chapter 5

Fortunately, Russell wasn't unconscious for very long. He suspected it took him longer to figure out where he was after he came around than the time he was actually out. But by the time he got his brains unscrambled and got himself re-orientated, the rapist, the van, and the girl were all gone. So were his bow and his last two arrows.

Which left him with a bit of a predicament.

He didn't know whether to run like hell, walk up to the convenience store, or just hide in the bushes to see if the cops were going to show up. Either of the latter two options being the only way of knowing if the girl had actually made it to the convenience store. If not, she could have been recaptured and stuffed back in the van— only this time the guy could be speeding off to some new hideout where no one would ever find her.

Russell didn't run.

To do that would be the same as abandoning the girl in the first place. He also did not walk up to the convenience store to see what if anything was going on. To do that would get him more deeply involved than he wanted to be at the moment. The cops would want him to tell what happened, make him go with them back to the ramshackle house and explain about the arrows sticking in the wall and ceiling.

He wasn't about to volunteer for that.

Instead, he picked himself up, dusted himself off, went back into the kitchen, ripped off the shades and took a look around. He was very glad he did. He found a small ditty bag tossed in the corner. There wasn't much inside the bag except a few T-shirts and under things, mostly dirty, an open pack of cigarettes and a couple of matchbooks, some toilet articles, and a single photograph of a black woman and small boy standing in front of a white house. There was a real estate sign and the back end of a car in the bottom corner of the picture.

The bag obviously belonged to the kidnapper.

Russell surveyed the back porch and kitchen one more time to make sure he hadn't missed anything, then started back towards his car, bag in hand. That's when it hit him. The arrows he'd fired at Maria and that guy on the beach had been wiped clean and he'd been wearing latex gloves—not so with the arrows still sticking in the wall and ceiling of the abandoned house. He ran back in and was about to rip the arrow out of the wall, when he realized that would be a mistake. He had been hoping to leave a false trail of arrows across part of Florida. *How perfect was this?* He pulled out his handkerchief and carefully wiped the exposed part of the arrow sticking in the wall, then looked around for something to stand on to get at the one sticking in the ceiling.

It was a bit risky but he had to get up on the beat-up table to wipe the arrow sticking in the ceiling. Hopefully, he hadn't left any fingerprints on the embedded part of the shafts. He also took a minute to wipe any doorknobs and such that he might have touched, then headed back towards his car again.

...

Mama Jo had pretty good radar. One look at the little girl told her that something was drastically wrong. The girl's face was porcelain white except for the dirty tear-stained tracks down her cheeks. She was panting like a racehorse and had her tennis shoes in one hand. There was no sign of any stockings.

"Lorda mercy, child!" Mama Jo exclaimed. "Y'all seen a ghost … or what?"

The child could not answer.

"You come on back here behind the counter, honey." Mama Jo continued, pulling herself more up right on her stool in case she might have to get up. "You come on back here and let Mama Jo get a good look at you."

The child seemed rooted in front of the counter.

"Come on, honey" Mama Jo persisted, raising a meaty arm to encircle the child in case she accepted. "You let Mama Jo he'p ya."

The roots gave way and the child moved around the end of the counter and slipped under Mama Jo's inviting arm, her nostrils flaring unexpectedly at the sudden impact of the smell of Mama Jo's armpit.

"What's your name, honey?"

"W-wendy."

Mama Jo was not actually from Florida and she had no children of her own. The nickname came from handing out candy to local children. Her southern accent acquired from living and working in Lake City all those years after Eugene had left her here. When she got excited, her speech reverted back to that of a reservation girl who'd worked off the reservation—an odd mixture of Indian and northern European, clipped and guttural.

"Vas den?" Mama Jo urged, studying the child. "Vhat happ'nd?"

Wendy could not find her voice.

There were a lot of things that could have explained Wendy's tears and apparent fear—snake bite … falling out of a tree … getting hit by another child … being lost—the list could go on and on.

"It vas a man, yah?" Mama Jo said intuitively.

Wendy sniffled and nodded in the affirmative.

"Vhat happ'n?"

Mama Jo's jaw took a firm set. *She knew it!* Ever since that skinny, drunken relic of a Cherokee cowboy/Indian from Oklahoma had dumped her in Florida she figured men were lower than the reptiles of the earth.

Had she thought otherwise, she might have taken the trouble to do more than her biweekly sponge baths in the crappy little trailer she lived in. She might have gone on a diet, spruced herself up a bit and gone after some local cracker. As it was, she was happy enough sitting on her stool behind the counter doling out candy to the local kids who were willing to do little chores for her.

"Y'all hurt?" Mama Jo asked, hoping Wendy would get her meaning. She had no experience talking to children about things of a sexual nature.

Wendy shook her head. She had all but forgotten about Mama Jo's offensive smell. It was nice to have this sisterhood with Mama Jo—something women shared regardless of their respective ages.

"Vhere is dis man?" Mama Jo asked.

"In that old house—"

"Dat old shack up the street?"

"Yes."

"Oh, well—you just hold on child," she pushed Wendy away a bit. "You just let Mama Jo get up 'n call da police—"

...

Russell had just tossed the ditty bag onto passenger-side front seat and was about to climb into the driver's seat when a Sheriff's car come barreling around the corner and parked at the convenience store, lights flashing.

So much for that unanswered question!

For the first time in days, Russell felt like something had finally gone his way for a change. He fired up the Escort and made an immediate U-turn with the intention of "getting the hell out of Dodge." But the human body was only meant to be able to handle a specific amount of trauma during any given period of time. Thus, if you went off to war and got shoot and bayoneted and knocked over a cliff within a few short hours, you might not die—but you'd definitely go into shock. And that was what Russell was feeling immediately after leaving the crime scene. His hands started trembling and his head started throbbing. He was quite surprised to discover it was still barely past 12:00 O'clock. He still had all of the junk food left from his purchase at the convenience store, but suddenly he wanted something more substantial. Which raised an issue he hadn't given very much thought to until now.

Money!

He had taken $200 cash out of his ATM before he'd left home for Menomonie, chastising himself for *poor memory* because he still had nearly $150 in his pocket at the time. "Oh, well" he had rationalized. Maybe he'd just stop by the casino at Turtle Lake.

Only he hadn't gone to the casino. Instead, he had rolled on down to Jacksonville, spent two nights in a motel, plus what he'd spent on food and gas and the $10 for the bow. At some point, very soon, he was going to have to come up with some more cash or he was going to have to start using one of his credit cards—which meant leaving an unacceptable, very undesirable paper trail.

Gas was the biggest problem.

He could sleep in the car. He could go for days without food. The one thing he would not be able to deal with, even though the Escort got really good gas mileage, was how to get home on fumes.

Instead of going back on the interstate, he drove north on U S 441 and found a somewhat secluded spot to park along the Suwannee River. The trees hung down like they were draped with forks full of seaweed. He wasn't sure if it was Spanish moss, wild cucumbers, or what because he could never remember the names of plants even after he was told. But ever since Vietnam he'd come to think of vegetation as a friend. The U. S. had spent millions of dollars on Agent Orange and napalm trying to burn *Nam* bald so the enemy wouldn't have any place to hide. If you found yourself being the enemy, vegetation was your friend.

Which meant he needed lots of vegetation, because right at the moment he felt like public-enemy number-one. Unfortunately, where he was parked, the grass was pretty matted down, which meant a lot of traffic and that it probably wasn't such a good place to expect to hide. But then, he wasn't even sure he needed to be hiding yet. *Who knows?* He still hadn't had a chance to read the newspapers he'd bought. *Another big mistake!* Maybe he'd get lucky and some dumb fisherman would come along and he'd be able to corner the night crawler/minnow market. He could certainly use the money.

Actually, what he really needed was sleep. But he was too wired for that. What little sleep he'd had in the past few days had not been very refreshing.

He slid the car seat back and tried to relax, but his head was still throbbing. He rummaged through the glove box and managed to find a beat up aspirin tin with four chalky looking lumps he assumed to be aspirin. He washed the entire lot down with stale coke and then polished off all of the junk food.

He wasn't sure if the emptiness he still felt had any thing to do with actual hunger, or whether it was the emotional turmoil he was going through. Technically, after three years in the Army and a tour of duty in Vietnam with the Air Force, he had to be classified as a trained killer even though he had never actually killed anyone before Maria. At least not that he knew of. And if he was a killer now, he had Luisa to thank for that. It galled him so he felt like going back and killing her. Not that she was responsible for everything.

Being a cuckold was a God-awful thing. Not that he had any actual proof. Just a gut feeling and a lot of little things, like coming back from Puerto Rico early with Kalina while Maria stayed behind. *What was that about?*

That was another thing he hated—woman who wouldn't talk about things. To be a man meant you had to have a God damned crystal ball to figure out what was bugging your woman. First time anything goes wrong, they clam up and you gotta play guessing games, and would they even tell you if you got it right. Take

Kalina, suddenly insisting that she had to go home and that she didn't want to talk about it. He was pretty sure she had seen Maria and Manny doing something they shouldn't have been doing—whether it was just kissing or something more serious, he couldn't be sure. To this day, as far as he knew, Kalina was still not speaking to her birth mother.

Then there were all of those so-called business lunches of Maria's. Supposedly all legit, one of the heavy prices you had to pay for being in public service, for getting yourself appointed to about a zillion committees. Russell had to give Maria credit for that. She definitely knew how to get a lot of mileage out of being a minority, but to be a Puerto Rican and a woman and a small business owner—well, that was just about carte blanche. *How was he supposed to know whether she was legitimately out to lunch or off screwing some guy?* Marriage is supposed to be based on trust. It would have been the easiest thing in the world to lie about lunch. And there were a couple of guys in particular he had some pretty strong suspicions about.

Like that Chad Blitzer, sales engineer from Martin Marietta—the way they'd kissed that time they all went to lunch together. *Since when do marketing people greet each other with kisses?* That Chad was a wolf in sheep's clothing if there ever was one. Chad was married but Ralph was pretty sure he wouldn't turn it down if a woman offered herself. And that Catholic Priest Maria always talked about … that Father what's-his-name? She was definitely in love with him. Whether it had gone beyond that … well, that kind of depended on whether the good father was into women or choirboys.

Truth was, Russell wouldn't have been very surprised to learn that Luis, her own father, was maybe guilty of some inappropriate behavior. Luis was definitely an arrogant son of a bitch when it came to women—and definitely a major contributor to the depression Maria seemed to have fought most of her adult life.

It was all pretty confusing. Like the church thing. Before they were married, Maria had gone to some holy-roller church but had all the trappings of a good Catholic. When he asked her about it she was pretty elusive at first. Turned out she had been married to some guy in Puerto Rico who had three teenage daughters from another relationship. Maria had supposedly tried to be mother to them, but wound up getting her butt beat for her troubles. Divorcing that creep had somehow meant she was no longer a good Catholic and could no longer attend Catholic mass.

Russell had never been much of a church person, so he didn't think much about it when Maria suggested a civil ceremony would be fine. For the first five years of marriage she never said a word about going to church. It was only after learning that her ex-husband had died that she'd started making noises about church.

"Do you think you could become Catholic?" she'd asked one day out of the blue when her mother was visiting.

Chen had come to Minnesota for knee replacement surgery in the world famous surgical unit at Rochester.

"I don't know," he'd shrugged, caught a little off guard. "I guess I could go to church okay … you know, learn the rituals, but I don't think you can lie to God—if you know what I mean?"

She'd given him what he'd thought was a puzzled look. Now it seemed like she might have just been angry. She'd never said another word about it.

The next thing he knew, months later, she was asking him if they could talk. There was something ominous about the way she'd said it. "I guess," he'd muttered, waiting for the other shoe to fall.

"I'm leaving you," she'd said. "I have a truck coming tomorrow."

Some talk! She'd never even said a word about divorce. The next day the truck came, along with Luisa's kids Sean and Carrie—to help load—and away they went.

There weren't even any tense moments. They loaded up most of the furnishings she'd brought into the marriage. There wasn't even any bickering about which pieces of furniture she should take. If there was something they'd bought together, she left that for him. Like she didn't want any reminders of their life together—except for Bud, one of their damned dogs.

"Mother wants Bud," she'd announced.

"Why don't you take Max," Russell had countered, feeling strangely guilty that she would be taking the dog he'd considered broken, instead of their feisty little Maltese. They already knew about Bud's fatty tumors and that he was going to have to be put down.

"Mother would rather have Bud."

"Didn't you tell her he has tumors?"

"I'll take him to the vet—"

The bitter memory of the conversation suddenly brought the tears welling up in Russell's eyes. "Fuck you God!" he screamed, slamming the heel of his hand into the steering wheel so hard he thought he might have broken it. He clinched both hands into fists and raised them toward the heavens and let out a mighty roar— then broke into uncontrollable sobs.

Chapter 6

When Russell awoke it was after six. Crying himself to sleep was not the kind of thing he did on a regular basis. In fact, he wasn't even sure it was something he had ever done, even as a child. If he had, he no longer remembered the event. Considering how crappy he now felt, he thought it might be something he would remember.

What he did remember was that he was in big trouble. Here he was more than fifteen hundred miles from home, guilty of a major crime, most likely murder, and he was down to a couple dollars. *How was he going to get home without leaving a paper trail?*

It didn't take him very long to realize the answer to his problem was obvious. If you don't have the money to buy something you need, then you either had to find a way to get some money or steal the item in question. Filling up your tank and driving off would be too stupid to consider, so there had to be another way. He ran his mind quickly over all of the possibilities he could come up with.

The only possibilities that made any sense all involved a siphon hose—which he didn't have. But he did have a roll of duct tape that he could no longer remember why he'd bought, and, if he was lucky, maybe enough change to make up the difference.

He started the Escort and drove back to the hardware

store where he'd bought the duct tape. Luckily, they were open until 7:00 p. m., which gave him just enough time to pick out a small copper fitting, a clamp, and ten feet of clear plastic tubing.

"I guess I'm gonna have to do it a different way," Russell told the disinterested clerk, "so I need to return this tape and get these other things."

Fortunately, the clerk didn't bat an eye. Probably had a hot date and was far more interested in the clock than any plumbing project Russell might be in the middle of. Which pleased Russell no end. If the guy showed the least spark of interest, he would have had to invent some long-winded, boring explanation that had nothing to do with stealing gas.

As it was, stealing gas was not something he expected to be very good at. It was pretty risky parking close enough to another car to get the siphon hose into operation. It seemed like there were a lot of variables that had to be taken into consideration. He'd have to find a car that had the gas cap on the opposite side as the Escort so that when he was parked beside the *tanker car,* the gas caps would only be a few feet apart. His piece of hose wasn't long enough to do it any other way. It would also have to be a car that didn't have a locking gas cap and one that had enough gas in it in the first place to make it worth the risk. It would never do to get the siphon hose all hooked up and then discover the tanker car was all but bone dry. Or to try to siphon someone's gas in a public place where there was a lot of activity.

The only sensible possibility involved farmer's fuel tanks out in the middle of open fields. Risky, of course, but less risky than any of the other possibilities that involved trying to do the job in a more populated area. Besides, he already knew where there was a good prospect. All he had to do was wait until it got good and dark.

...

It was well after 9:00 O'clock when Russell turned into the field driveway. He hoped that anyone looking would just assume he was just going to turn around, but instead of backing out, he cut the engine and lights. He'd planned on sitting there long enough to make sure that no one was paying any attention to what he was doing. There was no point in wasting gas while he was doing it.

After twenty minutes of sitting in the dark with no cars going by, he started the Escort, put it in low gear, and let out the clutch. He kept his eyes focused in the distance and his foot off the accelerator.

It seemed like it took a quad-zillion years to get to the tank. Following the hard-packed road across the field had been easy enough without lights because of the contrasting color between the road and field—just like plowing after dark. Seeing what he was doing after he got there was quite another thing.

There was no way Russell could risk turning on his headlights, so he had to do the job by feel. His plan was to use his pocket-knife to make a small hole in the farmer's fuel tank filler hose, then screw in the fitting he'd purchased, clamp the plastic tube to the fitting and turn on the gas by flipping the valve where the hose was attached to the tank. It would probably leak a little bit where the fitting was screwed into the rubber hose, but so what? The only problem was the valve was padlocked on the nozzle end of the filler hose.

What was he going to do now?

He rummaged around in his brief case, which didn't have much in it except his corporate tax class books, a couple of pens, and a calculator. He did manage to find a single paper clip in the bottom of the brief case by using the dim light from the calculator to search. Of course, that killed his night-vision for a bit, but by the time he got the paper clip bent into the shape he wanted, it was back.

It was a good thing. The moon was no longer full and somewhat hidden behind hazy clouds. Besides that, he'd never attempted to pick a padlock before, with a paperclip or otherwise. And it wasn't working.

Totally frustrated, he fumbled around in the trunk until he found a tire iron. He tried whacking the padlock at first, but in the dim light, he couldn't be sure where he was hitting. Then, it occurred to him that by whacking the padlock he might actually create a spark … set the thing on fire and blow himself up.

Not knowing what else to do he held the padlock in one hand and guided the end of the tire iron through the loop, twisted the tire iron slightly, and jerked down as hard as he could with his other hand. To his amazement, the padlock popped open.

Which scared him half to death. The end of the tire iron flew up and clanged into the fuel barrel with a god-awful clatter that was probably heard by everyone within a four-county radius.

Russell held his breath for a couple of eons listening for the sound of sirens or dogs barking or something. When it finally seemed safe, he flipped the valve, popped the gas cap on the Escort and squeezed the handle ever so gently. By listening very carefully, he could hear the sound of gasoline rising in the tank neck and was able to release the handle without spilling a drop.

Once, as a kid, Russell had swiped a grease pencil that a grocery clerk had been using to mark prices on canned goods. He'd felt so guilty about that he'd wound up chucking the pencil so he didn't have to look at it. Now he wondered if he'd feel the same way about the farmer's gas. That he could go ahead and kill his ex-wife ... wife, whatever she was, and not feel a thing was crazy ... but steal a few gallons of gas—

It didn't make sense!

He picked up the padlock from where he'd left it on top of the car and hooked it back in the valve, then tried to snap it shut. Either he'd broken it, or it was corroded and it had never been closed in the first place. He decided it didn't matter. He twisted it into place so it would sort of look like it was closed and climbed back into the Escort.

Now all he had to do was get out of the field without getting stuck.

Which was easier said than done. The driveway into the field ended at the fuel tank. That meant he either had to back out the way he'd come in, or turn the car around. And, if the front wheels of the car got off the narrow, hard-packed driveway he not only might leave tracks, he might possibly get stuck. And with the night being as black as it was, getting back on the highway in one piece was going to be a good trick.

...

When Deputy Dick McIntyre called Wendy's parents and asked them to come down to the Sheriff's office to

59

pick her up he advised them not to bother hurrying. The plan was to take her back over to the ramshackle house across the street and have her tell her story to the Sheriff when he arrived. In the mean time, Dick planted one half of his skinny butt cheeks on the corner of the counter and watched Mama Jo fuss over the child.

Dick McIntyre was thirty-one years old with one of those narrow heads that had a hairline that started at eye level on one side and went around the contour of his head just above his ears to end at the other eye. In other words, he was prematurely bald. He took a lot of good-natured ribbing about his baldness, but he was a good father. His son Michael was twelve and his daughter Julie nine, which meant she was probably in the same grade as Wendy and the kids probably knew each other. He had been in Mama Jo's many times to buy bait to take his kids fishing, so he knew Mama Jo pretty well and didn't see any need to bring in a county social worker to do what Mama Jo was already doing—comforting Wendy and getting her to relax.

The shortest route to the truth is trust. Dick had serious doubts that a county social worker could do as good a job as Mama Jo.

"You gotta tell exactly what happened," Mama Jo encouraged Wendy when Sheriff Bremer arrived. "Dat man gotta go to jail."

Wendy was still visibly shaken, but with Mama Jo's encouragement she was able to relate the circumstances of her abduction and rescue. An officer was dispatched to pick up her bicycle. Then McIntyre and Sheriff Bremer took Wendy across the street to the house and made her tell the end of the story again, the part that took place in the house.

"What did this other man look like?" the Sheriff asked.

McIntyre had lifted Wendy onto the table in the same position she'd been placed before, only this time she was fully dressed, except for her stockings, which were probably still some place on the grimy floor.

Wendy shrugged. "I don't know. I couldn't see him very good." She looked around the room, somewhat puzzled. "It was darker before—"

McIntyre nodded. "Look at this, Boss," he said, picking up one of the shades. "Looks like the shades were ripped off ... like somebody was looking for something. We need to get the state crime lab boys down here."

"I see what you mean," Sheriff Bremer said, thoughtfully surveying the ramshackle kitchen. "Lookee here!" He took three quick steps across the room and bent over, hands clasp behind his back, to peer down at the arrow sticking in the wall at gut level. "Didn't we have a report of some woman in Jacksonville taking a target arrow in the breast the other night? Probably would have killed her if it hadn't hit a rib."

"Right," McIntyre agreed. "Another guy out walking his dog tripped over another arrow that just happen to be passing between his legs."

"Lordee, Lordee, Lordee—" Bremer shook his head. "What the hell we got goin' on? Some crazy Robin Hood out scarin' folks and rescuin' kids from perverts?"

McIntyre smiled. "Ain't that something?"

They both knew there was probably a whole lot more to the story than such a simplistic explanation. Sometimes a simple leap of faith could get you there, but most of the time law enforcement was just the slow, steady grinding out of the facts and then linking them together—like putting together a jigsaw puzzle.

When they got back to the Sheriff's office hours later, Sheriff Bremer took Wendy's mother into his office and filled her in on what had transpired. "You understand, Ma'am ... that we are going to have to have Wendy examined by a doctor. And it's not that we don't believe her—it is just something we have to do. You know, just in case she's too scared to tell us what really happened."

"You think she might have been raped?" Wendy's mother said solemnly.

"Oh, God no!" Sheriff Bremer tried to sound reassuring. "It doesn't look like the guy ever got a chance to do anything like that. He had her jeans and underpants off but we think that's as far as he got ... let's just say Wendy was very lucky. Some guy with a bow and arrow showed up and put a stop to things before anything really bad happened. I mean, I don't mean to minimize what happened to Wendy ... but it sounds like it could have turned out a lot worse."

"W-what do you mean?" Wendy's mother had a feeling Sheriff Bremer was implying something more than rape.

Bremer shrugged. "Don't mean to start no rumors ... and it's just speculation on our part, but there have been quite a number of unsolved missing girl cases all across the south in the past few years. Might just be coincidence—but we might also have ourselves a serial murdered on our hands."

"Are you serious?" Wendy's mother was aghast.

"Afraid so … if it hadn't been for this Robin Hood guy stepping in—"

"I don't understand," Wendy's mother said. "Who is this Robin Hood guy? Where is he? I'd like to thank him for saving my daughter."

Sheriff Bremer chuckled and shook his head. "We don't know who he is or where he came from ma'am … but I wished to God we did."

A New Beginning

Chapter 7

Normally, I am not much of a drinker ... maybe a beer or two on a really hot day when I've been working hard, say digging up the garden or something. When Maria and I first got married, she was all gung-ho to have a garden and lots of flowers. My mother had always been a flower person, so I was happy to oblige and we spent some really enjoyable afternoons working in our garden and flowerbeds. The last few years, however, Maria had started coming home from her tax office in the early afternoon, since she had to be open only one day a week during the summer, and going straight to the bedroom to take a nap, leaving me to do the gardening alone.

Now, after a nerve racking evening stealing gas, I was in dire need of a good stiff shot of brandy rather than a beer or a nap. Unfortunately, I didn't even have enough money left for a coke. I thought briefly about ordering a drink someplace and then pretending I'd lost my wallet. The only problem with that is that they would likely take the drink back if I didn't pay for it. Of course, there was always panhandling, something I'd never had to consider before.

In the meantime, I drove around Lake City trying to decide what to do. Lake City was one of the strangest cities I'd ever been in. To begin with it seemed to sprawl all over the place. In places the streets were very narrow with odd little diagonal parking-spaces carved out next to the side walk that didn't go full length of the block. There were half a dozen highways running through it. The businesses along the highways were for the most part like in any other city. Then there were the ramshackle houses. I have never seen so many shacks in a single town in my life. Even a lot of the houses that weren't shacks were pretty junkie, with used appliances and tables and what not on the porches. Seemed like the best clue as to whether someone live in a house was whether there was a car or pickup parked in front and a TV antenna on the roof.

At night most of the side streets were downright spooky. Or maybe my nerves were just shot to hell. Actually, while out steeling gas in the middle of a dark field I had no expectation of another human being popping out of the shadows. That was definitely not the case while driving around on these poorly lit side streets.

What I should have been doing instead of meandering around like an idiot, like was usually my case, was seeking out Interstate 75 and *getting the hell out of Dodge.* But for some reason I had this overwhelming compulsion to find some human companionship. I felt like I had been sneaking around in the dark forever and the part of me that had inflicted pain and maybe even death on Maria was closed off. My mind refused to even go anywhere near those thoughts. It wasn't that I had trouble believing I had done such a thing, it was just so inconceivable that I could have done such a thing without feeling anything even close to remorse. Now, it was like I had just stepped out of the fog and could not get back in again.

While driving down one particular dark street I was

suddenly surprised to happen upon a sprawling blue building with quite a few cars parked under the large live oak trees surrounding the place. The building seemed to be on the other side of a railroad track so I had to go another block or so to find a place to cross and go back. I thought the place must be a bar or supper club, but it turned out to be an American Legion Post. I decided to park on the outer edge of the parking lot and smoke one of *el creepo's* cigarettes while I decided which way to go—*a little larceny, or a risky paper trail?*

Actually, I had never really smoked cigarettes. I had smoked a pipe for years, but had quit a few years back. But in my current mental state, the thought of a cigarette had a certain soothing appeal. Something about drawing in the smoke and blowing it out had a way a calming a person.

To my amazement, when I tried to get a cigarette out of the pack in the dim light I fumbled around and discovered a neat, quad-folded $100 bill between the inner foil wrap and the outer cellophane wrap of the package of Camels.

Unbelievable!

I stuffed the cigarettes and one of the matchbooks in my shirt pocket and headed for the bar. One drink certainly wasn't going to hurt anything. And since it was already a few minutes after eleven, I didn't have time for much more than one drink.

The bar part of the legion wasn't very crowded. Most of the people were scattered in small groups at a couple of tables——and they all looked at me like I had just dropped in from outer space … like the Pope in a pigsty, or something.

"What'll it be, cowboy?" a voice said, practically in my ear.

The diminutive waitress was standing between the two bar sections of the open bar pass-through. She wasn't much taller than the top of the bar, rough guess about five foot two. She was wearing black jeans, a big, floppy T-shirt with the word "*Gators*" printed on the front, and red tennis shoes with white trim. I've never been very good at guessing women's ages but I figured she was somewhere in the late thirties to early forties. She had a pert face with collar-length curly, light-brown hair and blue-green eyes. She was not exactly what you would call stunningly beautiful—just cute as hell. Her smile was like an oasis in the desert.

"Red eye," I replied, returning her smile.

"Is that kinda like sarsaparilla?" she quipped with a grin, glad to find someone with enough of a sense of humor to pick up on her teasing line from the movies.

"Sort of," I nodded. "Make it a double Southern Comfort."

"Whoa!" her grin got even broader and one eyebrow went up in recognition of the intended double entendre. "Sounds like somebody had a rough day."

"More like a rough week," I grinned.

I unfolded the $100 bill and took the creases out it with my thumbnail while she poured the drink. "I just printed it this morning," I joked, handing the bill over when she set the Southern Comfort in front of me.

She didn't bat an eye at the bill. "I bet," she said, turning toward the cash drawer.

There was a TV above the bar and the 11:00 O'clock news was still on, although the set was turned down so low it was barely audible. I sat there on the barstool nursing the Southern Comfort and dividing my attention between lip reading the news and watching Miss Blue Eyes putter around behind the bar. Somehow, I had completely missed the era of free love and I started to wonder what it would be like to pick up a woman in a bar and take her to bed. I didn't even know this cutie's name.

When the Sheriff came on the TV screen, my heart kicked into high gear.

"Could you turn that up a bit?" I asked Blue-Eyes when she came back towards me. It was all I could do to keep from jumping over the bar and planting one on her—but that would have been just too stupid.

"Sure," she replied, glancing at me as if to say, "I was kind of interested, but now you want to know about the Sheriff. What gives?"

According to the Sheriff, the abducted girl's parents were delighted to have her back in one piece and very grateful to the mystery man who had rescued her by shooting a target arrow into the sheet rock of the old house where she was being held. The police were looking for a black man driving a blue van, make unknown, but thought to be a Dodge or Plymouth. They would also like to question the man, thought to be white, who had pulled off the daring rescue—

"Ain't that something?" Blue-Eyes asked, jarring me back to reality.

"S-sure is," I stammered, not knowing what else to say.

Her eyes locked on mine for a second, probing.

"Wouldn't like to give a girl a ride home, would you?" she asked suddenly.

I was so stunned by the offer I nearly fell off my barstool.

Obviously my surprise showed because she offered a quick explanation. "Well," she grinned. "You're obviously not black … and if you're the white guy, you're some kind of hero so I should be safe with you. Besides, anybody who drinks sarsaparilla on a regular basis is okay in my book."

"Is that right?" I muttered, not actually answering her question. It was pretty obvious that I would be taking her home—and that I wasn't going to be telling her that her knight in shining armor might actually be a killer himself.

"Lynn," she offered her name without my having to ask.

"Russell," I reciprocated. "What time do you get off?"

"Another twenty minutes."

"I can wait," I nodded.

…

It turned out that Lynn didn't really need a ride … that she had driven to work in her red Chevy Malibou. I didn't want to leave the Escort sitting in the now empty Legion parking lot, so I agreed to follow her back to her apartment in White Springs. It was about a fifteen-minute drive and I must admit I was starting to get cold feet. The smartest thing I could possibly do was get on Interstate 75 and go like hell—but I never claimed to be that smart. Her apartment was a bit off the beaten path so I felt pretty relaxed about leaving the Escort beside her Chevy while I followed her upstairs.

"Would you like another drink?" she asked, planting me on a floral print couch.

"Sarsaparilla?"

She grinned.

"Better not," I shook my head. "I wouldn't want to pass out on you."

More double entendre, but she didn't seem to notice. "How about some coffee?"

"Sure,"

She went off to the kitchen and I could hear the little noises of cupboards being opened and closed, the soft clink of coffee cups being placed on saucers. I felt as if my mind was spinning out of control. Maybe that's what I missed the most. Being married and living with someone, there's always those subtle subdued noises of what your partner was doing … the shower running … pots and pans clanging in the kitchen—

I got up and walked in to the kitchen. "If I stay on the couch," I said, sitting down at the kitchen table, "You're going to have to get a crowbar to pour that coffee down me."

"This is way better anyway," she suggested, sliding a cup and saucer in front of me. She opened a cupboard and took out a small bowl and a package of cookies, dumping some cookies into the bowl. "You like these?"

"Sure … I like everything."

When she brought the coffee pot to pour the coffee, I reached up with my right hand, hooked it behind her neck, and pulled her gently down to kiss her on the lips without getting up.

73

"I was wondering if you were ever going to get around to that," she murmured, sitting the pot on the table without pouring any coffee. She stepped around my legs, turned, and planted her behind on my lap and put her left arm around my neck. A good kissing position.

We kissed for a long, long time. For me it was a painful reminder of the not-so-good-old-days when as a teenager I'd managed to find the nerve to kiss a girl but not the nerve to take things to the next level. Back then I was just chicken. Now it was an entirely different deal. I had the nerve, and I had the desire—but I wasn't sure I had the right.

"I don't think I even want any coffee just now," Lynn said finally, slipping off my lap. "I'll be right back."

I had absolutely no doubt about what she was up to. It was the old "let me slip into something more comfortable" routine, which I wasn't sure I was going to know how to handle. I poured myself a cup of coffee and tried to get my thoughts straight, but before I could, the Southern Comfort kicked in.

I must have been snoring like one of Santa's reindeer when Lynn returned a few minutes later all slicked up in a soft blue negligee.

"Let me help you to the couch," she murmured, helping me to my feet.

Chapter 8

What exactly are you supposed to tell a girl when you leave her stranded at the alter, so to speak, I wondered when I sat up in an attempt to get my head to emerge from the Southern Comfort fog the next morning. I was still on the couch and still fully clothed. *Damned fool,* I chastised myself, realizing I'd never been very good at holding my liquor. For just a brief moment, I wanted to slink out of Lynn's apartment and never look back. But she was too nice to be treated that way.

On the other hand, I couldn't exactly remember when I'd bathed last. I hadn't exactly left home planning on a long stay. The one change of clothes I'd brought along was sorely in need of an oil change. I felt like a scumbag and a complete idiot.

"Well, I see you didn't die," Lynn said, suddenly appearing from the bedroom.

I gave her my best sheepish smile. "No such luck."

"How do you feel?"

"Stupid."

"No need," she said, pushing my arm aside and seating herself on my knee with her legs between mine. "I could tell you were pretty exhausted last night. I was too. How about some breakfast and we'll start over?"

"What are you, Florence Nightingale?" I laughed. I

gave her a peck on the lips. "Sounds like a great idea but I need to get cleaned up a bit first, if you wouldn't mind."

"Actually," she gave me a big, goofy grin. "I took the liberty of going down to your car. Seems like you're traveling pretty light. You've got two bags—one of which I don't think is even yours—and there isn't much for clean clothes in either. I brought up the bag I figured was yours and I set out some of my ex-husband's clothes—"

I stared at her in total amazement. "I take it back … you're not Florence Nightingale! You're that gol' danged Sherlock Holmes. How'd you figure out which bag was mine?"

"For one thing, the picture of the black woman and child—"

"Smart!"

"Then, too, you're carrying cigarettes … but I don't think you smoke. You don't smell or taste like a smoker, and I didn't see any tobacco stains on your hands."

"Boy … you are a regular Sherlock Holmes."

She seemed a bit downcast. "Not really. There were a couple of things that really puzzled me though. You have a container of night crawlers and minnows, but no fishing equipment. Your license plate is from Minnesota, land of ten thousand lakes. I don't think you'd drive all the way to Florida to buy bait without bringing your fishing equipment."

"Maybe I accidentally threw my rod into the river."

"I doubt that … buying two kinds of bait suggests that you would have a tackle box of some kind. It's not likely that you would throw both in the river."

"Maybe my boat sank,"

"Then your bait would have floated away."

"Pretty smart, aren't you?" I said, beginning to enjoy this little game a lot more than I should have. If I didn't watch it, she'd have me pegged for the wife killer I really was. "I suppose you got me figured for some kind of weirdo that goes around stealing bags of dirty laundry."

"Not exactly."

My heart jumped into my throat. I'd just been kidding, but the way she said "Not exactly," I could tell she had something specific in mind. I pretty much hated the idea of asking what. "Well?" I prompted, holding my breath for the answer.

She wiggled her butt on my knee and grinned. "I think you must be this white guy Robin Hood … the one that foiled the kidnapping and rape. What I don't get is why you were shooting at some woman and guy in Jacksonville. You're lucky you didn't kill someone."

I nearly dumped her on the floor. "W-what did you just say?"

"What?"

"That stuff about the woman and guy in Jacksonville— did you say they didn't die?"

"Right. It was on the news. The police figure this Robin Hood guy that rescued the girl also shot at a woman in Jacksonville and some other guy walking his dog. The woman was wounded in the breast, but will recover. The man just tripped over the arrow as it went whizzing by. The police claim it has to be the same guy … I guess the arrows matched up or something."

"Yes!" I yelled, jumping up and almost dumping Lynn on the floor "Yes! Damn it! Yes!" I had never felt such relief in my entire life. I grabbed Lynn's hands and began jumping around the living room with her like a maniac.

"I take it you're pleased?" she said between bounces.

"You might say that." I grinned at her.

"And you are this Robin Hood guy?"

I stopped, wondering just how she was going to react if I said, "Yes." After all, I'd only known her a few hours, and I'd been asleep most of that time. But after this sudden exhilarating turn of events, I was beginning to think I just needed to learn to go with the flow.

"What if I am?"

She smiled again. "I think I'd be interested in hearing your explanations."

"Really?" I could hardly believe it.

"Why not? You obviously had your reasons."

"Maybe—but before we get into all that. I sure would like to get cleaned up."

Lynn led me into her bedroom, pointed out my bag and her ex-husband's clothes that she'd laid out on her bed, and gestured toward the adjoining bathroom. I was well into my shower when she parted the curtain and climbed in with me.

...

For me, the idea of sharing my life with a woman again was kind of like having the sun come out from behind a persistent cloudbank, not that I was ready to trot down the isle again. Technically, I wasn't even divorced yet. But thank God I was not a widower either! In retrospect, it was hard to fathom how I could have sunk so low as to actually fire an arrow at another human being—let alone someone I had been married to.

It was also hard to understand why Lynn wasn't running down the road screaming bloody murder. After all, if I was not guilty of murder, I was definitely guilty of attempted murder. The only real difference was the degree of "success" or "failure" depending on how you looked at it.

"So what gives?" I asked, polishing off the scrambled eggs she'd fixed for me.

"What do you mean?"

"How come we're sitting here eating this lovely breakfast when we both know that I am, at the very least, a would-be murderer?"

Lynn smiled and looked down at the plate in front of her. She was sitting sort of sideways on her chair. "It's not really that complicated." She took her fork and pushed the scrambled eggs aside so she could trace along the feathers of the big red rooster painted in the middle of her china plate. "I told you I was divorced—"

"So?"

"So … when I found out my husband was cheating on me I followed his girlfriend home one night and torched her car."

"No kidding?"

Lynn's blue eyes took on a devilish grin. "No kidding—and I loved every minute of it too! They might have suspected I was the one, but at that point I wasn't even supposed to know about them, so—"

I gave her an understanding smile. "They do say all is fair in love and war—"

"Right! And it's a lot more fun when they don't even know the war is on. I waited a couple of weeks after torching her car to catch Steve in another lie about being at work when he was really out fucking his girl. When I confronted him about it … told him that I had gone to his plant to find him, he finally told me the truth. Then I got to have all the normal wifely reactions. I took some of his clothes, dumped them on the lawn and poured red paint all over them. I was trying to do a big scarlet "A," but the wind wrecked it, so he never got the point. But it was fun anyway."

I nodded and took a sip of my coffee. "I see what you mean. It's the same for me. In case you haven't guessed … the woman in Jacksonville is my ex-wife—no scratch that. I should have said, 'soon to be ex-wife' since the divorce isn't actually final yet. Actually, it's pretty much final except for signing the papers. I was going to sign them but then I came down here on the spur of the moment because I thought she was starting a new tax business with money that should have gone to pay off our debts. The way it is now, she walks away scoot free while I get the 'shaft' so to speak. I just fired the arrow at the guy walking his dog to throw the police off. Pretty stupid, huh?"

Lynn shrugged.

"You know what it is?" I asked, hoping to make her understand. "Pain is like sitting on a flagpole … if you don't do something to get off, it can ruin your whole outlook."

She nodded her head in agreement. "Right! And divorce can be way worse than if your spouse dies. If the spouse dies, you only have grief to deal with. If you wind up getting divorced because your spouse cheated, you have to deal with rejection and betrayal as well as the actual loss of your spouse."

I got up from my chair and moved to her side of the table. I squatted in front of the corner of her chair so that my left knee slid under her legs and my other knee pushed against the side of the chair. I pulled her head forward with my right hand to kiss her on the lips. It was an enthusiastic kiss that found my tongue searching, probing— My left hand slid up to cup her bra, as if it had a mind of its own.

"Sorry," I said, breaking away after a few seconds.

"It's okay." She gave me a quick peck on the cheek.

"Things are happening pretty fast here—"

She nodded.

Relationships generally have their own kind of pace, depending on the two people and the type of relationship involved. You could meet someone and know from the very first second that it was going to be nothing more than a one-night-stand. Or you could have a relationship that went on for years with nothing more than smoldering glances and furtive looks. Or that first glance could flash back "soul mate" and everything after that was hung on a kind of blind trust that "soul mates" have for each other.

For the first time in my adult life, I felt like I was dealing with "blind trust" issues. I'd met and married my first wife in Germany and it was only after it was too late that I realized her major goal had had more to do with marrying a G.I. and getting to the states than it did with love or me. And Maria, of course, was too much of a rebound deal.

"How would you feel about a quick trip to Minnesota?" I asked, standing up and moving back to my chair on the other side of the table.

"Don't you think I should know you a little better first?" Lynn grinned.

"Maybe—I just didn't want you to think I was running away. I kinda need to get back and take care of a few things ... you know?"

"Sure."

"If I'm gone much longer people are going to start wondering where I've been—if they haven't already. I've been gone nearly five days as it is ... and I've got a tax class coming up that I shouldn't miss—"

"No, no, I understand." She waved me off with a pensive look, then pushed the knuckle of her folded right forefinger against her lower lip and sort of chewed at her lip in thoughtful repose. "I want to ... it's just that I'm not sure if I can get the time off or not."

I nodded. "Maybe we should get a few things established first," I said. "You do understand that we are only having this conversation because I need you to know how smitten I am with you. I don't want this to be any "slam, bham, thank you ma'am" kind of deal. And up until now I didn't have any good reason to come back to Florida ... in fact, just the opposite."

She nodded.

"What I should do," I continued, "is go to the police and tell them everything I know about this guy who kidnapped the girl—I mean, who knows if this was the first, or if this was a crime of opportunity. The guy could be a serial killer for all we know."

"That's what they're saying on the news."

"Really?"

"Yes."

"That kind of settles it, doesn't it?" I said, making

a decision. "Somebody needs to do something about this creep … and I damned sure don't want to go to the police. I mean, I committed a crime and I should be made to pay for what I did to Maria, but I don't think it will do anybody any good if I spend the rest of my life in jail."

This was nothing more than pure "*rationalization,*" a process that I understood very well. It was what I did when I went back to smoking the pipe that first time after I'd tried to quit. Seemed like no one had noticed that I wasn't smoking the pipe that was always hanging out of my face. "No one noticed," I'd rationalized, "So nobody cares." One puff and I was right back to smoking. Never mind that my mouth was always sore like I'd been sucking on a blowtorch. Never mind that my clothes and hair smelled god-awful. Never mind that people gave me looks of disgust when I lit up in public. It wasn't until the oral surgeon pulled out my tongue and whacked off a piece for a biopsy that I got the message, that I was able to turn the rationalization around with a simple "why am I killing myself with this stupid habit?" Oh, yes, I understood rationalization quite well.

"What do you have in mind?" Lynn asked.

I grinned sheepishly. "How about you give me a helping hand … help me track this son-of-a-bitch down?"

"Are you serious?" She wasn't sure whether to believe me or not.

I grinned again. "I'm not sure whether I'm serious or not. Sounds pretty far fetched, doesn't it? But if we don't track this guy down, who will? We could send what we have to the police but that would be taking a chance …

they could probably trace it back to me somehow. And I'm certainly not anxious to go to jail, and maybe get you in trouble for harboring a criminal."

The trouble with rationalization was that it doesn't really differentiate between the so-called "good" and "bad," or "right" and "wrong." What it really does is differentiate between "I want" and "I don't want." And what I really wanted was for Lynn to help me track down this potential serial killer—whether out of guilt for what I'd done to Maria, or because I just wanted to spend a lot more time with Lynn, I wasn't sure.

"How long would it take to go back to Minnesota to take care of what you need to do?" Lynn asked, causing my heartbeat to quicken. "I think I can probably get some time off. I'm just not sure how much."

. . .

As it turned out, Lynn wasn't able to contact her boss until late Sunday afternoon and he wasn't about to let her off with such short notice. He did let her switch shifts and work the Monday day shift so we didn't actually get to leave until after 4:00 O'clock Monday evening. We spent the time between Sunday morning and Lynn's Monday shift just enjoying each other and getting better acquainted.

Chapter 9

Minnesota was a tad more than a stone's throw from Lake City, Florida … in fact, a tad more than a couple of stone throws. Coming down, I had been so engrossed with getting there I was hardly even aware of where I was half the time. Going back was way different. I was absolutely overjoyed and enthralled by the pert figure sleeping against the door in the tilted-back passenger seat when it was my turn to drive. When she was driving, I was so busy sneaking peeks to make sure she was still there I hardly got any sleep at all.

By the time we got to the Wisconsin Dells area, I was so wired I asked Lynn to curl up with me in a rest stop area so I could relax. It was a little after 8:00 O'clock in the morning, but cloudy and gray. We had been driving through a mist for a couple of hours and it was getting me down. Besides, I needed an excuse to hold her in my arms again.

Five hours later, when I woke up with a god-awful crappy taste in my mouth, I wished I had opted for a motel. Lynn felt so good snuggled against me, I didn't really want to move, but I didn't want to kill her with my breath either. I twisted around until I could reach my bag on the back seat; rummaged around with one hand and found what felt like my toothpaste, retrieved it, unscrewed the cap and squirted a dollop into my mouth, all the while being very careful not to wake her.

"Me too," she murmured, squinting at me through one half-opened eyelid.

The way she held her mouth ready to receive the toothpaste reminded me of a baby robin waiting for a big, white grub worm, except the toothpaste was actually mint green. We spent the next couple of minutes smacking our lips and rubbing our teeth vigorously with a forefinger.

"Aaaggh!" I declared finally, smacking my lips in disgust. "We should have gotten a motel."

"We still can," Lynette murmured, twisting slightly to receive the kiss I offered.

Her willingness to oblige set my mind awhirl trying to do some mental calculations. We still had at least eight hours of driving to get to my house, and if we just grabbed a few things and headed right back to Menomonie that would be another four hours—

"You know what," I suggested. "I was planning to go home first and come back to Menomonie for my class on the way back to Florida, but it makes a lot more sense to do it the other way around. We should drive on to Menomonie and get a motel … I'll go to my class tomorrow and then we can go to my place from there."

"Fine with me."

"Great! But right now, let's get something to eat. I'm starving."

The restaurant was nothing to brag about.

…

The motel on the other hand was one of those quaint places with roses painted in primary colors of red and green on the white shutters. The shutters had hearts cut in the center. The room itself had basic motel furnishings, bed, dresser, TV, microwave and micro-refrigerator, writing table and one straight-backed chair with a ruffled, floral seat cushion. Every wood surface in the room was newly shined and smelled of furniture polish.

"This okay?" I asked.

"Lovely," Lynn barely glanced around. Throwing her bag on the bed, she started peeling off her clothes. "If you don't mind … I'm gonna take a shower before you throw me out."

I smiled and thought briefly of joining her. I opted to get a few things organized instead and spent some time skimming over the material for my upcoming tax class. I had to admit I was still a little puzzled as to why I had ever let Maria finagle me into taking over the tax franchise in the first place. It was one thing to be doing taxes because you wanted to, quite another to be doing them just because you could. What in the world had ever made me think I was qualified to run a business with more than a dozen part-time employees? True, I did have some supervisory experience, but still—

For me, taking over the tax franchise was a lot like skating on thin ice. It seemed like I always had to be holding my breath because I was really not very positive about what I was doing. Oh, sure, it wasn't such a big deal remodeling the office the way the franchise director wanted it; it wasn't even such a big deal buying all those new computers, a server, and a printer—what sucked was dealing with the riffraff. I had never dreamed there were so many people in the world anxiously waiting for the chance to rip you off, claiming they needed their tax prep fees back because you made a mistake. Most of the time the mistake was something they'd neglected to tell you, whether by accident or deliberately. I was beginning to think it was mostly deliberate.

I didn't really have time to do justice to the week's assignment and was going to have to plead stupidity if called upon to answer any questions. I glanced quickly over the next chapter in the textbook, then went out to the car and brought in *el creepo's* bag and set it on the writing table. I was just staring at the bag like it was a ticking bomb when Lynn came out of the shower all pink and fluffy around the edges, still wrapped in a towel.

"My turn?" I asked.

"If you say so."

She gave me one of those wry smiles women use to say, "you can stay stinky if you want to, but if you're planning to come anywhere near me in the hope of getting a little sugar, you'd better get your butt into the shower."

Our relationship still had that snappy, flirtatious zip to it that made meeting a new special person so totally exciting. Hopefully it would never wear off.

I wasn't about to jeopardize that. Besides, I needed a shower.

When I came out of the shower, Lynn was seated at the writing table, the free motel writing paper in front of her, my pen in her right hand and the picture of the black woman and little boy in the other. She had apparently been making notes; there were a few scribbled lines on the first sheet of paper. I was pleased to see she was holding the picture very carefully by just the tiniest bit of the corner.

"What do you think?" I asked, starting to climb back

into my clothes. "Can we figure anything out from the picture?"

"Maybe— It would be helpful to have a magnifying glass though."

"I have one at home."

"Okay. What about finger prints? You got a finger print kit at home?"

"No … but it's not the kit we really need. It's someone to run the prints once we have them, if you know what I mean?"

She was thoughtful for a moment. "Actually, I might be able to do something about that. After I dumped paint on Steve's clothes, he had me arrested and they did fingerprint me to see if they could connect me to the torching of his girl friend's car. Fortunately, being the master criminal that I am, I wore gloves that night." She giggled.

"Is that right?"

"Hhhmm," she nodded. "The thing is … the guy who did my prints was kind of flirting. If I talk to him real nice he might do it for us."

"Not if I'm around," I laughed.

She stared at me, her eyes sparkling with glee. "You'll just have to learn to trust me to be alone with him, won't you?"

Right at the moment, I did and would trust her with my life. "Okay … let's say we got that covered. What have you learned from the picture so far?"

"Well, I think we might actually be able to track down where it was taken."

"Really?"

"I think so … see the sign on the lawn? That's a real estate "For Sale" sign. With a magnifying glass we should be able to read the name of the company and trace it back to a city or two."

"Only a city or two?"

"Hopefully it won't be a really big company. We should also be able to read the house number with a magnifying glass. We won't know the name of the street, but if the town's not too big we could get it figured out."

"Isn't that kind of like looking for a needle in a haystack?"

"Maybe—but I think we can get zeroed in pretty good. I can almost read the license plate number on the car and that should at least get us in the right state and maybe into the right year."

"Really?"

"Sure … and judging by the flowers in front of the house and the shadow on the ground next to the car, the picture was probably taken sometime in early June about 2:00 O'clock in the afternoon. The house is on an east/west street on the north side of the street—"

"Holy mackerel, Sherlock" I exclaimed. "The next thing I know you'll be telling me this woman is wearing pink underpants!"

"No way!" Lynn grinned widely. "White bloomers … a woman like that would definitely wear white bloomers."

"I'll give ya white bloomers," I quipped, giving her a friendly tweak on the nose and a quick peck on the lips. "Let's get something to eat before you solve the case."

…

When we came back from eating, we made love in a slow, sensuous way that had me wondering how my life could have gone so wrong. You start out thinking that life is like a blank page. You fill in one event, and then another, and then another. The next thing you know the whole page is full and you have this happy-ending story. *Wrong!* In life, you start down one path and things start veering off course—you wad up that scenario and chuck it. You make a new entry on a clean sheet—only to have to wad that and throw it. The next thing you know, you're over the hill and up to your waist in wadded scenarios.

Now I ask you, is that fair?

Afterwards, we lay snuggling in each other's arms for a long time without talking "You still awake?" Lynn asked, breaking the silence.

"Hhhmm,"

"Counting sheep?"

"Something like that," I murmured, "more like regrets, I guess. I wished to God I would have met you sooner—before I painted myself into a corner."

She let my comment hang in the darkness for a long time.

"You didn't really want to kill your wife, did you?" She asked finally.

I gave her a quick, "Thank you for understanding" squeeze. "No … not really. I guess I just wanted her to share my pain. I thought we were happily married. I mean, I knew she wasn't totally happy … that she was fighting some depression. But I guess I just thought the depression would go away by itself."

"I know what you mean," She agreed. "Don't you think we kind of see just what we want to see. We have 100% hindsight. If I hadn't been quite so blind, I would have realized Steve was looking for an out long before I caught him cheating."

"Hhhmmn," I laid there a long time thinking about what she'd said. One of the things I had missed the most towards the end of my relationship with Maria was exactly what we were doing now—talking quietly in bed at the end of each day. "It's all about communication, I guess," I said finally.

Sleeping beauty did not respond.

Chapter 10

At first it was like watching the images unfold from some sort of eye in the sky, like maybe an eagle soaring overhead—everything around the periphery sort of bluish-gray and foggy while the center is clear and in focus. The scene is basically of a huge log building in a clearing in a valley in the mountains. I can't tell for sure, but it seems like the building is some sort of store but not modern, like a *Cracker Barrel* before *Cracker Barrel* became *Cracker Barrel*. The clearing is surrounded by pine trees, rock outcroppings, and blue sky with billowy white clouds. There is a cargo wagon and team tied at one of the hitching posts and several scraggly brown chickens pecking in the hard-packed ground.

The second thing was that I was conscious of the fact that I was dreaming. It was like watching a movie when you're in a drowsy mood.

About the time I was settling in to enjoy the movie, getting ready to reach for the popcorn, the scene suddenly shifted. Suddenly I was a small boy of about eleven, but small for my age and I was riding on a flatbed on a small train. There was something really odd about the train. There weren't many cars, maybe six or seven and they were shorter and narrower than I expected. Looking back I could see the store back in the valley and that the track was a much narrower gauge than I was used to. The train was moving very slow, working hard to climb the grade up out of the valley. Fascinated, I watched the gravel along the track half expecting the train to start sliding backwards.

When the putrid, rotting white horses head passed slowly by it didn't even register at first—and when it did, I was immediately transported to another place and another time.

This time the log building was much smaller, a simple two room cabin on a hill some place in Missouri. Don't ask me how I knew it was Missouri, I just did. The hills around the cabin were covered with oak stumps six to eight inches in diameter that looked like they had been chewed off by a beaver. Don't ask me how I knew they were oak stumps, I just did.

Before I could even adjust to the scene I suddenly found myself in a bed that was heaped high with quilts. My breath was like fire and the bed seemed permeated with the smell of urine and sweat. There was a young woman moving about the bedroom. She was dressed in a long brown dress with billowing skirt that reached the floor. The dress had long sleeves with tiny round black buttons at the cuffs. The room was cold, but I knew the shawl, petticoats, and her concern over me kept my mother warm.

My Mother?

Suddenly I was awake—but not really able to move. My mind did not seem to want to work right, like it had gone on vacation. *Who knows, maybe it did?*

My first impression of the dream—dreams—was that I must have been watching a civil war movie sometime in the not too distant past. The only problem was that I could not remember ever watching a movie that included such specific details as those that were included in the dream, such as the narrow gauge track. *Did they have narrow gauge track back in the civil war days? And why the rotting horses head?* Even the scene in the cabin bedroom had a realness about it that one wouldn't have gotten from a movie—such as the temperature of the room, the smell of urine and sweat, my fevered breath.

Then too, there was a different consciousness. The boy in the dream did not think he was about eleven. He knew he was eleven and small for his age and that the woman in the room was his mother and that she knew he was dying of a fever and there was nothing she could do about it. He also knew his name was Marshall Lincoln but his mother called him Marsh.

"Russ—Russell?"

I heard my name but I wasn't sure where it was coming from.

"Russ? You in a trance or what?" Lynn said, suddenly jarring me back to reality.

She was kneeling over me, her face wrapped in concern, but with a wry twinkle in the corner of her eye as if she thought I might be trying to trick her.

"Still asleep I guess," I murmured, grinning.

"Really? But your eyes were wide open."

"What does that prove?" I laughed. She was still wearing the big, floppy T-shirt she'd put on for a nightgown the night before and I couldn't resist running my hand up under the fabric and copping a feel.

She responded with a quick kiss on my lips, but Mr. Johnson seemed to be out to lunch so I pushed her aside and got up to take my shower.

...

There is nothing in the whole wide world quite so boring as a droning monologue on corporate taxes when your heart isn't into it. To begin with, I had a really difficult time getting my mind off the warm, wonderful slip of a girl—woman, who was suddenly in my life firing-up my enthusiasm like never before. In one short week I'd gone from crushing maniacal depression to almost absolute elation.

The only thing was, if I didn't come up with some sort of redeeming counter act for my so-called "attempted homicide," I'd likely crash and burn. *Or was I just being overly melodramatic?* You'd think if I had really intended to kill Maria I would have had sense enough to use something a little more potent than a target arrow. I wasn't exactly sure what I was worried about. Maria didn't really have any reason to suspect me of "criminal intent." Technically, I was the one divorcing her. She had never even asked for a divorce. She'd just left me. So on the surface it just looked like we had agreed to part. Still, my current situation left me with a feeling of impending doom despite my elation—like there was a big black cloud hanging on the horizon.

As the class droned on I found myself reviewing all the little things in our life that had led up to Maria's departure. Thinking back, it seemed like there might have been a single night during that last year's tax season that might have triggered her flight. In all the prior years, I was always in the office helping her, but not so that last year. I had been doing freelance engineering work and didn't have the time. Maria's biggest fault as a boss was that she didn't always delegate the way she should have. After Maria's four or five long grueling days at the office one week, I might have been a little too persistent about making love. Men can be like that.

It was like I had flipped a switch and turned her off.

Our relationship was never the same after that. And when Maria received a letter from Puerto Rico that spring claiming her father was living in a pigsty, she had dropped everything like a good daughter should and hurried off to rescue Luis. He was apparently recovering at home alone after undergoing some sort of surgery—and using ice cream pails to relieve himself instead of going to the bathroom.

After two weeks in Puerto Rico Maria had spent nearly a month in Jacksonville with Luisa and her mother and finally started going to mass again. I still didn't understand how or why her ex-husband's death had changed the church going thing.

Anyway, it didn't matter now. It was all over but the fat lady singing.

"Aren't you going to go on break, Rusty?" Jody Hansen, one of the many single ladies in my class asked when I didn't get up for the first of the three well-needed ten-minute breaks we got after every hour in class.

"Not today." I told her.

"Rough night?"

"More like a rough week—"

My quick comment gave me an instant feeling of déjà vu and I wished Jody would just shut up and leave me alone. I wasn't exactly in the mood for conversation. At least, not with her. It wasn't any big secret that some of the single women in the class considered me a potentially

97

good catch when my divorce became final. Maria's office—my office—was comparatively large in relationship to a lot of the offices in the district. So there were times when these eager ladies made me feel like one of the lobsters on display in the tank up front at Red Lobster.

"Anything serious?" she asked.

Jody was several years younger than I was, but I actually considered her too old and not exactly my cup of tea. "No, just didn't get time to read this weeks chapter."

I opened my textbook and pretended to read.

Thankfully, she respected my use of that "*never fail*" ploy and I was able to let my mind wander back to Lynn. I would have loved to bring her to class and set a few tongues wagging. The people who own and work for tax prep franchises are kind of a close-knit family. They have that common ground of "*actually liking to do taxes*," and being "math geeks." Bringing in an outsider would have really rocked their world.

...

To my surprise, Lynn was not waiting for me in the parking lot where she had dropped me off for class. We'd had to check out of the motel and that left Lynn with four hours to kill and no place to do it, so I'd given her the keys to my car. *No big deal ... right?* The thought that she would take the car and leave me stranded was ridiculous. *Why would she?* She had a much better, newer car back in Florida.

Still, where was she?

I waited ten minutes before I remembered that we had exchanged cell phone numbers before we'd parted four hours earlier for exactly this situation. I dialed her number and held my breath. The phone rang over and over again but there was no answer.

What gives?

Had she gone out on the highway and had an accident? Anything was possible with that clunky old Escort of mine. It should have been put out to pasture a couple of years ago. Maybe the danged thing just died on her. The timing belt had crapped out once already. The only problem with this theory was that you'd think she'd call—

Unless she really had gotten into an accident—

I paced back and forth for awhile before finally deciding to call the police and see if there had been any accidents reported.

The thought of that was driving me crazy. That would just be my luck!

"I was wondering," I said, when I finally got a receptionist on the line, "have you had any reports of car accidents in the past few hours?"

"Why do you ask?" the voice on the phone said, sending a spike of panic through me. *What if they were on to me?* I half expected the guy to say something like: "You're that Robin Hood guy, aren't you? You stay right where you are!"

"Ah … my-my, ah wife was suppose to pick me up half an hour ago, that's all." I managed to stammer.

"Probably just the traffic, Sir. It can get a bit crazy this time of day."

Yeah, right! I thought, hanging up. *You're probably having a traffic minute!* That was my little joke about traffic jams in small towns. Traffic jams in bigger cities was one thing I really hated.

I tried Lynn's cell phone a couple more times, then sat down on the curb in dismay. *What in the hell was I supposed to do now?*

I was about ready to call the police again when the Escort came tooling around the corner practically on two wheels, and parked in the parking spot next to the one where I was sitting. Lynn was so excited she was out of the car and standing in front of me before I could get to my feet.

"Guess what!" She beamed down at me. "I found it!"

"What's that?" I demanded, trying to maintain a stern face as I struggled to my feet. It was a losing battle. I was so glad to see her I couldn't hold back my grin.

"The real estate broker—" she told me excitedly. "I found the real estate broker whose sign is in the picture."

I stared at her in amazement, my anger quickly subsiding. "You're kidding!"

"No, really … come on, I'll show you."

I opened the passenger door for her and went around and climbed into the driver's seat. By that time she had popped open the glove box and produced the picture of the black woman and little boy and a magnifying glass. "See! It says *Courtland Realty* … plain as day!"

I gave her a warm smile as she handed over the picture and magnifying glass. She was almost a naïve as I was. It was one thing to read a name on a sign with a magnifying glass, quite another to track down the actual real estate broker. "Yes, but—" I was chuckling like a schoolboy who'd just pulled a prank on his best girl. "Where exactly is this real estate broker located?"

"In Courtland, Mississippi, of course—" She beamed at me as if she'd just found her lost puppy.

I was beginning to think I hadn't taken her as seriously as I should have. Then I noticed the sign wasn't as clear as she'd claimed. It had what looked like a glob of something (probably mud) splattered between the "Co" and the "rtland."

"How can you be so sure?" I asked, still skeptical. "Looks to me like the name isn't all that clear. The 'Co' is pretty clear; and the 'rtland' is fine—but that letter in between the 'o' and 'r' could be almost anything."

"Not really." Her smile was beginning to fad. "Some letter extend upward like the 't, l and d.' Some go downward like the 'y—'"

"Right … but that still leaves 'c, e, m, n, o, r, s, u, v, w, x, and z.' How did you manage to decide it had to be the 'u?'"

"Simple. It's the only one that makes sense."

"But that's not a guarantee—"

"I know." she grinned somewhat sheepishly. "But after I bought the magnifying glass and figured out what I thought the name was, I went to the local library. They have computers there that anyone can use to go online. I started out by doing a search for the city or town by the name of 'Courtland'. At that point, I didn't know if it was a brokerage named after a person or a town. I know lots of real estate agents use the name of the town they're from and that seemed to make the most sense. Besides, I've never met a person by the name of 'Courtland'."

"That doesn't mean they don't exist." I was still skeptical.

"I know … but I had to start some place."

"Okay … so how does that get you to Courtland, Mississippi?"

"Simple. It was the only Courtland that was in Mississippi."

"And how may I asked did you arrive at the fact that it had to be in Mississippi?"

"Piece of cake, Watson … the car has Mississippi plates."

I couldn't help grinning, but I was still a little peeved at her. "Pretty much a smartie, aren't you? So tell me, how many other Courtlands are there?"

"Quite a few—there's one in Alabama, one in Virginia … even in Ontario. There's even one in Minnesota. There's also a Cortland, Ohio and a Cortland, New York—but I ruled those two out because of the spelling."

"I hope you don't think I'm just giving you a hard time." I said, wondering if she wasn't beginning to think I was working a little too hard to prove her wrong. "I'm not, you know … I just don't want to go off half-cocked on some wild goose chase."

"I know," she said, almost on the verge of tears. "That's why I tried to take into account all of the other things in the picture. I think those shrubs along the house might be potentilla … and the flowers here by the steps look like peonies—these are all plants that start blooming in late May and early June in the mid-west. So that didn't necessarily prove any thing. But I'm pretty sure the car license plate is from Mississippi."

I thought her argument was a little weak. The picture was black and white and not in very good shape. The flowers and shrubs looked like black blobs to me … definitely not clear enough to enable anyone to identify the flowers. And to me, her comment about the shadows indicating that it was 2:00 O'clock in the afternoon seemed wrong. If the house really was on the north side of an east west street the shadows would indicate something more like five or six O'clock depending on what month it was and how far north it was. No, I wasn't convinced we'd ever be able to glean anything concrete from the shadows. But the fact that she wanted to try made me tear up a bit. And there was nothing wrong with her logic.

"Of course, I could still be wrong—" she admitted.

"Let's not worry about that now," I suggested. "We still have a good four hour drive ahead of us and I'm starving again."

We were on the road nearly an hour after eating before I finally decided to tell Lynn that I'd been a little pissed about her being late. Poor communication had been the downfall of my last relationship with a woman—it might be worth a little extra effort to keep this relationship on track. But that definitely required a little tact.

"I have to admit," I told her. "I'm a little surprised by your enthusiasm about tracking this guy down … I mean, I've put your life in total disarray over this thing and here I am dragging you halfway across the country—"

She smiled in the dim light. "Maybe I needed a vacation."

"No, seriously … I think there's more to it than that, if you know what I mean."

"I do." This time she was serious. "To start with … I'm a woman and I don't think there are many women who condone rape—especially when it involves underage little girls."

"I can see that."

"Besides that," she continued, "I guess I didn't mention it before … but I have two daughters. They're both in college and not underage little girls any more, but you never stop being a mother."

"I see your point," I said. My need to tell her that I'd been pissed because she was a little late suddenly dissolved and I found myself hoping that I'd know this lady for a long, long time. Not only was she cute as the dickens, she seemed to have all the right attitudes. I had to resist the temptation to pull over to the side of the freeway and smother her with kisses. Cops are known to frown on that.

…

It was nearly midnight by the time we got to my house. There had not been a woman in the house since Maria left, and needless to say, that was pretty well reflected in the housekeeping status of the house. The bed was still unmade from the previous week, the sink was full of dishes, and there wasn't a single thing that would have passed a white glove inspection. Not that I had been involved in many white glove inspections since the service, but I didn't want Lynn to think I lived in a pigsty either.

"Give me a minute to put some clean sheets on the bed," I said, dropping my bag on the bedroom floor and setting hers on the bed. "Did you want to shower?"

She shook her head. "I'll help with the sheets."

Minutes later, after a quick brushing of teeth, we were snuggled in bed.

...

It was nearly 4:00 O'clock in the afternoon before I finally got around to scanning the picture into my computer. A lot of the engineering work and technical writing that I'd done involved scanning pictures into various software programs such as Publisher and PhotoShop. I'd gotten pretty good at doing a lot of things with pictures on my computer. Enlarging various sections of the picture, such as the car license plate was a piece of cake.

"I hate to tell you this," I told Lynn when she came into my office after putting some feminine touches on the disarray of my house. I had tried to talk her out of that but it seemed to be a waste of breath. "But it turns out "Courtland Realty" is actually "Courtlund Realty." I still had the enlarged realty sign up on the monitor.

"Really?" She said, leaning closer to confirm what I was saying.

It was hard to argue with the enlarged version of the sign. The "u" between the "o" and "r" was spattered with something. What we had thought was an "a" between the "l" and "n" turned out to have what looked like a bullet hole and spatter of mud, or whatever it was, turning the "u" into an "a."

"What a bummer," Lynn muttered, letting me know she agreed with me.

"I know," I agreed, not bothering to hide my disappointment. "But that's not the worst part." We had already established the date of the picture, based on the stamp on the back to be 1969. I clicked a couple of things and brought up the license plate. "See," I told her, "The year on the plate is 1961."

"You're kidding!"

"Afraid not."

"Bummer," she said again, placing her hands on my right shoulder from behind, then leaning forward to place her chin on the back of her hands. I could feel the amazing warmth of her breasts against my shoulder blades.

"You were right about the state, though." I said, trying to keep her from getting too bummed out. "The plates do seem to be Mississippi plates."

That was like saying, "Got the motor started okay ... but the boat's leaking pretty bad and we don't have a bucket!"

"Oh, goodie, goodie," Lynn lifted her head slightly and let her arms slide down around me and gave me a hug. "All we have to do now is find that needle in the haystack."

Chapter 11

The weight on my chest was unbelievable. My arms felt like I was wearing a nightgown with incredibly long sleeve that someone had twisted up in knots until every last drop of fluid was squeezed out of my arms. Try as I might, I could not get my arms loose. And every time I tried to breathe I felt an incredible tickling in my nose but I could not sneeze. Anger and panic engulfed me like hot oil and I began to thrash about wildly until—the bubble burst and fleece was fluttering down around me in the golden light like tainted snow. I reached out and grabbed a handful of the tainted snow and was surprised to discover I had a handful of straw and that I was about to be buried alive again. I gave a mighty lunge—

And all but threw myself on the floor.

"Russell, honey!" Lynn exclaimed, rolling over in the bed to grab me by the arm. "What is it? Are you okay?"

I shook my head to clear away the cobwebs and Lynn slowly came into focus. The top button on the plaid flannel shirt I'd given her to wear as a nightgown had popped open, revealing the creamy white slope of one breast.

"Whew," I muttered, trying to rub the sleep from my eyes. My heart was still pounding. I rolled back toward her and pulled her into my arms. "I guess maybe I had a little too much of the hot tamales last night."

"Bad dream?"

"Something like that."

"What happened?"

"I don't know. I think maybe I was looking for that needle in the haystack you were talking about, only it was a straw stack and I got buried and I was about to suffocate—"

"You okay?" Lynn asked, snuggling against me.

I smiled, cupping an inviting breast in my free hand. "You keep that up and I will be," I said, kissing her gently.

The one thing I liked about this new relationship was that we had never discussed the "side of the bed" issue. Maria had always insisted she sleep on the left side of the bed. Lynn automatically took the right side and that seemed a much better fit to me. Lying on your left side left your right arm free and since I was right handed in most things—

"I suppose we better get to it," I continued, throwing back the covers. "If we're ever going to find that needle in the haystack."

She didn't argue. It was time to get up and get back on the trail.

That was another thing we didn't really have to talk about. Obviously, there was nothing forcing me to become a detective and go chasing around the country in pursuit of a sexual predator and possible murderer. Nothing, except of course, my own desire for redemption. Some times a criminal act could be boiled down to a simple movement of a finger such as squeezing of a trigger— an infinitesimal movement that could change your life forever.

Thank God my moment of weakness had been with a stupid target bow and arrow and my "*good luck*" was to have the "*bad luck*" of hitting a rib. Hopefully the police would be willing to chalk the incidents up to some maniac running around in the darkness of night randomly firing arrows into the mist.

Besides, how was I ever going to have any kind of life with Lynn if I didn't track down the kidnapper? At least, that's what I was thinking as I prepared breakfast while she showered.

...

There was no such place as Courtlund, Mississippi. Nor was there any listing for a Courtlund Realty that we could find. In fact, there didn't seem to be a "Courtlund" any place. And that wasn't the worst of it. Records for businesses from the 60's were hard to come by and, although the date wasn't exactly confirmed—the picture was clearly stamped "Aug 69" on the back and the license plates were from 1961.

So what now?

Either the car license plates weren't up to date or the film had been lying around for years before being developed, or maybe a little of both. I was momentarily at a loss to tell which, so I let Lynn play around on the Internet while I went to town for some supplies. Money was in danger of becoming an issue. Most of my income was from tax preparation and that came in the first three and a half months of the year. It was pretty good money, but it had to last the rest of the year. And since we were already well into October, I had to be a little bit careful. I couldn't go around splurging on motel rooms for long periods of time. Since the weather was still pretty good in the south, camping made a lot of sense. Besides, I kind of liked the idea of sleeping out under the stars with Lynn.

When I returned from my shopping trip Lynn had road maps and smaller maps she'd printed off the Internet scattered all over my desk. She was hunched over the computer apparently trying to chew the end off one of my pens. I wrapped my arms around her from behind and nuzzled her hair aside.

"What'd you find out?" I murmured, nibbling at her earlobe.

She twisted around and pecked me on the lips. "Nothing for sure … other than that printing city maps off the Internet takes a lot of time."

"I bet," I agreed, planting my butt on the corner of the two-drawer file cabinet next to my desk.

"What I've been trying to do is match the street name with one of the "Courtland" cities we came up with. I don't know if you noticed or not, but there is part of a street sign showing. Wanna see?"

Without waiting for an answer she rummaged under the maps and came up with the picture and magnifying glass and handed them to me. I was pleased to see she had found a plastic bag to keep the picture in. I tipped the plastic bag to slide the picture out part way and looked through the glass at where she was pointing.

Once again, she was right. There was a part of a street sign showing, but unfortunately a tree branch hung down over it in such a way that only part of the name was legible. All I could make out between the leaves was "*ington.*" Not a lot to go on.

The street name could be almost anything and I didn't mind saying so.

"Don't be so pessimistic," Lynn chided. "A lot of cities use the names of presidents for street names. I'll bet we're talking about "*Washington*" something … you know, street or avenue or whatever."

"What if there's more than one "*Washington*" whatever?"

She smiled deeply. I could tell she was really enjoying this.

"Well, we cross that bridge when we get to it. I'm guessing from the shadow from the car that the street it's parked on runs east and west. That means 'Washington' whatever runs east and west."

"Okay," I challenged, tapping the end of her nose with my index finger. "What if there are two "*Washington*" street and they both run east and west?"

Lynn shrugged. "Then we'll have to check them both out.

I had to agree.

The one thing we hadn't talked very much about was why the kidnapper had been carrying a picture that was more than thirty-five years old. The woman almost had to be the kidnapper's mother or some close relationship like that. Was the kidnapper the little boy in the picture? Or was the picture just some sort of memento from a kidnapping?

We hadn't talked much about the car either. It was a 1957 Chevy Impala, which made it about twelve years old at the time the picture was developed. And judging from the somewhat dilapidated condition of the house, the people involved were not terribly well to do. Unless

I miss my guess the picture was intended to capture a moment in time before the people involved moved away, as suggested by the fact the house was for sale. And judging by the damage or mud splattering on the "for sale" sign, I wouldn't be surprised if there was racial prejudice involved some way—like the Rosa Parks deal, for example.

"We have another route we can take," Lynn suggested, bringing me back to the moment at hand. "We have the phone number on the sign that gives us the area code and the prefix for the town. The only problem with that is that some phone numbers might have been changed since then—you know, with the splitting up of Ma Bell in the south and creating all those baby Bells, stuff like that."

"Speaking of that," I said, suddenly remembering we had a couple of matchbooks that had belonged to the kidnapper. They obviously wouldn't be a link to the past, but they might give us some idea as to where the kidnapper had been shortly before the kidnapping. Every little tidbit of information we could muster would help.

"Tell you what," I continued. "You keep doing what you are … and I'll see what I can come up with from the phone numbers. Okay?"

...

Traveling by Internet was a hell of a lot faster than rolling down the highway. It made a lot of sense to stay at home and glean as much information from the Internet as we could before setting off to actually track down our villain. Besides, I had to be back in Menomonie for my tax class again on Wednesday so it really made more sense to wait until then to head back south.

The lucky thing about it, living in the country the way I did, no one paid much attention to whether I was home or not. Actually, it was hard to tell. Sometimes I would put my car in the garage every time I came home. Other times I would go for a week at a time without bothering. It all depended on my whim at the moment. So it would be pretty easy to convince anyone who bothered to ask that I'd been home all week. The only one who might have some idea would be my mailman. If I got a lot of mail, it would start to pile up and old man Clarkson, my mailman, would figure something was up—although, there were times when I just got too busy to pick up the mail every day. Mr. Clarkson already knew that. Chances were pretty good it would never be an issue.

But, just to be on the safe side, I decided to spin a few tales with some of the people I knew, like Joe Nelson at the Army surplus store where I occasionally bought gas and had gone in search of camping equipment. I'd known Joe for years and we always shot the shit about the little stuff in our lives like, "Been fishin' lately?" Not that I was any kind of fisherman, it was just a Minnesota thing.

"Goin' campin', huh?" Joe gave me a big Scandinavian grin, when I tossed the double sleeping bag on the counter along with a used tent I'd picked out.

Actually, Joe didn't really sell that much Army surplus stuff anymore, a few canteens and stuff like that. Mostly he pumped a little gas, sold some bait and fishing tackle, and whatever used camping stuff he could get his hands on.

I nodded. "Yeah … got to. I'm taking this tax class once a week over in Menomonie. The drive home at night is killing me, so I thought I might try staying down there. No way in hell I can afford that kinda motel bills."

"That would be a bitch," Joe agreed. "Hope you got somebody to fill out the other half of this sleeping bag," he said, trying to muster up a sinister grin in the hope of getting me to divulge some tasty tidbit. "You could freeze you're ass off if you don't."

Actually, Joe knew all about my impending divorce and had a bad habit of trying to get me to "spill the beans" about any new relationships on the horizon. That might have had a lot to do with Joe's wife, who weighed close to 400 pounds and was rumored to like to watch a lot of television.

"Nobody yet," I told him, "but maybe I'll get lucky." We both knew the double bag was the only one Joe had.

"Here's to getting lucky," Joe said, giving me one of those lop-sided macho grins guys reserve for each other when they're trying to stimulate a little "kiss and tell" session about their various romantic escapades.

"Right." I murmured, not taking the bait. I signed the debit card slip and gathered up the sleeping bag and stuff and headed for the door. "See ya later."

"Getting lucky," had a whole lot bigger meaning for me now than it had in a long time. These days I spent an extraordinary amount of time hashing over the events of the past year or so—ever since Maria dropped her bombshell. Actually, Maria's employees had been nearly as stunned as I was. Everyone we knew thought we were happily married. Never mind that Maria was suffering from a little depression because the franchise director wouldn't approve her purchase of Clyde Dillman's Riverbend franchise. Clyde was having some back problems and having more than one office was beginning to be a burden. Selling the smaller office to Maria would have helped them both. I could certainly understand Maria being depressed about that—but did she have to go off the deep end about it and leave me? After all, it wasn't my fault.

Or was it? Women want a guy who will stand up for them, protect their dreams. And it was pretty easy to see why Maria would fantasize about building a tax-business empire to show her macho father that she was worthy.

I was beginning to think that our achievements in life have a whole lot to do with "getting lucky" in the various choices we make at those so-called "forks in the road." If the bow and arrow set I'd bought on a whim had been a hunting-set instead of a target-set I would now be a murderer and no amount of time and effort spent trying to track down a sexual predator would redeem that.

And then there was Lynn.

Telling God to go fuck himself might seem like a rash thing to do, but the truth, I realized now was that it was a sort of "last fling" expulsion of my grief over losing Maria. It cleared the slate, as it were. I could move on.

And, I loved it.

Lynn was like the non-sullen side of the Maria coin. Her smile seemed to come from somewhere deep inside and left me with a warm glow that refused to fade. And she was smart as a whip. Especially when it came to Internet things.

I was fairly computer literate, but when it came to the Internet I had what one would classify as a "fatal flaw." I had a tendency to be sucked in by the quagmire of information available. It wasn't that there was not enough information ... there was too much.

Take the *"ington"* part of the sign that we were trying to identify for instance. Nearly every Courtland on our list, including the Cortlands, had at least one street with *"ington" in* it—Washington ... Huntington ... Harrington ... Darlington. How were we ever supposed to know which one was the right one? Lynn had suggested that the car shadow made it an east west street, but that was a bit *iffy*.

When I got home, we talked about it for a while and then decided to sleep on it.

Only I couldn't sleep. I found myself laying on my back staring out my bedroom window at the moon plowing through a scuddy sky like a golden schooner plowing through frothy waves. Sometimes it seemed like the moon was moving and the clouds were fixed. The next second it seemed like the moon was fixed and the clouds were moving. *Which was it?*

Before I could decide, I found myself waking up in Lynn's lovely warm embrace, greatly relieved that I hadn't had another nightmare—if that's what they were. When you start dreaming about stuff that you have no way of knowing about, like the civil war, you start to wonder about little things like your sanity.

But then, they do say if you start to think you're crazy chances are pretty good that you're not because a crazy person never questions things like that. I had no idea whether that old adage was true, or not, but for the moment it made me feel better.

We busied ourselves with the morning bustle of

showering and breakfast before I put my concerns into words. "Well, what do you think?" I asked, drying the last dish as Lynn wiped off the counter. We could have used the dishwasher, but doing the dishes together by hand was a lot more fun.

"I think we should start with Courtland, Mississippi."

I was pleased that she hadn't asked "Think about what?" It was good to be on the same page. "And if that's not right … pop over to Courtland, Alabama?" I suggested.

She nodded in agreement.

"And if that's a bust … we'll go on to Courtland, Virginia. They're all in the south and actually, pretty much in a straight line when you go across the country. If you think about it very much, it seems like we have to be talking about the south. The only other Courtland, besides the one in Minnesota, is the one in Ontario and I don't think it can be either one of those because the woman and boy are black and that probably means we are talking about the south. I also think we can discount Cortland, Ohio and Cortland, New York because the spelling is wrong. Besides, there are a couple of other things."

She gave me a "what would that be" look.

I gave her a little "see, I'm not totally stupid either" grin and continued. "For one thing, there's a military emblem and another sticker on the back window of the car. They are too small to make out clearly, but they could still be good clues. The sticker's probably for "on base" parking and emblem for whatever military outfit the car owner belonged to."

Lynn nodded her head, duly impressed.

I wasn't finished. "We still have to finish with the phone numbers if we can. I know we might be stymied there because of the breakup of Ma Bell, but—"

"So we better get to work?"

"There is one other thing."

"You mean this," she laid the wash cloth on the sink and plastered her body against me. She put her arms around my neck and pulled me down for a kiss.

"That too," I grinned. "But I was thinking more along the lines of taking this operation into my office in town. I have more phone lines there and plenty of computers. That way we can both be on the Internet at the same time.

...

Lynn seemed properly impressed with the tax office. "Your wife has got to be crazy," she said, nodding her head as she looked around with approval. "A woman would have to be crazy to walk away from this."

"Or have a really bad husband," I offered.

She gave me a dubious look. "You're the one that's crazy if you believe that."

"Thanks for the vote of confidence," I muttered, showing her around and then escorting her into my office. "I'll let you work in here on my computer," I told her, settling her in my big "boss" chair. "I have to do some physical hook-up work to get a second computer on-line."

Chapter 12

The next few days slid by like a seal down a slippery slope. We spent hours thrashing through the quagmire of the Internet learning everything we could from the clues we'd gleaned from the picture. In between working and sleeping we lingered over long, comfortable meals which we prepared as a team.

It was one of the things I had missed most about the old Maria. In the beginning, we had handled mealtime chores as a team. I wasn't one of those old-fashioned men who couldn't boil water. Actually, I loved to cook. But in the end it seemed like Maria was doing all the cooking and I wound up doing the dishes. The only problem with that was she loved to fix chicken with red beans and rice, a popular Puerto Rican dish. The only thing was she didn't like to stir the rice, so it always got baked onto the bottom of the pan and I wound up spending hours scraping and scrubbing to get the pan clean even after it had soaked for hours. That wasn't exactly my idea of domestic fun—or fairness either, for that matter.

Besides, it's way more fun to do things together.

The one negative aspect of doing things together was that time literally flew by. We were back on the road to Menomonie in what seemed like a blink of the eye—which left me with an uneasy feeling that we didn't have enough information to do justice to this search for a pedophile. On top of everything else, I wasn't as prepared for my tax class as I should have been. Researching things on the Internet can truly be a plunge into quick sand.

"Can you believe the incredible number of missing kids?" I asked Lynn when we passed a school playground loaded with kids.

"I know," she said pensively.

"I mean, it's hard to image there's even one missing child … let alone literally thousands."

Lynn nodded.

"I know a lot of them are from broken marriages where one of the parents absconds with the kids, but still—"

"I know what you're saying." Lynn said, nodding toward the playground. "We look at these kids and see kids playing—but for sex perverts … they probably see these playgrounds like a shopping mall. It reminds me of those movies about the way Cheetah hunt antelope, how they pick out the most vulnerable before they charge. It's a little scary that the human race hasn't managed to progress much beyond such basics."

"You can say that again."

It was a sobering thought.

We really had our work cut out for us. The only actual fact we had was that I had rescued a young, white girl from a black man who'd very obviously had sexual intentions. Had the girl been his first victim? At this point, we had no way of knowing. I did have a gut feeling that this wasn't his first victim and very likely, none of his victims were still alive. That just seemed to be the way this pedophile thing worked. The perpetrator selects a victim that he can physically handle and sexually molests her—then has to kill her to keep from being incriminated.

So, the first task was to identify this man. And the only way we would be able to do that was from the clues we had gleaned from the picture. And it was entirely possible that the only reason this creep had the picture in the first place was that it was some sort of sick souvenir from one of his victims. And if that was the case, how in the world were we ever going to connect a single child out of a staggering list of missing children to our predator?

First things first.

While I was in class, Lynn went back to the Menomonie library to do more research. We had brought along my laptop, but because of the battery situation it was better to use public computers whenever possible.

This time Lynn was right there to pick me up after class, which worked out well. Normally, I would have greeted her with at least one kiss as I got in the car. But this time I knew Jody Hansen had followed me out of the building so I gave Lynn a couple of extra passionate kisses for good measure.

"Does that mean you missed me?" she teased.

"Either that … or I'm damned glad to be out of that class."

"I bet," Lynn said. "But guess what! I got a surprise for you."

I was too busy watching Jody buzz by with her nose in the air to answer.

"What's that?" I asked finally, turning my attention back to Lynn.

"I got bored with the library … so I found a camping spot and pitched the tent."

"Hey," I laughed. "You're my kind of woman!"

"Actually," Lynn had one of those "*mouse ate the cat*" kind of grins on her cute little freckled face. "The place was closed for the season … but the lady said if we were brave enough to try it we could have the spot for nothing."

The light dusting of freckles on Lynn's face went along with the hint of auburn in her hair, just enough to let you know there was a bit of a "*stinker*" behind those blue-green eyes. Sometimes it was hard to tell when she was teasing.

"Like I said," I mustered up my best macho face. "My kind of woman."

It was a sentiment I was to repeat many times over before the night was through. Camping in west central Wisconsin at this time of year was not quite the same as it was going to be down south. I was very glad I'd wound up with a double sleeping bag. We spent the night naked and wrapped in each other's arm. Under other circumstances it might have been marathon sex. As it was, Mr. Johnson was just glad to have a warm place to park. By sheer persistence, we did not freeze our asses off.

"The next time," Lynn grinned, after the waitress served our coffee the next morning. "I'm checking the weather forecast first."

"Aw, come on," I teased. "You know you loved it."

Lynn gave me one of those sideways double takes. "Actually, I did," She said, her eyes twinkling.

Somehow, I knew it wouldn't be right to shove the dishes aside and ravish her right there on the table, but I sure wouldn't have minded.

…

Courtland, Mississippi seemed to be a complete bust. First of all, there wasn't a single street name that ended in "*ington.*" In fact, there were barely more than a half dozen streets in the entire town and hardly any businesses on the main street. There was no way it could have anything to do with the picture.

"You do realize," I told her as we drove back north to Batesville to find a place to eat. "We have to check out surrounding towns around here as well. I mean, we only talked to a couple of people. Just because we didn't find anyone who remembers a "Courtland Realty" around here back in 1969, doesn't mean there wasn't one. The street doesn't have to be in Courtland … it could be in any of these towns."

She didn't argue, but that didn't make our task any easier

It turned out that Batesville also had no streets ending in "*ington*" and it seemed like another dead end. It did have a "Court Street" but that was pretty much a stretch.

We spent the night in a campground on Sardis Lake just off Highway 6. By connecting my cell phone to my laptop, we were able to go on the Internet and checkout most of the smaller towns in the area without actually having to drive to them. To tell the truth, most had very few streets and hardly even qualified as towns.

It also turned out to be another colder-than-average night and we had to huddle together again to keep from freezing.

"I think you planned this whole thing," Lynn teased as she struggled to get dressed inside the sleeping bag the next morning.

I was already dressed and had just come back from checking on the public shower. "What makes you say that?" I grinned.

"Cause you're sadistic and I'm freezing! How were the showers?"

"Public and colder than a witches behind at the North Pole," I laughed.

Not exactly my usual euphemism, but one you might expect. It always took me a long time to get around to swearing in front of people I hadn't known very long, even a lady I was sleeping with.

"So what are you going to do about it?" she giggled.

"Want me to warm you up?" I said, diving on top of her and capturing her in my arms, sleeping bag and all.

"You better feed me first." She said, returning my offered kiss with enough ardor to make me wonder if she was kidding about eating first.

Rather than go backwards to Batesville for breakfast we continued down Highway 6 to Oxford, Mississippi. Lynn went back on the Internet while I drove. That way we could check the street names in towns along the way without actually driving around in or even through every town. It turned out to be a good plan.

Oxford actually had a "Washington Avenue." Unfortunately, there were very few houses on that street and it turned out to be not the right one, but we learned a couple of valuable lessons in the process. First of all, streets can sometimes be interrupted for one reason or another—such as pothole, or a large rock outcropping, whatever. And, secondly, street names don't stay the same forever. Street names get changed to honor an important person from the area, or, as in the case of Martin Luther

King or President Kennedy, just an important person. It was like looking for a needle in a haystack and finding a nail.

Is that confusing enough, or what?

One of the reasons for continuing on Highway 6 was that it was the most direct way to get to Courtland, Alabama from Courtland, Mississippi. We would take Highway 6 to Tupelo, Mississippi and then take the Natchez Trace Parkway to the Lee Highway near Cherokee, Alabama—just a hop, skip and a jump from Courtland.

Tupelo, Mississippi also had a "Washington Avenue," but it was not very long and it had mostly industrial buildings on it. Obviously it was not the right street. By the time we got to Courtland, Alabama it was late in the afternoon and I was convinced we were not only looking for a needle in a haystack, but we were still looking for the damned haystack.

Besides, I was beginning to feel apprehensive about returning to Florida. First of all, it was not inconceivable that the police were looking for me there; and, secondly, it could mean that my time with Lynn was running out. Something I wasn't exactly ready for yet, but I wasn't sure I was ready to make a permanent commitment either— which could be a little like jumping out of the frying pan into the fire, which was what I'd done the last time. Maybe my relationship with Maria would have lasted longer if I hadn't been so quick to jump into it in the first place.

At any rate, Courtland, Alabama turned out to be rather intriguing. Not that there were tons of streets that ended in "ington," but there were a number of street that were potential possibilities, such as Clinton Street, Jesse Jackson Parkway, and Martin Luther King Drive. In North Courtland there was a Rosa Parks Street, a Joe Louis Lane, a Hank Aaron Road, and finally a Harold Washington Avenue. Way too many possibilities to investigate in a single evening.

We spent the night in a campground in Joe Wheeler State Park—at least, most of the night. The weather was still unseasonably cold and damp so we got up a little after five, dressed, broke camp and packed up the car.

"If you don't get some hot coffee in me in about the next five minutes," Lynn said, clutching the turned-up collar of her sweatshirt against her neck while her teeth chattered, "I'm gonna pound a knot on your head."

"What kind of knot?"

"A big one!"

"Again with the threats," I laughed, slamming the trunk. I roughed her up playfully then escorted her to the passenger side and opened the door for her.

Nana's Country Café was the only place we could find open at such an early hour. The décor fit the restaurant's name and so did the clientele—a motley collection of older white men in overalls, plaid shirts, jackets, and John Deere baseball style caps.

"You folks are out early," a nice waitress named Anita said with a smile.

My guess was that she was someone's grandmother and owner of the place. "More like froze out," I quipped, returning her smile.

My razor sharp morning wit didn't seem to register and she stood poised, pencil at the ready over her pad, but with one eyebrow raised in a frozen quizzical look.

"We were camping up at the park," I explained, resolving to shelve the wit and be more direct in the future. "And we're in desperate need of some hot coffee."

For a few seconds it seemed like every old geezer in the place picked up on the "camping up at the park" bit and turned to look at us, like birds on a wire when someone fires a shotgun. I half expected the lot of them to go fluttering through the windows in panicked flight.

"Coming right up," the waitress said, taking flight herself.

The Café was quite spacious with somewhere around twenty-five tables and had obviously been through a few transformations in its day—like maybe a pharmacy with a snack shop. "What brings y'all to these parts?" the closest farmer asked, turning his chair to face us. He was wearing unlaced boots, blue jeans with a gray T-shirt, an open red and black plaid flannel shirt as a jacket, and a beat-up straw hat with the brim rolled macho cowboy style. He was only about thirty. "Y'all look a little lost," he concluded.

I nodded, feeling a little like I was on stage in an auditorium. "I guess you could say that ... we're kind of on a mission. We're looking for Courtland Realty. Did you all ever have an outfit like that around here?"

The man shook his head, looking around at his buddies for confirmation that no one knew anything about any Courtland Realty. There was a lot of negative head shaking and the show was over as suddenly as it had begun. The men still seemed curious about what sort of mission Lynn and I were on, but I had a feeling their Southern upbringing made it difficult for them to pursue the matter further without knowing us better.

"We do have a picture," I said, hoping that would help.

I left Lynn drinking her coffee and went out to the car and got one of the enlarged pictures that I had printed out. When I came back Lynn was laughing at something our amiable farmer had said and I have to admit feeling just a twinge of jealousy—which was ridiculous. Lynn was almost old enough to be the guy's mother.

"We think this picture was taken in 1969," I said, ignoring my twinge and offering the enlargement for viewing. "At least it was developed in 1969. And as you can see by the stickers on the car, we think it might be somewhere near a military base."

Most of the other men in the room, five or six came over to bunch around our cowboy friend and study the enlargement.

"There was an air base here at on time," one of them said. He was dressed in blue overalls, light blue shirt, and John Deere cap. His face wore the wrinkles of many hours in the Alabama sun. He took the enlargement for a moment and then shook his head. "Like I said … there was an air base here at one time, but this doesn't look like anything I've ever seen around here."

His word was apparently law because the gang dispersed, shaking their heads.

After breakfast, Lynn and I went back to the car and onto the Internet to learn what we could about the area. Courtland turned out to be two towns that were once divided by the highway—Courtland and North Courtland. During the 70's a bypass was built around the town and that part of the Joe Wheeler Hwy became Martin Luther King Dr. Which no doubt had a lot to do with the meager crowd at Nana's Country Café. Bypasses have a way of killing downtown businesses wherever they're built.

During World War II the government built an air base just outside Courtland to train fighter pilots. In its heyday Courtland Army Airfield had four runways, a PX, a theater, and enough barracks to support 500 planes. They even had their own bank.

Lynn and I drove out to look the airfield over but there wasn't much to see—the foundation of the old guard shack divided the road onto the field like a rectangular skeleton slammed down in the grassy strip. The only buildings there were hangars and such for the Lawrence County Airport and some others that resulted from trying to turn the airfield into an industrial park.

As near as we could learn the life of the airfield had been relatively short—only from 1943 to 1948 when it was turned over to the state. Toward the end of the war the government had transferred the training of B-24 Liberator pilots from Maxwell Field at Montgomery, Alabama to Courtland, but by 1951 they were raising chickens in what was left of the tar paper covered barracks.

There was no way this Courtland fit the time frame we needed. Even so, we were determined to thoroughly explore the town before moving on, just in case a street name had been changed or something.

Rosa Parks Street and Hank Aaron Road in North Courtland seemed to be the only two prospects in the name-change category that ran east and west. Of course, Lynn could be wrong about the significance of the shadows in the picture, but I tended to agree with her. In the end, we wound up going to both city halls and the post office to get the full story on all of the streets in question. All to no avail, we were obviously in the wrong haystack. Which meant we had a decision to make.

To my dismay, Courtland, Virginia was much further away from where we were than Lake City, Florida and Lynn's time off was coming to an end. If we tried to go to Courtland, Virginia at this time Lynn might loose her job. I sure didn't want that.

Actually the decision to not go to Courtland, Virginia at this time was more a fluke than a decision. We had stopped in a Food & Fuel on the south side of Courtland, Alabama in our last swing through town to fill up with gas and get ready to hit the road. I was browsing the map display while Lynn went to the bathroom when I spotted a brochure for *The First White House of the Confederacy.* For no particular reason, I picked it up and glanced through it. When my eyes spotted the address, my heart stopped. It read: 644 Washington St. Montgomery, Alabama—and going through Montgomery was practically mandatory if you were going from Courtland, Alabama toLake City, Florida.

Chapter 13

The drive to Montgomery took just a little over three hours, and this time we didn't even consider pitching the tent even though the weather was better. A hot shower was going to feel pretty good and both the computer and the cell phone batteries were in need of recharging, which is a little hard to do in a tent. Besides, in a major city like Montgomery, places to camp within the city-limits were not exactly a dime-a-dozen.

We checked into a Days Inn just off the Martin Luther King Junior Expressway on Zelda Road. From the looks of the map of the surrounding area, the city fathers must have been fans of F. Scott Fitzgerald because there was an F Scott Drive, a Gatsby Drive, and a Zelda Circuit connecting to Zelda Road. None of which had anything to do with what we were trying to do, but I was amused just the same.

The motel was a large U-shaped two-story building with a swimming pool in the center of the U. There must have been about 150 rooms, which meant no one paid much attention to our presence—a fact that did not displease me. Once in a while I like the anonymity of a city, but generally not. So it occurred to me that I might still be worried about being a wanted criminal.

"I asked the desk clerk about places to eat," I told Lynn as I unlocked the second-floor room. "He said there were a lot of places close by, including next door and across the street, depending on what we're in the mood for. I think we should get cleaned up and just walk until we find something that suits our fancy."

"Fine with me," Lynn agreed.

It was the only motel I've ever been in that had a granite shower surround, which got me to thinking about home. The area around St. Cloud, Minnesota produces a lot of granite stuff and this seemed kind of extravagant for a motel.

"See," I told Lynn jokingly. "I take you to nothing but the finest places."

She was naked except for the bath towel wrapper. "I know," she murmured, her eyes twinkling. She reached out and gently traced the back of her hand against my beard stubble. "Now if I could just get you to shave."

Having been put in my place, I hopped into the shower.

...

By the time we finished cleaning up it was after five. We walked south on Zelda Road for about a mile and made a right turn on Carter Hill Road and walked about another mile. There were quite a few fast food restaurants along the way, but I was looking for more of a sit-down place. We settled on a place called Martin's in the corner of a parking lot for a Winn Dixie store.

Martin's turned out to be a good selection. The wall over the cash register was plastered with framed awards and the décor was nice. The walls were paneled in what I guessed to be Butternut paneling with worm holes, with a large 48 pane window in both the north and east wall. The window treatment was two-inch wide wooden blinds. The tables were covered with green and white checkered oilcloth.

We both ordered Martin's famous fried chicken, which came with green beans and candied yams and really hit the spot. We had an unusually quite meal, then started back in what I estimated to be the general direction of the motel. Walking cross-country would save us at least three-quarters of a mile and I had always been pretty good at getting my physical directions right when heading cross-country. It was my emotional directions that gave me problems.

"I think we need to talk," I told Lynn, taking her hand.

The minute the words were out, I wished I'd taken a different approach. It almost sounded as if I wanted to brush her off. Nothing could have been further from the truth. When she didn't reply, there was only one thing to do.

"I think you'd agree that we don't exactly constitute your typical one night stand," I said bluntly.

"You think?" she said, squeezing my hand.

She wasn't making this any easier. "What I'm trying to say is that tomorrow is about the last day we can spend together before getting you back ... then we have to decided what comes next. With us, I mean."

"I know," she said softly, staring at the ground in front of us as we walked.

We walked for another block in silence. It was starting to get dark and I was beginning to wonder if taking this way back was all that smart. There were lots of houses, but I didn't see any people. Given Montgomery's history of racial violence maybe this wasn't the best route we could have chosen. There had been quite a few blacks in Martin's and I hadn't really given it much thought. But I wasn't exactly sure if walking my new lady friend through a black neighborhood at dusk was a good idea.

"Given my track record," I said finally, "you should probably run like crazy."

"Why do you say that?"

"Oh, no reason … I've been married twice and both times I divorced them, not the other way round. I'd think that would scare you to death."

"Maybe … but it seems to me you told me you're divorcing your second wife because she left you, and the first one because you were completely incompatible and you didn't want to spend the rest of you life living with a women you didn't love."

"That's true, but—"

"Besides, who says we have to get married?"

I shot her a quick glance. Her implication was clear and it was something that had not even crossed my mind. "You know what … you're right. I know quite a few people who've been together for years and years— even bought houses and cars and stuff like that together, and they're not married. When it comes right down to it, a marriage license is just a piece of paper, albeit an expensive one."

She stopped walking to grin at me. "Did anyone ever tell you, you talk funny?"

"I know," I laughed, tousling her hair playfully. "When I first went in the Army at the age of seventeen all the other guys thought I had such a stiff upper lip, you know, like the English, that they had me running for president. This one Cajun guy from New Orleans wanted to beat the crap out of me because I didn't swear enough to suit his taste."

"They have swearing standards in Louisiana?"

"Something like that—at that age in the service, I think it's every other word. At least that's the way it seemed. Personally, the only reason I didn't swear like the rest of them is because my mother did have swearing standards, which she reinforced with a lath off a peach crate."

"Whoa!" Lynn's eyes twinkled in the growing dusk.

I gave her a quick kiss and looked around to get my bearings again. We had just crossed what appeared to be an old rail bed in which the tracks had been removed. I was hoping the street we were on would run back into Zelda Road, but now I was having some doubts. Come to think of it, I didn't remember any connecting streets on Zelda Road until you got to Carter Hill Road. That's why we had turned right there.

"How do you feel about getting lost on your first night in Montgomery?" I asked.

"Fine, as long as I'm with you."

The buildings around us seemed to be warehouses, probably from the railroad days, so I decided to go another block east before turning north. It was a good plan. We ran smack dab into Ann Street and from that corner I could see the restaurant on the corner beside the Days Inn.

"You know what's bothering me the most?" I asked as we headed down the home stretch.

She had a way of not answering with words, but a

quick glance let me know I should go ahead with my thought, which I did.

"What if we actually find the guy tomorrow. Say we find the house, go and knock on the door, and the guy actually answers the door. What do we do then?"

Chapter 14

The house stood like a beacon on a cliff overlooking the sea—not that there was any sign of a cliff or a sea either, for that matter. It's just that it was the only house on the north side of the street in the 1500 block of E. Washington Street. And it was clearly the house in the picture, even though the trees and flowers were gone.

And what was even more astounding we had practically driven right to it. A quick check of the area on Internet maps the night before had shown there to be three sections of street with "Washington" included in the name in downtown Montgomery. First, there was a nine-block section smack dab in the middle of the Capitol area called "Washington Avenue," which was where *The First White House of the Confederacy* stood. Then, a block to the east, a two-block continuation that appeared to be "*residential*" that was also called "Washington Avenue." And finally, just on the other side of the striped-out rail-bed, another five-block section called "E. Washington Street." There was also a Washington Ferry Road and a Willie Washington Street, but they were on the outskirts of Montgomery and may not have even existed in 1969.

We drove through the two-block section of Washington Avenue first, but the houses were all brick and too up-scale. So we went on to the five-block section of E. Washington Street—and it was kind of like winning the lottery.

"Can you believe this?" I asked Lynn, almost shaking in my boots.

"I see what you meant last night when you were wondering what do we do now," Lynn said, giving me a sheepish smile.

Walking to the door was like going to the playground to meet the school bully. If my knees weren't knocking, they were darned close to it. I gripped Lynns hand a little tighter, pulled myself a little taller and pushed the doorbell button.

There wasn't much traffic on this street, but I suddenly became conscious of the steady hum of traffic to the north. I had not heard a doorbell ring, nor did I hear the sound of anyone stirring inside. Maybe the doorbell didn't work. I glanced at Lynn, shrugged, and rapped on the door a couple of times.

I was about to rap again when the door suddenly swung open.

The black woman wielding the doorknob was at least as tall as I am if not taller with salt and pepper hair set in a style that made her look like an older colored version of Princess Leia from Star Wars. She was very thin, straight as a ramrod, and wearing glasses with thick pinkish rims. "Can I help you?" she asked, pursing her lips while giving us a quizzical look. She appeared ready to slam the door shut on a moment's notice.

"I hope so," I said, not really sure where to start.

"We're looking for someone," Lynn offered. "And all we have to go on is this picture." She held up the picture for the woman to see.

I wasn't even aware that Lynn had brought the picture along.

"Oh, my Lord!" the woman exclaimed, quickly covering her mouth with her hand.

"You know these people then?" I asked, looking quickly at Lynn.

"Of course." The woman was visibly shaken. "That's me and my grandson William. Where in the world did you get that picture?"

This was not a turn of events that we were prepared for. I looked deep into Lynn's eyes with my best "what do we do now" look. "That's kind of a long story," I stammered.

The woman studied us for a moment … as if trying to decide if we were ax murders, or what. "You'd better come in then," she said finally.

She led us across a foyer and into what I had an urge to call a "parlor." It was a page out of time. There were hardwood floors with throw rugs, chintz curtains, a brass lamp with a half-moon milk-glass shade with crystal-like glass danglies all around the rim. You'd have to look in an antique shop to find anything similar. She seated herself in a wooden rocker and waved us toward an antique love seat.

"My name is Ruby McPherson," she told us in very business-like tones. "And I'm sure dying to know how it happens you have a picture of me and my grandson. Last time I saw that picture, William was just a boy."

I looked at Lynn again, wishing we had talked about this situation a little more before knocking on Ruby McPherson's door. "I guess to start with," I said. "I have to asked you if your grandson is still alive?"

Ruby all but glared at us. "Far as I know … don't hear so much from him any more now that he's grown."

"Well," I hesitated, uncertain how to proceed. "We got this picture from a man who is … is most definitely a sexual predator. What we don't know is whether that man is your grandson … or whether your grandson may be one of this guy's victims, or maybe just a friend—."

I have seen storm clouds gathering before, but Ruby's face was suddenly as black and as ominous as any storm clouds I've ever seen. Her eyes could have made laser cuts across a plate of steel.

"How long has it been since you heard from your grandson?" Lynn asked.

Ruby's eyes softened a bit and I was glad Lynn was along. "About six months, I guess," Ruby said. "He was working in a place down in Florida. Lake City if I remember right. I don't always remember things exactly right any more, if you know what I mean."

"I hate to tell you this, Mrs. McPherson," I was beginning to feel like the scum of the earth again, "but that kind of fits. I got this picture from a guy in a house in Lake City, and from the looks of things he was about to rape an eight year old white girl."

"Oh, Lord a mercy!" Ruby exclaimed, the color draining from her face. "I was afraid of something like that."

Lynn and I exchanged glances.

"What do you mean?" I asked.

"That'd be my long story, I guess," Ruby sniffled, a tear suddenly rolling down her cheek. She took a tissue from the box on the oak table beside her chair and dabbed at the tear while we waited.

"I should tell you," I said, after a minute. "If your grandson is a sexual predator there is also a good chance that he is a murderer as well. That's what these guys do. They rape some child ... then wind up killing them to keep from getting caught."

Ruby nodded. "I understand." She murmured. "I was a schoolteacher here in Montgomery for more than forty years. I heard more than a body should ever have to about the rape and murder of innocent children."

Lynn and I were both on the verge of tears. Life can be pretty unfair some times. We waited patiently for Ruby to collect her thoughts.

"Could I have that picture?" she asked finally, her voice filled with hope.

The request caught me completely off guard. The picture was actually evidence in what could be a capital murder investigation. There was no way we should give up the picture, even though technically it probably belonged to Ruby.

"I'll see that you get a copy," I promised.

Ruby sat silent for another long minute. "William was always a good boy," she said finally, "but it's not surprising that he'd do such a thing ... under the circumstances."

Lynn seemed just as puzzled as I was, but neither one of us wanted to push the elderly woman too hard.

"Let me show you," Ruby said, rising from her chair with dignity.

She disappeared in the direction of what I guessed would be a bedroom. The house was one of those long, narrow affairs that people call a *"shotgun shack."* She came back in a few minutes carrying a letter. "Read this," she ordered.

Lynn and I sat huddled on the love seat reading the

letter like a couple of school children. It was not a very long letter and if it was supposed to clear things up, it had the exact opposite effect. According to the envelope the letter was from Evelyn Mattson, Avenger Village, Sweetwater, Texas to Charles McPherson, 1524 E. Washington St., Montgomery, Alabama. There were no zip codes. The letter was postmarked 10/25/1944. It read as follows:

Dear Charles,

I hope you don't mind me using your first name, but after the events of last week I don't see how I can call you anything else.

First of all, I pray that my letter does not cause you any trouble because I can certainly see how it might. At any rate, I just had to write you and thank you for the comfort you brought me—a virtual stranger. I think you were probably as much surprised by what happened as I was and that just points out that we don't know very much about our so-called human condition, if you want to call it that.

At any rate, when I heard of Kathy's death, I don't know what I would have done if you hadn't been there to bolster me. I also know that what we did was wrong, even though it felt right at the time. And like I said, I don't mean to get you in trouble, but I will love you forever for what you did for me.

Love Always,
Evelyn Mattson

Lynn and I looked at each other to confirm that each had finished reading the letter and maybe to see if the other had any idea what the letter meant. Apparently we were both finished but neither knew what the letter meant and our faces showed it.

"That's what started it all," Ruby said, satisfied that it was okay to continue. "This letter kind of seems like a love letter … but judging by the formal signature, it's not exactly. As you can see, it was mailed to my husband back in late 1944."

Lynn and I waited for Ruby to continue at her own pace.

"You folks have heard of the Tuskegee Airman, right?"

We nodded.

Ruby's Story

Chapter 15

According to Ruby McPherson what may have been the single most important event in her life started out as having nothing whatever to do with her. It was only through a bizarre set of circumstances that other people's lives spilled over and impacted hers in such a dramatic way.

...

It wasn't until Kathy Henson realized that her watch had stopped that she began to realize that she was in real trouble. And it was all the fault of that damned maintenance jackass back at Stuttgart. Her AT-6 trainer engine had been plagued with occasional backfiring since the baker's dozen had left Avenger Airfield at Sweetwater, Texas, earlier that day. Instead of going to dinner with Evie and the other girls she'd stayed on the field to get someone to check out her engine. But instead of working on the problem, this six-handed arrogant Arkansas jackass had backed her into a rolling maintenance platform and tried to grope and kiss her.

"Get your hands off me—" Kathy had protested at the time, struggling to get her hands free to push him away.

Stupid grease monkey, she thought. That's what she

should have called him. She probably should have just let him kiss her. *That's what Evie would have done.* But at the time she was worried the Lt. Kramer would see them. *Mrs. Leonard Kramer,* she tried the sound of that over again in her mind for the umpteenth time.

Her mind was like a humming bird, flitting from flower to flower. She should have paid more attention, not let herself get trapped behind the plane that way, out of sight of the other men on the field. She distinctly remembered her wrist slamming into the handrail of the maintenance platform steps at the time, but she'd never thought to check her watch—why would she? She was busy fighting off that octopus jackass.

The nerve of the guy! He actually had the gall to get angry and yell some stupid crap at her about how women should stay home and have babies instead of learning to fly. *He was probably just jealous.* Not everyone could afford to learn to fly. There was a world war going on.

Mrs. Lt. Kathleen Kramer. Now that had a nice ring. She let her mind drift awhile trying to decide what proper military etiquette was for naming wives.

The good lieutenant was supposed to be behind her, the last one to take off, the leader of the baker's dozen— twelve civilian WASP trainees and their Army flight leader. Only when they'd reached the Mississippi River they ran into some rapidly developing thunderheads that no one had bother to mention. In an attempt to fly around the storm and avoid flying through cloud cover they'd lost sight of each other. Then the damned engine started backfiring again. *What the hell was she supposed to do?*

According to her map and everything she's been told

Courtland Army Airfield was a short distance southwest of Courtland, Alabama. The highway ran east and west through the town. If she overshot she'd hit the bigger city of Decatur, Alabama—which must be what she was seeing ahead. She put the AT-6 "*Texan*" into a left bank, did a 180 and headed back toward the sinking sun. Time was becoming critical. If she didn't find the airfield soon she'd wind up putting down in a cow pasture after dark.

The fuel gauges were also beginning to worry her. She should have plenty of fuel, but with the backfiring could she trust that? *What if the engine was backfiring because it was getting too much fuel?* She didn't know enough about the mechanics of the Wright Whirlwind radial engine to know if that was possible.

Another thing that worried her was the terrain. She'd first learned to fly, before she could even drive a car, back at Reno Sky Ranch near Sparks, Nevada. Out there on the desert if she ran out of fuel she could just flare out and let the plane settle onto the sand. It was an entirely different story here. This part of the country was rougher, with trees and fences and gullies and power lines galore, not to mention cows if she had to put down in that cow pasture.

Kathy let the "*Texan*" drift a little to the south so that the highway was on her right. That way when she approached the town of Courtland she should be in direct line with the airfield. *Only there wasn't any damned airfield where it was supposed to be!*

She put the trainer into another tight bank, did a180 over the highway heading back east and counted *one mississippi, two mississippi* for about a minute, then did another 180 back toward the town again. Thankfully, the engine was beginning to run better. One of the guys had told her that engines sometimes run better at night because of the increased moisture in the air. Apparently that was true.

Why are there so damned many trees, she wondered, watching the terrain skim along beneath her. She'd thought the area around Courtland was supposed to be cotton country. *And where's Wheeler Lake?* According to her maps Wheeler Lake, formed by the Wheeler Dam on the Tennessee River, should be just a few miles north of Courtland.

Damn, it would be nice to have a watch that worked! If she ever saw that stupid maintenance jackass again, she was going to kick him right in the *in-betweens.* At least that's what Evie called them. She thought briefly of her friend and roommate. They'd be spending the night in Courtland and there was a good chance that they might get to meet some of the Army's pilots in training. Something they all had looked forward to with nervous anticipation.

Only right now, she had to find the *damned airfield!*

Kathy made another pass—going a little farther to the west this time. Still nothing! *This is crazy! It's got to be there!* Airfields are big long strips with control towers and hangers and airplanes and trucks and what not. *How could she be missing it?*

She made yet another pass, letting the AT-6 drift out farther from the highway this time in case she'd been missing the airfield on her left because her attention had been on the right. Still she could not spot the airfield! And the sun was dropping like a rock. She could tell by the lack of shadows on the ground that is was only her altitude that kept it visible for her. If she didn't land soon, she'd be doing it in the dark.

She made another shorter pass around the town, picked out what appeared to be a fairly level hayfield where the airfield was supposed to be, and hit the landing gear control knob to put down her landing gear. Uncertain as to how much room she had, she cut back on the power to make sure she began her landing at the edge of the field. It was then that she suddenly realized she was about to hit a power line. She slammed the throttle forward and pulled back of the stick—and thankfully the engine didn't backfire. This time, thanks maybe to the fresh evening air, the AT-6 engine surged with power and the craft suddenly leaped upward, fighting for altitude. As she passed over the power line there was a sudden jolt, but she kept climbing.

I bet I hit the damned power line, she thought, expecting the aircraft to go cart wheeling through the air. But it didn't. Thankful to have remained airborne, she thought briefly of sitting her baby down on the highway instead of the field, but the road seemed suddenly abuzz with traffic. She had no choice but to try the hayfield again.

Considering the way the AT-6 had bucked, she had to have broken the power line with her landing gear. *Hopefully there was no damage to the landing gear.* Anyway, now it certainly should be safe to make another approach on the same hayfield. She really had no other choice. It was getting quite dark. As she sank into her glide path, she opened the canopy and tried to lean out so she could see the field better. *It's like flying in a coal mine,* she thought, reluctantly releasing her shoulder harness so she could lean out farther to get a better view of the hayfield.

I hope Lenny will be proud of me, she thought, easing off on the power. At the very last second she realized her mistake. She was too low! Her landing gear clipped the fence at the edge of the hayfield, snapping the fence and collapsing her landing gear—and sending her head catapulting forward into the canopy frame and oblivion—

...

The area just outside Base Ops at Courtland Army Airfield was unusually congested on the evening of October 16th, 1944. In addition to the normal traffic of white pilot trainees stationed at Courtland, there was also a contingent of black Tuskegee pilot trainees, as well as the baker's dozen from Sweetwater. Being a good flight leader, Lt. Leonard (Lenny) Kramer had waited around to make sure all of his chicks made it safely to roost. When Kathy Henson hadn't landed by 19:15 hours, he initiated action to find out what, if any thing had happened to her. There had already been nearly a dozen women killed in training accidents since the program began. He dreaded the thought of Kathy Henson becoming just another statistic.

Most of her fellow trainees hung around as well. Everyone's mood was quite somber. One trainee in particular, Evelyn Mattson, seemed particularly agitated. She spent most of the time pacing back and forth. Lt. Kramer thought she might have been one of Kathy's two roommates.

Lenny was a bit surprised when Mattson stopped to

speak to the *coons* that were hanging around Base Ops. *It's bad enough that we're training women to fly,* he thought. *Now we gotta worry about the blacks.*

The blacks weren't even supposed to be here. They were supposed to have left before his ladies landed, but one of them had had engine trouble so they all stayed rather than fly back after dark—which they didn't have enough experience for yet. Not that Lenny had anything against blacks, but where he came from respectable white women did not socialize with blacks. The *niggers* were probably hanging around because they had no way of getting the mile or so into town. And besides, he realized, there was probably no place for them to stay in such a small town, at least not one that would be safe after dark.

One black in particular, a light-skinned one named McPherson, always seemed to be waiting expectantly when Mattson reached the spot where he was standing, like he was waiting for word on Henson too. The pair always seemed to exchange a few words before Mattson turned to pace back toward Lenny.

"Why don't you plant it some place, Mattson?" Lenny demanded at a quarter to eight. "You're wearing out the tarmac."

"I'm worried about Kathy."

"Well, pacing ain't gonna get her here any sooner."

"I know—"

"So what's with the spooks?"

Mattson turned to give him a concerned look. In the light from the Ops windows, it was hard to tell if it was surprise or scorn. "What do you mean?" she demanded.

Lenny took a last drag off his cigarette, weighing

his options. "I heard blacks have really big ones," he was tempted to say. "Is that what you're interested in?" Instead, he snuffed out the cigarette, ran his hand over his blonde crewcut, and let his blues eyes wander up and down her pert figure for a few seconds. "I mean," he said slowly. "I was wondering why you keep talking to those black airmen."

Evie smiled at his exaggerated tact. "I don't … that one just keeps asking me if we have any news on Kathy yet, that's all. Is that okay?"

"Sure … whatever?"

"Honestly—you men." Evie snorted. "Sometimes I'm not sure what upsets you more … women's suffrage or the black emancipation?"

"Like I said," Lenny snapped back angrily. "Whatever!"

When word came fifteen minutes later at 20:00 hours that Kathleen Marie Henson had crashed in a hayfield up near Walnut, Mississippi at 19:35 hours, time stopped while the question of her survival was put forth. "No!" Evie Mattson shrieked, bursting into immediate uncontrollable sobs. She did not, however, throw herself into the arms of flight leader Lt. Leonard Kramer. Instead, she turned toward Tuskegee pilot trainee Charles McPherson.

Now … don't that fry the spaghetti? Lenny thought as he watched McPherson first awkwardly pat Mattson on the back, then open his black arms to receive her sobbing form. He wasn't surprised when they moved out of the Ops building's circle of light.

…

No one ever knew for sure whether Kathleen Henson had gotten confused and made the mistake of assuming that Corinth, Mississippi was Decatur, Alabama. If she had just kept following Highway 72 she would have eventually made it to Courtland Army Airfield. Nor did anyone ever know or even suspect that the six-handed mechanic at the Stuttgart, Arkansas airfield was as guilty of murder as surely as if he'd deliberately jammed up Kathy's fuel lines.

Chapter 16

In the spring of 1941, nineteen-year-old Charles McPherson was looking over the butt end of a team of cantankerous old brown mules when his sixteen-year-old sister, Hattie came a running. Charles was busy trying to keep the worn-out plow share of the walking plow cutting a straight furrow in the red earth near Hardaway, Alabama, so he didn't notice Hattie until she yelled at him.

"Charlie ... Mamma says you gotta come right away!"

"Whoa!" Charles commanded the team, glancing at his sister as he transferred his hands from the plow handles to pull back on the reins. He always kept the reins tied in a knot and looped over his shoulders while he was plowing so he could keep both hands on the plow handles. "What's the matter?" he demanded of Hattie.

She was tall for a girl, nearly as tall as his six feet, but much darker in color. A lot of people didn't even take them for brother and sister. In fact, Charles was the only one in a brood of six with such fair skin and wavy rather than curly hair.

"It's Poppa ... he's much worse."

Charles studied his sister a moment trying to assess how bad the situation was. Hattie was wearing the usual cotton dress she always threw on after she got home from school. It barely came halfway between her butt and knees, and she was barefoot.

"Mamma want me to go for the doctor?" he asked.

"Huh-huh … at least, I think so. Or maybe jes' that Mrs. Maybrury."

"What good will that do?" Charles snorted, slipping the reins over his head and commencing to unhook the double tree. Normally, he'd catch it but good leaving the plow in the furrow in the middle of the field like that.

"Don't ask me," Hattie shrugged, watching him.

Charles picked up the reins again and started to turn the mules to cut across the field toward the house.

Hattie took a couple steps to follow then grimaced as Charles looked back to see if she was following. "Kin I ride, Charlie?" she asked. "This stubble hurts my feet."

Normally, he would have made fun of her in a situation like that. This time he didn't. "Maybe that's a good idea," he said. "Here, I'll boost you up."

The mules must have sensed the situation was serious. They'd been ridden before, but never while harnessed. So it was hard to know what to expect. Fortunately, Molly, the smaller of the two mules, barely batted an eye when Charles boosted Hattie up. He then walked around to Lady's flank and jumped up so he landed on his stomach on her back, then he pivoted on his stomach to swing his legs around and straddle the bigger mule. Gathering up the now extra long reins, he folded them in one hand until a couple of feet at the ends hung free and used that to whip the team into a trot.

When they got to the house Charles told Hattie she could do the unhitching.

…

Hiram McPherson was not an old man by any standard of measurement, except that of appearance.

Twenty some years of share cropping, like his father before him and his grandfather before that, had left him bent and broken and all but spent. Then he went and got himself bitten by a raccoon.

At first, he did nothing. But then, when the bite got red and swollen, he had hobbled the two plus miles to Edna Maybrury's shack and got something to put on the bite—an obnoxious mixture of glycerine, laudnum and kerosene oil. He knew the proper thing to do was go to Hardaway and have Dr. Rinker give him a rabies shot, but the white doctor would not accept a chicken as payment.

He would have been better off chopping the head off the chicken and throwing it in a pot to make chicken soup. At least that way he would have gotten some food into his stomach. Within a day the swelling of the bite became worse, his body became racked with fever, and a couple of whitish lumps developed under his tongue. He no longer had the desire to eat.

Now, Edna Maybrury might have been damned good at her craft back *in the day*, but her day was long past. Some folks claimed she was over a hundred years old. No one seemed to know for sure. Whatever the case her second recommended so-called remedy (the chewing of poplar bark) was just one more coffin nail.

Hiram McPherson was dead long before Charles got back from Hardaway with the Dr. Rinker.

"How much we owe you, Sir?" Charles's mother asked, when Dr. Rinker nodded his head to confirm that her husband was indeed dead.

Dr. Rinker shook his head. "Nothing … I expect. I didn't do anything. The man was already dead when I got here." He was a big man with big ears and a red pock marked nose that suggested heavy drinking. The reddish, flabby skin on his neck made one think of a turkey wattle. He looked around the room ruefully. "From the looks of things you folks went to that damned Edna Maybrury for Hiram's treatment. The county ought to have locked that danged fool woman up years ago for all the mayhem she's caused. It's a damned shame!"

Charles wasn't sure what he should do. Tears were streaming down his mother's face, but she stood her ground.

"Hiram knew he shoulda went to town for y'all," his mother said defiantly, "But we ain't got but a few dollars to put in a crop. He didn't want to risk loosing that."

"Well he risked a lot more than that, didn't he?" Dr. Rinker snapped, moving toward the door like a huffing steam engine.

"We still need to pay y'all for coming out," his mother suggested. "We always pay what we owe."

Dr. Rinker laughed. "I suppose I could take a chicken," he said sarcastically. "But what the hell would I do with a chicken? No, it looks like you've got plenty to worry about without worrying about paying me." He started toward the door, and then stopped. "You got folks that can take care of the burying I presume," he said.

Charles's mother nodded, not bothering to wipe away her tears.

After Dr. Rinker left, Charles pulled himself up tall and put his arms around his mother. "Don't you worry, Mamma … you got me to help take care of these young'ns."

Only his mother wouldn't hear of it. After burying

Hiram she packed them up kit and caboodle and moved them to Tuskegee, the nearest big city, so she could find work.

...

As he stood there in the shadows of Base Ops at Courtland Army Airfield, an older and hopefully wiser Charles McPherson was immediately reminded of the other time in his life when he'd put his arms around a grieving woman. Only this time was way different.

The other time it was his black Mammy. This time it was a white woman that he didn't even know. This time he could have easily gotten shot or hung for even thinking about what he was doing, let alone doing it. But still, his compassionate heart would not let him walk away.

Evie Mattson seemed to sense his discomfort.

"Oh, my God!" she sobbed. "I'm sorry ... I shouldn't be doing this."

"It's okay," he assured her. He reached in his back pocket and handed her his white, newly starched handkerchief. "You've just lost your friend. Times like this a body needs someone to lean on for comfort."

"I know," she dabbed at her tears. "But I don't even know you ... you must think I'm terrible."

"Not at all," he assured her.

"You sure?" she sniffled.

She was still leaning against him but seemed to be getting her crying under control—and things were getting confusing. The warmth of her body in the evening October air was beginning to cause a reaction that he neither expected nor wanted. *Now what?* He thought, hoping she would either move away or that his rising erection would just go away by itself. *Maybe the earth could just open up and he could drop into it.*

No such luck! Her breathing became a little faster now and he noticed that her eyes took on a heavier appearance that seemed to make grief indistinguishable from desire. *Or was that his imagination over reacting in the dim light?*

All at once he had an overwhelming desire to kiss her. *That was crazy! He was a happily married man.* But apparently his now rock hard erection could have cared less. He tried to put a little space between them without actually seeming to push her away, but she might as well have been magnetically attached. Now, the least little movement of her body threatened to burst his trousers.

"Where can we go?" she said suddenly, to his delight and shock and dismay.

His erection was no longer his little secret—and there was nothing little about it.

...

"You son of a bitch!" someone yelled and Charles felt himself stumbling backwards, fighting for consciousness.

He hit the ground with a thud and stayed there.

"Knock it off!" someone else yelled. "It's time you monkeys hit the rack."

There was a confusing minute of scuffling and a lot more yelling, then suddenly Evie was kneeling beside him and helping him up. The white guys who had assaulted him had been sent on their way and he was going to have to let her go or be in real trouble.

"Are you okay?" she asked tenderly.

"Fine," he chuckled. "I'm probably going to have a black eye where that guy popped me … but that probably won't even show."

She smiled at his bravado. "I won't ever forget you," she said.

Obviously, it would be suicide to try and kiss her again in public.

"Me neither," he murmured, and then she was gone.

Charles proved to be right about his eye. Whatever discoloration there was around his right eye hardly showed at all. The problem was not with appearance—it was with function. By the time it was his turn to take off the next day, he was having extreme difficulty focusing on his instruments. The return flight to Montgomery was not going to be easy, not in the least.

Charles proved to be right about that too. Somewhere on the down leg of their landing pattern he got too close to his white flight leader's plane. Their wing tips touched for a second and the next thing Charles knew he was slipping into a sideways stall. It was about the last thing he would ever know.

…

It might be a stretch, but like the six-handed mechanic at Stuttgart, the unnamed racist at Courtland who popped Charles McPherson in his right eye for trying to comfort a grieving fellow student pilot, should have at least been charged with accessory to murder.

And no one ever questioned whether there should be an investigation into the racial attitudes of his white instructor and flight leader.

Chapter 17

News of Charles McPherson's death was an especially devastating blow to Ruby Ann, Charles's young wife of just twenty-six months. Ruby Ann was the youngest of five children born to William Henry Rudolph and Emma Mae Spangler Rudolph and the only girl. The problem was that William Rudolph likened himself to William Randolph Hearst in that he considered himself a self-made man and didn't like to let anyone forget it.

Having met Charles at the Montgomery Colored USO Club on Monroe Street while she was a student at Alabama State University, Ruby Ann had gone against her Father's wishes in first dating and then marrying the young aviation cadet.

"Why you got to marry some dumb share cropper?" William Rudolph demanded when his daughter started flashing a cheap engagement ring after just a few dates.

Ruby Ann stared at her father in total dismay. He must have thought she didn't have a clue how he'd gotten his start—which wasn't all that glamorous. He'd started out with just a team and wagon back during the First World War. In no time at all he was running a taxi service with a second hand Buick, hauling soldiers from Fort Benning near Columbus, Georgia across the Chattahoochee River to the Phenix City honky-tonks for beer and prostitutes. After the war he quickly expanded the taxi service into a trucking company, then a contractor business, and finally, with the onset of World War II and the construction of Craig Field at nearby Selma, into full scale real estate development. His rapid rise to affluence was commendable but no reason to look down his nose at Charles.

"You weren't always so well fixed, Daddy," Ruby Ann tried to argue. "You got to give Charles a chance. He's gonna be a pilot and then who knows—"

"Most likely jes' get hisself killed." William Rudolph scoffed. He was a stubborn man—shorter and darker than his daughter with a barrel chest, a grizzled face, and one gold tooth, which he proudly displayed. "Besides," he concluded unceremoniously, "they ain't never gonna let no Negroes fly planes in this war!"

"You're contradicting yourself, Daddy." Ruby Ann was determined to stand up to her father. "First you say he's gonna get himself killed … then you claim they ain't gonna let no Negroes fly planes in the war. You can't have it both ways. What d'you think … he's gonna get hit over the head with some dumb pots'n pans working in the mess hall?"

It was a reasonable argument and one that should have worked—but it never quite achieved the desired result. Her Daddy was suddenly too busy to even attend their wedding. Ruby Ann's only consolation was that his wedding gift was the down payment on a house in the capitol district of Montgomery. But even with that, their relationship remained strained.

When a baby boy was born just 10 months after their wedding, Ruby Ann was still miffed enough to name the baby Charles William McPherson Jr. If she'd named the baby the other way round—William Charles, everything might have been different. Their relationship might have gone back to William Rudolph's original philosophy "Daddy's little girl can't do no wrong."

When news of Charles death came, Ruby Ann had a terrible time facing the "I told you so" looks of her father. If it hadn't been for her mother's help she never would have made it through the funeral, or gotten her life back in order enough to finish school and take a teaching job. But then, what Grandmother could resist the innocent antics of her daughter's only child?

Not that Emma Mae Rudolph was a dawdling old fool.

"I'm fine with helping you," she told Ruby Ann early on. "But you need a man in your life to help with your baby. Young'ns need a man's firm hand … and you got your own needs too."

Ruby Ann was well aware of what her mother was getting at, but at this stage in their relationship she was not exactly comfortable discussing things like that with her Momma. "I—I got all the men I need, Momma," she told her mother awkwardly.

Emma Mae shook her head dubiously "What? You mean that Ray Galston … that friend of Charles's? That boy just plain moon-struck!"

Ruby Ann laughed. "I didn't mean that, Momma … I was talking about Daddy and my brothers."

"Humph!" Emma Mae scoffed.

Ruby Ann knew her mother was not pleased with her father's stubbornness, but she didn't want to argue about that now so she held her tongue.

"Your brother William got all he can do with them

four young'ns of his," her mother continued. "And with Henry and Robert off in the Army—that only leave Joseph, and between college and helping your Daddy, he ain't got time for nothing."

"Like I said, Momma … that's enough for me. Besides … if things get bad, I can always get Ray's help if I need it."

Emma Mae looked at her daughter with real concern. "I still don't see why you don't just go on ahead and marry that boy. I know he asked you least a dozen times."

Ray Galston had been a Tuskegee aviation cadet with Charles, but after Charles's death had washed out and moved to Montgomery. He was trying to convince Ruby Ann that he felt honor bound to take care his friend's wife and infant son.

"After Charles," Ruby Ann told her mother. "I don't want no relationship with no danged man anyway."

Emma Mae just shook her head in dismay. "You got to be crazy, child," she told her. "I think you need to go talk to someone."

But Ruby Ann never did.

The years that followed turned out to be like the trees zipping by on a bobsled ride down a mountain—just a blur.

After graduating from Alabama State Ruby Ann took a teaching job within easy driving distance from the house in Montgomery. Emma Mae continued to baby sit until Charles Jr. was old enough to start school. She was, of course, no longer needed by then because Charles attended the same school where Ruby Ann taught.

After a few years Ray Galston married another woman—but he never quite gave up on Ruby Ann. Or maybe it was because of Charles Jr. that he continued to come around. Charles Jr., although much shorter than his father, was an exceptional athlete, lettering in both football and basketball. In a way, Ruby Ann had Ray to thank for that, for all those early years of playing catch with the boy.

After graduating from high school in 1961, Charles Jr. announced the he wanted to follow in his father's footsteps. The only problem was that things had changed a lot since his father's day. The Tuskegee aviation cadet program no longer existed. And to go to the Air Force Academy, if he could get in at all, would take a whole four years—and with the situation in Vietnam escalating at the time, Charles Jr. wasn't sure he could wait.

Needless to say, Ruby Ann was devastated by Charles Jr.'s decision to join the Air Force as an enlistee. True, because he was still under twenty-one she had to sign the papers giving him permission. But when had she ever told him no?

After basic training at Lackland Air Force Base in California, Charles Jr. was sent to Keesler Air Force Base near Biloxi, Mississippi for 10 months of electronic training as a flight facilities equipment repairman. That was about as close as he would ever get to following in his Daddy's footsteps.

Except for one thing—

Chapter 18

They hung Charles William McPherson Jr. some time in February of 1962, a few months before his graduation from electronics school at Keesler AFB. The "they" was presumed to be a passel of rednecks with possible affiliation to the Klu Klux Klan in or around Pascagula, Mississippi.

Charles's body was found in a swamp by a coon dog hunting opossum. The presumption of hanging had to do with the fact that his hands were tied behind his back, there were enormous rope-burn bruises on his neck, and his neck was broken. National newspapers carried the story only a short time because of other racial incidents ongoing at the time. Some of the local gentry dwelled on the story a bit longer—eagerly repeating some crass remarks about Bubba's coon dog being a really good *coon* dog.

Fortunately for Ruby Ann, when the news of Charles' death came school only had a few months to run until the summer break. To say that she was devastated would be a gross understatement. By this time, both her Father and Mother had passed away and her brothers had taken over her Father's business and had lives of their own. Ray Galston made another bid at being there for her, but she could barely stand to look at the man. After Charles left for basic training at Lackland AFB, Ray let it slip that he might have been the one to suggest the boy join the Air Force, if that's what he wanted to do.

In the middle of March, Ruby Ann received an unexpected knock on her door.

"You Ruby McPherson?" the very white, very pregnant young girl asked.

"Yes," Ruby replied, puzzled. She didn't often see white folks in this part of the capitol district. "Can I help you?"

"I sure as heck hope so!" the girl exclaimed with a nervous laugh. "Otherwise I dunno what I'm gonna do."

Ruby frowned. She was beginning to get an ominous feeling. "What can I do for you?" she asked stiffly.

"Kin I come in?" the girl asked, bouncing up and down like she was about to pee in her underpants.

Ruby weighed the request solemnly. A man never would have gotten past the front door—but what did she have to worry about from such an obviously pregnant white girl, other than being forced into a sudden unexpected, unwelcome role as mid-wife. "I guess so," Ruby said, stepping back and swinging the door open.

"Thanks," the girl stepped across the threshold and glanced around while Ruby closed the door. "I know you don't know me," she said momentarily, "but I'm a friend of Charlie's … well, more than a friend, actually." She waited for Ruby's reaction.

It was hard for Ruby to react. In the first place, she wasn't exactly sure who this girl was talking about. To Ruby's knowledge, no one had ever called Charles Jr. "Charlie." And, secondly, she was totally unaware that Charles had any white friends. Then there was that "more than a friend" phrase to figure out.

"Charlie's the father of my baby," the girl blurted, when Ruby took too long.

This announcement left Ruby somewhat numb. They were still standing in the foyer and the March temperature suddenly became unseasonably stifling.

"Let's go in the parlor where it's a little cooler," Ruby suggested.

The girl followed along like an exuberant puppy and seated herself on the antique love seat Ruby offered. "Can I offer you some ice tea?" Ruby asked, not one to forget her manners though no ice tea was made.

"Oh, no ma'm … I'm fine."

That seemed rather like an absurd understatement because the girl didn't look at all fine. In fact, she looked on the verge of panic. Her shoulder length dishwater blonde hair was in total disarray, like she'd just gotten out of bed. Her face seemed puffy around blue eyes that had a sort of "wild blue yonder" look. Which made what Ruby had to do next all that more difficult.

"You are aware that Charles is dead?" she asked, bracing herself for the scream and subsequent wailing that was sure to follow.

No scream was forthcoming.

"Oh, yes, ma'm," the girl said, as calm as you please. "I read it in the papers."

Ruby made no reply. She simply did not know what to say to this strange girl who was claiming her Charles had fathered a child. The subject of the *birds and bees* was not one of the subjects she'd ever discussed with Charles.

"Sorry for coming here like this," the girl continued when it was obvious Ruby wasn't going to help her. "But

I didn't now what else to do. Oh, by the way, my name is Monique. Anyway, like I was saying … Charlie and me, was more'n friends. When he found out I was p.g. he wanted to marry me right away. He even got us a place to stay in Biloxi. It wasn't much, but I liked it. Charlie had to stay on the base most of the time, but he spent most weekends with me. We was gonna get married just as soon as he got graduated … you know, so I could go with him to the next place he got sent. But he got killed before that could happen."

Her rambling story was almost more than Ruby could absorb at one sitting. Was this the rambling of a love-smitten schoolgirl who thought she'd figured out a way to scam some poor unfortunate serviceman's mother? Or was she just a fruitcake? Ruby was kind of leaning toward the latter.

"Anyway," Monique continued. "After Charlie got hisself killed I didn't have no way of paying for the apartment … and nobody would give me a job because I'm so close to having the baby. I tried to go home … but when my Momma heard Charlie was black, she said she just wouldn't have it. She said the fact that Charlie got hisself killed proved that us raisin' a black baby wasn't gonna work. So I come here."

The last pronouncement was about as weighty as a really loud fart in church and as such it left Ruby mentally spluttering for some sort of truth—some straw of reality to grasp onto and hold tight.

"Where are your things, dear?" she asked finally, stalling.

Monique shook her head. "This is it … I don't have

174

nuthin' else, 'cept for a couple of dollars. I had to spend mosta what I had just gettin' here on the bus."

"I see," Ruby muttered, suddenly understanding the deal with Monique's hair.

Monique's bombshell was something that needed sleeping on. Based on the way Monique talked she was from a poor, most likely, single parent family. There was no mention of a father—other than Charlie being the father of her unborn child, which may or may not be true. Stranger things have happened.

"How do you know Charles is the father of your baby?" Ruby asked.

"He's the only guy I was ever with."

"You sure?"

"Oh, yes ma'm … you'll see when the baby comes. I bet he's gonna look just like Charlie—"

There was a kind of finality to Monique's statement that made it seem as if there were no other options available. She had arrived at Ruby's house to have Charles's baby and that was that.

There was also something very prophetic about the statement. William Charles McPherson turned out to look enough like his father at birth that Ruby would have had to be completely off her rocker to raise any questions about his paternity. Besides, by then (April 1st, 1962) the grandmother thing had kicked in. Monique demonstrated her gratefulness to Ruby for taking her in by letting Ruby name the baby. Ruby went the other way round this time as an act of contrition for stubbornly refusing to honor her father while he was still alive.

The only fly in the ointment came about six months after William Charles McPherson was born.

"You think maybe we could hire a babysitter for awhile?" Monique asked one day after Ruby came home from school. "You've done so much for me … I'd like to see if I could get a job to help out."

Ruby was astounded. "You'd hardly make enough to pay a sitter," she told her.

"That don't matter … I just want to feel like I'm helping. Besides, it would give me a chance to get out some."

Ruby should have paid more attention to the "besides."

Monique's first job was as a dayshift waitress at a nearby restaurant. Ruby was able to find a woman with grown children from the neighborhood to come and be nanny to young William while she and Monique were at work. For awhile, things went pretty smoothly—except Monique wasn't very strong. Most evenings, it was Ruby who wound up feeding William and changing his diapers.

It wasn't long before Monique suggested that since Ruby was doing most of the work in the evenings anyway, maybe they would be better off if she found a better paying job on the evening shift—at a lounge maybe, where the tips would be better. Within the week she was working at the Capitol Bar and Grill a few blocks up the street.

Talk about handwriting on the wall. Ruby would have had to be deaf, dumb, and blind not to have seen what was coming next before it happened.

And she did see it.

She just didn't care.

Frankly, she was never able to quite understand what Charles Jr. found so darned appealing in Monique.

In Ruby's estimation, the girl didn't have much of a backbone. The least little things would put her in bed for two days. And the amount of money she earned as a waitress would hardly even buy William's diapers. Then, too, there was the smoking. Why a young girl would want to ruin her health with such a filthy habit was completely beyond Ruby. She sure as heck wasn't going to allow it in her house.

But it wasn't until Monique brought a man home after work that Ruby lost her cool.

"I'm just not having that in my house," she told the dumbfounded girl when she caught them necking in her kitchen. "It's okay a man walk you home and you offer him a cup of coffee for his trouble … but we ain't having no hanky-panky here!"

Monique gave her that big *wild blue yonder* stare, but the man got mad.

He glared at Ruby for a moment, as if he was contemplating throwing her on the table and ravishing her (she was still a handsome woman) and then glanced down at the skimpily dressed wild-eyed white girl he'd just been mauling. "Fuck this!" he declared shoving Monique roughly aside. "You ladies can just go on ahead and fuck yourselves!"

And with that, he stormed out of Ruby's house.

Monique did not come home from work the following night.

At first Ruby thought she was just being defiant and spending the night with some man. When Monique didn't show up on the next day, or the day after that, Ruby realized there was something more going on. She went to the police and reported the girl missing, but they didn't seem to care much. They did go to the bar where she was working, but concluded there was no evidence of foul play—that she had simply gone off looking for greener pastures.

It did occur to Ruby that Monique might have simply gone back to her mother's place now that she no longer had a black baby to worry about. She was hardly more than a child herself. And for a white girl to try and raise a black child in Montgomery with all the racial tension that was currently going on was a little crazy. Seemed like the news was nothing but civil rights skirmishes these days. Having Monique go back to her mother's was probably the best thing that could happen.

Yes, indeed … that'd be just fine, Ruby told herself, thankful to God for giving her a second child to raise.

Chapter 19

William's presence in her house really turned things around for Ruby. During the year that Charles Jr. was off training she found herself going to church more. Of course, she always did go on Sundays, but after Charles was gone she started letting herself get involved with some of the evening things as well. After all, Pilgrim Rest Baptist Church was just a few blocks down the street. Made for nice evening walks, if nothing else.

The only negative thing about the church was that it was nearly as bad as her mother had been in trying to get her hooked up with a man. All the ladies seemed to think that a woman raising a child, even if it was a grandson, needed the help of a man. What they didn't understand was that she had her reasons for not wanting a man and the subject wasn't open for discussion.

"Why you wanta be like that?" her friend Sadie said every time she brought the subject up and Ruby cut her off. "You a handsome woman!"

"I don't see what that has to do with anything … it's not a crime to keep ones self fit. I'm a professional. I'm supposed to look nice—set an example for the children."

"Well, lah-de-da … I bet you fixin' all up cause there's some married hunk in yer school you fixin' to drive crazy so he'll dump his woman—"

"Don't be absurd!" Ruby snapped knowing full-well Sadie was teasing.

Sadie cackled like a hyena.

Ruby smiled sheepishly. Sadie was just jealous. Sadie was the kind of woman men called "banjo butt" because her behind was disproportionately larger than her ample breasts. Ruby, on the other hand, was like a ramrod. Her breasts were not so large, but nice. And her hips, such as they were, would have looked really nice in a pair of tight fitting jeans—not that she'd ever be caught dead in such a get up.

That was about as far as these episodes ever went. Sadie always seemed to be satisfied once she got Ruby's dander up.

For a while, Ruby felt like she was on that bobsled ride again. Life seemed to be flying by. Rosa Parks' famous bus boycott was ancient history even before William was born. By the time William started school even Dr. King's assassination was in the history books and segregation was finally loosening its grip.

Ruby was thankful for that. William was surprisingly dark considering that his mother was white and blond. The reason for that was fairly obvious. As he grew older he looked more and more like her father—the same stocky build, the same dark kinky, curly hair. Naming him William had been the right choice. He looked more like his Grandfather than his Uncle William did. Hopefully, he'd have a better shot at life than his father and grandfather had had.

That was the odd thing. When Ruby was younger, back in the days when she was in college and in the early days of her marriage, she'd felt like the world was her oyster, that she was blessed with opportunities that weren't yet available to many blacks. But after twenty years of teaching her vision narrowed. In a way, raising William was not so much a second chance as it was a limitation of opportunity. Some days she felt just like a mule hitched to a plow that was cutting a furrow across the entire state.

Fortunately, those feeling were mostly supplanted by the joy she found in young William. When Ray Galston started coming around again she reluctantly gave in and let him spend some time with the youngster. If William became as good at sports as Charles had been there would no doubt be opportunities for scholarships in colleges all across the country. That alone was worth a little sacrifice on her part.

It wasn't until William was nine years old that the sacrifice became a burden. As time went by, Ray had started spending more and more time at Ruby's until finally, his wife got fed-up and demanded a divorce. In the first place, she claimed she didn't believe there was nothing going on between Ruby and Ray. And in the second place, she insisted, it didn't matter whether it was true or not because he was spending so much time there that he obviously wished that it would be true.

Ray did not argue the point.

And it obviously took away Ruby's most potent argument. She could no longer put Ray off by saying "What about your wife?"

Still, she held him off, hoping that his renewed ardor would eventually give way to acceptance of her determination to remain celibate. He insisted that she was just being stubborn—that he knew she wanted him as badly as he did her, she was just afraid. The argument was ridiculous but it didn't matter. It was her decision.

Everything was fine until one day when young William decided it was time Gram started letting him walk the half dozen blocks to the Dairy Queen up by the Capitol Bar and Grill for an ice cream cone. He and Ray had just finished a grueling session of catch football and Ruby was about to fix them an ice tea like she always did.

"Please, Gram … kin I go to the Dairy Queen?." William persisted. "Other kids do it all the time."

Ruby waited, expecting Ray to jump in and support her position. Instead, he took the boy's side.

"He be fine, Ruby. It's only about six blocks."

"I know how far it is," she insisted.

"What's the harm?" Ray countered, eager for some time alone with Ruby. "You know you can't keep the boy under your wings forever."

"Please—" William chimed in.

"Oh, all right," Ruby finally gave in. "But you hurry right back."

"I'll even buy," Ray chimed in, handing the boy a five-dollar bill.

"You still want that ice tea?" Ruby asked after William had scampered out the front door. She had been half-expecting Ray to go with the boy.

"Why wouldn't I" Ray grinned.

He must have been kidding, because the minute they got through the door to the kitchen he pushed Ruby up against the wall, jammed one of his thighs between hers and tried to kiss her.

"Ray, please—" she put up her arms and tried to fend him off.

"Damn it, Ruby!" he snapped, not bothering to hide his anger. "My wife divorce me on accounta you … you think that would count for something. What the hell am I suppose to do, pretend I don't want you—act like nothin' happened!"

It was Ruby's turn to be angry. "I didn't ask you to divorce your damned wife," she snapped. "And I ain't been askin' you to spend time with William and me … that's your own idea."

"What's the big deal?" Ray persisted. "It's not like I'm askin' for so damned much. All I wanted was one little kiss. Don't seem like that's a lot to ask after all I've done for you and the boy."

Ruby had to admit that he did have a point. "If I let you kiss me … will you just drop it and leave me alone?"

Ray sucked on that a minute. "Have I ever disrespected you?" he asked finally.

"Not until now."

"Well, okay then."

The conversation wasn't really making any sense, but the issue seemed to have been settled for the moment. Somehow, an agreement seemed to have been reached. Ruby would allow one kiss with no resistance offered and Ray would then go off and peddle his danged fool papers.

Or so it seemed.

Ruby stood ramrod stiff—except for her lips. There was nothing she could do about their soft warmth or the fact that Ray was determined to linger over them for as long as she would let him. She had to give him credit. There was nothing touching during the long kiss except their hands and their lips.

"Okay," she declared, pulling away abruptly. "You've had your kiss."

He stared at her in dumb amazement. "You gotta be kidding!"

"No … I'm not. You said you wanted one kiss and you would go away after that. Well … I gave you one kiss. Now go away!"

"I'll be damned if I will!" he declared, pinning her against the wall with an arm on either side.

"Ray, please—" she tried to duck under his arms. "You promised!"

"I didn't promise a damned thing," he insisted. He forced one arm around her waist and jammed his right thigh between hers again, while holding her chin with the other hand and forcibly kissing her on the lips.

The soft warmth was gone. She locked her teeth firmly together and pulled her lips into taut steel ribbons against his lips. Giving a mighty heave, she shoved him back and made a break for the parlor.

She had no idea where she thought she was running to—but it didn't matter. She barely got halfway across the parlor before he tackled her and they went crashing to the floor. From then on, it was a fight to the finish. Every time he grabbed one of her breasts she grabbed the offending hand and tried to bite it. When he tried to force her legs apart she tried to slam him in the balls. On the floor like that, he definitely had the advantage. He was bigger and heavier.

She tried to get to her feet, but he kept pulling her

back. The odd thing, in the midst of all this kicking and screaming, scuffling and rolling around on the floor, her ears started burning something fierce—and then it happened.

Suddenly she wanted him like she'd never wanted a man in her life.

"Not here, damn it!" she growled. "What if William comes home?"

When the love making, if you could call it that, was over she put on her robe and waited for him to dress. "You ever come darken my door again," she said simply. "I'm gonna shoot your ass dead."

Ray would've been a fool not to believe her. Besides, his quest had been fulfilled.

The very next day she called a man she knew from church who had a real estate business and put her house up for sale. It was a very confused Sadie who agreed to come over and take a picture of Ruby and William standing beside the real estate sign. She did not know whether to be sad that Ruby wanted to move or glad that she'd hired such a hunk of a real estate agent.

"Why you call your business Courtland Realty, Mr.Mintendorf?" Sadie asked, sashaying her ass around for him as they went up the walk for that ice tea Ruby had promised.

"Oh, that's simple," Mr. Mintendorf beamed, wondering if he should maybe take up the banjo. "I do most of my business here in Capitol Heights … and this is just a stone's throw from where they make the laws, so I think that's a perfect name, don't you agree?"

Sadie did indeed.

So much so that Mr. Mintendorf found very little time

to work on selling Ruby's house and in the end wound up marrying Sadie. He ultimately had to let the real estate business go in favor of getting a real job to support Sadie in the life style she wanted to become accustomed to.

...

"Anyway," Ruby concluded, bringing us back to the present. "That's why Mr. Mintendorf's real estate business was named Courtland Realty."

I think both Lynn and I were feeling a little guilty about badgering this dignified woman into airing her dirty laundry, so to speak—even though Ruby seemed relieved to finally be talking about it.

"I don't know how much you folks know about them days," she continued, " but back then we had young people training to fly all over the south, even foreigners—we had boys from England, boys from France. We had the Tuskegee Airman in the Montgomery area, women folk out in Sweetwater, Texas, white men up at the Courtland Army Airbase. Anyway, that's what started the whole thing, a series of unfortunate circumstances. Some of the women from Sweetwater were supposed to fly cross-country to Courtland at the same time as my Charles. He just happened to be in the wrong place when this Evelyn—"

Ruby paused for a moment, letting Lynn and I fill in the word "bitch" for her.

The little surge of anger subsided and Ruby's face took on a soft, wistful look. "Charles was always a very big hearted guy," she said sadly. "I sure can see that when this Evelyn woman broke down about her friend, he'd feel it was his obligation to comfort her. That's the kind of boy he was. I can even see how they could get a bit carried away—but you'd think a body wouldn't want to have no sex at a time like that—"

Neither Lynn nor I knew what else to do but nod.

"Course, I never would have known a thing about it if Charles hadn't got killed. That Ray I told you about seemed to think Charles's accident was no accident ... but back in them days we was killing so many young folk in training accidents no one bothered to do anything about it. Be near impossible to prove anyway, and it wouldn't bring him back none. They said Charles's flight leader probably would have crashed too, except he had more experience and was able to right his plane. I guess I was disappointed that he never came to the funeral or to talk to me. Kind of made me think Ray might have been right."

She stopped again and for a long time seemed lost in her thoughts.

And I was feeling more than a little confused. "I'm not exactly sure I understand what all this has to do with William," I said finally. "Are you saying that you think your grandson might be taking his anger about loosing his father and grandfather out on white girls because it seems like white girls caused the problems in the first place—"

"Oh, Lord no!" Ruby seemed shocked.

Lynn and I gave each other probing, puzzled looks.

"I can see where you might think that," Ruby continued. "We could never say one way or the other whether my Charles was killed for consorting with a white woman or if it was an accident. And we'll never know if they hung my baby just because he was black, or whether they done it because he got a white girl pregnant, or just because they felt like doing it. They claimed to have investigated the case, but no suspects were ever found.

She stopped again, reliving the painful memories.

I wasn't sure what we were supposed to say to a woman who has to live with that kind of grief—that they hung her son just because he was black?

I could see Lynn was struggling with the situation as well. "Jeez!" she muttered, tears suddenly sliding down her cheeks.

I was having trouble holding tears back myself, but I thought I was beginning to understand what she was getting at.

"You might have noticed," Ruby went on, as if reading my mind, "the car in the picture has Mississippi plates and they're from 1961. It was my Charlie's car and he had it down at Biloxi. We finally got it back some time after Monique left and I just let it sit all those years. William put new tires on it years later and drove it to college—"

"So what you're saying," Lynn said, about three steps ahead of me. "Is that despite what happened … you never talked about blaming anyone, black or white, and you just went on with your lives?"

Ruby nodded. "Something like that—"

"But at some point you obviously had some concerns about your grandson," I offered. "That his life wasn't going the way you thought it should?"

Ruby sighed heavily. "Seems like that boy never gets ahead … he don't seem to stay in any one place for more than a couple of years. Makes a body wonder if he's got a drinking problem. I know he smokes them cigarettes, but didn't seem like he cared much for drinking. Just every couple of years, 'Zuppp!' he up and moves."

I still wasn't convinced. I hated to think that my own grandmother would be that quick to accuse me of a series of foul deeds on such flimsy evidence.

"Lots of people move around a lot," I suggested. "You must have more of a reason than that to suspect your grandson might be up to no good."

Ruby leaned back in her rocker and stared at the ceiling as if it was a movie screen clicking off scenes from the past frame by frame. "There was a girl," she said reluctantly. "Went missing years ago, before William left home. After desegregation I transferred to Lee High School to teach because it's closer and that's where William would go. I just stayed on there after William graduated and started college. Anyway one of my students, a freshman I think she was, come to see me all the time for help … though didn't seem like she needed that much help—"

"What do you mean?" I prompted when Ruby seemed to space out. She had that far away look people get when they're running out of gas.

Ruby shook her head and kind of chuckled. "Seemed like she was more interested in William than me—but she was too young for him. He was twenty and in college, she was just twelve or thirteen. Anyway, she turned up missing shortly after William dropped out of school and moved to Atlanta to get a job. I can tell you I didn't much like him quitting school … but what could I do? I didn't think much about it because William was already gone when the girl come up missing."

"Was the girl white?" Lynn asked.

"Lord, no!" Ruby exclaimed. "But she was very light-skinned. Gorgeous thing!"

"You know what?" I said suddenly feeling uncomfortably guilty. "We might be rushing to judgement here ... we need to sit down and work out a plan—"

The comment sounded stupid because we were already sitting down. What I was really trying to say was that I wasn't very comfortable telling some poor old lady that her only grandson was some damned evil monster who preyed on innocent young girls.

"I could use some coffee," Lynn offered, apparently reading my mind.

"Right," I agreed. "How about we take Mrs. McPherson up the street for a cup of coffee and see if we can't get our heads screwed on a little straighter."

"I could make iced tea," Ruby suggested.

"That would not be right," I insisted. "I mean, for us to barge in like this—"

Chapter 20

The Capitol Grill was in a strip mall just six or seven blocks from Ruby's house. I had remembered seeing it on the drive over from the Days Inn when we were looking for E. Washington Street. For some reason it reminded me of that restaurant on TV called "Mel's Diner" or whatever it was—all I could remember for sure was that it involved an owner named Mel and a waitress named Alice, or was it Vera. In this case, the owner's name was apparently Dimitri.

"Hello, Dimitri," Ruby said politely to the middle-aged man sitting on what looked like an old bus seat in the glass-enclosed entry. "How are you today?"

Dimitri smiled broadly. He was wearing blue jeans and a short-sleeved blue and white shirt that looked plaid but was actually a cross-hash of blue and white lines. The softness of the shirt seemed to match the gray-white of his hair, which was combed straight back from his forehead without a part. He had obviously known Ruby for some time and was glad to see her. "I'm fine Ruby," he beamed. "How you doin'?"

"I'm just fine Dimitri," Ruby paused. "Say, I'd like to have you meet my—ah, friends Lynn and Russell."

I didn't blame Ruby for hesitating on the *"friends"* part, but Dimitri didn't seem to notice. He was on his feet with a quickness you wouldn't have expected from his slightly stout frame. "Nice to meet you," he said, offering first Lynn and then me a warm, friendly handshake. "What brings you folks out today?"

"Just coffee," Ruby said, moving to the inner door but waiting for me to open it for her. "Just coffee."

I couldn't help wondering if that was Ruby's way of saying, "I know you're curious, Dimitri … but we're not ready to talk about it just yet."

The restaurant was divided down the middle with a pale blue half-wall with a foot high white lattice on top. It was like two separate but almost identical rooms with soft blue leather booths and black/brown tables down one side and tables and chairs on the other side. The back wall could have been off-white kitchen cabinets out of someone's house. There were numerous hanging pots of philodendrons and what I think my mother called "spider plants" strategically placed on the booth side of the rooms. There was a huge tan leather corner seat with at least three separate tables directly opposite the cash resister in the front of the room. What was left of the walls was a pale green with quite a number of pictures with a Greek theme, like the Acropolis, hanging on them. The floor was covered with random odd-shaped pieces of tan and red clay tile randomly mixed in a black matrix that made it look like a jigsaw puzzle.

"I take it Dimitri is Greek," I said, noting a black and white framed menu item on the wall explaining what was served with a Greek omelet.

"Oh, my yes," Ruby laughed. "And rightfully proud of it. His entire family attends the Annunciation Greek Orthodox Church we passed on the way here."

"Really … have you know him long?" I asked.

"Oh, my yes … almost forever. Or at least since I transferred to the Robert E. Lee High School, which is just a few blocks away. A lot of the teachers from school come here and Dimitri is always very nice to us regardless of skin cooler."

"I think we drove by that school on the way over here," Lynn said. "That's where you taught?"

"It's where I was teaching when I retired. Before that I taught in a black segregated school and Lee was for whites only."

"Seemed to me the students were mostly black," I said, remembering the throng on the street on the drive over.

"Yes," Ruby nodded. "I guess that's true … but that's mostly due to economic factors and not segregation. As a race we still haven't caught up with the whites when it comes to money.

"You mean white men," Lynn said, grinning at me. "A lot of white woman haven't gotten out of the starting gate yet either."

I hadn't given that much thought and was about to ask her what she meant when a blonde waitress in black jeans, green smock and white tennis shoes showed up. "What would you like Mrs. McPherson?" I asked, taking charge.

She gave me a proper smile. "Some tea would be nice."

"Okay … how about some pie or a cookie to go with it?"

Ruby beamed. "Lord, no … I don't eat much between meals."

"Well, one cookie wouldn't hurt—"

"I'd take a cookie, if you wouldn't mind," Lynn said, sneaking a sly grin at me and I suddenly realized she was hinting that it was lunchtime and maybe instead of cookies we should be talking about soup and sandwiches. She was right. We took another look at the menu and ordered a proper meal for everyone.

"You two aren't married, are you?" Ruby said after the waitress departed with our order. It was more of a statement than a question.

"How'd you know?" I grinned, glancing at Lynn.

"Too much affection ... folks that been married awhile take each other too much for granted."

Seemed like a fair statement to me, but it also seemed like we were making a lot of small talk, avoiding issues. "If you don't mind my saying, Mrs. McPherson ... you're being awful nice to a couple of people who are accusing your grandson of all kinds of nasty, vile things."

Ruby shrugged. "Being nasty to you wouldn't change the truth none."

"I guess you got a point there," I said, wondering if Lynn was as impressed with this lady as I was. I did have to wonder what it had been like for William though, being raised by his straight-laced grandmother. "I hope you understand," I continued, "we're not exactly out to crucify your grandson. If he's only guilty of molesting young girls, and not something much worse ... then he needs some help. If he's guilty of rape or worse then we need to get him off the street as quickly as possible. But what I'm trying to say, is that even if the worst is true, he still needs our help. I've been around enough to know that some times things happen that are beyond our control. It can happen to the best of us—"

"What Rusty's trying to say," Lynn said, coming to my rescue. "Is that we want to work with you to get your grandson the help he needs … and we're sorry for the pain we know that's going to cause you."

Before Ruby could answer Dimitri came by the table to make sure we were being taken care of properly by his staff. Or maybe he was just curious about what Ruby was doing with a couple of white people.

"Oh, yes Dimitri," Ruby told him, "We're just fine … we even decided to stay for one of your fabulous lunches.

He nodded his approval and disappeared for a moment only to return with what looked like the framed cover of *Martha Stewart Living* with a Thanksgiving layout. It was obvious he was very proud of the success the Capitol Grill had achieved and rightfully so. The food proved to be excellent.

Afterwards, we thanked Dimitri for his hospitality and went back to Ruby's house to see what additional information we could get about William. Ruby still had all of the letters William had written her and was generous enough to let us read them. I'm not sure what I thought that would accomplish other than give us a better understanding of what made William tick. Normal boys don't just grow up ready to rape and maybe kill. Besides, it might also give us some clue as to where he might go next.

"Didn't William ever come back for visits?" Lynn asked at one point.

"Not too much," Ruby conceded. "Seemed like when he moved to a different city I'd get a letter saying he'd moved, but he wouldn't come to see me for a long time

... then he'd start coming every few months, depending on the distance—then he'd move again."

"What about school?" I asked later. "You mentioned that he was in college and having trouble—"

"Wasn't no big surprise," Ruby snorted. "I taught school long enough to know it's not how smart a kid is that gets 'em in trouble ... it's whatever demons they got driving them. William had a lot of trouble understanding why he didn't have a mother to raise him instead of his grandmother. And I can't say I blame him for that."

"You never told us what happened to his mother after she left," Lynn and I said almost in unison.

"Didn't I?" Ruby looked puzzled, like she was struggling with her memory. "Then I probably didn't tell you that Dimitri's used to be the Capitol Grill Bar and Grill either. Dimitri's cousin owned it back when Monique worked there. I guess he got tired of the drunks and converted it into a restaurant. Anyway, Dimitri's family tried to help me find out what happened to Monique. I even went down to Biloxi a few times before William started to school, but I could never find out what happened to her. In the end her mother threatened to call the police if I didn't stop bothering her."

Lynn got up and moved quickly around the kitchen table to put her hand on Ruby's shoulder. It was the kind of thing that the sisterhood of women did when one of their sisters was in pain—it didn't matter what the age difference was, or if they were of different races, or different religions, or any of that.

"So William doesn't even remember his mother?" I asked stupidly.

"He doesn't even know she was white," Ruby said solemnly, blowing both Lynn and I away.

"You're kidding," we chimed in unison.

"Why tell him," Ruby said defensively. "I never had a picture of her or any way of getting one. And her mother made it pretty obvious she didn't want to have any thing to do with no black babies. So, it just seemed better to let things be."

"So what did you tell him about his mother?" I asked, thinking about Maria's Kalina. "I can't imagine any child not wanting to learn as much as he could about his birth mother."

Ruby nodded her head sadly. "You're right about that ... but what could I tell him? Certainly not the truth, that she probably went away with some man and wound up living on the streets, prostituting herself or worse. Later on, when William was older, I just decided to tell him the truth—"

"That you had no idea where she was?" Lynn finished the sentence for her.

"More like she'd gone to look for work and never came back."

Obviously Ruby was not one to kid her self about the realities of life. Back in those days a lot of black families wound up with the father going off some place to try and get a new start in life, or to just avoid their responsibilities. Black woman just picked up the gauntlet and carried on. Only in Ruby and William's case, it was a hapless teenage mother that ran off.

"Didn't William ever question that?" I asked.

"Yes, of course. He even tried to track her down himself. But since he was given his father's last name and

Charles and Monique were never married, he didn't get very far. I don't even remember now what her last name was."

I had an objection but Ruby continued before I could voice it, almost as if she was reading my mind. "I don't know," she said remorsefully. "Maybe that wasn't very fair of me. Maybe I was too hard on Monique, expecting her to do for William like I did my Charles—maybe I was even blaming her somehow for what happened to my Charlie—"

"You can't blame yourself for that," I told her. "That was just part of the times."

"Oh, I know," Ruby laughed wistfully. "Sure is a shame though, ain't it … the way we go around killing each other in the name of skin color and religion."

"You got that right," Lynn and I seconded the notion.

Basically, what we were trying to do was work our way through William's letters to establish where he'd lived and worked in the nearly twenty-five years since he'd left home. That would give us some idea of what kind of man he was, and secondly, it might establish links to any unsolved crimes that might have occurred where he'd lived.

There was still one thing that was bothering me. "You said William had trouble in college … did he have trouble in high school as well?"

Ruby sat a long time before answering. "Not at first, as I recall," she said finally. "Seems like it all started over some sports thing. He wanted to play basketball, but he was never very big … took after my father in that way. Anyway, the way William told it, the coach told him he wasn't big enough to be on the team and some of them other boys started picking on him about it. They demanded to know when his birthday was. They just kept badgering until he gave in and told them."

Lynn and I exchanged puzzled looks. "What's wrong with that?" we asked simultaneously.

Ruby smiled knowingly. "What's the worst possible day a child can be born on?"

"Maybe Christmas—" I suggested. "I've heard kids say they hate it because they only get presents for one and not the other—it's either a Christmas present or a birthday present, but not both."

Ruby shook her head with a wry smile.

"We give up," Lynn conceded.

"April 1st," Ruby exclaimed triumphantly.

Some New Twists

Chapter 21

"Is your head spinning as bad as mine?" I asked Lynn when we finally got back in the car after spending so much time with Ruby.

Lynn shook her head and shuddered. "Worse probably."

"Man … I can hardly believe it. This morning seems like about a million years ago. And you know what … I have no idea what's supposed to come next."

"I think we need to talk about that," Lynn agreed.

We had checked out of our motel before going to Ruby's and it was still nearly 300 miles to Lake City. Starting out to on a drive like that after 5:00 O'clock in the afternoon didn't make any sense. Ruby had offered us a room for the night, but— "I think we've imposed enough for one day." Lynn was quick to suggest. I had to agree.

"What if we drive for a couple hours and then get a place to stay?" I suggested.

"As long as you feed me some place along the way." She agreed.

"Jeez!" I exclaimed, easing the car into the rush hour traffic. "Why didn't you say something? We probably should have offered to take Ruby out for supper. I never even thought about it. Do you think we should go back?"

"No way ... she's probably ready to kill us as it is."

I nodded in agreement. "You're right. Can't say that I blame her much for that. To tell the truth though ... I almost dropped my teeth when she asked why we didn't just go to the police and tell them what we know about William. Thanks for coming to my rescue."

...

The couple of hours turned out to be a real grind. The traffic was pretty heavy and we only got as far as Troy, Alabama. When I spotted another Days Inn I turned in without even asking Lynn if that would be okay. She didn't object. Nor did she get out of the car. I went in and registered, then asked the clerk for an eating recommendation.

"The clerk recommends a place called "*The Pines*," I told her, climbing back in the car. "He said it's the only sit down place close by ... even told me how to get there."

...

"How old do you think Ruby is?" I asked later that night, after lying awake for what seemed like hours.

We really should have been talking about what was going to come next in our relationship. We were actually a day late in getting back to Lake City. Lynn was really supposed to be at work tonight instead of lying awake in a motel room some place in Alabama. She'd called her boss and had been informed that one extra day would be okay, but she better not take any more than that—not if she wanted to keep her job.

"About eighty-five, I would guess," Lynn replied. "What difference does it make?"

"None, I was just thinking—"

"About what?"

"Oh, you know … how much our lives have changed over the years."

"What do you mean?"

I propped myself up on one elbow. We always slept with the shades wide open, even in public places like motels, because we liked to wake up early with the sun streaming in the windows. Besides, in situations like this, Lynn was very beautiful in the moonlight. She had a child-like innocence with her hair splayed out on the pillow like a movie star.

"It's probably a little different for you than it was for me," I told her. "But when I was a kid on the farm we didn't even have electricity until I was in the fifth or sixth grade. We never had in-door plumbing. I never lived in a house with indoor plumbing until I went into the service."

"You're kidding!"

"Afraid not. Never lived in a house with a furnace until then either. For all practical purposes, my early childhood was no different than my father's … no different than it was in the pioneer days."

Lynn's eyes sparkled in the moonlight. "That must mean you had horses, right?"

"Yeah, we had a team. We had a couple of different tractors too … but we did quite a few different things with the team as well. You know … like hauling hay and wood. And we used them for picking corn."

"You mean you picked corn by hand."

I laughed. "Didn't everyone?"

"Did you have to fight Indians too?"

"Of course … didn't everyone? We had to walk to school—a country school, and it was up-hill both ways—"

"Now I know you're kidding," Lynn giggled, playfully punching me on the arm.

"Maybe a little," I assured her. "But you see what I'm getting at … how life was so much different for people of my generation. Actually, Ruby is from my father's generation … except she's black. Life had to be dramatically different for people like her back then."

"I'm not sure I know what you mean."

"I'm probably not explaining it very well. I probably never told you, but I was stationed at Keesler Air Force Base in Mississippi when I first went into the service. I took electronic training their to be a flight facilities equipment repairman. But this is the scary part. I got sent there in September of 1961 and before I left the next June there was some talk about a black man being hung in Biloxi—now I'm wondering if that could have been Ruby's son Charles."

"Wow!" Lynn muttered.

She was silent for a moment mulling what I'd said over.

"So just how old are you?" Lynn demanded finally. Age was not something that we had talked about much. I knew she was forty-two and that she had two daughters away at college. Somehow I'd never bothered to mention that I was nearly twenty years older than she was.

"Old enough to be your father," I laughed.

"I always did like mature men," she murmured, pulling me down to kiss my nose.

"You're not getting off that easily," I teased, flopping back to shove my elbow-prop under her pillow and scoop her into my arms.

...

Lynn had nearly a dozen messages on her answering machine from her daughters when we got back to Lake City the next morning. Her daughter Julie was a drama student at the University of Florida in Gainesville. Andrea was a business major at Florida State University in Tallahassee. Julie's messages seemed the most frantic.

"Mother," the last message was almost pleading, "where are you? You need to call me right away. I've talked to Daddy and Andrea and I even called your job. Nobody knows where you are! I don't want to have to call the police!"

"I take it you didn't tell them about me yet?" I asked, knowing full well she hadn't and feeling more than a little guilty.

"What was I going to tell them?" she snapped. "That I was running off with some crazy old man that I picked up at work who goes around shooting arrows at his wife?"

I smiled sheepishly. "I see your point."

"I'm sorry," Lynn said quickly. "I didn't mean to snap at you ... it's just that—" Tears welled up in her eyes as she took my hands in hers. "You know it's a lot different when you have daughters. With daughters you have to set an example. A man with boys can just brag about his conquests."

"That's not exactly true," I assured her. "But I do understand what you're saying. Boys are a lot easier in that way. You just tell them how to behave and hope to God they don't go bonkers crazy the first time they get that close to a girl."

"You mean hormone crazy?"

"Right!"

"Girl's have hormones too, you know. The right guy comes along and—"

I laughed. "Just be glad girls don't have the same hormone drive as boys. You'd have spent guys draped all over the place and half the population would be pregnant."

"Oh, you think so, do you mister?" she exclaimed, sliding her hands up under my armpits and trying to tickle me.

I was glad to see a smile on her face again. "Seriously," I continued. "I've been avoiding talking about it because I wasn't sure what my priorities were … or what my capabilities actually were—"

"Do you always talk in circles?"

"Doesn't everyone? No, seriously … I know you need to give your daughters some sort of explanation about where you've been. And I don't think you particularly want to lie to them. I suggest you tell them the truth— that you've met a man and you wanted to explore where the relationship would lead. If it'll help, I'd love to meet your daughters—"

"You're not some kind of sex pervert, are you?" she said, giving me the damnedest hug I'd ever gotten from a woman in his life. It was a wonder she didn't crack one or two of my ribs.

"Most definitely not," I chuckled. "You'd be in big trouble if I was."

"And who says I'm not in trouble—"

"Tell you what," I could hardly believe the words tumbling out of my mouth. "I can't really afford to go running back and forth across the country every week, so I've decided to drop the tax class. It's not a mandatory thing anyway. It's not a part of the franchise agreement that I provide corporate tax expertise. It's just something you do to improve your bottom line. Besides, I can always take the class again next year if I'm still in the tax business."

"Meaning what?"

"Meaning that I want to spend more time down here … I can get someone to handle my one day a week commitment to having the office open … maybe go home once a month or so—"

"Are you sure?"

I nodded. "Getting William McPherson off the street seems like a far more important thing at this point, don't you think?"

Lynn nodded.

"If you want me to," I offered. "I'll even get my own apartment so your daughters don't have to worry about their mom living with some sleaze-bag old guy."

"Not on your tintype, buddy!" Lynn exclaimed, giving me another one of her super power-hugs.

I could hardly believe the turn around in my life. A few weeks ago I'd impulsively driven to Florida to see if my soon-to-be ex-wife had gone off surreptitiously and started a new tax business without me. Now I was going to be living with a different woman in a different part of Florida and my life was completely up in the air.

I offered to do our four days of travel laundry while Lynn took a nap so she wouldn't be dead on her feet at work. Of course, the first thing on our agenda was for her to call Julie and Andrea to let them know she was okay. She told both girls that she had just decided she needed to take a vacation and she hadn't wanted to bother them about it. To reassure them, she invited them both to dinner on Sunday—for a surprise.

Having lived in an apartment for quite a few years, I was completely at home doing the laundry. While the first load was washing, I set up my laptop on Lynn's kitchen table and went on the Internet to research the various cities William McPherson had lived in since leaving Ruby's home. I had a feeling we might be able to link some of the various places William had lived with missing girls and unsolved rape cases from those cities. I also wanted to learn as much as I could about William's last known address, just in case he was still there. You never know.

Lynn's shift was from 4:00 p. m. to midnight., which didn't exactly thrill me. The American Legion post where she worked was on one of the darkest, scariest streets I'd ever been on in my life, and that was saying quite a bit. Besides, I really didn't like her being out alone that late at night, for obvious reasons. She tried to tell me I was being silly when I offered to drive her to work.

"Not really," I insisted with a grin. "Just look at what happened that night you picked me up."

How could she argue that?

...

When I got back from dropping Lynn off at work I went back on the Internet to kill some of the time. Working from the notes we'd taken on that afternoon with Ruby I attempted to put William's life in some kind of sensible order. The list of cities where he'd lived and worked almost seemed to be alphabetical at first. He started out in Atlanta and then moved on to Athens, Georgia, and then Augusta, Georgia. There also seemed to be an odd correlation between the length of time he stayed in any one city and the size of that city. The bigger the city, the longer he stayed. Most of the cities had a population of 50,000 or more.

There did not seem to be any rhyme or reason to the type of jobs that he had taken and in some cases he never even mentioned the type of work he was doing. All of the jobs were low paying positions that probably didn't require much of a resume to get ... pumping gas, fast food, warehouse work, things like that. Seemed pretty obvious that William was intent on going nowhere fast. Ruby deserved better than that.

All in all, the list included some thirteen cities that stretched over a period of nearly twenty-five years. We had been assuming that William's gypsy-like life style had some sort of connection to sex crimes in the various cities. Now, I was finding it hard to believe that a rapist/child molester and possible murderer could have committed that many crimes over that long a period without getting caught. But why else would William keep trying to start a new life if some one or some thing hadn't pushed him over the edge? I was totally convinced there had to be a connection. Nothing else made any sense.

It wasn't until I started searching for *unsolved missing children cases* by state that I realized what a monumental task I had undertaken. Just on the one web site alone over the past twenty years there were as few as nine in Mississippi, to as many as 137 in Florida. The missing children ranged in age from just a couple of years, to more than thirty-some years of age now. In order to establish the age at the time the child went missing, I would have to subtract the *missing date* from the *age now date*. There were blacks, whites, Hispanics, and a few other races that I wasn't even sure of based on the name. There were also quite a few boys.

In no time at all, my head was spinning and I decided to go early to pick up Lynn. I could always watch TV until she got off.

Obviously, my preconceived notion that William only molested young white girls was in jeopardy of being very wrong. Another thing I was forced to admit was that his victims did not necessarily have to be from the actual city William was living in at the time. Apparently, from what Ruby had told us, he'd been driving since he was eighteen. There was no reason to assume that all his victims were from next door.

Actually, there wasn't any real proof that there was even more than one victim.

I was actually hoping that would be the case—that the girl I'd rescued would turn out to be his only victim, for Ruby's sake. The girl that had turned up missing when he left home could just be a coincidence. In the single day we'd gotten to know Ruby I had concluded she deserved a lot more out of life than having her only grandson turn out to be some kind of monster. No one deserved that. It seemed like Ruby had made some major contributions to a lot of people's lives, teaching the way she had all those years. To have my worst fears about William turn out to be true wouldn't be fair, but then who ever said life had to be fair.

Lynn was talking to a Deputy Sheriff when I walked into the Legion bar. To my surprise, she motioned me to come over and sit down.

"You're early, honey," she said quickly. "Did you come down to have a drink before we close?"

I smiled nervously. "Something like that … maybe just a beer."

"Coming right up," she smiled a little more gregariously than she might normally have. She grabbed a bottle of beer out of the cooler a few feet behind her and popped the cap on the opener attached to the cooler. "Deputy McIntyre was just telling me about that little girl that was abducted here a couple of weeks ago. They still haven't caught the guy."

"Oh," I murmured, pushing a ten-dollar bill across the counter and taking a swig of the beer. I wasn't even sure what kind it was.

Deputy McIntyre was giving me a hard once over.

"Oh, I'm sorry," Lynn said. "I didn't even introduce you guys. Honey, this is Dick McIntyre … the big bad policeman I was telling you about that took my finger prints when my ex's girlfriend's car got torched. Dick … this is my boyfriend Russell."

McIntyre's handshake reminded me of dry husks from my corn picking days. I took an instant dislike to the guy, but I tried to be nice anyway. It seemed like Lynn might have had an ulterior motive in the way she'd introduced us.

"Can I buy you a drink Deputy?" I asked.

"Naw," McIntyre shook his head, holding up a can of coke. "I'm on duty. Maybe another time … if you're around that long."

I wasn't sure how to take that. For one thing, I had no idea what Lynn might have already told him about me. Obviously, she'd mentioned that she had a new boyfriend. Had she told him that I was just down here visiting? Or did he have something else in mind?

"You're not from around here, are you?" McIntyre asked.

I shook my head, wondering if he was trying to make small talk or starting an interrogation.

"Where then?"

"Up north."

"Where?"

Where the heck was this going I wondered. "Originally, from Wisconsin … but lately Minnesota. Why do you ask?"

"Sorry," McIntyre's smile was weak and insincere. "Old police habits, I guess."

He raised the coke can and took a drink. "What is it you do, if you don't mind my asking."

I smiled. "I'm kind of in between things at the moment." I made a mental note that the ring finger on McIntyre's left hand had a conspicuous white band where a wedding ring might have been. "I used to be in the tax business."

"No kidding!" McIntyre seemed impressed.

"Tell me Dick," I said meanly. "Are you recently divorced … I notice you're not wearing a wedding ring, but you've got a white mark around that finger."

McIntyre's face turned beet-red. "Oh, no … still married. I take my ring off when I'm on duty … you know, in case it'd get caught on something chasing the bad guys."

"Any children?" I asked.

McIntyre nodded. "Right … a boy and a girl."

"How old?"

"My son's twelve and my daughter's nine."

"I bet that kind of hits home, huh? You know … working a case in which the victim is about the same age as your own kids."

"You can say that again." McIntyre looked at me with a newfound respect. "To tell the truth if I turned out to be the arresting office on this case … I might shoot first and ask questions later."

"I wouldn't blame you," I nodded. "It seems like these creeps aren't all that fussy about who they choose for victims."

"You seemed to know an awful lot about this," McIntyre started getting wary again.

"Not really," I laughed. "Lynn and I were talking about the case earlier and I had some time to kill this evening so I went on the Internet and did a little research. It's pretty scary when you look at all the kids that have gone missing out there. I'd like to claim that I'm glad mine are grown, but that doesn't work either. I still have grandchildren."

Chapter 22

"Are you completely crazy?" Lynn demanded when she got me alone in the car. "I don't believe you!"

"Why?" I laughed.

"Well, to begin with ... I already knew that jerk was married. So you didn't have to go through with that macho charade to get him to admit it. Honestly, I thought you were just trying to piss him off so you could get into a fight. Jeez!"

I had to laugh again. "I'm not a fighter. I just wanted to let him know that you're my girl and that I'm not about to put up with a lot of crap from some on-the-make cop."

"Is that right, Mister?" Lynette said, grinning at me in the dim light. "Do you really think women are fooled by guys like him? Some, maybe—but I hope you don't think I'm that gullible. Besides, he's too young for me. And besides that, wasn't it awfully risky talking to him like that about this case. It would be awfully easy to let something slip that your not supposed to know."

"Like what?"

"I don't know ... but it seems to me like you were taking an awful chance."

"Maybe—"

Because I had arrived so early to pick Lynn up, I'd had to park on the back side of the parking lot under one of the big live oak trees. The tree didn't let much light get to that area of the lot, so I let the subject drop and gathered her into my arms for a forgiving kiss.

In a way, she was right. What I had done with McIntyre was like bungee jumping for the first time on an untested bungee cord, or throwing yourself belly first on one of those plastic water slides—it was a high risk proposition with no way of knowing exactly how it would turn out.

I wasn't even officially divorced yet and here I'd already moved in with another woman. Not to mention that I didn't even have a full year under my belt running the tax business and here I was gallivanting around the country trying to track down some sexual misfit. And on top of everything else, I was probably wanted for an attempted assault on my soon-to-be ex-wife and some unfortunate suburbanite out walking his dog.

"Y'all want anything to eat?" Lynn asked when we got back to her apartment.

I had to smile. Lynn was originally from Michigan and had only moved to Florida a few years earlier because of her ex-husband's work. She had stayed because her girls like the idea of going to college here and not having to put up with snow. Her occasional use of the vernacular "Y'all" always caught me off guard and made me smile. She did it so cute.

"What did y'all have in mind?" I teased.

She smiled and shrugged.

"I suppose we could eat breakfast now," I suggested. "That way we wouldn't have to get up to do it."

I fixed some scrambled eggs, toast, and juice—no coffee. Lynette changed into a nightgown, robe, and slippers and joined me at the kitchen table just as I was serving the eggs. I was amazed at how quickly and perfectly the domestic shoe fit. I was so totally comfortable and at ease with Lynn it felt like I'd known her all my life. Every thing before must have been someone else's life.

I almost hated to bring up my discouraging evening spent on the Internet.

"It seems like we might wind up chasing our tails," I told her finally. "Trying to connect William to any of the missing children cases over the last twenty-five years in this part of the south is going to be tough. There are literally hundreds—kids of all shapes, sizes, and colors. You name any category you can think of and there's probably at least one kid for that category. Even if we only took the white girls, say nine to twelve years of age ... we're talking about a mountain of work—"

"You're not giving up?" Lynn looked disappointed.

"Oh, no, no ... I'm just suggesting that we need to take a different tack. We need to concentrate on finding him first—which isn't going to be easy. We have next to nothing to go on in that regard."

"I know," Lynn agreed.

...

The girls came on Sunday—which gave me a certain amount of *angst*. One never knew what to expect when meeting your girlfriend's children, whether they were grown or not. Not that I had a ton of experience, but there had been a few times between Maria and my first wife when a girlfriend's child had created some *touch and go* moments. Barb's daughter Jessie, for example, was going to buy a whole cart full of clothes if I was willing to pay for them. I was pretty sure it was a test by both Barb and her daughter just to see how far I was willing to go in the game of supplanting her birth father.

Actually, Maria's daughter Kalina couldn't have treated me better, but that was different. Kalina never lived with Maria so she didn't have a relationship with Maria in the traditional daughter/mother sense. Since Kalina never knew her biological father, I was no threat to her relationship with Maria. And hopefully, since Lynn was already divorced from her children's father, I wouldn't pose any threat to Lynn's daughters. Still, waiting for them to arrive was like waiting to go on stage when your speech wasn't ready yet.

Andrea arrived first. She was twenty years old with a cute round face and short, straight auburn hair that framed her face in a way that reminded me of a bicycle helmet. She was at least a head taller than her mother and several inches taller than I was, or so it seemed. With the short plaid skirt and thick-soled clogs she was wearing it was hard to look at anything but her legs, which seemed to go on forever.

I felt my face burning and I half expected Lynn to declare, "Ha! Caught you looking!" *What was the matter with women, anyway?*

"Andrea," Lynn said, after Andrea had flounced in and bounced around and then came to a stop staring at me. "I'd like you to meet my new friend, Russell."

Andrea's reaction pretty much confirmed it for me. I had long suspected that women had some sort of secret communication channel they used to communicate with each other about secret stuff.

Andrea stared at her mother for about thirty seconds.

"MAhother!" she shrieked. "Why didn't you tell me?" And with two long strides she was across the kitchen and grabbing my hands in hers as she leaned forward, bused her cheek against mine and then kissed my cheek. "So happy to meet you," she murmured seductively in my ear.

"Andrea!" Lynn exclaimed. "For goodness sake … you'll scare the poor man half to death. I mean, really!"

"Sorry, Mother," Andrea flounced. "I'm just happy to see you finally decided to ah—meet someone."

I felt the crimson fire spread across my face and down my neck—just where in that mother/daughter interface had the information, "Yeah, that's right … he's banging me," been exchanged.

"Russell's in the tax business," Lynn told her daughter, giving me a chance to get my mind back out of the gutter and have a conversation like a normal human being.

"Really?" Andrea's big blue-green eyes showed some genuine interest. "I don't know if Mother told you or not … but I'm a business major at Florida State."

"She did."

Andrea and I made small talk about college while Lynn fussed over dinner. I'd gone to school on the GI Bill passed in 1966 and was already married with three boys at home by then, so it wasn't the easiest thing for me to find common college ground to talk about. In my entire college career I had never done anything on campus other than go to class.

By the time Julie showed up, I was beginning to feel about 90 years old.

Maybe I was. Thankfully, Julie saved the day.

"Mother," she said, barely in the front door. "This is

Jamal." She made a quick backhanded sweeping gesture toward the tall, light-skinned black man following her with a bottle of wine clutched in his right hand and a bag of groceries in his left arm. "He's—" She hesitated, catching sight of Andrea and me sitting at the dining room table. "He's going to be staying for dinner," she continued without taking her eyes off me. "I hope you don't mind my bringing him unannounced."

"Of course not," Lynn beamed. "Welcome Jamal … here let me take those."

She relieved the young man of his burden and graciously escorted the pair through the kitchen into the dining room to finish the introductions.

"Jamal's a cheerleader," Julie offered, as if that explained everything.

There was another quick mother/daughter exchange that said, "Yeah, that's right, Mother, he's black and he's banging me … what are you gonna do about it?" without a single word being said. Then Julie turned to her sister with a confused look on her face.

"Don't look at me," Andrea giggled, reading her sister's mind.

"Really?" Julie exclaimed, turning to her mother with a still puzzled look. "Is this true?"

Lynn actually blushed. "Yes," she said, confirming the silent communication. "If you can have a new friend, I guess I can too."

In no time at all Lynn announced everything was ready and that we could sit down to eat. Julie and Jamal made a handsome couple. Julie was tiny compared to Andrea. Barely five foot two, she had longer, darker hair that was nicely curled on the ends. She had the same blue-green eyes as her sister, although less prominent, and her lips were softer, fuller—more like her mother's. Andrea had a few freckles. Julie did not.

Actually, Jamal made the situation much more comfortable for me than it might have been otherwise. I was a little too old-fashioned to sit around with a bunch of women and have two of them thinking, "Who the hell are you—sleeping with my mother?" Jamal kind of shared the load, as it were. I even caught him sneaking a glance at those fabulous legs of Andrea's.

"You're not really majoring in cheerleading?" I said, coming to Jamal's rescue.

Jamal gave me a friendly smile. "No, Sir … I'm an art major. I just do the cheerleading because I wasn't good enough to make the varsity football team."

I nodded. "Football's pretty big down here I suppose."

"Yes, Sir."

I had about all I could take. "If you don't stop calling me 'Sir' Jamal," I told him with a grin, " I'm gonna have to pop you one."

He looked confused for a moment and then realized I was teasing. "Sorry," he muttered, "that's just the way my folks raised me—"

"Jamal's parents are both doctors," Julie added quickly.

"That's okay," I told him, ignoring Julie's so-called claim to fame. "Being called 'Sir' makes me feel either like I'm a customer and you're trying to sell me some danged fool thing, or that I'm getting really old. Either way, it makes me uncomfortable."

Jamal nodded. "I think some people think I do it

because it's a racial thing … but it's not. My parents just taught me to treat my elders with respect."

"Mine too," I admitted.

"So are you a racist?" Julie suddenly interjected, almost glaring at me.

"I hope not, " I laughed, noting that Lynn was watching me in a kind of bemused way. I wasn't sure exactly how far I should go in explaining my philosophies to her. "To tell the truth," I said, deciding to throw caution out the window. "My first wife was from Germany and my second from Puerto Rico … and I've seen racism in varying degrees on both sides of the pond, and I don't think I fit in either category."

"What do you mean?" Julie seemed completely baffled.

"Well," I hesitated, wondering what I'd gotten myself into. "In Germany, back during the war … we had all this Arian crap about the superior race, the attempted annihilation of the Jews. After the war there were thousands of black GI's who had babies with German women and that didn't seem to be that much of a problem."

"I'm not sure what you're getting at," Julie shrugged.

"In Puerto Rico," I went on, "the culture has been integrated for centuries. It is a completely homogeneous mixture of blacks, whites, Hispanics and native Indians and they claim no racial prejudice. But my wife's mother treats her black maid as if she's definitely inferior—"

"I still don't get it," Julie admitted.

"It's simple," I explained triumphantly. "In both cases, the prejudice is not racial—it's economic."

"I think you're right," Jamal agreed. "You should see my parents with some of their white doctor friends and then see how they are with some of our neighbors, most of which are black."

I was about to nod in agreement when Andrea spoke up. "I don't mean to nit-pick. But you said 'wife' Russell, not 'ex-wife' … is there something we should know?"

"Oops!" I exclaimed, wondering whether Lynn would prefer me to lie or what. "You caught me … my divorce is not final yet."

"But soon will be?" Andrea said with a questioning look.

"Right," I nodded.

"And Mom knows all about this?" Julie put her two cents worth in. "We know why Mom's divorced … does she know why you're getting divorced?"

"Girls!" Lynette exclaimed. "Knock it off! You're being rude."

"No, no, " I insisted. "I think they have a right to know … they're just looking out for their mother— which is only right."

"Yes, I know but—"

I launched into the my long, all-but-unbelievable story of how Maria had left me because her sister had divorced her husband and moved to Jacksonville, Florida and bought a house with a swimming pool because she always wanted a house with a swimming pool. Not because she was this fabulous swimmer, but because that's what she wanted, and that she had talked both her mother and her sister into leaving their husbands and moving in with her because that's what she wanted.

"You're kidding?" both girls exclaimed, almost in unison.

"Not really," I added. "It has something to do

with her ex-husband's death and the fact that divorced Catholics aren't welcome at mass. To tell the truth, it's a little confusing … but that's what happened. I didn't want to stay married to a woman who was going to live fifteen hundred miles away … so I filed for divorce."

"So where did you meet Mom?" Julie demanded.

I looked at Lynn and grinned. "She picked me up in a bar," I teased.

"Seriously?"

"I met him at work if you must know." Lynn said, giving me one of those "You're paying for this later and it will be more fun for me than it will you," looks. "Honestly, you girls are worse than the Gestapo."

"Actually," I was still trying to be the *good guy*. "Your Mother's right, I was on my way home from Jacksonville—"

"From visiting your wife?" Andrea didn't miss a thing.

"Aah, not exactly," I assured her. "We had separate bank accounts. My tax business was actually hers. She signed it over to me when she left, which sounds great, except it isn't paid for. It didn't seem right to me that she should be able to take all the profit from her last tax season and move down here and start a new tax business. I can do taxes fine, but running a tax business is not something I've been dreaming of doing my whole life. I just came down here to see if she'd started a new tax business. Seemed like the thing to do before I sign the divorce paper."

"So did she?" Andrea was persistent.

"No, I don't think so."

"So did you see her then?"

I was trapped. There was, of course, no way I could tell the truth—that I had seen Maria but hadn't talked to her—that I'd shot her with an arrow—

"That's just enough, Andrea," Lynn said, coming to my rescue. "Let's change the subject." Her voice had that tone that only Mothers get when they want you to know they are no longer joking around.

"Down from where?" Julie asked, immediately jumping on the bandwagon.

"Minnesota."

"Really … I suppose Mom told you we're originally from Michigan. Jamal is from Ann Arbor."

After that our dinner conversation drifted into safer topics like the difference between living in the north or down south until finally Julie informed her mother that Jamal was hoping to watch the Detroit Lions take on the Green Bay Packers at three O'clock. Mom said, "Sure, fine—" and Jamal and I were summarily dismissed to the couch while the ladies took care of domestic cleanup. It was the first time in my life that I ever drank wine while watching a football game with one of the boys. It felt really odd.

"So what did you think?" Lynn asked, with folded arms as we watched the girls drive away after the game. She was leaning against me, but not looking at me.

I gave one last wave and wrapped my arms around her from behind. "I think you have two very lovely daughters," I told her truthfully, "but I have to admit there were a couple of times they really put me on the spot."

"No kidding," Lynn laughed, pulling away. "Did it ever occur to you that it might be your own fault.

Honestly, sometimes you act like you have to tell everybody the whole truth and nothing but the truth, so help you God."

I took her hand as we walked toward the door. I was both shaking and nodding my head. "Hmm … I'm sure you're right. But I've never been particularly good at lying. I just figured it's best to tell the truth."

"I'm sure it is in your case," she laughed. "But some times it's not always the best thing to do … particularly if it hurts someone."

Chapter 23

My next step was an elusive one. I agonized over it almost day and night. On the one hand, I should go home and take care of my business. On the other … I could not imagine going anywhere without Lynn. She was like a comfortable pair of shoes that you wore every day regardless of how scuffed and worn they were.

To gain a little breathing room, I called Sam Turner, a farmer who had been one of Maria's best employees and was supposedly my friend and asked him to open the office one day a week. Sam had had an office key for years and generally wasn't too nosey. He agreed but was very curious. Just to be on the safe side, I decided to let Sam think I was down in Florida trying to win Maria back. *Boy would he be surprised*, I thought, conceding that maybe Lynn was right. *Some times a little white lie didn't hurt—*

That night I dreamed about being charged by a big white cow. When I kicked at the cow's head to scare it away, I nearly kicked Lynn out of bed.

"Sorry," I murmured, pulling her delicious warm body against mine. "I was out chasing cows and got a little carried away."

"I hope you don't do that too often," she murmured, snuggling.

"I guess I'm getting a little up-tight about our

situation," I admitted. "I'm not used to being supported by a woman."

"I'm not exactly supporting you," she scoffed.

"Oh, I know … but you know what I mean. I don't seem to be making much progress in figuring out what became of our Willie boy after his little foray here in Lake City. We have next to nothing to go on, except a gut feeling that he probably moved on, and that's only because that seems to be what he's done in the past. We don't even know for sure that he's ever actually raped a girl. All we know about is an apparent attempted rape that I stumbled in on and some suspicions that Ruby told us about. That's not a lot to go on."

"I know—"

"If you try to extrapolate a destination from Lake City based on the moves he's made in the past you come up with zilch. The only thing that's relatively consistent is that he's never gotten more than two or three hundred miles away from Montgomery."

"That might be our best hope … we do have the holidays coming up. Maybe he'll pay his Grandmother a visit on one of the holidays."

"Do you think she'd call us if he did?"

"Would you?"

"That's kind of a toughie. Is blood really thicker than water?"

It was a rhetorical question. We both felt that Ruby would indeed *rat* on William should he make the mistake of showing up on her doorstep. She just seemed that kind of lady, having taught school all those years and having lived through the racial turmoil of growing up in the Montgomery eye-of-the-storm, as it were. By now, I had gotten enough black history off the Internet to know that even during the war years black women in Montgomery had lagged behind what most of the black women in other Alabama cities had been able to achieve.

How had Ruby jokingly put it? "The war got nigras out of the kitchen every where but in Montgomery."

What she was really trying to say was that because Montgomery was the seat of Alabama's government, white leaders at the time tried to make it clear that the Federal government was infringing on states rights by trying to force the hiring of blacks in defense jobs. At the time, it was almost unheard of for a black woman like Ruby to go to a four- year college.

Her beloved Charles had come straight off a tenant farm up Tallassee way before entering into the Tuskegee flight-training program.

Ruby's father had apparently been an exception.

"So what do you think?" I asked, suddenly realizing Lynn hadn't answered my rhetorical question. She did not answer this question either, apparently having taken advantage of the lull in conversation to fall asleep.

I should be so lucky, I thought, gently turning on my other side so I wouldn't wake her. I spent the next couple of hours trying to come up with a solution to my problems, but to no avail. My biggest problem, I finally realized some time before morning, was that I was trying to solve too many problems with a single solution. To begin with, I couldn't be in two places at once. Which meant that I either had to stop worrying about my business at home and concentrate on the business of finding William, or drop the project altogether and go home. And because of Lynn, I wasn't about to do that.

Since I wasn't sleeping anyway, I got up and went back on the Internet.

...

"I feel like I'm beating a dead horse," I told Lynn at breakfast, which was more like a late lunch since it was already after one O'clock. "I've tried address searches for William using every search engine I can think of. The last address Ruby had was Valdosta, Georgia and that's more than a year old. When I do a reverse address search on that address I get a woman's name. So either he became a woman or I have some sort of computer error—I don't know what to think. Valdosta is close enough to Lake City that he could actually be commuting from there."

"That sounds a little sadistic."

"I know. But crazy as it sounds it could be true. I certainly hope not. If it is I'll probably have to start physically searching of all the towns within a hundred-mile radius of Lake City. I have a feeling our William hasn't gone all that far, but—"

"Isn't there some other way?" Lynn asked. "That could take years."

"I know," I continued. "I had this crazy idea that maybe we could get Ruby to file a missing persons report, but then I realized we don't have enough information to make that work. It was about then that I realized we don't even have any pictures of William as a grownup. You could be standing right beside him and wouldn't know it."

"My God, I never even thought of that—"

"If we assume," I went on, "that he committed a rape or attempted rape every time he moved and the moves are getting closer together time wise … then the distances probably are too. I'm ruling out Jacksonville for now … because he hasn't backtracked so far and besides, it's too big to search. That leaves either Valdosta and the slim possibility that he might still be there or that he's no longer bothering to change his address. He could be living in Lake City, or Gainesville, or any of the smaller towns around here—"

I could see the thinking-like-a-mother wheels start turning in Lynn's head and realized I'd made the mistake of mentioning Gainesville in the same breath as William.

"Oh, hey … don't worry." I tried to reassure her. "Even if he's in Gainesville your girls are far too aggressive for someone like him. From what I've read there's a reason why guys like him pick on little girls. Besides, the odds of him picking up one of your girls on a college campus is about a zillion to one. Not while he's hanging around playgrounds."

"I know," Lynn sighed. "But I am still a mother—"

"And a darned fine one at that," I reassure her.

I was still thinking about the moment an hour later after Lynn had gone to work, when there was a knock on the door. My first thought was that Lynn was knocking as a warning in this little teasing game we played. "No bimbos in here," I said, throwing the door open wide.

It wasn't Lynn.

"Julie, er … Andrea!" I exclaimed. "I thought it was your mother."

Andrea gave me a skeptical look. "Do you always have to get the bimbos out when Mom comes home?"

I smiled sheepishly. "It's one of our little jokes."

We both just stood there, each waiting for the other

to unravel the awkward moment. "I think I lost my bracelets when I was here on Sunday," Andrea said finally. "Did you guys find them?"

I thought it odd for a daughter to be referring to her mom as *you guys*. "Er, not that I know of … your Mom didn't say anything." I stepped aside. "You'd better come in and look for them."

"Thanks."

For no reason in particular I went into the kitchen rather than through the entry and down the hall to the living room. It's just what you did with walk-through kitchens. As I followed Andrea toward the dining area I let my eyes wander over the countertops, just in case she'd left the bracelets there. Andrea was wearing a different skirt than she'd worn on Sunday, except it was even shorter, if that was possible.

"Any idea where you might have lost your bracelets?" I asked awkwardly in an attempt to get my mind off her cute little behind.

She turned toward me, shaking her head. "No … not really."

Her breasts aren't bad either, I thought, realizing I shouldn't be having such thoughts. They weren't particularly large—just what you'd call pert. And the fact that the top button on her blouse had popped open revealing a smooth, white slope of cleavage wasn't helping.

"I-I'm not sure I remember bracelets," I stammered. "What'd they look like?"

"Three gold rings … about this big and this wide." She formed a semi-circle with her thumb and forefinger about the size of an orange, then let her thumb and forefinger come almost together to create a gap about a quarter of an inch wide. "They were linked together and had little embossed flowers on them."

"I'll help you look," I offered, "Now that I know what I'm looking for."

The thing about two-bedroom apartments is that there are not a lot of places to hide something the size of the bracelets Andrea was describing. It took about five minutes to search every conceivable surface in the kitchen, hall, bathroom, and dining room. We both ended up on the couch stuffing our hands down between the cushions in case the bracelets had fallen in there.

"Did you look in your car?" I asked.

Andrea was almost prone on the couch, her head jammed up against the armrest, one arm buried behind the cushion up to her elbow, and her butt turned in such a way that good portion of her white panties were clearly visible.

"Before I came," she told me.

"Oh," I murmured, pretending not to notice that I could see halfway to China.

"You don't suppose Mom put them away in her bedroom?" Andrea suggested, sitting up and tugging at her skirt.

I was starting to get real uncomfortable. "I doubt it … but I could look if you like."

"Would you?"

Her lips had that little V-shaped peak just under her nose that made it seem like she was pouting. It was kind of an awkward moment, like in the movies when the guy and the girl are leaning toward each other about to kiss but not quite making it and you're ready to shout, "Well kiss her for God's sake! We haven't got all day."

Fortunately, I took her question to mean that she would let me do the looking in the bedroom and not the other thing I was trying hard not to think about. "Sure," I told her.

I had just finished giving the bedroom a quick once-over and had paused at the foot of the bed to make sure I hadn't missed any obvious spots when Andrea appeared in the doorway. "I'm afraid I didn't find anything," I told her, feeling a little guilty about poking around in Lynn's personal stuff while she wasn't there.

"I saw the way you were looking at me Sunday," Andrea said, ignoring my comment and closing the gap between us in a couple of slow, sensual strides.

"Wh—what d'ya mean?" I felt trapped.

"You know what I mean," Andrea smiled devilishly.

For just a moment I felt a surge of anger. What the hell was wrong with women—girls? Did everything have to be about them?

"Oh, hey … look, Andrea—I'm sorry." I stammered. "You are a very beautiful young lady, and—"

"And what?"

Instead of backing down or apologizing, she pulled her blouse out of her skirt and started unbuttoning it. Before I could object in any way, she pulled her blouse open, moved against me and began kissing me on the mouth.

To my horror, I felt myself responding to her advances.

"Hey, no … Andrea, please," I pleaded, pulling her arms from my neck. "I can't be doing this—"

"Humn—" she struggled, trying to pull me back into her embrace.

This is crazy, I thought, my anger returning. "Andrea, no!" I barked, almost as if scolding a dog for misbehaving. I pulled her hands down and held her firmly at arm's length.

Her big brown eyes filled with sudden panic and she jerked herself free and fled from the bedroom.

By the time I got into the living room Andrea was back on the couch sobbing her eyes out. This time I wasn't much worried about the complete exposure of her white panties. I stood there for a confused moment debating whether I should call Lynn or try and patch up the situation by myself.

I opted for the latter.

"I'm sorry, Sweetie," I said, flopping down on the floor beside the couch. "I sure didn't mean to give you the wrong idea Sunday … it's just that—"

I honest to God didn't know what to say. If women didn't want you to look at their butts … then why the hell did they have to dress that way?

Andrea ignored me completely and just kept sobbing.

I tried rubbing my hand awkwardly across her shoulder blades. "Really, Sweetie— I haven't known your mother very long, but I'm very serious about her—"

Andrea suddenly rolled against the backrest of the couch. "You won't tell her will you?" she demanded, wiping at the tears streaming down her face. "I'd rather die—"

I suddenly felt tears surging up in my own eyes. "Of

course not," I murmured, blinking back the tears. "It'll just be our little secret."

"I'm so stupid—" she blurted, stabbing at her tears with a vengeance with a tissue she'd gotten from some secret place.

I wasn't sure whether to laugh or cry.

"It's okay, honey," I told her. "We all make mistakes some times. Fortunately we didn't make a bigger one by letting this get out of hand."

"You mean like with my Dad—"

For just a moment, I thought I hadn't heard right. Then I realized, from the stunned look on her face, that she'd let something slip that she'd never intended. I could almost see the wheels turning in her head as she tried to figure out how to take it back.

"Are you saying what I think you're saying?" I asked gently.

"No, no … of course not," she was angry now because we both knew what I was asking her. "I just meant—you know … that maybe I drove him away."

"You learn that in Psychology 101?" I scoffed.

She flashed me the hint of a sheepish grin. "Maybe—"

It was like there was suddenly a secret agreement between us that there were certain things we weren't going to discuss. And for the moment, I was pretty damned happy to let that *sleeping dog* lay. But the truth was I wasn't sure what kind of a can of worms we had opened.

"Should I tell your mother that you were here?" I asked, walking her awkwardly to the door after a few minutes of equally awkward silence.

"Hmm," she nodded her tears all gone now. "You can ... I found my bracelets when I was thrashing around on the couch." She held up her wrist and rattled the gold rings. "Can you believe that? Besides ... I had a double reason for coming here today. Julie wants to know if you and Mom can come to the Gators football game on Saturday."

I couldn't answer right away. First of all, I wasn't sure if I believed her about the bracelets. Secondly, I had no idea what Lynn would say about the game.

"Are you going?"

She grinned broadly. "Sure ... I'll bring my boyfriend. I don't have a boyfriend yet, but I bet I can have one by Saturday."

"In that case," I returned her smile. "We wouldn't miss it."

. . .

Speaking for Lynn was not something I was used to doing just yet. That would come later. But for the moment, I had committed us to a Saturday football game and now I had the unexpected task of explaining to Lynn how I could have been so presumptuous without violating the promise I'd made to Andrea. I kind of felt like I needed a running start for that.

"What are you doing here?" Lynn asked when I showed up at the Legion half an hour later. "I thought I drove myself to work."

"You did."

I set my laptop down on a corner table and waited for her to bring me the beer that she automatically assumed I'd want. "Thanks, honey," I gave her a quick surreptitious peck on the lips before sitting down. "I just figured I could work down here as well as in the apartment."

"You were just missing me," she grinned.

"That too," I nodded, returning her grin.

"Making any progress?" Lynn looked like she wanted to sit down but wasn't sure if she should. All of the other employees already knew we were an item, but the question of acceptable latitude in our behavior at her job was one that hadn't been fully answered yet.

"Not much," I shook my head. "How about Deputy McIntyre … has he been around lately?" I had no idea why I asked that.

"Not lately." Lynn picked at the edge of her bar apron as if she wanted to ask "Why?" but didn't.

I suddenly realized that what I really wanted was to talk to Lynn about Andrea and I was pretty sure I didn't want a pain-in-the-ass nosey deputy butting in on the conversation. It was one thing to not tell Lynn about some harmless little flirtation by her daughter—quite another to withhold information about a potentially serious mental health issue. Andrea was obviously a little confused about what a daughter's relationship with her mother's boyfriend should be—

"I had an unexpected visitor today," I announced.

"Really?" Lynn looked puzzled. "Who."

"Andrea—"

Lynette looked even more puzzled.

"She lost her bracelets in your couch on Sunday."

"Really? I didn't even remember that she was wearing a bracelet."

"Me neither … but that's where she found 'em."

"Oh," Lynn seemed at a loss as to what to say.

"She also said Julie wants us to come to the football game on Saturday," I blurted, realizing this was going to be a lot harder than I'd anticipated.

"Really?"

By this time I began to figure out that her answers were a little strained and that she obviously suspected there was a lot more going on than I'd said so far. "I'm not exactly sure how to tell you this," I said, keeping in mind the old adage: *you can't make an omelet without breaking some eggs.* "But your daughter made a pass at me."

"What?"

Watching Lynn's face was kind of like watching the space shuttle take off. For a few seconds there was the flair of fire around the base, and then slowly, as the vehicle lifted the flames stretched out and became a fiery torch in rapid ascent toward the heavens. And so it was with Lynette's burgeoning realization of just what I had said.

"Are you kidding me?" she said in disbelief.

Somehow I could not keep a stupid, silly, guilty grin from spreading across my face. "Afraid not," I admitted. I had no idea what she must be thinking.

She just glared at me.

"Why would you tell me such a thing?" she demanded finally.

"Actually," I told her. "I promised Andrea that I wouldn't tell you, but—"

For a few moments I was kind of hoping the floor would open up and swallow me. I was well aware that when any relationship comes to an abrupt end, as both our marriages had, the issue of trust is paramount in developing a new relationship. And I could see that she was really struggling to find a way to cling to the trust we had already developed in our relationship. I really had no choice but to tell her the truth.

"Look, Sweetheart," I started fumbling around for words, "I know this isn't going to be easy to hear … and I'd rather take a beating than to have to tell you this—but there's something I have to ask you, and—"

I broke off and studied her face for a moment. It was really hard to judge how much more bad news she would be able to take before exploding.

"I really hate to ask" I took the plunge, "but was there ever any indication that your ex-husband ever molested either one of your girls?"

It was like watching the fire on a burning fuse race towards the dynamite. Then, suddenly, it fizzled and exploded.

"Oh, my God!" Lynn exclaimed very slowly. "That son of a bitch!"

Chapter 24

Lynn was so upset her boss gave her the rest of the evening off without either of us resorting to little white lies. Deputy McIntyre was not quite so generous. We were sitting in my car, Lynn crying softly against my chest because she was beating herself up for not being there for Andrea when her husband crossed the line, when pain-in-the-ass McIntyre suddenly rapped on the window with his flashlight.

"Yes," I barked, turning to glare into the light, which he was now shining on us.

"Is there a problem here?" McIntyre demanded.

"Nothing that concerns the Sheriff's department," I snapped back.

"Is this your car?" McIntyre asked, butting in where he wasn't needed. "We had a report that the driver of a blue Escort is wanted for questioning by the Highway Patrol."

"Well, it's not me ... besides, I've already talked to them."

"Really?"

Obviously, McIntyre didn't believe me. "Yes ... a Patrolman Peterson, if I'm not mistaken," I told him, surprising myself. I had no idea I'd read the Patrolman's nametag, but there it was in the recesses of my mind like a lighthouse beacon.

"So what's going on here?" McIntyre was determined to be tenacious.

"You want to get that light out of my face?" I made my own demands

"You didn't answer my question," McIntyre was bound and determined to play the Gestapo roll.

"Look Deputy," I said, turning my body toward the door and reaching for the door handle. "Lynn's dog got run over if you must know … now if you don't get that light out of my face I'm gonna come out there and shove it up your ass!"

"You can't talk to me that way—"

"Can't I?" I popped the door handle and started to push it open.

"Okay, okay," McIntyre said quickly, turning off the light. "It's my job to check things out, you know?"

"That's fine," I said, relaxing.

"Sorry about your dog," McIntyre said, turning to leave.

"Say, Dick," I called after him. "Lynn's too upset to drive … we're gonna leave her car here for tonight, okay?"

"Which one is it?"

"The red Chevy."

"Got cha!"

"Thanks, honey," I murmured under my breath, watching him walk away.

"Remind me not to mess with you," Lynn said, crying and giggling all at the same time. "In case you weren't aware of it, policemen have guns."

"I know," I laughed, suddenly shaking like a Colorado aspen. "But sometimes that guy really pisses me off."

All at once she was all over me like a teenage *nympho* smothering me with kisses and trying to light my fire.

"Whoa," I muttered, pushing her back a bit for breathing room. "If you aren't careful you'll have Dickie boy back here waving his gun around. I only have so much self control you know."

The light wasn't very good under that big, old live oak, but it was good enough to see the sparkle in her eyes. "Sorry," she whispered huskily with a grin.

I didn't believe her. "I'm sorry to be the one to tell about Andrea's unintentional slip of the tongue, but I really thought I had to ... you know. Once we start violating each other's trust by keeping secrets—" It was a sentence I didn't have to finish.

"I know," Lynn said, wiping away her final tears. "So what are we going to do about Andrea?" she asked.

"Get her the help she needs, I guess." I told her, glad to hear it was a "we" problem. "Andrea's probably going to be pissed at me for a while for violating her trust, but once we get her some help and she sees we're on her side, I think she'll be fine."

I fired up the Escort and we headed home. Lynn was still trying to beat herself up for not being the perfect mother— "I can guarantee you you're not the first mother in history to fail a daughter in exactly the same way," I told her. "That kind of thing is way more common than most of us realize."

"You've got to be kidding—"

"'fraid not!"

After that, we might as well have been welded at the hips. There's nothing that will bring about closeness quite like standing together as a team to nurture a child, even if that child happens to be twenty years old. And, I decided *once a parent … always a parent*.

…

With that in mind, I got on the phone the following day and called Ruby to see if she had any pictures of William as a grownup. "If you do," I told her, after she had agreed to look, "You could just drop them in the mail here at Lynn's address—"

"Lord, child—" Ruby interrupted. "Why don't you just come for Thanksgiving … you can pick 'em up then."

Now there's a kick in the head for you, Ruby calling me "child."

Before taking Lynn to work we called Andrea to make arrangements about the football game the next day. Andrea was to come over to Lynn's apartment and we'd drive down to Gainesville together. Naturally we'd take Lynn's car since it was the nicest, which meant I didn't have to pick Lynn up since she'd left her car at work the night before.

I had all but stopped listening to Lynn's half of the conversation when I heard Lynn say, "Boyfriend, what boyfriend?"

"Here," I said, jumping up quickly. "Let me talk to her."

Lynn handed me the phone, puzzled.

"Hi, Andy," I could feel Lynn's eyes burning in to me. "Look, honey … I don't mean to be blunt, but this guy better be some guy you've known for years. Otherwise he's not welcome. We want to spend the time with you not some dumb guy."

"Are you sure that was a good idea?" Lynn asked, after I hung up.

"No," I told her, "But I'd heck of a lot rather she came alone than with some guy she thought she had to pickup—and I'm pretty sure you feel the same way."

"Yes, I know … but you sounded so much like her father, it scared me."

"I know," I agreed. "But that was on purpose. I think she's feeling very confused about what's the right thing to do. I just wanted to make sure she understands that we want her just the way she is—"

Lynn stared at me for a long time. "Where the hell were you when I was looking for a good man?" she asked finally.

All I could do was grin.

...

Saturday dawned like a canon blast over the horizon. Actually, it was Andrea pounding on the front door. With Lynn working until after midnight every night, we were not used to getting up very early. Fortunately, I had brains enough to slip on a pair of pants before answering the door.

"Hi, Andy," I murmured, feeling enough like a scuzz-bucket to try and comb my hair with the heel of my hand.

This time I was the one not properly dressed, since I usually slept only in my under shorts. I always found the sleeves on pajama to be too restricting. Andrea, on the other hand, was wearing a very pretty forest green dress with pleated knee-length skirt, long sleeves, and little round black buttons. She had on elegant black sandals with a sexy one- inch heel.

"My … don't you look nice," I said sincerely.

"Thanks," she murmured.

Normally, I would have been embarrassed by the situation—going to the door like that to greet my new significant other's grown daughter when it was so obvious that I'd just gotten out of her mother's bed. This time, I just felt proud.

"You're gonna have to give us a minute," I said, paddling back toward the bedroom. "We don't get up very early when your mother works late."

"I know," Andrea grinned. "I always have a hard time getting used to Mom working late. She always used to work during the day. Daddy was the one who worked late—" She broke off, embarrassed that maybe she shouldn't have gone there.

By the time I finished my shower, mother and daughter were sitting at the dining room table drinking coffee. There was a plate of bacon, eggs, and toast in front of the chair where I always sat.

"We ate already," Lynn informed me.

"I can see that," I laughed, noting they each had a saucer with nothing on it but toast-crumbs. "You ladies are really hell on toast."

While Lynn went off to shower and get dressed, I tried to eat without acting too much like an idiot. There was nothing like a nubile, young girl to make you feel like you were about nine hundred years old. It was true, I surmised: *there's no fool like an old fool.* Still, I tried my best to make small talk.

"You told her, didn't you?" Andrea said, suddenly cutting to the chase.

There was nothing I could do but nod.

"I figured you would."

What could I say? "Listen, Andy," I said, leaning back and taking a sip of my coffee. "We don't have to talk about this today … there's not much we can do today anyway. But first thing Monday we're going to try and get you some counseling."

She sat there for a long time without speaking, so long in fact, that I began to wonder if I'd even said anything—that we were maybe talking about something totally different, or that she was simply trying to muster the courage to yell at me. Then, she got up and walked around the table and kissed me smack dab in the middle of the forehead.

"Thank you," she said simply.

It was a simple kiss, but it spoke volumes.

…

Fortunately, the drive to Gainesville took less than an hour and the game had a three O'clock kickoff. It was also fortunate that Lynn knew exactly where to go and that Julie was there to meet us as she had promised. Since the game was about to start, Jamal had to be down on the field with the rest of cheerleaders.

For me being in a football stadium on a college campus was an entirely new experience—the only thing comparable had been going to a circus once in Germany where we'd nearly gotten trampled to death before the gate finally opened. It was, I assumed, also a lot like going to a rock concert, something else I had never experienced.

I had never gone to a big event like that with a mother and two grown daughters before either.

"What d'ya think?" Lynn yelled in my ear while she was jumping up and down with Andy and Julie when the Gators got their first touchdown.

"I think I might be getting old," I yelled back with a grin, thinking I had developed a whole new perspective on the word "pandemonium."

At halftime Jamal joined us for a few moments, and then agreed to accompany me to the snack stand to get something to drink for the girls. The stadium was too busy for us to have much to say to each other beyond, "Hi, how are you." and "It's good to see you."

When it was my turn to place our order at the refreshment stand, I found myself staring at the shocked face of William McPherson.

For a moment, I was too stunned to react. At first, Ruby's grandson simply stared at me. Then, slowly, disbelief spread across William's face. For a few seconds, he was poised to take my order—then, suddenly he was making a mad dash toward the back of the refreshment stand.

Jamal looked completely mystified.

"Do you know the back way out of here?" I demanded, grabbing Jamal by the arm and shaking him.

"Yeah? I guess so."

"Well, quick," I insisted. "Show me."

We weren't quick enough. By the time we got to the back, William was long gone.

"Where are our drinks?" Julie demanded, when Jamal brought me back to our seats empty handed. "I thought you guys were getting us something to drink!"

Jamal could only shrug.

"I'll explain later," I promised. "After the game."

The girls didn't like it much but the game was about to start again so they let it drop. Lynn didn't give up quite so easily. I could feel the questioning look in her eyes without even looking at her.

"You'll never guess," I said to her as the crowd hushed for the kickoff.

"You've got to be kidding!" she exclaimed, guessing immediately.

I could tell she was dying to hear more, but the ball was already in the air.

By the time the Gator's receiver caught the ball and returned it twelve yards and got tackled, I realized I shouldn't be just sitting there watching a college football game. There were a few more things in life more important than a football game and I could be missing a great opportunity to catch William McPherson.

"I'm gonna go drive around for a bit," I told Lynn, pulling her close so I could yell in her ear. "I'll bring you back something to drink first, though."

"That's not necessary," she mouthed the words.

I waved her off, went and bought the drinks and delivered them, then made my way out of the stadium. Like a lot of college campuses, this one kind of sprawled and parking was always a bit of a struggle on game day. I would have to get lucky to spot William's van on the crowded streets, but with the game still on it was worth a try. Of course, there was always the possibility that William was no longer driving the same piece-of-junk—

When I spotted a van that looked like William's I got so excited I nearly took the taillights off the car in front of me. The van was nearly a block away and going in the opposite direction. I tried to make a left turn to pursue, but unfortunately the street was a one way street going in the opposite direction. By the time I got straightened around and got on the right street, the van had disappeared. And I really couldn't be sure whether it was William's van or not.

I drove around for awhile hoping to get lucky, but it was hopeless.

Fortunately, by the time I got back Lynn and Andy were waiting outside Ben Hill Griffin Stadium. I was lucky to even find them again, since we'd never really discussed how we were going to meet up after the game. I'd been cruising around hoping to snatch a parking space near the gate when I spotted them on a corner, looking a little lost.

"Boy am I glad to see you," Lynn exclaimed as they piled into her car. "I wasn't sure you'd ever find us again."

"It is pretty much a madhouse," I agreed.

"Julie and Jamal are going to meet us at some restaurant," Lynn informed me. "I'm not sure how we're going to find it ... but Andrea's suppose to know the way."

"So who won the game?" I asked.

"We did." mother and daughter chimed in unison.

"Go Gators," I added my two cents. I know Lynn was dying of curiosity about William, but she was kind enough to wait and let me just deal with the traffic.

Finding the restaurant turned out to be a snap. All we had to do was follow the flood of traffic that was going that way. Actually, it made no sense whatever to go to a place that was so crowded, but that's where part of the football gang always went and Jamal and Julie were part of that gang. It did make it really difficult for me to explain to them why I was chasing some black guy all over Gainesville.

Not that I had any good explanation that I could offer without digging myself into a deeper hole. If you go around telling people you're chasing some black guy because you know he's a sexual predator, they are going to want to know how you know he's a predator and why you don't just call the police. And that would just be for openers.

"So what gives?" Jamal asked during a momentary lull in the din of noisy students.

"It's a long story," I told them, watching Lynn to see if she was going to help me. "The short version is that this guy is the grandson of a lady we know. We think he has some information about a rapist wanted by the police. Ruby, the guy's grandmother, wants us to convince him to come home so we can asked him some questions."

"He must have thought you wanted something else," Jamal concluded. "Cause he sure took off when he saw you!"

"Maybe you should call the police?" Julie suggested, before I could get comfortable with the idea that I might be off the hook.

I wasn't exactly sure what Julie was getting at by suggesting we call the police, but I didn't want to appear deliberately obstinate. "We could do that," I suggested. "We could stop by the police station on the way home."

Fortunately, the pizza we'd ordered arrived at that moment and the subject was dropped for the more important questions: "Which do you prefer, sausage, pepperoni, or Canadian bacon?" I was amazed at how much pizza a bunch of ladies who can generally survive on toast could actually put away. *Women! What an enigma!*

...

"I thought you were going to stop at the police station," Andy said from the back seat when we were back on the Interstate 75 heading out of Gainesville.

"I—ah," I glanced over at Lynn for some help. "I guess I forgot."

"We could go back," she suggested.

"I—I'd rather not," I said. "It's getting late ... we could do it some other time."

"Tomorrow is Sunday," Andrea reminded them. "Never put off to tomorrow what you can do today ... isn't that what grownups always say?"

"Yes, but—" I was hoping Lynn would jump in any second now with a legitimate excuse. "I don't even know where the police station is."

"We could ask."

"I'd rather not," I said firmly. "I'm pretty much shot for the day—"

Andrea let it drop and we rode in silence for awhile. I was feeling a little guilty about putting Andrea off that way and I knew she was far from being satisfied. I was also glad it was such a short drive back to Lake City. Hopefully Andrea wouldn't stick around too long. *College kids had homework,* didn't they?

"Can I ask you something, Russell?" Andrea asked just before we got back to Lynn's apartment. There was an ominous tone in her voice.

I tried to locate her face in the mirror. "Sure," I said when my eyes locked on hers in the mirror. "What's on your mind?"

"You're that Robin Hood guy they were talking about on the news, aren't you?"

An *eon* is that period of time between when the thing you least want to happen in the world goes from *possibility* to *reality*. It can happen in the blink of an eye and feel like a year—or in this case, a couple of centuries.

"Wh—what makes you say that?" I stammered.

"I just know it."

I glanced over at Lynn for some help. To my surprise, she had a kind of silly smirk on her face. "I should have known," I muttered, shaking my head.

"What's that?" Lynn was about to bust out into titters.

"That you didn't raise any dumb kids—" I grinned.

"I guess that means I was right," Andy chimed in.

Feeling like I'd just taken a high dive off a hundred-foot high cliff and didn't know how to dive or swim I nodded. "Yes," I conceded. "You're right."

So what now? Pick up your game piece and go straight to jail?

Suddenly I was not nearly so anxious for Andrea to go back to school tonight and apparently Lynn was reading his mind.

"Why don't you sleep on the couch tonight?" she suggested to Andrea.

"I didn't bring any clothes, Mother,"

"I can find you something," Lynn offered.

"Do you have any homework?" I asked.

"Yes … but I have my books along."

"Then it's settled."

. . .

I took Lynn and Andrea to Tucker's, a steak, seafood and Italian place a few blocks from Lake de Solo in downtown Lake City, for supper. It was money I couldn't afford to spend, but some times a guy's gotta do what a guy's gotta do. At least, that's what I told myself as the host showed us to a table.

Actually, I just wanted to show off. Tucker's was the premier *fine dining* place in downtown Lake City, just a couple of buildings up the street from Ruppert's Bakery & Café where I'd eaten breakfast. It was in the back half of the ground floor of the Blanche Hotel, which according to the owner, Brian Tucker, had once been the stomping grounds of Florida's Governor Cone and Al Capone. Walking past the huge staircase in the middle of the Hotel lobby was like taking a walk back in time. The wood-and-brick interior was cozy with blue table clothes over white and the food was unbelievable.

In reality, I didn't just want to show the restaurant off to the girls—I wanted to show Lynn and her daughter off to the world. I'm old enough to be Andy's grandfather rather than her father, but somehow that didn't matter. Age is relative anyway, isn't it? Except when it comes to guys molesting kids!

. . .

After Lynn got Andrea settled on the couch for the night, a part of my mind kept circling like a bird of prey over the image of Andy's nubile, young body sleeping on

Lynn's couch. *Was I crazy? Or are men simply hardwired that way?* It was hard to believe that I could ever in a zillion years seriously consider sexually exploiting Andrea, even though in her present mental state she might welcome it. Still the image persisted.

For once, this was a situation that I didn't feel comfortable discussing with Lynn. But to tell the truth, it did seem to help me understand and empathize with the situation that William McPherson had apparently gotten himself into. It wasn't such a big stretch to see how a guy could get off on the wrong foot, sexually speaking. The problem, of course, was that sex wasn't supposed to end with murder.

"Can I asked you something?" I asked Lynn when I realized she wasn't sleeping either. I really wanted to make love to her, but I wasn't comfortable with the idea of doing that with Andrea on the couch.

"What's that?" she said softly.

"Well … I've just been laying here trying to figure out what makes a guy like Ruby's grandson tick … you know, what makes them rape instead of going for normal sexual relationships? Then, I got to wondering just what is considered *normal?*"

"What d'ya mean?"

"Oh, I don't know. I just got started thinking about how it was growing up. You know, when you first start finding out about sex. One of the first things I remember was seeing a guy and a girl coming up out of a road ditch and the girl was putting her belt back in her jeans. I figured they had to be, you know, ah—fooling around."

"So?"

"So that just got me thinking about what we do as

kids and how that can effect the rest of our lives. Did you ever have any cousins that you know were ah—fooling around?"

"Now that you mention it … yes. But what's your point?"

"Did you ever make it with one of your cousins?"

Lynn giggled. "None of your damned business."

"So did you?"

"No … but we did kind of mess around."

"Playing stink finger?"

"Russell … honestly! What's gotten into you?"

I laughed softly. "See you knew exactly what I meant. You know why? Because that's something that a lot of people go through as kids. And, obviously we're bound to experiment with people we're comfortable with—like cousins."

"I still don't see what you're getting at."

"Well most of that stuff turns out to be harmless enough, even though it would be considered wrong. You experiment with a cousin and, regardless of how far you go, it turns out to be a lifelong secret, but a part of your learning curve about sex. But say, for example, you were raised by someone who was pretty ridged in their attitudes and your first sexual experiments went drastically wrong?"

"You mean like William McPherson?"

"Yes. I think Ruby is a really nice lady … but I'm not sure being raised by your grandmother would be all that conducive to achieving a real healthy attitude about sex, if you know what I mean."

"You might have a point," Lynn admitted.

"It's pretty easy to imagine the worst when you think

about a shy boy being confronted by a hot-to-trot young girl … and that's kind of what Ruby implied—"

"So how do we know William was shy?"

I laughed again. "I think most boys that age are shy when it comes to sex. I can tell you this much … I was myself. I remember a neighbor girl coming over to our place when I was about seventeen. She seemed to have a thing for me but she was only about twelve, so I ignored her. I was doing some work in the yard and happened to look up, and there she was, standing in the haymow door with her skirt pulled up over her head. I'm never knew for sure what she had in mind … but I know I was terrified enough that nothing would ever have happened."

Lynn giggled. "You were just a big chicken, that's all."

"It's a good thing. That first time can be pretty traumatic."

"Was it for you?" Lynn asked, surprising me.

"Yeah … I guess so. I'm not proud of it, but it was in a whorehouse in Juarez—" I stopped, letting my mind wander back over the bizarre experience. "I was just an eighteen-year-old kid in basic training at Fort Bliss, Texas." I told her. "I went with a bunch of guys to Juarez on a Saturday afternoon. I was too dumb to know that most of the guys wanted to go because of the women. I didn't even go into the first place they went in, at first. I just stood outside on the sidewalk and prayed for my raging hormones to let me be."

"So what happened?"

"What d'ya think," I laughed. "The hormones won … of course."

"Really?"

"That wasn't the worst part," I continued. "I was so stupid that I thought only girls had a cherry, you know. I was never circumcised and when I first put it in, I guess I went a little crazy. After I came, I was bleeding all over the place."

"You're kidding?"

"No, seriously … if the woman hadn't been older and kind of motherly, I could have wound up being emotionally scarred for life.

"You mean you could have wound up like William McPherson?"

"I can see where it could be possible. Say it's a guy's first time with a girl and they start goofing around, only the girl gets scared and he doesn't want to stop. She starts fighting him and he winds up forcing her. What's he gonna do afterward? Most likely he'll get scared that she'll go to the police and—"

Lynn shuddered. "Now you're scaring me."

"Sorry."

"Speaking of these nasty things," Lynn continued. "What do you think we should do about Steve? Have him locked up and throw away the key?"

I thought about that for a while. "It's kind of up to Andrea isn't it," I said finally. "Depends on what kind of relationship she wants with her father and that might depend on whether he did anything with Julie or not. What do you want to do?"

"Boiling oil would be nice?"

I smiled. "No one ever said being a parent would be easy, did they?"

"Guess not," she agreed.

Chapter 25

"So did you guys fool around all night, or what?" Andrea demanded at breakfast.

Lynn and I stared at each other a full minute before either of us could find our voice. "Andrea!" Lynn exclaimed finally. "That's kind of personal, don't you think?"

For just a second, Andrea looked like she'd been slapped. "I was just kidding, Mom." She muttered. "Jeez—"

It was one of those moments that truly qualify as an "awkward moment." Andrea and I had made a sort of connection—but I wasn't ready to joke about my sex life with her just yet. And I was pretty sure Lynn wasn't ready for that either.

"Actually," Andrea continued sheepishly. "My ears were burning. I thought maybe you guys were talking about me."

Suddenly, the world flopped back into orbit.

"Actually," I conceded. "We were talking about you … at least, part of the time. Since it's no longer a secret that your, ah—"

"Father's a full-fledged son of a bitch," Lynn finished for me, though not with the exact words I would have chosen.

"What your mother is trying to say," I went on, "now that we know there were some things going on that shouldn't have been, we want to get you some help. Girls are not supposed to learn about sex from their fathers, at least not like that. Your father crossed the line."

I glanced over at Lynn and saw that she was on the verge of tears. She was watching Andrea very intently.

"We know these kind of things are not easy to talk about." I added.

"But we're here for you, honey," Lynn said, a tear rolling down her cheek.

"I know, Mom," Andrea murmured, her eyes suddenly filling with tears. "I should have told you—"

The damn finally broke. The next thing I knew mother and daughter were clinging to each other and bawling like babies. I was about ready to cry myself.

The rest of Sunday passed quickly. We spent part of the time playing badminton, me against the ladies. It was a way of being together without dwelling on serious things. I was pretty sure Andrea wanted to ask some questions about the Robin Hood thing, because the newscasts had indicated that the so-called Robin Hood was suspected of committing a couple of assaults in Jacksonville. That was not something I was anxious to discuss with Andrea. I was also knew Lynn was bursting with curiosity about whether her ex-husband had molested Julie as well, but we weren't ready to talk about that yet.

Later that evening after Andrea had gone back to Florida State, Lynn and I went back on the Internet and made a list of potential places in Tallahassee where we could take her for sexual counseling. I also researched part-time employment with the University of Florida in Gainesville so I'd know where to go to start tracking down William McPherson in the morning.

As Sherlock Holmes or someone put it, I thought excitedly, "The game's a foot." With any kind of luck I could be hot on William's trail and get the suspense over with. Having your life totally up in the air because of some sexual predator was not a very comfortable feeling.

"Are you going with me tomorrow?" I asked Lynn when we were snuggled in bed for the night.

"Not if I can get an appointment for Andrea ... but that probably won't happen on such short notice."

"You're right about that. That could take a couple of weeks."

"I hope not, but with the holidays coming up, who knows?"

"Speaking of which—are we going to Ruby's for Thanksgiving?"

"We should. But I don't know what the girls want to do yet."

That stopped me for a moment. Being divorced with grown children kind of put the holidays under a different set of rules. It seemed to me like a lot of grown children of divorced parents continued to spend the holidays with their mother. Fathers, on the other hand, got pity invitations to whichever one of the kids was willing to put up with them.

"You know," I suggested, "maybe we should take the girls up to meet Ruby. That would kill two birds with one stone."

"How do you mean?"

"Well, since Andy's already figured out that I'm the Robin Hood marauder, maybe we should explain everything to them, Ruby included, and just trust them to let us do the right thing."

"Are you kidding," Lynn exclaimed. "The girls might understand okay, but you're likely to give poor old Ruby a heart attack!"

"I doubt it. Besides ... that would kind of help me. I really should go home for a couple of days and make sure my business hasn't burned down. If we did that, you could ride up to Montgomery with me and back home with whichever one of the girls drove. That way I could go home from there—unless of course you want to quit your job and go home with me."

"Don't tempt me," Lynn laughed, but not for long.

...

The girl in the University employment office was short, overweight, and black. Not that there was anything wrong about her being black. It was just that to have a white couple come in and asked about a black man who does part-time soda-jerk work in one of Ben Hill Griffin Stadium's refreshment stands on Saturdays raised some suspicions.

"What did you say you needed Mr. McPherson's address for?" Cecilia (according to her nametag) asked, looking up from the computer screen in front of her.

People who insisted on being deliberately obtuse made me want to scream. "I didn't actually say, " I told her, "But if you must know ... his grandmother is sick and she asked us if we could find him for her."

"You some kind of lawyer?"

"No—"

"So how come you know his grandmother?"

"What difference does that make?"

I could feel Lynn squeezing my arm, probably trying

to encourage me to not loose my temper and start yelling. "She's a friend of the family," Lynn told her.

Obviously, Cecilia wasn't buying. "I don't mean to give you folks a hard time, but we have privacy rules. We can't just go givin' out personal information—"

"I understand," I told her. "Isn't there some way?"

Cecilia softened a bit. "Maybe if you'd bring a note from the grandmother—"

"Maybe we could do that, honey," Lynn said quickly, squeezing my arm again. "We are going to see her again on Thanksgiving."

I fought back an urge to go off like a Fourth of July rocket. "If that's the best we can do. Ruby's gonna be disappointed if Willie can't make it for Thanksgiving though."

Normally, I wouldn't have dreamed of telling little white lies and putting on such an acting job, but this time I was glad I did.

"Whyn't you folks do that," Cecilia suggested, glancing down at her computer screen again. "I'll be able to help you then." She looked at her watch and then flashed us a thin smile. "If you're gonna be in town for lunch … I could recommend a place called "Decadance.""

"Really?" I raised an eyebrow. "How far is it?"

Cecilia hesitated a moment as if distracted by something on her computer screen. "Not far … it's just off University Avenue down on 2nd Street."

"Thank you," I told her, "We'll give it a try."

"What the heck was that about?" Lynn asked immediately once we were out in the hall. She was still clinging to my arm. It wasn't even eleven O'clock yet and it had only been a couple of hours since we had breakfast.

I smiled knowingly. "I don't know … but I have a feeling it will be worth our while to check out this place. It might explain a few things."

She looked up at me, puzzled. "Like what?"

"Like how a forty year old man survives on what he earns as a soda jerk on a few Saturdays a month."

This time she got it.

The drive to the restaurant only took a couple of minutes—only it turned out to be more of a bar than restaurant. It was a small single-story brick building with glass block windows on either side of the boarded up front door. There was a sign at the top of the building that read, "Girls! Girls! Girls!" There were a few cars and pickups parked along one side of the building and an open door. I wasn't sure if the place was open for business or if the vehicles belonged to workman in the process of remodeling it. Either way I was pretty sure I didn't want to take Lynn into such a place. But she insisted.

We ordered coffee with cream and sweetener.

"We were wondering if you have an employee named William McPherson?" I asked when the waiter brought the coffee.

The waiter nodded. "Sure," Before I could stop him he turned his head and yelled toward the kitchen, "Hey, McPherson … someone's here to see ya."

"Why'd you do that?" I demanded, holding back an urge to smack the guy.

The waiter shrugged. "Ya wanta see him, don't ya. Wait! I'll go get him."

He was the only one surprised William McPherson was no longer in the kitchen.

"I don't suppose we could get his address from you?" I said, not trying too hard to hide my disappointment and anger. I didn't like jerks much more than I did obtuse people, and this guy was maybe a little of both.

"Sure," the guy said to my surprise. "If the boss ain't got the office locked, that is. You never know about that."

"Are you sure that would be okay?" I asked. "We wouldn't want to get you in any kind of trouble."

"Hey, no problem."

William must have known his fellow employee fairly well. By the time we looked up his address on a newly purchased map and figured out how to get there he was already gone. And it didn't look like he would be coming back any time soon. The door to his one room apartment was open and there was nothing left behind.

Oddly enough, I wasn't sure whether I was disappointed or glad.

Chapter 26

After dropping Lynn off at work later that afternoon, I went back on the Internet to see if I could figure out William's next move. There was so much I didn't know—like how much personal property the guy had. If he was able to pick up and move on a moment's notice, as seemed to be the case, then he had to be almost living out of his van. If that wasn't already the case, it could easily be his next move. I was suddenly remembering the guy on the motorcycle swiping the purse all those weeks ago. If William took to the road, we'd never catch him. If that happened, about the only thing I could do would be hand our information over to the police. And how was I ever going to do that without implicating myself in the assault on Maria.

Once, that wouldn't have mattered much. Now it did.

When I arrived to pick up Lynn later that evening, Deputy McIntyre was there busy making a nuisance out of himself. The guy still rubbed me the wrong way.

"How's the vacation going?" McIntyre asked, making no mention of our previous run in. I thought he might ask if I'd gotten Lynn a new dog, but he apparently had other fish to fry. I distinctly remember not having told McIntyre that I was on vacation, which could mean he'd taken the trouble to call Patrolman Peterson cause now he was acting like I'd claimed to be on vacation.

"Fine," I told him, hoping that would quell his curiosity.

"Catching any fish?"

Well, now, I thought, *that ought to make me feel at home.* Asking about fishing was what people in Minnesota did to visiting tourists. Only trouble was, the question kind of put me on the spot. If I said, "Yes" then McIntyre would want to know how many and where and what kind. I knew there had to be plenty of places to fish around Lake City, but I really had no idea what kind of fish you would get or where,

"Actually haven't had much time to do any fishing," I told him finally.

"So what keeps you so busy?"

I laughed. "You mean besides Lynn?" I waited a minute for that to sink in, then added, "Oh, I've just been doing a little business research, I guess—you know, looking around to see what's shaking, that's all."

I realized that was a mistake even before the words were out of my mouth.

McIntyre's eyes perked up like a robin that had just spotted a juicy worm. "Business research, huh? You planning on opening a business down here?"

"Maybe," I lied. "I'd have to sell the one up north first though."

"I thought you already did that." McIntyre jumped on my slip.

I'd forgotten that I'd told him that I used to be in the tax business so he wouldn't have to go on and on about what the tax business was like. "Oh, no," I finally decided just to tell him part of the truth. "I just meant I used to be in business during the tax season ... you know, from

January 1st to April 15th. Not much going on during the rest of the year."

It was an outrageous stretch to cover a silly lie that need not have ever occurred, but McIntyre was apparently buying it.

"So you starting another tax business down here?" he asked.

Now, there ... you see? I told myself. *You tell one silly lie and then you have to go on lying forever to cover your butt.* I was well aware that in some places in the south there were very large H & R Block franchises that included whole areas rather than just a city or two. I just wasn't sure if that was the case in this area. Whatever the case, I wished McIntyre would just dry up and blow away.

"It's too early to tell," I said, continuing the charade. "What about you? Are you working tonight? We were wondering if you guys ever caught that rapist."

"You gotta be crazy!" Lynn said when she got me alone in the car. "It's like poking a bear with a stick asking that guy about the rapist!"

I smiled sheepishly. "I know, but it's the only way to shut the guy up."

...

Nothing much happened during the next few days other than I spent a lot of time on the phone talking to Sam Turner back home about different things that had come up with the tax business. Our pursuit of William McPherson had come to an abrupt dead end. Andrea's appointment with a psychologist in Tallahassee was scheduled for after the Thanksgiving holiday, so there was nothing to do there. I spent most of my time playing around on the Internet trying to come up with a miracle.

There were several missing children that could be linked to William's different addresses over the years if you took into account some short diving distances. There were only a couple of missing children that turned up missing from an exact city that William was living in at the time—but none of them were young, white girls. That could either mean that I was wrong about the *young, white girl* theory in the first place or that there never was a connection other than coincidence.

At any rate, the time flew by and the next thing I knew we were on our way back to Montgomery to Ruby's for Thanksgiving. The prospect of that left me with very mixed feelings. On the one hand, I was well aware that a lot of older people would do just about anything to avoid spending the holidays alone and I was pleased to brighten Ruby's day in that way. But then, I was also going to be bugging her for more information to help track down her grandson and put him in jail. That didn't feel so good.

I also felt a little guilty about ascending on Ruby with Lynn and her daughters. For that reason, I was glad that Jamal was going along to help take the onerous stigma of four visiting whites off Ruby. Although, I didn't really think that kind of racial thing mattered much any more.

Ruby was a very good sport about the whole thing. She let Lynn and the girls take over her kitchen while Jamal and I entertained her in the parlor. The one area that was a little touchy was the fact that I hadn't told Jamal and the girls that the black guy I'd been chasing in Gainesville was actually the rapist and not just someone with information about a rapist. I had also implied that we were mostly trying to find William for Ruby because she was getting old and he was her only grandson—which, of course, did not explain why he'd bolted like a scalded rabbit. Andrea and Julie had no problems with that, but Jamal wasn't so easy to persuade.

"He should have stood his ground and heard you out," Jamal insisted after bringing the subject up. "Why run away if you've got nothing to hide?"

"Maybe he thought I was a cop?" I suggested.

Ruby stopped rocking for a second and looked at me. "I can't believe that. You don't look anything like a policeman to me, Russell. Lordee, no." She shook her head in disbelief and chuckled. "No way ... not the way you dress."

I met her gaze and grinned. "What's wrong with the way I dress?"

Ruby chuckled. "Well, for one thing ... policeman don't wear tennis shoes."

"Mrs. McPherson has a point," Jamal agreed.

"Maybe he thought I was undercover."

"Why would you be after him then?" Jamal insisted.

"Unpaid traffic tickets, maybe—" I was beginning to feel put on the spot and I couldn't help wondering if Ruby had forgotten about our agreed upon lie. She was not making the situation any easier for me. It was bad enough that Andrea knew about my assault on my wife—or soon to be ex-wife, if the divorce papers were ready to be signed when I got home.

"Maybe he thought you were from the IRS—" Jamal suggested suddenly, throwing the whole conversation out of kilter.

"That was probably it," I laughed. Sometimes I just

271

marveled at how hard it was to tell what people were thinking. It's probably a good thing we don't walk around with a little CRT screen in the middle of our foreheads that prints out our thoughts. If we did, there'd probably be a lot more rapes and murders than there already is.

Ruby chose that moment to asked Jamal if he played sports, but before he could answer Lynn informed us it was time to eat.

Chapter 27

Ruby had just finished the blessing for the meal when an unexpected dinner guest arrived. Actually, he was not a totally unexpected guest, but his timing did catch me by surprise. So did the gun he was waving around.

"Hello, William," I said, taking charge. "I don't think you really need a gun in your Grandmother's house. We're all friends here."

"Who the hell are you, Mister?" Willie boy demanded waving the gun menacingly.

I smiled and tried to remain calm while everyone else seemed busy looking shocked. "To start with, I'm a friend of your Grandmother's and we're actually here to help you."

"What are you doing waving that gun around, William?" Ruby demanded.

"What are these people doing in your house, Gram?" William demanded back, ignoring her question.

"We can talk about that William when you put the gun down," Ruby said.

"No way," William declared, waving the gun some more and positioning himself so that he blocked the door to the kitchen. Any one trying to leave by the double door to the parlor would be an easy target. "Not until I know what's going on."

"I think it's obvious that you know who I am," I said, standing up.

"If you don't want to end up dead, Mister," William threatened, gesturing with the gun. "You'd better just sit yourself right back down." His eyes were large with fear.

"Okay, okay," I muttered, quickly sitting back down. "Don't get excited."

For a moment everyone just stared, waiting to see what William would do. I tried to think of some way to lighten up the situation—like offer William some dinner, get him a chair, anything— But that didn't seem like the thing to do just yet.

"You remember me interrupting you in that old house in Lake City, don't you?" I continued. "So there's no use pretending about that. You know we know you're guilty of attempted rape."

William just glared at me.

"You're just hurting your grandmother by waving that gun around," I said, hoping the *'family card'* would take some of the tension off.

"How'd you find Gram?" William demanded his eyes a mixture of fear and anger.

"Oh," I let out a little nervous laugh. "That's quite a story. Actually, it was from the picture in your bag. Oh, by the way, I still have your stuff. It's in my car. Anyway, finding your grandmother with nothing to go on but that picture—well, that was something. Lots of false trails— actually, it was just a big stroke of luck."

I knew I was babbling, but I figured as long as we were talking nothing bad would happen. And the more I could get William to talk the better off we'd be.

"I know your name is William," I rambled on. "But I

have this urge to call you Willie. Is that what people call you, Willie?"

"People don't call me nothin'," William snapped. "So you can just shut up."

Well, okay, I thought, *the man's got a gun. I probably shouldn't argue with him.* I looked around to see how the rest of the gang was taking the situation. Andrea and Julie both looked pretty scared. Lynn, on the other hand, was watching me with loving, trusting eyes. Jamal just looked wary. Ruby, however, looked as if she was about to pop a button.

"William," she said sternly. "You just put that gun away! No need for no fool nonsense like that here!"

"What are these people doing here, Gram?" William demanded ignoring her admonition.

"Why they'se invited to Thanksgiving dinner, child … what's wrong with you? What happened to your manners?"

I was surprised by the way Ruby's speech had slipped back to the way folks had talked back when she was a kid. Next thing I knew she'd be saying things like, "Ya sir, Massa. What ch'all want?"

William looked a little surprised too. "What's got into you Gram? Why you inviting white folks to dinner? Ain't like they ever done one damn nice thing for you."

"White folks never did me no harm child." Ruby protested.

"Didn't they? What about that white bitch that got Grandpa killed?"

Ruby's jaw dropped in amazement. "W-what do you know about that?" she demanded. "That was long before you were born!"

William laughed coldly. "I know all about it Gram," he said. "Uncle Ray told me the whole story about Grandpa getting' killed cause he fucked some white bitch pilot—"

Ruby's eyes were suddenly spitting fire. "You just watch your mouth William! What happened to your grandfather all those years ago ain't got nothin' to do with you!"

"Don't it? I don't exactly see it that way Gram. My daddy wouldn'ta gone off and got himself hung if it hadn'ta been for what happened to Grandpa. And you can't tell me that ain't the truth of it."

"That ain't got nothing to do with this," Ruby insisted.

"Your Grandmother's right," I joined the fray. "What happened back then doesn't have much to do with what's happening now."

"I thought I told you to shut up." Willie said, swinging the gun back toward me. "I don't know what gives you the right to say anything any way. Aren't you the one that goes around shooting arrows at people? I kind of thought so, cause I sure'nuff have your bow and arrows."

"That doesn't have anything to do with this either," I said, standing my ground, but watching a puzzling cloud pass over Julie and Jamal's demeanor.

"I told you to shut up!" William declared emphatically, raising the gun and firing a quick shot over my head.

Several of the girls let out a scream, but I was never sure which ones. Maybe it was even Jamal. It didn't matter. We were all startled. What did matter was that the question of what William was willing to do … how far he was willing to go, was no longer up in the air. I also noted that the shot was actually not very loud, which meant the pistol was a small caliber one.

Exactly where that information got us, I wasn't sure—except if you were shot with a small caliber your chances of surviving were better. I wasn't feeling real anxious to test that theory, however.

"William!" Ruby all but screamed, coming to her feet. "You just give me that damned gun!"

"Sit down, Gram!" William ordered coldly, leveling the pistol at her. "I don't want to shot you … but I will if I have to."

"Well, this is ridiculous," I muttered, suddenly deciding to try a different tact. "We came here for some Thanksgiving dinner and here we are sitting around chewing the fat."

It was, of course, a ridiculous statement. But I had every intention of backing it up with action. I grabbed the nearest bowl and began slopping mashed potatoes on my plate. Ruby was sitting at the head of the table, on my right. I passed the potato bowl to her and said. "Mighty fine looking dinner, Mrs. McPherson."

Ruby hesitated just a second, then took the bowl and began serving herself. "Thank you, dear," she said, flashing me a tiny, but devilish smile. "I'm glad to hear you like it. Lynn, honey," she continued without hesitation. "Why don't you start those yams around?"

All at once dinner was under way, everybody passing food and digging in, even making small talk—as if William wasn't even there.

"Are you God damned people crazy?" William yelled, waving the gun around some more. "What do you think this is … some damned pea-shooter?"

Ignoring his question, I leaned back in my chair and rested my closed fists on either side of my plate, the fork in my right hand sticking straight up toward the ceiling. "We known you're there waving a gun around, Willie ... but frankly, your grandmother went to a lot of trouble and I hate to see this meal go to waste, you know—"

William looked like he was about to pop a cork.

"Maybe you'd like to join us?" I knew I was skating on pretty thin ice. "Maybe you could get Willie a plate, Mrs. McPherson?"

I wasn't sure where I was going with this, but I was pretty sure Willie wasn't going to trust anyone leaving the room but his grandmother. I had no idea what Ruby would do if she was allowed to go to the kitchen. What I did know was that Ruby knew that she hadn't prepared the meal ... that I was grabbing at straws to find a way out of our dilemma.

"He can get a plate his own self," Ruby said stubbornly, to my surprise. "He knows where they're at."

"Sure," I murmured, scowling softly at Ruby to let her know she'd let me down. Before I could say anything else, Willie went into the kitchen and returned in just a few seconds with a plate and silverware.

"Let me get you a chair, William," Lynn said, getting to her feet without waiting for permission. "Here, Jamal," she ordered. "You can move around by Julie. You wanted to sit by her anyway, didn't you."

Bless your little heart, I thought, bursting with pride at Lynn's courage. I'd have to get her a cape so she could take her rightful place with that weird '*Superman*' guy back on the street corner in St. Cloud.

Everyone quickly shifted and the extra chair in the corner

of the room was brought up to the table. That put William at the other end of the table opposite his grandmother, and since he was the one with the gun, that was now the head of the table. We started passing food around and patiently waited while Willie served himself with his left hand so he wouldn't have to lay his gun down.

I was beginning to understand why Ruby had refused to get William a plate. If we made it too easy for him, he would not bother to eat regardless of how tempting the food was. Ruby apparently knew her grandson pretty well. By refusing to get him a plate she had counted on him being stubborn enough to insist on eating—even though it meant using his left hand. The situation reminded me of some old TV show where the spy said "Very clever!" with a strong German accent.

I was now beginning to think the best thing to do was just let the meal go on as if nothing unusual was happening. Given enough time, Willie might relax his guard and we could jump him. The only problem with that was that the jumper would have to be some one close to him. Unfortunately, Jamal and Andrea were the closest to him. Jamal was on the opposite side of the table—good enough for eye contact, but any kind of signal beyond that would be tricky.

In the interim, I decided to try drawing Willie out with a few innocent questions. "You still driving that same van, Willie?" I asked.

The question got completely ignored.

"You must be ambidextrous?" I noted, trying to make it sound like ambidexterity was a good thing.

"William was always good with his hands," Ruby chimed in. "Isn't that right William?"

That question also got ignored, leaving me with a sincere wish that William would be one of those people with a CRT screen on his forehead.

"Might be easier to eat if you'd lay the gun down." I suggested. "I don't think there's any danger of Andrea making a grab for it … is there, Andy?"

"No way," Andrea replied nervously. "Guns scare me."

Willie paid no attention to either of us. He continued eating with his left hand and holding the pistol at the ready with his right hand.

I began envisioning the outcome of different scenarios that were running through my head—some dangerous, some fanciful. "How about an after dinner nap, Willie?" Or: "How about brandy and cigars?" Those were the fanciful ones. The others, the dangerous ones, all ended the same way. One of us jumped Willie and got shot.

"You know, Willie," I said finally. "The penalty for attempted rape might not be all that severe—"

Willie suddenly slammed the butt of the pistol down on the table. "I thought I told you to shut up, Mister! Where the hell do you get off calling me Willie anyway? Is that some damned racial thing where you think you're better than me?"

"Sorry," I muttered. "I didn't mean anything—"

Although I had seen William several times before this was the first time I got a really good look at him. Aside from being relatively short and stocky, he wasn't that bad looking except that the way he had his hair cut made him look like someone had tried to squash his head down with a nutcracker. His head was wider at the ears than it was from top to bottom

"Well, for your information, Mister," he snarled. " I

know what happens to child molesters when they get put in jail. You think I'm about to volunteer for that? If you do, you must think I'm crazy!"

I had to choke back the urge to keep from say, "Well, yeah."

"Besides, there's Sheniqqua—"

Ruby suddenly gasped and brought her hand up to cover her mouth. "Oh, no, William … don't tell me—"

I knew immediately what she meant.

"Was that the young student you were telling us about, Ruby?" I asked.

Ruby nodded.

William studied us both for a moment, then nodded his head, apparently satisfied that Ruby and I were far more in cahoots than we'd previously let on. He laid down his fork and just sat there.

"If you really want to know … that thing with Sheniqqua was an accident, " He said to no one in particular. "She just kept coming around. And then when I tried to do stuff … she got all scared. It was an accident, Grandma … I swear to God!"

"Oh, William—" Ruby sighed.

"Don't look at me that way!" Willie exclaimed, angrily glaring at his grandmother. "It's not like I did anything different than you did with that Ray Galston—"

If Ruby looked deflated before, her demeanor did a sudden about face. "What do you know about Ray Galston?" she snapped angrily.

Willie let out a low, sinister laugh. "Everything, Gram … everything."

"Oh, my Lord no—" Ruby gasped.

William's Story

Chapter 28

When William went running up the street with a five-dollar bill clutched in his hot little hand in search of ice cream he made the mistake of not putting the bill in his pocket. His arch neighborhood nemesis *Butt-head Hadin* (they called him butt-head because it was the major tactic he used in fighting) was on a similar mission. Butt-head was older, bigger, and meaner than William and considered anything that William possessed to be fair game in his little "I rule the Capitol Heights neighborhood" war.

By the time William recovered from the blind-sided head butt that sent him sprawling into the gutter, Butt-head had already relieved him of the five-dollar bill and was standing gloating over him.

"Thanks, fool!" Butt-head said, making sure to rub salt in his wound.

William had already learned long ago that it did no good to scream and carry on any time Butt-head victimized him. Butt-head had been calling him "Fool" ever since he'd started school and word got out that his birthday was the first of April. There was nothing to do but suck it up and go home. If Ray expected change from the five, he'd have to get it from Butt-head—although William was planning to lie and say the wind blew the money away.

To make the lie convincing, William didn't bother to do anything about the silent tears streaming down his face as he opened the front door.

That was unfortunate.

At first William was too stunned to fathom what was happening before his young eyes. His first reaction was that his Gram and Ray had decided it would be fun to wrestle while he was gone. Then he realized their wrestling had a ferocity that reminded him of dogs he'd seen fighting. *This was serious stuff!*

Just when he decided that Ray was trying to hurt his Gram and that he should jump on Ray's back, Gram suddenly stopped fighting and let Ray kiss her on the lips. It was something he had seen on TV a few times, so he decided, *Oh … no big deal!* But then Gram said something to Ray and they immediately got up and went into Gram's bedroom.

That seemed kind of mysterious and William was surprised that they hadn't seen him and asked about his lack of ice cream and his tears and why was he back so soon. Almost in a trance, he followed along as far as the bedroom door, which he half expected them to close, but they didn't. Clothes were flying every which way. It wasn't until he saw Ray's rampant *thingee* that he realized they were actually going to be *doing it!*

It being that mysterious thing Butt-head and some of the other boys talked about.

Up until that point William hadn't had the vaguest notion of what *doing it* really meant even though he'd heard lots of kids laugh about it in school. From what William could see, it wasn't exactly a laughing matter. Ray's *thingee* seemed as big as a baseball bat and the way he was shoving it in his Gram didn't seem real. There was no way his little pee-pee could ever get as big as Ray's. *And why wasn't Ray hurting Gram?*

Or, maybe he was?

William was disappointed the next day when Ray did not show up for their usual afternoon session of catch football. He was also very surprised when some greasy real estate guy showed up instead and pounded a *For Sale* sign into the front lawn and Gram's friend Sadie materialized with a camera to take pictures.

The way Sadie was carrying on with the real estate guy William wouldn't have been surprised to see them '*doing it*' on the front lawn. He didn't really care for Sadie because she was forever hugging his head in between her big tits, then laughing at his embarrassment.

He thought Sadie smelled bad too.

The "*For Sale*" sign stayed in their front yard for over a year. During that year William was puzzled about why Ray didn't come around any more, but he knew not to ask. He also knew it had something to do with Ray and Gram '*doing it*' and that it was some how bad. Just before the sign came down William overheard Gram and Sadie talking about Ray for what was to be the last time.

"You should have married that Ray," Sadie told Gram the day she announced she was going to marry Hugo Mintendorf and that most likely Gram was going to need a new real estate agent.

"Why would I want to do that?" Gram scoffed.

"Why?" Sadie was fit to be tied. "Ta get yo thiiing on, girl!" she snorted. "I know you ain't dead yet. Fact is … I know why that man stopped comin' around."

"What are you talking about?"

Sadie laughed sadistically. "What'm I talking about? You … that's what! You think I don't know, but I know what happened with you and that man—and you can't tell me no different. I know you heard that ole sayin' *Why a man gonna buy the cow when the milk is free?*"

That was about as angry as William had ever seen his grandmother.

"Why don't you just mind your own business, Sadie?" Gram had snapped.

"Okay," Sadie said glibly. "But I bet you ain't heard … cause I know you ain't done no askin'—but that Ray Galston done gone'n got hisself hitched again."

After that, there was no reason to move.

Ruby and Sadie went back to being friends. Ruby even stood up for Sadie in the civil ceremony she and Hugo had at the courthouse—which seemed appropriate. After that Ruby and William climbed back on life's bobsled and hung on.

Chapter 29

In the summer of 1982 their bobsled hit a tree. William was through high school, still living at home, and a sophomore at Alabama State University. He had a job at a fast food place but since Ray Galston had not been around to help him with the sports thing, there was no scholarship. Any question of an academic scholarship was out the window because his grades were barely good enough to get him into college in the first place.

School was not exactly William's thing. First of all because Butt-head Hadin made a career out of torturing him. Then later when the schools became desegregated he felt like he didn't fit in. Physical education class was another torture. There was no way he'd ever go out for any sport because he hated being naked in the locker room. By the time he reached puberty the die had pretty much been cast.

He was a full-fledged loner and satisfied to make do with that.

All that might have changed as William got older if Ruby hadn't started teaching summer school classes for extra money to help him with the college expenses. Even that might not have mattered if one of her students, a cute thirteen year old named Sheniqqua, hadn't come by the house one day and gotten a look at William.

Ruby did not teach classes at home, but had told the

girl she could come by to pick up a book. Sheniqqua was small for her age, barely five foot, with long black hair that she kept in a ponytail. She was quite slim with a small round face and tiny breasts, almost as if she hadn't reached puberty yet. Her mental state was far more advanced.

Sheniqqua was boy crazy—and she thought William was a dreamboat. "Do you have a girlfriend?" She asked the first day she managed to get William alone.

He simply shook his head, staring at the loose button at the top of the white blouse she was wearing. She was obviously not wearing a bra. Since he was taller than she was he could clearly see the beginning slope of her tiny breasts and he was intrigued. Most of the time he felt threatened by girls his own age—particularly those with larger breasts. Sheniqqua was different. She was being friendly, but because of their obvious age difference she was not threatening.

"I'm surprised," Sheniqque continued. "You're too cute not to have a girl friend."

William didn't know what to say. No girl had ever called him cute before.

There was something about making a guy blush that sets girls off like a dog after a bone. Once you get a reaction like that, you gotta go after the juggler—or in William's case, his warm full lips.

"I bet you'd like to kiss me," Sheniqqua said boldly.

"What makes you think that?"

She giggled. "I can see the way you're looking at me fool."

Now calling him a fool was not exactly the smartest thing Sheniqqua could have done because it reminded him of Butt-head Hadin's terrorism and for a moment

Scharlie R. Martin

his anger almost got the best of him. But then, he really did want to try and kiss her. He managed to get a grip on his anger and then started to wonder where the hell his Gram was. She was almost always home by this time of day, and if she had told this twerp to come over to pick up a certain book, then why wasn't she here? He really didn't want to start any thing and have Gram come busting in on him.

"You're crazy," he told the girl. "Why would I want to kiss you. You're just a little baby."

Now if she had made a mistake in calling him a 'fool,' he made an even bigger one in calling her 'little baby.'

"No way!" she declared angrily.

The argument could have taken a childish 'are too' ... 'no way' spin, but for reasons that William didn't fully understand it didn't. "How can you tell I want to kiss you?" he asked in a shaky voice.

"Just because ... I can see by the way you're looking at me."

"So?"

"So ... you want to kiss me. I know you do."

Suddenly kissing her didn't seem like such a scary idea.

"What if I did?" he asked.

"So do it!" she exclaimed, shutting her eyes and offering up her lips.

If she hadn't shut her eyes, he might not have ventured to do it. But since she did, he saw no reason not to proceed. He put his hands on her shoulders and touched his lips gently against hers. To his surprise, her lips parted and he suddenly felt her tiny tongue probing through his lips. He was also aware that she had put her arms around his waist.

At first, he resisted. But then his tongue began to do some probing of its own. She opened her mouth wider and let his tongue slide in deeper. Suddenly his mind was swimming in the warm sensations of his first boy/girl kiss. Almost of its own volition his right hand slid from her shoulder down across her chest to the open button and beyond.

For just a second, there was no response.

Then Sheniqqua quickly pulled away. "Don't," she cried, clutching at her blouse with one hand. She looked scared.

But now it was William playing the role of *dog after a bone*. After all, she'd started it—and he just wanted to feel what it was like to have his hand on her breast.

What happened next was unbelievable, even for William. The more Sheniqqua fought his advances, the harder he tried to get his hand on her breast—which should have been easy because he was much bigger than she was and much stronger. But she was very wiry and squirmy. And, although it was crazy, the more she squirmed, the more he wanted to captivate her in the exact same way Ray Galston had captivated his Gram.

"See," he said suddenly. "I knew you were just a little baby."

"Am not," she declared.

"Then why don't you let me look at your tits."

It was the first time in his life that he'd ever said the word 'tits' and the way it rolled off his tongue had an immediate reaction on the growing bulge in his trousers. To his surprise Sheniqqua didn't get angry.

"I'll let you look at me if you'll let me look at your *thingee* first," she said boldly.

William felt his face and eyes burning as if someone had thrown hot acid at him.

"I bet you think I won't," he laughed nervously.

The air was suddenly stifling. "So show me," Sheniqqua challenged.

"Okay," William heard his distant voice say. He wasn't about to let this snip of a girl get the better of him. At that point, he really should have taken her into his bedroom but he was too excited to think about that. Not daring to look at her, he unzipped his jeans and fumbled around trying to separate his burgeoning erection from the stubborn folds of cloth. He had all but forgotten Sheniqqua was in the room by the time he got himself unfurled.

That's when the really bad stuff started happening.

He had never actually handled an erection before. Oh, he'd had wet dreams, but the erection was gone by the time he woke up. His first reaction was that there must be some mistake. He couldn't be sure, but it seemed like he was actually larger than Ray Galston had been. His second reaction was to notice that Sheniqqua's eyes were bigger than her breasts and she was snickering.

"Why are you laughing you dumb jerk?" he demanded.

"Cause you look funny," she snickered. "Your *thingee* looks like a boomerang."

"I'll boomerang you!" he declared angrily, making an embarrassed lunge for her.

She let out a little shriek and tried to jump past him, but he was too quick. He grabbed her by the shoulders and shoved her back against the wall. Now, he was more determined than ever that he was going to see her breasts. Holding her flat against the wall he shoved his right hand between their bodies and grabbed a handful of blouse. She wasn't about to give him what he wanted without a fight.

When Sheniqqua finally broke away William had a firm grip on the button side of her blouse. The buttons gave way suddenly and she stumbled backwards, causing more pressure on the blouse material than it was capable of standing. William was suddenly left holding a ripped piece of blouse as Sheniqqua crashed against the doorframe.

For a long minute William stood staring at the unconscious girl, his mind racing wildly. Then he did something that he couldn't believe he was doing even as he did it. He bent down and scooped up Sheniqqua and carried her to his room. Having learned at least one lesson from his grandmother, he closed the door before proceeding.

Chapter 30

Looking at the unconscious girl on his bed was like looking through a double-barreled kaleidoscope. William's eyes felt like onions that someone had peeled away the outer layers of flesh, leaving freshly moist stunned orbs. The strangeness of this feeling lifted him past those normal barriers of propriety that had left him a virgin at twenty when two-thirds of the guys he'd been in high school with were either already married, engaged and doing it, or had knocked someone up and moved on. He felt like a monk in a whorehouse with a *carte blanche* ticket.

Sheniqqua's white blouse was missing a triangle-shaped piece where the material had torn away but was still partly buttoned. His fingers felt like fat grubs as he bumbled with the tiny, flat white buttons. He managed to work two out of the three buttons without giving in to his rage, but the third succumbed to a yank and went spinning through the air like a tiny coin-toss coin.

William felt guilty about the blouse, but also felt the transgression was worth the risk. Sheniqqua's nipples were like two tiny cherries atop a double mocha chocolate sunday. Her skin was even lighter in color than his skin and he suspected that at least one of her parents had to be either Hispanic or Indian or something like that. If looking at her small breast made his erection feel like a stick of stove wood, the small rise around the inward slope ringing her '*innie*' belly button made it feel like a cannon.

Just looking at her on the bed like that was driving him crazy and she was still half-clothed. He stood to one side of the bed with his left hand absently on his erection and reached out and ran the black grubs of his right hand over the black slope of her crotch. She was wearing black pedal pushers and white tennis shoes. He gave no thought whatever to the tennis shoes but the pedal pushers had to go—only he didn't know how girl's clothes worked. He looked first on the left side of the waistband and then on the right where he discovered a strap held in place with two buttons.

Consequences no longer mattered and the black grubs were hungry for action. He shoved one grub into the slight loop formed at the top of the zipper that lurked there and gave another yank, sending one flat black button into the coin-toss realm. Another yank sent the remaining button spinning through space and the strap was free. That left only the cantankerous zipper.

The only thing was, Sheniqqua was beginning to moan and make soft grunting noises. William was very familiar with zippers, having worn blue jeans for most of his life—but the little pull thingee on the zippers on girl's black pedal pushers was definitely not designed for easy operation by the thick black grubs of bumbling boys. Instead of being substantially flat and brassy, the thingee was a tiny skinny black oval that had to be held at just the right angle while pulling the zipper taut before it would operate the slide. It was a near impossible task for black grubs under the influence of raging hormones.

William tried another yank but that brought a loud

moan from Sheniqqua and he knew that wasn't going to work. He thought briefly of just giving up, but that meant enduring all of the penalties of transgression without any of the perks. Tears of frustration squeaked out of the corners of his eyes and he found he was sweating profusely. He wiped angrily at the tears with his black grubs and then directed them to get control and make the damned zipper work.

His triumph was doubly rewarding in that when the zipper finally surrendered to his demands and he could pull the black pedal pushers down, Sheniqqua's white panties went with them. He pulled the cargo load below her knees and shoved her knees as far apart as he could get them without actually removing her pedal pushers and the impeding tennis shoes. There was no way he'd ever get the pedal pushers off over her tennis shoes and he wasn't about to waste time trying.

Especially not after he finally looked at the treasure his transgressions had revealed. He felt like he was waiting for a bomb to explode. Sheniqqua was beginning to stir as if she might be regaining consciousness and he could not permit that to happen without achieving his goal. Consequences no longer mattered.

He put his left knee on the bed beside her right knee and lowered himself over her motionless body. She was starting to moan louder now, so he put his left hand over her nose and mouth and then reached down with his right hand to try and find the center of his target. He had, of course, never had his hands on a girl's privates before and the sensations that he should have been treasuring were pushed aside in the urgency he felt to achieve his goal. When the black grubs finally found the tiny slit beneath the crown of black curly hair he was at first overwhelmed by a sense that there had to be something wrong. Men and women fit together in that way—Gram and Ray had proven that. He had seen it with his own eyes! But still it didn't seem like it could work.

And he was right!

Try as he might, he could not get even the tip of his erection started into the target area and Sheniqqua was beginning to squirm around and try to buck against him. The way he was lying on top of her holding her nose and mouth with his left hand meant her right arm was pinned beneath him. As she came around, the only thing she could do was flail away at his back with her left arm and try to twist her head from side to side to free her nose and mouth.

Since William weighed half again Sheniqqua's barely 100 pounds he felt he could hold her while he searched again for the target area and proceeded to force an insertion. The one thing he couldn't understand was the way non-lubricated skin stuck together and how was he supposed to do anything about it with only one hand—

"Hhhrggg!" he screamed suddenly, giving in to his rage.

Sheniqqua never had a chance.

Like a child that had thrown itself on the floor in the midst of a tantrum William flailed away at the unfortunate teen. To Sheniqqua's credit she managed to free herself enough to almost get free. If she hadn't been hobbled by her black pedal pushers she might have been able to kick William off her. Unfortunately, her near freedom led directly to her demise. As she pushed herself away from him in a crab-like fashion, she was working herself closer and closer to the head of the bed and freedom. Unfortunately, one of William's flailing blows snapped her head back against the headboard, stunning her enough to take the fight out of her momentarily, but not enough to render her unconscious again.

It was then that the black rage of frustration took over. William grabbed the limp girl around the throat with both hand and squeezed his eyes tight shut as his black grubs dug mindlessly into her flesh. It was only then that he experienced his first sexual climax outside of a *'wet dream.'*

Talk about bitter sweet! The lubrication that he had been so in desperate need of only moments before was abundantly plentiful in the gobs and gobs of milk-white slime covering almost everything. The only problem was that his once rampant erection vanished more quickly than Halley's Comet flashing across the sky.

His rampant erection and the feelings that went with it were replaced by extreme sensitivity to touch and a burgeoning remorse. While he busied himself trying to clean up the mess and gird himself for the impending doom of his crime, tears flowed freely down his face. The tears were damned maddening. *What was he, some God damned baby?*

The answer to that question came as a shock.

It wasn't until he was wiping his semen from Sheniqqua's naked stomach that he realized her inert form was a bit more than just unconscious. He didn't know thing one about how to determine if someone was dead or not, but that's when he realized that her eyes were still open. He didn't think that was a good sign. Nor was it a good sign that he could find no evidence of a pulse, even though he had only the faintest of ideas how to go about taking a pulse. Nor was it a good sign that he could see no telltale signs of chest movement beneath her tiny mocha breasts.

Amazingly, the burgeoning remorse that was about to engulf William suddenly took flight on the wings of hope that he wasn't going to get caught.

But he would definitely have to hurry—

Chapter 31

William did not know when his grandmother would be home. She could be at a meeting at school or simply have gone shopping—which meant that he had to get Sheniqqua out of the house first. He pulled the Chevy up to the spot where Gram normally parked. Then he wrapped Sheniqqua in the bedding from his bed and carried her out and shoved her between the front seat and the back. Before going back into the house to pack he took a minute to fluff the top of the bedding in such a way that made it look like it was just tossed on the floor of the car to make room on the seat for boxes or whatever.

He didn't bother to pack a lot of stuff—just enough to make the note that he wrote to Gram convincing. The note read:

Dear Gram:

Went to Atlanta for a few days to check out transferring up there to go to school. I wanted to stay and talk to you about it, but I wasn't sure when you'd be home and I wanted to get there before dark. Oh, yeah, I took the bedding off my bed in case I wind up sleeping in the car a night or two.

Love
William

He did not tell his Gram that he took all of his money out of his bank account, nearly a thousand dollars. Nor did he tell her that he wasn't planning to come back for a long, long time—if ever. He also made no mention of Sheniqqua.

...

At first, he just drove without any idea of where he might be going. He made a left turn onto Federal Drive because he knew it went past Maxwell Air Force Base. His reason for that decision was kind of murky and didn't matter because he didn't stop there. Federal Drive gave way to U S 231 and he was headed toward Wetumpka—but that area was far too populated to even consider dumping a body.

Actually, if he had seriously been heading toward Atlanta it would have made far more sense to take Interstate 65 out of Montgomery.

For awhile he just drove north toward the Talladega National Forest. If he waited until it got dark he could just carry Sheniqqua out into the woods and leave her. But there were a couple of problems with that plan. First of all, could a person walk in the woods at night carrying a body without falling over something and breaking your neck. Secondly, if you just dumped a body in the woods without covering it somebody might find it in a day or two, then where would you be?

It wasn't until William saw the sign for Gantts Quarry near Sylacauga that an actual plan sprang fully formed into his head. He remembered from his high school Alabama history that Alabama was a major coal producing state and there had been a lot of talk on the news lately about safety hazards posed by abandoned mines and the state was working to close them up. He also remembered that one of the areas of coal mining was a narrow finger along the Coosa River north and east of Birmingham.

He stopped at a gas station and bought an Alabama map to confirm what he had been thinking. It seemed he was right. Instead of staying on U S 231 he took Highway 21 and headed toward Talladega, where he turned off on smaller roads but continued to head north towards Gadsden. Sooner or later as he got closer to the Coosa River he would find what he was looking for.

It took the better part of the next morning driving around in the Coosa River area south of Gadsden before he found what he considered to be the perfect spot. The thing that made it perfect was the ongoing dirt moving with heavy-duty construction equipment. He went to a hardware store and bought a flashlight and shovel, telling the clerk he was fixin' to dig some night crawlers for fishing.

He returned to the construction site later in the afternoon while the dirt moving was still on going so he could pick out the best spot to bury Sheniqqua. The flashlight would be a risk but he had to make sure no part of her body would be visible when the cat skinners returned to work the next day. Which also meant he'd have to return to the site early in the morning to make sure that no wild dogs or other animals had uncovered any part of her body during the night before the bulldozers could finish his burial task.

As William sat in his car a second straight night waiting for darkness to pull her eyelids over the intended burial site he let his mind wander back over his memories of the slip of a girl scrunched up on the floor of the car behind his seat. To his surprise, he actually felt his penis swelling at the memory of their struggle. Almost against his will, he felt himself giving in to the idea of taking another stab at accomplishing the penetration he hadn't been able to achieve back in Montgomery. Sheniqqua certainly wouldn't be fighting back this time.

The only problem was that when he tried to lift her up to position her on the seat, he discovered rigor mortis had set in and her flesh was cold and clammy. And the flash of Halley's Comet made a sudden unexpected return visit far sooner than the expected 74 years.

Another stroke of luck was that the moon did not come up immediately. By walking very slowly he was able to get to the exact spot he'd picked out in the complete cover of total darkness. He could tell he had arrived at the right spot when his next step sent him pitching forward on his face because of the sixty-degree rise of the soil in front of him. For reasons William didn't understand, tears were streaming down his face and when he righted himself and wiped at them his face became streaked with dirt and mud.

Just as he was about to start digging the crown of the full moon popped above the horizon and in just seconds the site was illuminated enough to accomplish the burial without the aid of the flashlight. His plan was simple. He would dig a notch at the base of the built up soil, throwing the dirt on the bank above. When he got a big enough space shoveled out, he would place her body against the backside of the notch and roll the dirt down over her. He was sure the workmen would never notice any slight increase in the soil volume created by the addition of her body. By the end of the next day, her body would be buried so deep it would never be found.

The most difficult moment with the burial came when William attempted to remove Sheniqqua's body from the bedding. Rigor mortis did not want to release its stubborn grip. His first thought was to just leave her in the bedding—but that would be traceable evidence should she ever be accidentally found. By using a little extra force he was finally able to free her and shove her into place.

The only other nerve racking moment came the next morning when after watching the bulldozers make him smarter than he deserved to be, he drove to the river and found a secluded spot to toss the shovel. To his great surprise the shovel did not sink completely beneath the surface as he had expected, but rather sank until only the tip of the handle was showing and that went bobbing along in the stream's muddy current like a bland, telltale fishing bobber.

Who gives a shit, he told himself, dismissing the shovel from his mind as he walked back towards his car.

. . .

The drive to Atlanta was almost an accident. The euphoria William felt after he'd tossed the shovel kept his mind afloat like a hot-air balloon as he wended his way cross country toward Anniston, Alabama. When he saw the sign for Interstate 20 he suddenly realized that he had to be some place—that he couldn't just wander around forever. He sure as hell wasn't ready to go back to Montgomery and face Gram. And since he was already headed toward Atlanta it suddenly made perfect sense to at least live up to part of the content of his note to Gram.

Once he got to Atlanta he could mail her a letter claiming he had decided to transfer there to finish his education and she'd probably never be the wiser. Transferring to Atlanta to finish his education, however, seemed more like an impending nightmare than fulfillment of any dream. Besides, it wasn't his dream anyway and he'd already had about all the education he could stand.

Chapter 32

At first Atlanta was overwhelming—which made no sense because William had grown up in the city of Montgomery and wasn't one city pretty much the same as another. The difference, of course, was that he'd spent his growing up years learning little things about Montgomery as time went on. His initial experience with Atlanta was like opening the first page of a huge textbook. He had no idea what was on the next page ... what was around the next corner.

William spent his first night in Atlanta in his car again because he afraid to ask what a motel room would cost. His money wouldn't last very long if he spent it on motels without any new money coming in. Which meant finding a job and that meant having an address to put on a job application.

The next day William discovered he hadn't gotten very far into Atlanta, which was okay. *What would a twenty-year-old black man do in downtown Atlanta?* After driving around a bit without straying too far from Interstate 20 he discovered an area with three colleges: Clark Atlanta, Morehouse, and Spelman—just what he was looking for. He drove around until he spotted a "Room For Rent" sign on a house near an old Army fort named Fort McPherson that caught his eye. That had to be a sign.

The room wasn't much. It was on the third floor of a

house that didn't originally have a third floor. The owner had finished off the attic many years before to rent to college students. The room was barely big enough for the single bed and a small table. It had one window and two doors—one to get in and out, and one for the small closet. There were no kitchen facilities other than a small, ancient refrigerator and the bathroom was down on the second floor. It wasn't much, but it was cheap.

Finding a job turned out to be a lot easier than William had expected. He spotted a Taco Bell nearby and simply asked if they were looking for help. The clerk shrugged and yelled at someone in the back.

"Yes," a taller black man said, coming to the counter.

"I—I was wondering if you need any help?" William stammered.

Instead of giving William an application, the man said, "When could you start?"

William shrugged.

The man never said a word but disappeared into the back for a few seconds. When he returned he threw a cap and apron at William and said, "How about now?"

William shrugged again.

"We need to get your vitals," the man said later that evening.

"W—what?" William stammered again.

The manager stared at him for a moment. "Your vitals … you know—name, address, social security number … stuff like that."

"Oh," William felt like an idiot but was relieved to know what "vitals" meant.

"I'll give you a *job ap* to take home … you can fill it

out tonight and bring it back in the morning. I'll keep you on dayshift until I see how well you handle yourself."

William was put on the nightshift the very next week with a new boss, a nightshift manager named Doug.

After settling in to his job, William wrote Gram and told her about his luck with Taco Bell in Atlanta and that he would be starting the fall semester at nearby Spelman College. He also asked her if they had any relatives that had anything to do with a Fort McPherson, and promised he would come back home for a visit as soon as he could.

Being on his own was more of a challenge than William thought. He no longer had Gram to take care of things like keeping his car insurance up-to-date, maintaining a bank account, and taking car of his car. That was the only thing he liked about the nightshift, it gave him time to take care of those kinds of chores and to do his laundry. Nightshift did put a damper on having any kind of social life—especially when you worked weekends.

His life began to take on a very predictable pattern: be to work by 4:00 p. m., go to bed by 4:00 a. m. He maintained the same schedule on his nights off because any change to his schedule on those nights seemed to screw him up something awful. And his schedule left next to no opportunity for meeting girls.

There were plenty of girls coming to the Taco Bell but they were either already on a date or with a bunch of other girls. Either way, that left him no opportunity. And to be perfectly frank, after what had happened with Sheniqqua, asking any girl for a date was not going to happen except under very special circumstances.

In the meantime, William started driving to different

neighborhoods where he could buy men's magazines like *Playboy* and *Hustler*. Now that he was no longer under Gram's watchful eye he felt free to explore his own sexuality. At first he carried his *Hustler Magazine* downstairs to the bathroom to masturbate. But after his first encounter with another tenant while carrying the magazine he gave that up in favor of pulling his window shade and doing it in his room. After he discovered the college girls in the rooming house next door loved to party he didn't even need the magazine. He would sit for hours with one hand holding the drawn window shade a few inches away from the window frame and the other hand holding his erect penis while peering down at the unsuspecting girls.

Of course, that only worked on William's nights off. And since his nights off were during the week, the girls didn't have as many parties as he would have liked. In the end, he finally got up enough nerve to go to an X rated movie theatre in one of the seedier parts of town. The movie experience confirmed what he already suspected—that his penis was seriously malformed. It was much thicker at the base than any of the men he'd seen in so-called adult movies, with a serious bend in the middle that did indeed make it look like a boomerang from the side. On top of that, he had never been circumcised and the way the foreskin came together at the end made it look pointed. In short, he was a freak.

This conclusion had an unexpected impact on his life. Instead of going out and trying to find a girl capable of dealing with his abnormality, such as a fat whore, William found himself gravitating toward cruising playgrounds. For months he did nothing more than cruise and look.

Eventually, however, he grew bored with the activity and started picking potential partners out of the throng of youngsters to follow.

At first he followed a different girl each time, massaging his penis through his blue jeans as he watched the unsuspecting girl from a distance. When the girl got a block or so away he would drive up behind her and stop and watch her walk away. He repeated the sequence over and over again, leapfrogging down the street for as long as it took him to achieve a climax.

The only problem with this scenario was that it was messy.

For awhile William chastised himself for being chicken, for being afraid to unzip his pants and pull out his penis in the open car. Then he began to fantasize about what it would be like to actually have nerve enough to pick up one of these girls. Before long, he was following the same girl over and over again—stalking, actually.

Several times he actually went so far as to stop the girl and ask her some stupid question about how to get to some fictional business place. Of course, they never knew what he was talking about and he would use that opportunity to try and turn their lack of knowledge into conversation. The ploy never worked because he would chicken out before he was able to capitalize on the situation. And, of course, after that he would have to find a new prospect to keep the different girls from suspecting they were being stalked.

Fortunately for these girls, William had his memory of Sheniqqua to hold him back. She'd been gone now nearly two years. Long enough for William to convince himself that he was not a bad person and that her death had been mostly an accident. After all, it wasn't like he'd deliberately gone out to find a girl to rape and murder. If she'd just left him alone in the first place—

William's sexual activities might have stayed at that same level forever if Doug hadn't hired a new girl named Tracy. Tracy was eighteen but looked every bit of twelve—and she was interested in William. She was also a student at Spelman College. For some reason, it seemed to bug Tracy that William was such a loner.

"What chew hidin' from Willie boy," Tracy challenged, "Life?"

William wasn't sure whether to be angry at the question or delighted that another human being had taken a moment to include him in their momentary reality.

"What's it to you pip-squeak?" he challenged right back.

Tracy grinned broadly. She was just barely five feet tall and tipped the scale at a whopping 98 pounds. Her face was narrow and crowned by thin, black curly hair—what William called a helmet cut because it made her look like she was wearing a helmet. Her skin was more tan than brown or black.

"Just wondering," She said finally.

That was the end of their conversation that day, but the beginning of a tit-for-tat daily exchange that went on for weeks before William finally blurted, "Can I give you a ride home tonight, Tracy?"

To his surprise, she accepted.

To his further surprise, she was in more of a rush than he was. The first night they kissed a couple of times. The second night the kissing lasted for a good half an hour.

On the third night even longer and it was becoming obvious that Tracy was getting frustrated. On the fifth night she took William's hand and placed it on one of her small breasts. He basically copped a feel and told her that he had to get home because he had laundry to take care of.

The next week she was distant.

"You mad at me, Tracy?" he asked.

"No ... I thought you might be mad at me."

"Why would I be mad at you?" William was puzzled.

"Well, you act like it ... like you can barely stand to touch me. You're not a queer are you?"

At first William didn't know what she meant. "W-what ... Oh, you mean do I like guys? God no! It's just that—"

Tracy stared at him for a moment, then grabbed him by the arm and raised up on her tiptoes to whisper huskily into his ear. "You tryin' to tell me you're a virgin?"

"What if I am?" he blustered.

Tracy got a big twinkle in her eyes. "We'll just have to see what we can do about that later," she grinned, going back to her workstation.

Needless to say, William flubbed up with food orders about a dozen times before he and Tracy got out of there that night. But that was only the foreshadowing of what was to come. William drove her to a secluded spot that he knew of out past Fort McPherson and shut off the engine. They kissed for awhile before she suggested.

"Let's get in the back seat."

William didn't argue.

This time he didn't wait for her to put his hand on

her breast. He boldly unbuttoned her blouse and pushed up her bra. She let him have his way as he explored with the black grubs that had so devastated his life before. This time he wasn't going to let that happen. He unhooked her bra and pushed it further out of the way so he could lean down and kiss her perky nipples. He felt the tiny raisins harden as he pulled first one and then the other into his mouth to suck on them.

By this time his erection was ready to split a seam, but still he didn't rush. He undid the button on her blue jeans, then unzipped them. She was very cooperative, arching her butt and spreading her legs so he could slide his hand inside her panties. When the black grubs found her slit he had to stop to keep from climaxing.

"Do you have a rubber?" she asked heavily.

For a moment, it felt like she'd thrown a bucket of cold water on him—although it had no affect on his erection. "Ah, no—" he stammered stupidly.

"Don't worry," she told him. "I always carry one in my purse … just in case."

Under other circumstances, he might have been shocked at her comment. *What the hell was she, a Boy Scout?* As it was, he was greatly relieved. She wiggled out of her blue jeans, then leaned over the back of the front seat to find her purse while he slipped off his shoes and struggled out of his jeans. Under other circumstances, undressing in the back of a car might have wreaked havoc on his erection—not so this time. If any thing it was more massive than ever.

Not that Tracy was at all alarmed by the massive tent William's erection formed in his under shorts. Perhaps it was the dim light. Or perhaps she was merely preoccupied with retrieving the rubber and opening the package. She used her teeth to start a crack in the foil package and then pulled it open to remove the rubber before turning her attention to the cotton tent before her. It wasn't until she pulled the tent aside and inadvertently placed her hand on the base of his cock that she panicked.

"On my God!" she exclaimed, probing with her hand to make sure she was feeling what she thought she was feeling. She was both fascinated and terrified and started to pull away.

William was lost. "Tracy, please—" he exclaimed, not even knowing what he meant.

Tracy's fear got the better of her fascination. "There's no way in hell I'm letting you—" she exclaimed, fumbling around for her jeans.

William was stymied. "Wait—" he pleaded. How could he make her understand that it was only the base of his penis that was so thick? That it was relatively pointed and if he only put it part way in it wouldn't be a problem? Then, he realized with horror, that the only way to accomplish that would be to turn on the dome light and let her get a good look at him, which of course meant that she would see his deformed shape and wind up laughing at him the way Sheniqqua had.

There was only one thing to do.

He grabbed Tracy roughly by the shoulders and threw her back on the seat, then forcibly inserted his body between her thighs. She was strong and wiry, but no match for his stocky frame. He wasn't about to be denied a second time.

William's actual insertion only lasted a split-second

and his penetration was minimal at best. His premature ejaculation took care of that.

What happened next was never very clear to William. In that moment of climax he was overcome with shame and flopped back on the seat. In that split-second, Tracy yelled "You bastard!" at him, kicked him in the stomach, and jumped out of the car and started running. *What was William to think?* She would obviously call the police and report that he raped her—and he wasn't even sure if that was actually true.

In a panic, William pulled on his jeans, threw himself over the front seat and tore out after her with the Chevy. It only took seconds to catch up to her. She probably thought he was trying to run her down because she started zigzagging as he tried to pull up beside her to beg her to stop. One second she was beside the left front fender and he was yelling for her to stop. The next second she vanished from view and there was an immediate, sickening thump and bump.

William slammed on the brakes and ran back to find her, but it was already too late. The back tire had run over her shoulder and neck. Her neck was broken.

"Noooo!" William bellowed, pounding his fists against the ground.

Chapter 33

A pickle is something that no matter how you twist and turn it, no matter how you try to doctor it up, no matter what you do the sour taste comes through when you bite into it. And that's one thing William knew for sure—he'd really gotten himself in a *pickle* this time. He was not sure if anyone from work knew he had left with Tracy. Obviously, if he just took off then Doug would question why neither he nor Tracy showed up for work and he would wind up being wanted by the police, if only for questioning.

No, he needed a better plan than that.

Fighting back tears, William opened the trunk, gathered up Tracy's things from inside the car and put them in the trunk. Then he gathered up Tracy and deposited her on top of her things. It was not the best plan in the world, just the riskiest.

"Where's Tracy?" Doug asked the next day, about an hour after her shift was supposed to start.

William shrugged. "Haven't seen her yet today," he said, wondering if technically that was a lie. It was true in a sense. He hadn't looked in the trunk of his car where he knew her to be. He hadn't seen her since last night, but since that was after midnight—

"I thought you two were a thing," Doug said, interrupting his internal argument.

"Are you kidding?" William laughed. "What would I want with a skinny pip-squeak like that?"

Doug looked a little puzzled.

William was ready for that. "Oh, you mean because you saw us leave together a few times? I was just giving her a ride home. She has a boyfriend."

"Really?"

"Yeah ... a guy that goes to Morehouse. I dropped her off there last night because he was having car trouble."

Doug was still giving him the dubious once over.

"It's too bad," William continued, trying to put on a face of disappointment.

"Why's that?" Doug seemed surprised by his comment.

"The guy's a real stud," William answered, trying to pretend he was jealous of Tracy and that he'd let something slip that he hadn't intended.

The ploy worked perfectly. Doug's "Oh," reply was loaded with a meaty "That explains a lot" tone.

Hopefully, the jealousy charade was something that wouldn't have to go on for very long. "I think they were talking about running off and getting married," William added the *coupe de grâce*.

"Ain't that a bitch!" Doug exclaimed dismally.

The only other tense moment came the night before William's night off. Doug had just come in from completing his nightly inspection of the grounds the way he always did.

"You walked past the back end of that car of yours lately, Willie?" he asked.

"What?" William said obtusely.

"Your car ... stinks something awful. It's enough to gag a maggot!"

"Oh, my God—" William exclaimed, making a big show. "I forgot all about it."

He had been hoping to take care of Tracy's body on his night off and hadn't realized how quickly it would start to smell.

Doug gave him one of his usual dubious looks.

"Fish!" William explained, almost enjoying the lie. "I caught some fish the other day and put them in the trunk. Then my grandmother called me and I forgot all about them. I'll got out and put them in the Dumpster right away."

"You do," Doug said firmly, "and I'll nail your God damned little ass to the God damned side board! Why would I want stinkin', rotten fish in my Dumpster?"

Needless to say, William didn't argue.

The next day after closing his bank account and packing his things in the back seat of the car, William called Doug and told him the final lie. "My grandmother called again and she's really sick. She wants me to come back to Montgomery and I'm not sure I'll be able to come back. I thought I better let you know ... you know, so you can get someone to take my place if you have to. I'm really sorry to do that to you ... you know with Tracy gone and all."

"Forget it kid," Doug was very understanding.

...

Burying Tracy was the most disgusting thing William had ever experienced in his life. Doug was certainly right about that. The smell was enough to gag a maggot. It was a wonder there wasn't a huge swarm of flies following his car. William never even had to think about where to go to bury Tracy. It was almost as if the car had a homing device as he headed back toward Anniston, Alabama. Not that he expected to be able to put Tracy in the same ground as Sheniqqua. The area had so many suitable spots with different gravel pits, quarries, and different construction sites.

He stopped in some nameless town along the way to buy a flashlight, shovel, and some air freshener for the trunk. By midnight Tracy was ancient history and William made himself a solemn promise. He would never again let himself get involved with a woman from work or where he lived. It was just a lot safer to pick up a girl from a school ground.

...

Gram didn't seem glad to see William. She asked him what he'd found out about Fort McPherson, but he had long ago lost interest in that after learning that it was named after Major General James Birdseye McPherson, a Union general. He'd rather it had been a confederate general and slave owner, but he wasn't sure why. Mostly, Gram was preoccupied with her impending retirement, like she was facing the end of the world or worse. William didn't feel sorry for her. Her life was better than the life of drudgery he foresaw for himself.

He was a freak! There was no way he was ever going to have a normal life and he would just have to make the best of it. Which meant that he had to establish some ground rules. First of all, any town he decided to move to would have to be large enough to have an adult theatre and plenty of places to find work where they didn't ask a lot of

Scharlie R. Martin

questions checking up on your background. William was convinced he had covered his trail pretty well, but you never knew when a problem could pop up.

William moved on to Athens, Georgia without bothering to let Gram know where he was for a long, long time. In a way, he was subconsciously blaming her for his plight. If she hadn't been so rigid in her thinking he might have had a more normal life. All those times growing up when he should have been going out with other guys sowing his wild oats, he was busy minding his P's and Q's trying to prove to her that he was a proper young man that would grow up to make her proud.

Athens was factory work in an electronic assembly plant. William avoided forming any friendships with the people around him. This time he intended to be far more careful. Originally, he'd intended to cruise school playgrounds but after due consideration decided that had dangerous implications. Some one might actually notice his car and be paying close enough attention to get his license plate number. The streets around the schools became his hunting grounds. There were always kids coming and going, even in summer.

William's *modus operandi* had one other important change. After the fiasco with Tracy, he was thoroughly disgusted by the "burying of the body" part and decided he'd rather be identified by a living victim than live with the guilt of a disgusting memory. To his surprise, William also found he had a growing fascination with young, white girls.

His next victim was maybe ten, with blonde pigtails and freckles. He followed her for weeks before snatching her from his hiding place in the bushes where she cut

321

through a park alone each day. His car was already parked in a hidden spot.

"I won't hurt you if you don't fight me or scream," he told her as he dragged her to his car with his hand over her mouth.

She either believed him or was too terrified to scream or fight. Tears rolled down her face in a steady stream as William inserted one of his black grubs, but she only whimpered. To prevent the girl from totally freaking, William kept his body turned away so she wouldn't see his penis while he did his business. When he was finished he felt obligated to let her go with only a simple admonition, "You ever tell any one and I'll come back and do worse—" he warned.

After that, the years just rolled by. William actually lost track of the number of victims and he never gave a moment's thought to what he was doing. *Why should he?* He was a freak and this was just the way he was going to have to live his life. The unfortunate thing was that William knew he would never get ahead financially. First of all, he would never have a good paying job and there would always be a car to maintain. Plus, he always wound up spending quite a bit on X rated movies and magazines.

Through the years William usually let his Gram know where he was living, but not always. She had obviously long ago given up on his living up to her dreams for him, which was unfortunate but that's the way it was.

William's only tense moment came when the police in Macon, Georgia picked him up for questioning about a missing girl. It was one of those crazy "Now, ain't that a kick in the head" moments. He didn't know a danged thing about the girl. According to the picture he was shown she was black, older, and heavy-set—not his type at all.

The same could not be said of his cellmate. The minute William laid eyes on Jose Angel Rodriquez Ramirez they both might as well have been wearing "killer" name tags. It all had to do with Angel's introduction. "Most people call me Jose or Joe," William's new cellmate told him. "But you can call me Angel." William knew instantly what he meant, but he didn't know how or why.

"Don't worry, man," Angel told him. "I know you ain't got nothin' to worry about, if you know what I mean. These cops are just spinning their wheels."

William didn't know what to say.

It didn't matter. Angel wasn't done talking. "You got a car, don't cha man?" he went on. "Once the cops check out your car they'll let you go. I ain't got no wheels—at least, not that the cops know about. If they let us out at the same time, kin you give me a ride?"

Angel proved to know what he was talking about. The police put them both in a lineup, which seemed pretty silly since Angel was Hispanic and William Negro. The only resemblance between them was that they were both short and stocky and their skin color was nearly the same. Two hours later they were released. And judging by the newly cleaned appearance of the inside of William's 1984 Blazer, the police had apparently given his car a thorough once over. It was just a stroke of luck the 57 Impala had recently crapped out and had to be replaced. The Blazer was more than ten years old, but as far as William knew forensically clean.

"We'll have to do some shit together," Angel suggested when William dropped him off at his flophouse. "I'll give you a call in a couple of days."

William nodded, wondering how Angel was going to do that since he didn't have a phone and he hadn't told Angel where he lived. Angel was a man of his word, however, and two days later William got a knock on his door informing him that there was a call for him in the office.

"Kin ya pick me up?" Angel said. It was more of an order than a question.

"I'll be right there," William said, for reasons that mystified him.

"I don't know about you, man," Angel said the minute he climbed into the Blazer, "But I kinda feel like my welcome's worn out in this town."

William didn't argue, nor did he ever bother to ask how Angel knew where to call him. It went without saying that Angel could do pretty much whatever he wanted to put his mind to with William. That was just the way it was … like he had a window right into William's soul.

…

In the years that followed William took Angel home to meet his Gram once, but Gram took an immediate dislike to the younger man. "Why you want to hang out with white trash like that?" Ruby demanded.

"He's not white, Gram," William told her. "He's Hispanic."

"He's still trash!" Ruby told him.

William didn't go home as often after that. *What was the point?* Not that he spent all that much time with Angel. That wasn't exactly his way. Generally, it was Angel who suggested when it was time to go for a few beers. They only did one job together, which was almost an accident.

One night they happened to be in a bar when a young white couple tried to order drinks. The guy claimed to be old enough with a driver's license to prove it, but unfortunately, he looked like he was only about twelve years old. The bartender refused to believe him or serve him.

"You're crazy," the kid stormed. "Just look at my license ... that proves I'm old enough to drink."

"I don't give a shit!" the bartender told him. "You look like a kid to me and I ain't serving no kid in here! I could loose my license."

"Come on, man," Angel said, sliding off his barstool after the couple left. "Let's go give those kids a hand."

William was mystified but followed Angel out of the bar as ordered.

"You guy's wanta party?" Angel asked the couple before they could get in the guy's car.

At first the couple looked like they wanted to run, then the guy realized this might be his opportunity to get his girl a drink. "What kind of party?" he asked cautiously.

Angel shrugged. "You know ... sit around and have a few drinks, shoot the shit, listen to a few tunes."

Angel might just as well have offered a $1000 bill. They went back to Angel's where he produced a case of beer and a fifth of Jack Daniels. "How do you guys feel about boilermakers?" Angel asked, busy adjusting his radio for some tunes.

"What's that?" the girl asked.

"You don't know what a boilermaker is?" Angel laughed.

"Here, let me show you." He went to the cupboard and got out a couple of shot glasses and a couple of bigger drinking glasses. Dropping one of the shot glasses into one of the bigger glasses, he filled the shot glass with Jack Daniels and proceeded to show her how a boilermaker worked.

"Why do they call it that?" the guy asked.

"Who cares?" Angel laughed. "Wanta try?"

By the time William left with the girl, they were all pretty drunk. This, of course, was a new experience for him. He had never been with a full-grown, drunk woman before and he found the prospect very exciting. He found a secluded spot to park and proceeded to turn his black grubs loose on the girl's body. "Hey!" she exclaimed at one point before momentarily passing out again. "What happened to my boyfriend?"

"I'm right here," William told her.

"You're not my boyfriend," the girl slurred, making no objection to the sudden insertion of a black grub into her forbidden nether region.

When all was said and done the girl had passed out completely and the last vestige of William's virginity was ancient history. So too was his misconception that he was just too thick for a woman to handle. All you had to do was get them drunk. It would have been a great memory for William, except for one thing.

"Did you snuff her, man?" Angel asked two days later when they got together to compare notes about the adventure.

"No," William admitted. "I just dumped her."

"Man, you're just plain chicken shit," Angel exclaimed. "The cops are probably already looking for us."

Willie was afraid to ask what that meant.

At that point, William was ready to end his association with Angel and move on by himself. They were both killers but William thought they were somehow different. His problem, aside from being a bit of a freak, had been brought on by an unfortunate accident. Angel, on the other hand, though he never talked about his past, seemed to be a natural born killer!

In the back of his mind William felt there might be a chance he might be able to find a real woman and turn his life around. Judging by the way that girl had moaned during their intercourse there was at least one woman who didn't object to his size. Unfortunately, that kind of thinking made William like the smoker who started chewing gum to help get over the smoking habit only to discover that he'd become a gum-chewing smoker.

In William's case he was searching for a real woman to help him get over his odd addiction of working his black grubs into terrified young white girls while masturbating. Angel's "chickenshit" chastisement left him conflicted. He spent more and more time in bars in an effort to find that special woman, generally without success. When he did eventually give in and snatch another young girl off the streets, he had a tendency toward more aggression, resulting in more so-called accidents.

William's only adjustment to *modus operandi* after an accident was to just dump the body in the woods or a lake before moving on.

Through it all, Angel was William's only confidant. Angel was the only person in the world who understood what he had become. So, even though he really didn't want to, William allowed Angel to stay in touch over the years.

Impending Doom

Chapter 34

The world suddenly stopped spinning on its orbital axis. William and Ruby were the only two people in the room who knew exactly what the word "everything" entailed, the rest of us quickly realized that what ever it was, it wasn't good. William's eyes took on a cold, calculating determination that was blood chilling. I had been kind of joking about this being our last meal—now, all at once, it didn't seem like a joke.

Ruby's face suddenly took on the demeanor of someone who was the harbinger of extremely bad news. "Ray Galston was a friend of my husband's," she explained to no one in particular. Her voice was heavy with sadness. "He came around for years claiming he wanted to help me—"

"Ruby," Lynn said softly. "This is not something we need to know."

Ruby shook her head vigorously. "No, I want to tell—"

"No, really, Ruby," I put my hand on her arm. "It's none of our business."

"It was my fault," Ruby went on. "I knew all along he was after me … but I didn't want that. At first I just let him keep comin' around because of Charles, Jr. Boys need a father figure in their lives. I knew I wasn't being fair, but—"

Lynn and I were both shaking our heads trying to shush her but she was apparently feeling an overwhelming need to confess.

"Anyway," Ruby continued. "After Charles got hung, Ray was more persistent than ever—insisted that he wanted to marry me. When I wouldn't give in he went and married someone else, which was fine with me. Anyway, after a while … when William got to 'bout eight or nine he started comin' round again—claimin' like before … that boys need a father figure. Then one day he just snapped … was fixin' to rape me—"

If Ruby ever had *story time* in any of her classes, she must have had her kids perched on the edge of their seats like a hawk ready to dive on some prey. Everyone in the room, including William, was holding their breath.

"I fought him off at first—" Ruby seemed to be very far away. "Then … I guess I snapped too. Next thing I knew I was tearing my clothes off to get at that man—"

In the pin-drop quite moment that followed, Lynn and I both shushed Ruby, letting her know in no uncertain terms that she didn't have to go on.

"I guess that's what William saw—" she concluded.

Everyone just sat there for the longest time—not talking, not eating. We might have sat there forever if it hadn't been for Ruby. At first her laughter was a simple low snicker, but it quickly rose to an almost hideous howl like the tormented venting of some dark creature from the swamps.

"What the—"

Lynn and I exchanged puzzled glances and waited patiently with everyone else for Ruby to explain her outburst.

330

"What's so funny?" I asked finally when she seemed disinclined to explain.

"That day," Ruby explained. "I told Ray if he ever came around again, I'd get a gun and shoot him. Wish to God now that I had done that a long time ago."

Amen to that, I thought, realizing for the first time what the full implications of Ruby's story meant. At a very vulnerable age William had witnessed an adult act that was obviously more an act of rape and lust than love. It wasn't hard to see how he could have gotten the wrong idea of what love and sex was about and that had apparently culminated in the accidental death of his first partner.

"That's not even the worst part," Rudy said suddenly. "I should have realized what happened with Sheniqqua and done something about it. I just didn't want to know."

This time it was William who prodded her to continue. "How could you know, Gram ... you weren't even here."

Ruby gave him a patient smile that seemed to say, "You poor boy ... don't you know?" She got up from her chair and started moving toward the sideboard. "I'll show you," she said simply.

She opened one of the drawers and removed a triangle shaped piece of torn cloth and placed it in front of William.

"What's that?" I asked, noting that William had very little reaction to the cloth.

"My guess," Ruby said emphatically, "is that it was part of Sheniqqua's blouse."

"So what?" William scoffed. "That doesn't prove anything!"

"You're right," Ruby agreed. "It doesn't prove anything by itself."

"So what else is there?" William demanded, obviously loosing his cool.

"Well, for one thing," Ruby continued cautiously. "When you went to Atlanta and claimed you starting school there ... I knew you were lying."

"How could you possibly know that?" William scoffed. "You weren't there to see whether I went to class or not."

"I didn't have to be."

"Then how could you know?"

Ruby smiled. "You told me you were going to Spelman ... right?"

"So?"

"So ... Spelman's a girls college—"

William suddenly looked as if someone had switched on his light bulb. "I was wondering why you never asked me any questions about school. At first I just thought it was because you were mad because I'd moved."

Ruby nodded her head sadly. "I wanted so desperately to believe that you were still in school ... that you were going to go to Morehouse College, which is practically next door to Spelman, that I didn't even question it. I managed to convince myself that you had left out part of what you had intended to write. Then you came home for that first visit—"

William looked puzzled.

"That's when I knew for sure you were lying. By that time I had been teaching for forty years and the life just went out of me. I felt like that old team of mules that Charles used to talk about. After you left I put in for retirement right away. That was one of the lowest points in my life."

I could tell by Lynn's face that she was wondering the same thing that I was. How could a woman who'd lost both her husband and son to violent deaths be so devastated by what could only be classified as "peculiar behavior" of a grandson—unless she seriously did suspect what was going on. But what if she did? Suspecting wasn't a crime.

"I was seriously depress for a long time," Ruby continued. "Then you brought that Angel creep home—"

I think we all wanted to ask, "Who the hell's Angel?" but were afraid to.

"I still don't understand why you disliked him so," William said smugly.

"Humph!" Ruby snorted. "What is there to like about a snake?"

It was very obvious from William's demeanor that he'd heard about all he wanted to hear from his grandmother. By this time, most of us had lost our appetites anyway. You didn't have to be an Einstein to realize William's plan for us did not include a picnic in the park. He obviously figured he had nothing to loose by making this our last meal. It was a very sobering thought.

William made us do the dishes up spick and span, like there'd never been anyone there. He kept us all in a group with the gun, going from the dining room to the kitchen like some huge crab scuttling along over the hardwood floor. Once in the kitchen the dishes were done lickety-split like a bucket brigade, everyone doing their small part. Once the dishes were done we were forced to do the crab shuffle back into the parlor, where we spent the next several hours huddle in a group around Ruby.

The periodic chiming of the pendulum clock in the shadows of the parlor was like a death knell in the hallowed halls of *unjustice* as twilight descended.

Apparently William's plan was to wait until dark and then load us all in his van. As an extra precaution, he made me cut Ruby's good linen tablecloth into long, narrow strips. But instead of tying our hands together behind our backs like you might expect, he made me tie the strips from one person's wrist to the next, connecting us together like a bunch of preschoolers being marched to the playground. William carefully supervised the tying of each knot.

Any plans I might have had for attacking William with the scissors while I was cutting up Ruby's tablecloth were nullified by a very effective use of the gun. William made Julie sit on the floor between his legs while he held the gun to her temple. Looking at William it was hard to give him credit for being that smart. I had it pegged as craftiness born out of desperation. By using Julie as a shield he kept both men at bay. He apparently wasn't worried about the women. He also took my cell phone away, just in case.

After what seemed like eons of sitting in Ruby's antiquated parlor listening to the tick-tock of the clock and our own pounding hearts, we were all suddenly jammed into the back of William's van, all that is except Ruby. William had Ruby sit in the passenger seat and then tied her wrists in such a way that she could put her hands on her lap but could not get them close enough together to untie the knots. In no time at all, we were wending our way out of Montgomery.

The one thing about *immediate impending death*, if there's time to think about it, is that we each start wondering how we stand with God. Unfortunately for me, my last conversation with God ended with a hearty "Fuck you, God!" At times like these, from my point of view, it was pretty hard not to wonder if maybe God wasn't being more than a little vindictive. It reminded me of that phrase, "Fuck you, buddy … and the horse you rode in on!" that some of my new-recruit army buddies were so fond of throwing around.

I was not an expert on the Bible by any means but I was reminded of some verses that talked about not just killing the enemy soldiers, but wiping out their families and crops and livestock as well. *Was that supposed to make me cower at the wrath of god?* If it was, it wasn't working. The thought made me bristle. I was not going down without a fight.

"There's no way you're going to get away with this William," I admonished from my cramped position in the back of the van.

I had been forced to get in the van first, so most of the rest of the gang were kind of piled in on top of me. The van had apparently been some sort of maintenance vehicle. It had wooden bins built in on each side and my right shoulder blade was practically jammed into one of them. From what I could see, it looked like Jamal was jammed into a similar position on the other side. The back end of the van was piled full with what I assumed was William's entire worldly belongings.

"You hear me, William?" I said after it became apparent that Willie boy wasn't going to answer me. "The first chance we get we're going to rush you and take that little pea-shooter away from you. Why don't you save yourself a lot of trouble and pull over to the side of the road and let the police help you?"

It sounded like a good plan. From what I could tell from my position on the floor, I was pretty sure we were headed northeast on Interstate 85 toward Atlanta. If Willie would stop on the side of the highway, the highway patrol would be all over his ass in no time at all wanting to know what was going on.

Willie wasn't buying. "You could save yourself a lot of trouble, Mister," he said. "If you'd just shut up. But you kin keep flappin' yer lips if ya want. I don't really care."

"What are you planning to do, William?" Ruby demanded.

He turned to look at her. "Never mind, Gram'," he muttered, turning back to the road. "It'll all be over soon."

"Don't you 'never mind' me boy!" Ruby declared, tugging angrily at her bindings so hard she was rocking the van. "I gave you whuppings before … I ain't so old I can't do it again! You hear me?"

Well, if nothing else, I thought ruefully, *you have to admire her spirit.* I was also reminded of the old adage, *spare the rod and spoil the child.* I couldn't help but wonder if Ruby's somewhat old-fashioned and rigid attitude about discipline didn't have quite a bit to do with our current predicament.

At any rate, there was no changing the past. All of the little things that had gone into turning William into an apparently cold-blooded killer were hidden somewhere deep in his past. And at the moment, nothing we said seemed to reach him.

"I have to go to the bathroom," Julie whispered at one point.

Now there's a dilemma and not something that killers probably give much thought to or care about. If it's parents and a carload of kids going on vacation and the subject gets brought up as Dad is whizzing down the road, Dad turns and yells, "Well, that's something you kids should've thought about before we left home." And he keeps driving—until they reach the nearest gas station or restaurant.

"Julie has to go," Lynn told me, even though we both knew I had heard Julie in the first place.

"William," I picked up the gauntlet. "We're gonna need a potty break back here before too long. Okay?"

Silence.

"William McPherson," Ruby said in a low tone, after maybe another five minutes of whizzing down the road had passed without any response from Willie. "I didn't raise you to be mean. Now you find a place that girl can go to the bathroom and you better be quick about it. You hear me?"

William didn't answer her either other than suddenly taking his foot off the van's accelerator. The next thing we knew we were being bounced around something fierce as William drove down some sort of logging road. I could see what I thought must be kudzu vines growing in the overhanging trees. We bounced along for another couple of minutes, then William abruptly stopped behind a huge pile of smaller logs cut in eight foot lengths, pulpwood no doubt.

William grabbed a flashlight from the glove box, cut the engine and shut off the headlights. The van only had two doors in the front and a bigger double door in the back, which was blocked. Willie got out, flipped the driver's seat forward and flashed his flashlight in our faces and ordered me to untie Julie's wrists.

Her predicament must have been urgent because she was bouncing around pretty good until I got her loose, then she was out the door.

Now run, I thought, *you can worry about peeing later.*

"Hold it!" William ordered. "If you're gonna go … you're gonna go right here."

Julie's voice was like a little mouse. "You expect me to go with you watching?"

"It's that or nothing. Suit yourself."

William had the flashlight shining half in the van and half on Julie. While his attention was on Julie, I reached over and quickly untied Lynn's right wrist. My plan was to tie that tablecloth strip to Julie's wrist when she got back in, instead of the one that had been linking her to Andrea and thus fooling Willie into thinking we were all tied together as before.

Unfortunately, William was a little too wary. "Come to think of it," he said as I retied Julie's wrists under his scrutiny. "As long as we're stopped … you all better go cause I'm not making another stop."

One by one he let us out to have our turn, making sure that each was retied correctly before letting the next person out. He apparently took his own turn before turning to his grandmother "What about you, Gram'?"

he said, flopping the driver's seat back in place indicating the *potty break* for passengers was about over.

Ruby shook her head adamantly. "I'll damned if I'll do that ... I'd rather pee in my pants than go with you holding a gun on me!"

"Suit yourself." Willie exclaimed, hopping back in the driver's seat and slamming the van door.

Within seconds we were jostling our way back out of the woods, and I was really beginning to kick myself. That old adage, *he who hesitates is lost* couldn't have been more true. *Why couldn't I have been more creative?* I hated to admit it, but it seemed like Willie was much better at being the arch villain than I was giving him credit for. It was only then that the full implications of the past twenty-five years began to sink in.

If, as the evidence seemed to indicate, William had been raping young girls and hiding his crime by murdering his victims for a good part of twenty-five years, then he was obviously either extremely lucky in escaping detection or more wily than I was prepared to deal with. But it wasn't like I was junior varsity having to go against the varsity—I couldn't just say things like, "No, you're too skilled ... I don't wanta play." I had to come up with a plan that would catch Willie off guard and put him out of action.

We rode for another hour before Willie suddenly took an exit ramp, leaving me to wonder if we were getting close to our destination or if we were getting off the Interstate for some other reason, such as getting low on gas. If so, this might be my only opportunity to signal to someone that we were being kidnapped. Before I could come up with a plan, however, Willie pulled into a gas station, cut the engine, turned in the driver's seat, and pointed his pistol at me.

"Give me your bank card," he said coldly.

I really couldn't see much of anything except part of the station canopy. I had no idea if there were any other people around or not. At that moment I couldn't hear anything other than the distant hum of traffic on the Intestate. I didn't have to ask why Willie wanted my bank card. That way he'd be able to buy gas without leaving the pump area or dealing with any clerks.

"What makes you think I have a bank card?" I asked, grasping at straws.

"Just give me your damned bank card!" Willie ordered. "Before I have to shot one of your sluts."

It was not exactly the kind of order one argued with. I handed over my bank card and began looking around to see what I could come up with to get us out of this crazy situation. I could see that both Julie and Andrea had been crying and that everyone in the back of the van was very solemn. I wasn't sure about Ruby. I could only see the top of her head.

"On second thought," Willie said, once again beating me to the punch. "You can come out and pump the gas."

He handed me back the bank card and motioned me to climb out over the girls. He marched me around the van with his pistol stuck in my ribs. While I pumped the gas, Willie stood beside the van with his left hand between the back of the seat and the window frame pointing his pistol into the back of the van. I wasn't sure Willie could actually hit anyone that way, but I wasn't about to risk trying to run or anything just in case. Also, to my dismay, the gas station was completely deserted except for Willie's van. It was only then that I remembered that it was still Thanksgiving.

The only good thing about that was it might mean there were more Highway Patrol on duty than might be the case on a regular night. That's why my heart skipped a beat when I saw headlights turning into the station just as I was finishing pumping the gas. Glancing at Willie, I put the pump nozzle back in place—but instead of turning back to put the gas cap back on, I turned part way and then tried to sprint toward the on-coming car. *Hopefully,* I thought stupidly, *Willie won't start shooting at anyone but me.*

Unfortunately, instead of breaking into a graceful sprint like a football receiver, I did what a lot of receivers do at the height of their first big game. I started running before all of the necessary elements, such as catching the ball, were in place. In my case, it was untangling my feet. My first step was with my left foot. My second step, with my right foot, caught the edge of my left shoe sole, ricocheted off the back tire of the van and sent me sprawling headlong into oblivion—

Chapter 35

When I regained consciousness I was considerably disoriented. At first I thought I must be in bed with Lynn because I could feel a warm cheek against mine, the tickle of hair against my face, and my right thigh was jammed between someone's legs. The thing that didn't make sense was the steady hum of the van engine and the darkness. It also felt like my hands were tied behind my back—and my head was throbbing.

"Huhmm," I murmured, trying to move.

"I think he's awake now, Mom," a voice whispered, practically in my ear.

"Are you okay, honey?" Lynn's husky whisper came from somewhere in the dark. "You had us worried."

"I don't know. What happened?"

"We're not sure. Another man showed up."

"What?"

"Another man—" the voice in my ear whispered.

It was only then that I realized I must have slammed my head into the corner of the cement pedestal that supports the gas pumps. William and this other man they were talking about must have taped my hands behind my back and just tossed me into the van right on top of Andrea, my thigh practically jammed in her crotch. "Sorry, Andy," I murmured, struggling to shift my position. "What's going on?"

"We're all tied up—taped up, actually." Andy whispered, wiggling to get in a better position. "Like we said, this other guy showed up—"

Andy gave me a minute to let that sink in. Apparently the car that had arrived at the gas station was some partner in crime of Willie's that he'd called in to help, probably while we had stopped in the woods. I squirmed around enough so I was able to see the rear view mirror. It seemed like there was a car following us pretty closely.

"Who's your buddy, Willie?" I called dismally suddenly feeling very disheartened. All along I had been thinking that if worst came to worst we could always rush Willie and we wouldn't all have to die. Six against one was pretty good odds. Six against two got you started remembering that one of the six was an eighty some year old woman, two of the six were young girls, and another was the woman you loved and you'd rather die than have harm come to her. It was a whole new ball game.

"I said, who's your buddy?" I called again when Willie did not answer. I was immediately sorry I did.

"Never mind," Willie said his voice full of a newfound cockiness. "You'll find out soon enough. Angel likes men."

"What's that supposed to mean?" I demanded.

Willie boy didn't bother to answer.

Well, there you have it, I thought, knowing full well the implications of Willie's comments and attitude, *we got ourselves some equal opportunity career fiends. One does girls ... and one does guys! How nice!* Ruby had called Angel a snake. Obviously he was that and more and ready to become Willie boy's partner in crime. And at the moment, they were in the catbird seat, everything was going their way.

Not only was the situation very disheartening, the ride was very uncomfortable. Five people with their hands taped behind their backs and jammed in on top of each other in the back of an old beat-up van was not very conducive to comfort. Especially, since we also still seemed to be tied together with the strips of tablecloth Willie had made me cut from Ruby's tablecloth. The darkness in the back of the van didn't help either.

"How long was I out?" I whispered finally.

It was kind of a stupid question, but certainly a natural one. Unfortunately, none of my fellow prisoners seemed to have an answer for that.

"Any body know where we're going?" I whispered hopefully.

No one had an answer for that either.

Judging by the sounds coming from the highway and the occasional flare of light from passing headlights, we were no longer on Interstate 85. It was hard to tell, but I thought we might be going west. Not that knowing that with a certainty would have had any impact on our situation. Whatever direction we were going, it wasn't good—Willie seemed to be driving with a real sense of purpose. And Angel was staying right with us.

"Where you taking us, Willie?" I demanded, trying to connect with Willie's eyes in the rear view mirror.

Willie didn't even bother to look in the mirror. "What do you care?" he muttered cockily. "You won't be coming back."

I had always thought of myself as one of those rare people who were not only not intimidated by a challenge but actually rose to the occasion. That's why when I thought that Maria had moved to Florida and started a new tax business with money that should have been used to pay off our debts, I just jumped in the car and went to check it out. Talk about jumping out of the frying pan and into the fire.

Maybe it's a big mistake to think you can do anything you put your mind to. Maybe one shouldn't go around half-cocked trying to do things you don't know anything about.

My biggest regret, thanks to my blundering, was that I was going to get five other innocent people killed—and one of them was the woman I loved.

"Lynn, honey," I whispered, wishing I could see her face. "You doing okay?"

"I've been better," she admitted.

I could almost taste the fear in her voice. "What about the rest of you?" I asked hoarsely. "Everybody okay so far?"

There was a lot of nervous muttering and joking, the consensus being that the next move would be *out of the frying pan and into the fire.* We rode for what seemed like a very long time in uncomfortable silence while I tried to come up with a rescue plan. It did occur to me that Willie might actually have something in his pile of stuff in the back of the van, such as my bow and arrows, that could help us, but it was awfully hard to do anything about that with your hands taped behind your back. And as far as I could tell we were all in the same predicament, except maybe for Ruby.

"You doing okay up there, Ruby?" I asked.

"I was," Ruby snapped, "'til I wet myself!"

I wasn't sure whether Ruby was kidding or not but I suddenly had the urge to yell out, "Well, bless your heart, Ruby," cause it really felt like she was telling William in no uncertain terms, "Piss on you … you little whippersnapper!" Her snappy reply raised my spirits considerably.

The human body is an amazing thing. After hours and hours of almost unbearable discomfort and boring fear, it just shuts down and you go to sleep. Never mind that you might not ever wake up—

I tried to rationalize the situation by telling myself that I had allowed myself to go to sleep so that I would be better able to deal with the crisis when the time came. Actually, it was a pretty sound argument. At any rate, when we finally jiggled to a stop a long time later and Willie cut the engine, I had no idea where we were, other than somewhere off a main highway. I figured it was probably in the wee small hours of the morning, judging by the position of the nearly full moon.

Willie's burly friend Angel helped us out of the van and into some sort of one-room building about twenty feet square. There was no furniture of any kind in the building and the windows seemed to be barred. Willie escorted his grandmother into the building and both men left without bothering to remove our tape or untie their victims. The only light in the building was from the waning moon.

I did not hear or see any vehicles drive away so I had to assume that Willie and his burly friend could return at any minute. We were going to have to act fast.

"Ruby," I said quietly. She was the only one who didn't

have her hands taped behind her back. "Can you come here and do something about this tape on my wrists?"

Ruby was happy to oblige, but the tape proved too tough for her aging fingers.

"Here, Jamal," I suggested. "If I can get you loose you can free the rest of us."

To get in the right position to unwrap Jamal's hands while we were back to back and my own hands were taped was like trying to wrestle an octopus in the blackness of a coal mine. As soon as I got Jamal free he undid me and we both set to work to free the others. I looked for a light switch but had already decided that if there was one I wouldn't turn it on just in case Willie or his friend suddenly came back.

If there was a light switch, I was never able to find it. There was a light off in the distance and I assumed that to be another building that Willie and his friend had gone off to decide what came next. In the mean time, I posted Jamal to watch out the small window in the door and then began searching the rest of the room for a way out.

It didn't take very long feeling around the rough-textured walls to figure out that it was a cement block building and that the crossed-bars on the windows were actually set in cement. For all practical purposes, it seemed that Willie and his friend had managed to put us in an abandoned jail. If I had to guess, I would have guessed it was a building that had once been used to store explosives and I wondered if we weren't on some sort of military reservation. The door did not seem to be latched, but was held firm in some way by something on the outside, most likely a padlock. It appeared that the bars on the door window were bolted on from the outside, judging by the extended end of the bolts and nuts on the inside.

"Everybody might as well try and get comfortable," I suggested after I had exhausted my search. "Jamal and I can take turns watching out the door—"

There did not seem to be anything else to say.

Jamal volunteered to take the first watch and since I thought there would probably not be much happening for a while I agreed. I had a strong feeling Willie and friend were probably sleeping since they'd been driving the better part of the night.

I decided I wouldn't have a better opportunity to catch forty winks so I told Jamal to wake me when it started getting daylight and flopped down on the floor. There was no way I was ever going to get comfortable without a blanket and pillow, so I leaned against the wall and invited Lynn to put her head on my lap.

The next thing I knew, I felt myself drifting. It was a really weird situation. Like a lot of people, I've had lots of dreams of falling where you never reach the bottom. This was different. Instead of falling, I was floating upward. At first, I didn't realize what was going on. Then I saw that I could look back and see my body still sitting—leaning against the wall with Lynn snuggled against me, her head in my lap.

Strange, I thought, all I have to do is just float away.

Oddly enough, it seemed that my new air-born body was controlled by thought. I started drifting toward the door where Jamal was still standing watch.

Better watch it Jamal, I thought, wondering if he would feel my presence if I just drifted right through his head. It wasn't until I felt the cold sensation of the glass in the door across the middle of my stomach that I realized that since Jamal and I were both at body temperature he wouldn't feel a thing and that I was drifting through the window.

That scared the crap out of me!

"Uhhh!" I snorted, jerking awake with a start.

Lynn raised up her head. "You okay, honey?"

"Just a little nightmare?" I informed her.

"Here I thought you were sleeping," she replied.

I was happy to see she still had her sense of humor.

Chapter 36

I had a feeling it must be getting near time for the sun to come up so I lifted Lynn into a sitting position, gave her a quick kiss and got up to relieve Jamal.

Once the sun came up, I could see that there was no actual ceiling in our prison—just exposed roof trusses that supported the single gabled roof. There was also an air vent in each of the gable ends, but unfortunately, these were barred from the outside just like the door. *Good luck with getting those loose with just your fingers.* There were also several good-sized wasp nests up in the rafters and on the underside of the roof. Judging from the rubble that became visible as the rising sun cast its rays over the area, we were somewhere near what appeared to be an abandoned open pit mine or quarry. I could make out some sort of office or hunter's cabin at the edge of some trees several hundred yards away.

Nice of the boys to leave us the cars, I thought ruefully, staring at Willie's van and the beat up Pontiac his friend Angel had been driving.

That pretty much confirmed that the boys, since they'd driven the better part of the night, had gone off for a nap before beginning whatever festivities they had planned for the day. There was no way of telling how much time we had before the pair returned. It also seemed fairly obvious to me that my first suspicions were right, that our prison was no makeshift prison. It clearly designed as a storage shed for keeping people out as might be the case if the mining company or whatever it was had something to store, like dynamite. Unfortunately, no one left any samples behind.

Willie had not bothered to search any of us before sticking us in his prison. None of the ladies, of course, had any weapons since Willie had confiscated their purses. Good thing for him that he did—the combined stuff from four ladies' purses could be enough to sabotage the whole building. Unfortunately, about the only things that Jamal and I could come up with to use as tools was a few keys and my tiny imitation Swiss Army knife.

With the ladies taking turns watching out the door, Jamal and I set to work trying to scratch the mortar out from between the cement blocks in an area toward the back of the building. We started with one block on the second row of blocks (because the bottom row of blocks might be bolted to the floor). Then went to two blocks on the next row (because the blocks were offset half a block). And finally to a single block on the next row. That would give us a rough opening sixteen inches wide by twenty-four inches high, enough for some of us to squeeze out.

"This is only going to take about twelve years," I said dismally, after scratching away for the better part of an hour.

"I know," Jamal agreed, "But like you said … what else can we do?"

We worked steadily for another three hours before trying to kick the blocks out of position. We had gotten most of the mortar out of the grooves as far as we could reach with the keys, but that still left the entire joints on the outside of the building. If we'd had a sledgehammer or maybe a couple of star drills or chisels, maybe it would have been different. But as it was, both Jamal and I slammed our feet repeatedly against the blocks so hard it was painful just to stand. And both of our hands were bloody messes.

"This is never going to work," I admitted, looking around for some other idea.

While I had been scratching away with the keys, there had been one idea nagging away at the back of my head—but I didn't know if the ladies would be up for it. "You know," I said finally. "These rafters are only sixteen inches apart."

Everyone gave me a puzzled look.

"I don't know if you ladies would be up to it … but I've done enough work in attics and such to know that a guy can lay crossways on these stringers and be fairly comfortable. What do you think would happen if Willie and his buddy came in here to get us and it looked like nobody was home?"

More puzzled looks.

"How would we get up there?" Julie asked finally.

"Jamal and I can boost you guys up," I explained, perking up. "What d'ya think? Should we give it a try."

"I don't know," Andy shuddered. "There's all kinds of wasp nest up there—"

"Would you rather be raped and dumped in some mine pit … or put up with a few minor wasp stings?"

"I think I'll take the mine pit," Andy joked.

"I bet."

"It's a good idea, honey," Lynn said, taking one of

my hands in hers. "But do you really think you guys can get a bunch of women up in the rafters? The girls maybe … cause they're young. But I'm not so sure about me … and I'm pretty sure that might be more than Ruby is up to." Without waiting for my answer, she pulled out my handkerchief, spit on it, and began dabbing at my wounded hands.

Once I thought about it, I had to admit Lynn was right. Jamal was a good sized, very athletic kid, but it was doubtful that between the two of us we'd be able to boost Ruby up into the rafter without killing her. *Another plan bites the dust.*

"There might be a way it could work," Lynn said after a moment, a devilish grin in her eyes. "What if just you guys get up in the rafters and the rest of us pretend to be asleep on the floor. You know, with enough skin showing to distract them. They might not even notice you guys are missing until it's too late."

"I think you might have something," I grinned. "What d'ya think Jamal?"

"Sounds like a plan," he agreed.

The only problem was that the unwilling participants did not show up for a couple of eons. Which in a way was good, because it gave us a chance to rehearse a few times and work out the bugs. We decided it would be best for Jamal and I to stay three stringer spaces apart, a distance of about four feet. That way we would have the best chance of surprising Willie and his friend regardless of where they stood in the room.

Of course, we had no way of knowing if both men would actually come into the building and we didn't know if they both had guns. In fact, we knew nothing about

Willie's buddy except his name and Ruby's declaration that he was a snake. The only thing Willie had told us was that Angel liked men and we didn't know for sure if that was true. That could have just been Willie's way of controlling the situation.

The only thing that seemed certain was that Willie's friend was there to help Willie, regardless of what Willie wanted to do. And that wasn't much of a recommendation.

"Get ready you guys!" Andy exclaimed and hour or so later. "I think they're coming."

Jamal and I scrambled up between the roof trusses and got ready. The girls made a quick dash to the far side of the room and sprawled around where Ruby was sitting. Julie went on her back with her knees up so the skirt of her dress fell to the floor exposing her legs and panties. Andy pulled her blouse open in a provocative way and lay on her side with her head on Julie's stomach and her legs spread apart. Lynn did her part by revealing a silky length of gam that had me ready to fall out of the rafters.

Nothing happened.

After what seemed like an eternally long time we heard the sound of Angel's car starting and apparently driving away. Andy jumped up and ran to the door for a quick look. "I can't tell if they're both in the car," she said after a moment, "but at least one of them is leaving. I don't see any sign of the other one."

Resolutely, Jamal and I dropped down out of the rafters. Staying perched up there required more energy than getting up and down and it wouldn't do to have muscles lock up when you were in a battle for your life.

The only thing now, we would have to post two look-outs at the door to make sure Willie or his friend didn't come from the house while we were busy watching the road for the return of Angel's Pontiac.

An hour or so later, Angel returned with what looked like a bag of groceries and at least one case of beer. It was a good thing we were locked in a building because we were all hungry enough there'd be nothing left but the bones if we got our hands on Angel. By this time, we were all a little stir crazy and wondering what had become of Willie.

It was nearly three hours later before our curiosity was resolved. Willie had apparently been waiting for dusk before making his move—which was just fine with me.

"I only see Willie," Lynn informed us as Jamal and I shimmied back up into the rafters. "I think he has his gun in his hand."

A few moments later the door swung open and Willie cautiously stuck his head into the room. He looked to either side of the door and then spotted the girls in a heap against the far wall. "Okay everybody," he announced, "Time to get up."

I had to wonder if he was really dumb enough to think we'd slept all day, as he probably had, or was he just confused. By this time, it was getting fairly dark inside the building with the falling dusk and it was probably going to take his eyes a few seconds to adjust to the dimmer light. It was then that I remembered the wasp nest in the next rafter space over from the one I was occupying. I could see from the dim outline that the nest was right over Willie's head.

Supporting myself with both hands and one foot, I

arched my back so I could stretch my left leg back and dislodge the nest with my foot. The nest actually missed Willie, falling harmlessly a few inches in front of him. The angry wasps that followed the nest down did not miss him.

"What the—" Willie exclaimed, suddenly batting at the air with both hands. "Ouch! What the hell!"

This time I was very careful not to screw up my move. Taking careful aim, I swung down from the rafters and kicked Willie in the chest with both feet. Willie flew backward and struck the edge of the doorframe and went down like a sack of wheat. Jamal was *Johnny-on-the-spot,* recovering the gun before either of us realized Willie was, in actual fact, totally unconscious.

"I'll be damned," I muttered, staring down at Ruby's inert grandson. "I hope you get one helluva head ache," I told his unconscious form.

Jamal stood shoulder to shoulder with me studying our tormentor. "You want the gun?" he asked, holding it out to me with his left hand. He was holding it by the barrel.

"No way," I wanted to say, but I had serious doubts that Jamal had ever held a gun before. "You ever use a gun?" I asked.

Jamal shook his head. "Naw … not unless you want to count paintball guns."

I grinned. "Maybe we shouldn't count those just yet," I said, accepting the pistol.

By now, the ladies were crowding around. "Is he dead?" Ruby asked.

"No," I informed her. "Just unconscious."

"So what now?" someone asked.

I stuck the pistol in my belt, stooped and fumbled through Willie's pockets until I came up with the van keys. "I don't know about the rest of you," I said, "but I'm all for getting the hell out of here."

No one was arguing.

Chapter 37

"What about his buddy?" Lynn asked, nodding toward Willie.

It was a very good question. One that I gave considerable thought to before answering. For one thing, we had no idea whether Willie's buddy had any kind of gun or other weapon. For another thing, we had arrived at our present location while it was still dark outside. We had no idea where we were or how you went about getting out of there. Judging by the length of time that Angel had been gone for groceries we were probably at least fifteen or twenty miles from the nearest town.

"I think we should just leave him," I said finally. "We don't know if he has a gun or not ... and I don't want to chance getting any of you ladies hurt. Let's just throw Willie in the back of the van and go for it. I doubt Willie's friend is crazy enough to follow us. And if he does ... we have the gun to fend him off. I'm for getting to the nearest police station as quick as we can."

"Amen to that," Ruby said starkly.

I took a couple of steps over to the doorway and surveyed the situation. There was no sign of Angel and I was hoping he was having a high old time drinking beer. The van was parked in a position that would leave us totally visible if we just walked out to the van in a straight line. "Here's what we need to do," I told them. "Jamal and I will carry Willie ... but we're not going straight to the van. We'll go along the front of the building real quick until we get the van between us and the cabin—that way if Angel happens to look out the van will block his view of us. Okay?"

Everyone agreed it was a good plan.

And it only took about two minutes to execute.

Once we got to the van, Andy opened the back door for us and we dumped Willie's unconscious form on his pile of stuff like a bag of dirty laundry. Jamal held the gun while I tied Willie's hands and feet with the strips of the tablecloth Lynn had thoughtfully brought with her. The girls climbed over Willie into the back while Ruby got in the passenger seat and Jamal got in behind the wheel. I climbed in over Willie and pulled the back door shut. We were all very careful to not slam any van doors.

"Everybody ready?" Jamal asked, turning the ignition key.

The engine turned over okay, but did not start.

I rose up on my knees and peeked out toward the cabin to see if Willie's buddy had heard the van. There was no sign of life, but it was hard to tell if it was dark enough for any lights from the cabin to show. "Relax, Jamal," I said. "Just pretend this is your car and you and Julie are just leaving on a date."

This time, the engine caught.

"Don't turn the lights on yet," I ordered. "Just make a U-turn here and drive real easy. Maybe we can get out of here before Willie's buddy misses us."

Everyone held their breath until the van had cleared the immediate area of the cabin and storage shed. The road was very crooked and rough so Jamal had to take

360

it really easy. Julie and Andrea were holding onto the storage bins on either side so they could raise themselves up enough to keep watch out the windows in the back doors. "Shit!" Julie exclaimed, just as we were all about to breathe a big sigh of relief. "A light just went on in the cabin—"

"Maybe it doesn't mean anything," I suggested hopefully. "Maybe it's just because it's getting dark."

"I hope you're right," Andy said, her voice filled with tension. "But I doubt it ... his car lights just went on!"

At that precise moment we came to a fork in the twisty road. "Which way?" Jamal asked, slowing almost to a stop.

"Let's try to the right," I suggested. "Leave the headlights off as long as you can."

We bumped along in silence for a while, with Julie and Andrea still trying to watch for headlights out the back windows. It was now getting so dark inside the van that I was getting concerned about Willie coming around without me seeing it. "Can you look in the glove box, Ruby? See if Willie put that flashlight in there."

The flashlight was there—and so was my cell phone. Unfortunately, however, either the battery on the cell phone was too low or we were in a bad area for reception.

"Maybe you can drive a little faster if you put the headlights on now, Jamal," I told him. I was beginning to get very nervous about our situation. It would help a lot if I knew where we were and where we were going. I wasn't even sure what state we were in. Obviously, to begin with, we had driven toward Atlanta. And I was pretty sure we were already in Georgia when Willie's buddy joined us. But there was something about our situation that made me feel like we had gone back into Alabama. I wasn't even sure why. Maybe it was just my innate sense of directions.

"We're never going to get out of here," Andy said dismally. "What is this road? A damned cow path?"

"I think it's an old mining road," I told her. "Hopefully we'll come to a major road any minute now."

"We better," Julie agreed. "I still see that guy's headlights every once in a while."

"Is he getting closer?" Lynn asked.

"It's hard to tell, Mom," Andy said. "They're just there for a few seconds and then one of us goes around a curve. I think we need to get out on a straight away so we can make some real time."

"Don't tell me," Jamal muttered. "Tell the road. I never saw such a crooked road in my life. It doesn't seem to go anywhere and I haven't seen sign one of any houses!"

"Speaking of signs … did you see any sign of that tape up there, Ruby?" I asked, beginning to wish I had taped Willie instead of tying him.

"No," Ruby informed me

"I think Willie's buddy is getting closer—" Julie exclaimed suddenly.

And, of course, at that moment Willie started moaning loudly.

"If you don't want to get shot, Willie," I told him, handing the flashlight to Lynn to hold. "You just stay right where you're at and relax. I have your gun and I'm not only not afraid to use it, I'm kinda hitchin' to do just that."

Willie craned his neck and squinted his eyes against the light "What the hell's that supposed to mean?" he growled.

"It means I spent nearly seven years in the service—killing vermin is something I know a lot about. The last time I just had a target bow. This time I got your handy-dandy little pea-shooter and I'd love to use it."

"Go to hell," Willie declared, flopping back on his stuff.

"That guy is getting really close—" Julie exclaimed again.

Willie looked puzzled for a moment. "You talking about Angel?" he said finally. "If you're talking about Angel … you better hope he don't catch you. That guy's crazy!"

It did seem as if Angel was indeed getting closer, but not directly behind us. He seemed to be off to one side and not only gaining on us, but apparently he was passing us. It suddenly occurred to me that he was on a parallel road—trying to cut us off at the pass, so to speak.

The thought was hardly formed when Jamal apparently figured it out too. All at once we were in a blind race and we had no idea where it would end. We didn't have long to wait to find out. Jamal swung through a sharp curve and tried to accelerate, but because he was unfamiliar with the road he didn't realize until it was too late that this was a mistake. For a few seconds the Pontiac seemed to be on a road that was a quite a bit higher than the one we were on. Then, suddenly, the Pontiac headlights swung toward us, and within seconds impacted the side of the van.

Jamal fought valiantly to keep the van in the road but

could not. There was no road ditch—but, unfortunately, a kind of pothole of major proportions. The van flew up in the air and landed with a crash that jarred the back doors open. Everything flew helter-skelter, including all the passengers. When I finally recovered the flashlight, Willie was gone.

"Can we still drive?" I asked quickly, my mind racing to figure out what the best thing to do would be.

Jamal raced the engine, but the van did not move.

"Shit!" I exclaimed. "We're stuck!"

"What now?" Lynn asked quickly.

"We're sitting ducks here," I declared. "We still don't know if Willie's buddy has a gun, but my guess is that he does and that Willie is well on his way to get it. It's too dark to try and get the van out now. We're gonna have to leave the van and try to hide in the woods."

"You sure that's a good idea?" Lynn asked.

"The van is the first place they'll look," I told her dismally.

Alone, I'd have no problem hiding in the woods. In fact, because of my country background, I had been very good at war games that required sneaking around in the woods to avoid or kill the enemy. But now, I had an eighty some year old woman, Lynn, and three grown kids to protect.

"We have to stick together," I said, sliding out the back of the van. I turned around and flashed the light back in so the others could get out. As I did so, I noticed that my bow and arrows were among Willie's junk that had gotten dumped on the ground. I stuck the pistol in my belt and grabbed the bow and two arrows. "We better hurry," I admonished. "I have no idea how much time we have before they come looking."

It really took some doing, but in a matter of minutes I had the entire crew lined up in front of the van, the van keys in my pocket, and everyone holding hands. I turned off the flashlight and told them I was going to wait a bit for my eyes to adjust to the dark. I also told them there would be no talking unless absolutely necessary.

"What does that mean?" Jamal whispered.

"That means don't say anything unless you see imminent danger," I whispered back. I had the pistol stuck in my belt and the bow looped over my neck. I had the two arrows and the flashlight in my right hand. I was also holding Ruby's right hand with my left. Unfortunately, the moon was not out yet so, you could barely see beyond the end of your nose. "Everybody ready?" I whispered, leading my people train into the abyss of blackness.

We moved very slowly. With the flashlight off, I was using the arrows as a kind of blind man's cane, slowly swinging my arm in front of me to detect any obstacles. Fortunately there was not a lot of small underbrush and the leaves on the ground were wet enough that we did not make a lot of noise. The trees were a mixture of deciduous and pine and not terribly thick. I was hoping to be able to lead my people train to a cluster of pine that would provide a secure hiding place without Willie and his bastard friend knowing where we went.

As we snaked along, I couldn't help thinking it should be Lynn's hand I was holding instead of Ruby's. But given Ruby's age, she'd obviously need more help than Lynn or the kids. So I had arranged the train in descending order of age except that I put Jamal on the tail end. I wasn't sure how old Jamal was. He was a good kid though.

Occasionally, I would stop, squat down, and try and pick out objects on the skyline. Pine trees formed a darker mass when silhouetted against the sky. It gave me something to shoot for. I also kept a running count of the number of steps I took and tried to keep a running tally of how far we had moved since leaving the van.

At one point, I stopped and looked back toward where I thought we'd left the van, but in the dark, even that was hard to determine. I kept going until I ran into what seemed to be solid wall of pine trees.

"You guys wait here," I whispered.

Dropping to my hands and knees I probed my way around until I found a slight opening. Cedar trees generally grow with limbs very close to the ground. They also grow in clumps that get started by little birdies sitting on a limb after they've had their fill of cedar berries, or whatever they're called. A little clump of cedar with an opening at the center was exactly what I was looking for, if I could just find my way into the center.

It took some time to find an opening with the limbs coming from two directions and kind of overlapping because I was going against the grain, but I finally did. Unfortunately, by the time I got things figure out and got the route to the opening firmly fixed in my mind, I was no longer certain where my people train was.

"Where are you guys?" I whispered.

"Here," someone whispered, practically in my face.

I was delighted to find my sense of space and object orientation still worked pretty well in the dark.

Chapter 38

Sometimes silence is far scarier than all the cannon fire in the world. Darkness can be a warm comforting blanket, but when you can't even see your own hands and you have to fumble around to find your own face, it gets a little unnerving. Crawling around on the ground also tends to remind one that going back into the earth is something we all have to look forward to. It also makes you feel like some low life vermin.

"You guys okay?" I whispered for reassurance.

"Snug as a bug," someone whispered back. I had no idea which member of my people train it was.

"Here's the deal," I told them in a gruff whisper. "They're probably going to come looking for us. I don't know if they have another flashlight or any more guns. What I do know is that they will have a hard time finding us here where I'm going to hide you. The moon will be coming up in a little while and then you'll be able to see a lot better. But if they come looking with flashlights try to avoid looking at the light. Also don't look at the moon. If they do find us ... I want everybody to run in different directions. Okay?"

No one argued.

I had spent seven years in the service, a year of which was in Vietnam—but I'd never been in combat. *Was this any different than combat? Probably not,* I realized. We were hiding in the dark and the enemy was out there in the darkness some where. Not knowing exactly where Willie and Angel were or what they were planning to do was the unnerving part.

Hopefully, the evil pair would just get in Angel's car and hightail it out of there, if Angel's car wasn't too badly damaged that is. The cars had impacted pretty hard—hard enough to send the van careening off that cow path that masqueraded as a road. It was possible Angel's car had been damaged to the point of not being useable. If that turned out to be the case, the pair would certainly be looking to find us if for no other reason than to retrieve Willie's van keys. It was a sobering thought.

"Now, this is the hard part," I whispered, explaining the rest of my plan. "We're standing right beside a good sized clump of cedars. We're gonna get down on all fours and crawl into the center of this clump. That way, if they come looking with flashlights they'll have a really hard time finding us … so just pretend you're rabbits hiding in a brush pile and don't move a muscle." I knew I had everyone's full attention, so I just plunged on. "I'm gonna go first. Ruby I want you to go next—then everybody else in the same order as before. Okay? Only, because we'll be crawling on all fours instead of holding hands you'll grab the guy in front by one ankle. Okay?"

I got a lot of murmured consent and we began the time consuming awkward task of converting my people train into what I thought you might appropriately call a *'choo-choo'* train. It was an easy mental image, arms and legs moving forward simultaneously like the drive arms on a steam engine.

"Everybody ready?" I tried to throw my whisper back toward Jamal, our caboose.

"Go for it," someone whispered.

Under normal circumstances we might have felt chilly from the cool evening air, as it was, we were too preoccupied. Any teeth chattering that occurred among us would likely be from nerves. When we got to the center of the clump I chugged my *'choo-choo'* train into a circle and told everyone to get comfortable as best they could. When I got them all settled in, I crawled into the feathery tunnel leading into our hiding place and stretched out on my stomach so I could survey the woods below.

As I studied the darkness, it occurred to me that maybe the rabbit analogy wasn't the best choice of words. My parents had an Elkhound named Mike that found a rabbit sitting exposed on the edge of a brush pile. The rabbit thought it was hidden and just sat there trembling until Mike grabbed it and crushed the life out of it. At the time I had wondered why the rabbit didn't run—or was that just the way it was supposed to be when you're just a link in the food chain. It was kind of a chilling thought. And if I didn't keep a clamp on my imagination, I'd have Willie and Angel grabbing us while we sat petrified.

I'm not sure which came first—the moonlight or the sound. After what seemed like quadruple eons I heard a faint "Clinking" sound in the distance, metal on metal, and almost simultaneously realized that the moon must be up because I was beginning to be able to make out the outline of trees. Much to my chagrin, our hiding place was not as far away from the van as I had thought. The van was barely a hundred yards away.

Angel's Pontiac was maybe twenty-five yards further

away and had apparently ricocheted into a tree after hitting the van. I could make out two shadowy figures tinkering around at the front of the car, apparently trying to get the hood open. They did have a flashlight, which they occasionally used to look up into the grill as if they were trying to figure out why the hood wouldn't open, but I saw no sign of a gun. The trunk of the Pontiac was open and it appeared they were using a tire iron as a hood-opening tool.

Now ain't that a bitch, I snickered to myself, my mind racing wildly to evaluate the different possible scenarios of what was to come. Obviously Angel's Pontiac had sustained some sort of damage that required opening the hood—which could be as simple as just flooding out. If they got it started, they might just flee the area. Or, perhaps getting the Pontiac started was just the first step in a more diabolical plan. If they couldn't get the Pontiac started, sooner or later, they would come looking for the van keys.

"Jamal?" I called softly. "Come up here beside me!"

A minute or so later I felt Jamal's hand patting his way up my leg. I almost laughed. I had never been "patted up" before.

"I'm not exactly sure what their problem is," I whispered to Jamal when the young cheerleader was up beside me. "But I don't think we should wait until they get it solved." I was surprised at how well I could see the young black's face in the moonlight. "Do you think you could protect the ladies if I leave you with the gun? Think you're up to that?"

"What are you planning to do?" Jamal whispered back.

"Damned good question," I admitted softly. "I don't know ... but I do know we wouldn't be in this fix if we had taken care of Willie's buddy before trying to get away. I don't want to make the same mistake twice."

Jamal nodded in agreement.

"I'm going to take the flashlight," I continued, "'cause it might give me an edge. If worse comes to worse and something happens to me, shoot first and ask questions later if they come your way. I think this gun is a .22 caliber Rueger. I believe it holds nine shots, but Willie fired one. I have no idea if he reloaded or if it was ever fully loaded in the first place, so its best if you wait until they get pretty close. Don't worry about aiming ... just point it at them and pull the trigger."

I showed Jamal how the safety worked, picked out a nice big tree off to my left, and started crawling into the darkness.

"Good luck," Jamal whispered as I crawled away.

It's gonna take plenty of that, I thought, making my way to the first tree. My plan was to get close enough to put an arrow in at least one of them. With an arrow coming out of the darkness, they'd be hard put to figure out what was going on. The only trouble was, I only had two arrows and shooting a bow accurately in the moonlight can be a bit tricky, as I'd already proven.

Keeping track of a bow, two arrows, and a flashlight while trying to sneak through the woods in the moonlight was also a bit tricky. It would have been nice to have a quiver, but I didn't and I was pretty sure the *sock thing* wouldn't work very well trying to crawl forward on the ground.

But I made the ten or so yards to the first tree without any problems.

Somehow in leading Jamal and the ladies to our hiding place I had been lucky enough to stumble my way through a fairly clear patch of woods. I could now see that by going a little ways to the left I could get behind some trees that would provide pretty fair cover for sneaking up on Willie and his buddy. If I moved in quickly enough, I could get them while they were still working on the Pontiac.

It would be really nice to have more arrows though.

It wasn't until after I'd crawled partway through a small thicket that I realized I was right in the middle of the solution to my arrow problem. As a former farm boy, I'd always carried a pocketknife. That's what farmers do. Once a farm boy becomes citified, he graduates to a penknife, which is smaller, cuter, and not very effective as a knife. I never quite fully graduated. The knife in my pocket was a so-called Swiss Army version about halfway between a penknife and pocketknife. The single blade was sharper than a penknife but it also had a screw diver blade and small pair of scissors.

If I hadn't totally wrecked the knife blade trying to scratch cement out of the block joints earlier, I might be able to do something about making more arrows. Fortunately, the screw driver blade was longer than the knife blade and I'd mostly used it on the cement. The underbrush around me was just the right size for making arrows. The only problem was that arrows don't fly very straight without the little feather fins on the back. It suddenly occurred to me that I had a way of solving that problem—it just meant cutting up a couple of credit cards.

Working quickly in the moonlight I cut a number of saplings and stripped the bark off them. By forcing my knife blade partway into the butt end of each sapling I should be able to form a slot that would accept half of a credit card. I really should use a whole card, but I was afraid a slot that deep would split the arrow completely. Besides, I did not have that many credit cards and I wanted at least four more arrows. After preparing the shafts I used the scissors on the knife to cut the cards in half, then forced them into place. By pulling the bark into thin strips, I was able to tie the card-halves solidly in place. I was also careful to wind enough bark into the slot behind the cards to make sure the arrows wouldn't hang up on the bowstring.

The extra arrows were pretty crude, but I had tapered them to a long, narrow point. Hopefully the arrows would pierce whatever I hit, instead of breaking.

Making the arrows probably took as much as half an hour, despite the feverish pitch of my efforts. Fortunately, Willie and Angel were not as successful with their efforts. *Girding my loins,* so to speak, I gathered up my handiwork and started inching my way toward the sound of their tinkering. It wasn't long before I could make out parts of their conversation.

"We should just hot wire the damned van!" Willie exclaimed at one point.

"I'm not leaving my car," Angel growled.

"We could always come back for it."

"Well, go ahead then … if you know how!"

Apparently Willie did not know how because the

sinister duo just kept banging and prying away at the Pontiac hood. Mostly, it was Willie holding the flashlight while Angel did the hood banging.

"There, damn it!" Angel declared finally. He handed the tire iron to Willie and jerked open the hood. "Give me the light," he snarled. "You get in and try it."

My timing could not have been better. I was behind a fair-sized tree barely thirty feet away from them. Angel was in front of the Pontiac on the driver's side just ready to take a plunge under the hood. Willie was to the right of Angel. They both had their backs to me and had their minds on Angel's car.

I had already decided to use one of the good arrows first and use the *made-in-the-woods* arrows for backup. I eased myself to my feet, then leaned my bundle of arrows against the tree for easy access, notched one of the good arrows and pulled the bow up just as Willie handed Angel the flashlight and turned to get in the car. Realizing there would never be a better opportunity I drew in a deep breath and let the arrow fly.

The whisper of the arrow 's flight was like music in a grand ballroom.

Angel's reaction was a total surprise, reminding me instantly of the time I'd tried to roll this big rock onto a skid loader with a pry bar. Just as I almost got the rock into the skid loader bucket I noticed a hog-nose snake slithering around my feet. The snake had startled me enough that I let the rock go and it landed on the snake in exactly the right position to cause the snake to expel the air in its lungs, making a sort of "Woofing" sound. It was the only time I'd ever heard a snake make a sound other than hissing, and it suddenly seemed very appropriate when Angel went, "Whoof," in the same startled, guttural way.

Take that you son of a bitch, I declared exuberantly to myself as I reached for the other good arrow.

"What the—" Angel declared, flailing around to try and reach the arrow sticking out of his backside. He was apparently hit in that soft spot between the bottom of the rib cage and the top of the hipbone. The arrow had entered more on his back than his side and it was hard for him to reach it effectively enough to pull it out with his left hand, as he seemed to be trying to do.

Just right to skewer the appendix, I thought, notching the other good arrow.

Angel slumped forward against the front of his car, still struggling to grab the arrow. In the process he lost his balance and slid to the ground in a heap on his left side. Again, it couldn't have been more perfect. When the arrow hit Angel he dropped the flashlight and it had fallen into the engine compartment.

"What's wrong?" Willie demanded, diving under the hood to retrieve the flashlight so he could see what was going on.

I waited patiently.

As soon as the flashlight revealed the arrow sticking in Angel's side, Willie looked out toward the darkness, but not exactly in my direction and screamed, "You son-of-a-bitch! I'll get you for this!"

Willie made the mistake of leaning over to get a closer look at Angel's wound—just as I let the second arrow fly.

Willie's reaction was even way more satisfying than Angel's.

"Hiiiiekes!" he screamed, immediately grabbing his ass and jumping around like a *peppered* hound.

Now here was the part of the plan that I hadn't given much thought to. *What was I supposed to do once I had these bastards skewered?* My first thought was to stay behind the tree and have Jamal and the girls come down. That seemed a little too risky, however, because I was too far away and I wasn't real sure how well my make shift arrows would actually work.

For want of a better plan, noting with satisfaction that Willie had dropped their flashlight again, I grabbed my makeshift arrows and started out of the shadows. As I walked I shifted three of the arrow against the bow so I could hold the three arrows and the bow with my left hand. Then I notched the fourth arrow and pulled the bowstring back partway.

"Unless you want to be wearing another arrow in your gullet," I advised sternly. "I wouldn't go reaching for the flashlight!"

The flashlight was shining up out of the engine compartment in such a way that the evil pair were fairly well illuminated and I was not.

Willie stopped hopping around and stared out into the darkness in the general direction of where my voice had come from. I could almost hear the wheels turning in Willie's brain.

"Last time I looked," he said right on cue. "There were only two arrows."

"I went to the arrow store," I snarled, letting the makeshift arrow fly so that it landed with a thud between Willie's legs.

"The next time I'll aim a little higher," I warned, notching another arrow.

Both men were apparently in considerable pain, but not really in any danger of dying or passing out. My first thought was to let them wear the arrows for awhile, but there were more practical reasons for having them removed.

"Jamal!" I yelled out without turning my head. "Can you hear me, Jamal?"

I waited for the faint reply and then yelled out for them all to come on down. I knew I would feel a lot better with Willie's gun in my hand rather than a bow with make-shift arrows. In the mean time, I decided to get the two good arrows back.

"Tell you what, Willie ... why don't you pull that arrow out of your buddy's side and bring it over here and stick it in the ground."

"I can just barely walk," Willie whined.

"It wasn't a request," I said firmly.

Willie did as he was ordered.

This time Angel let out a shriek. "Damn that hurts!" he exclaimed, writhing around on the ground as Willie took a few steps into the dark and stuck the arrow into the ground.

"Your turn," I said, motioning Willie back toward the car. "If your buddy can stop whining long enough to help you, that is."

Angel struggled to his feet and did as he was ordered.

By this time their flashlight was beginning to grow quite dim. I wasn't worried much about that, but I did regret leaving Willie's other flashlight at the base of the tree where I'd started my attack. Suddenly having a bright light flashed in your face was a good way of thwarting an attack, and I already knew from personal experience that Willie could become desperate enough to gamble and charge me.

I could hear Jamal and the ladies working their way down the slope, but without a flashlight they weren't moving very fast. I was beginning to wish to God they'd hurry up.

The wish was barely a thought before Willie and Angel made their charge.

I was already in the process of notching one of the good arrows when they came at me. Unfortunately there were two of them. I did manage to get the arrow fired off, but I was too rushed and maybe a little conflicted about which one to shot. The arrow flew harmlessly between the pair and I was sent sprawling backwards. I landed with a thud just as Jamal fired his first shot.

God Bless the boy, I thought as darkness closed off my mind for a second time in just two short days.

Chapter 39

"I'm sorry," Jamal said to me when I regained consciousness. "I let them get away. I didn't want to use up all of the bullets, just in case—"

The moon was now partway behind some clouds and it was difficult to see Jamal's face. "You did exactly the right thing," I told him. "In fact, I think you may have saved my life."

"Are you okay, sweetheart?" Lynn asked, emerging from the shadows just as the moon put in a new appearance.

"You mean other than my wounded pride?" I chuckled, wanting to kiss her so bad I could taste it. I decided to do exactly that.

She didn't object.

I looked around quickly, trying to assess our situation before the moon took another dive behind the clouds. I still had my left arm hooked around Lynn's waist and Jamal was just to my right. Ruby had one arm around Julie's shoulders and the other around Andy's. I wasn't sure if she was supporting them, or it they were supporting her. It didn't matter.

"Do you think they left for good?" I asked, not directing the question at anyone in particular. I had already made enough tactical errors to defeat a battalion. I didn't really want to make any more.

"It sure looked like it," Jamal laughed. "They were sure in a hell of a hurry."

"How long was I out?"

"Not very darned long," Jamal informed me excitedly. "When I fired that shot they jumped off you and grabbed that flashlight, did something quick under the hood, slammed the hood and took off. I don't think the hood was even latched … and they only have one headlight. They were just disappearing from sight when you came around. We could still probably catch them if we hurry."

"Let's not," I sighed, thankful that everyone was safe. "We need to find us a police station and let them take care of that."

"How we gonna do that?" Andy quipped. "It's so dark out here I couldn't find my ass with both hands."

Everybody laughed.

"I see your point, honey," I said, tears welling up in my eyes. "You guys wait right here and I'll see if I can find Willie's other flashlight. I think I know right where it is."

As soon as I retrieved the flashlight I got everyone herded back to the van. For reasons that I really didn't understand at the time, I took a moment to round up the bow and all the arrows. I removed the credit card halves from the make shift arrows and stuck them in my pocket, and then tossed the shafts. I tossed the bow and the two good arrows in the back of the van and held the light while Jamal and the girls loaded Willie's stuff.

I wasn't exactly sure why we bothered with Willie's stuff, other than it might contain some important evidence—and besides, it was in the way in case we had to back out of the pothole.

Getting unstuck with a vehicle was something I'd had a lot of experience with over the years. A quick survey of the situation with the flashlight revealed that the pothole wasn't really a pothole like I was used to back in Minnesota. I didn't think there was even any water in it. It was just a little depression that a dead tree had fallen across. The van had simply bounced into the air and land on a piece of the tree big enough in diameter to keep the drive wheels from touching the ground. All we had to do to get unstuck was find another piece of dead wood big enough to force under the wheels to get traction.

We were back on the road in no time at all.

Jamal and the girls made a sort of bed in the back for Ruby with Willie's stuff and let Lynn and I have the front. I elected to do the driving.

And the driving.

And the driving.

"Anyone got any spare women's intuition?" I asked finally when my head started spinning. "We might be driving around out here forever."

Andy's head popped up between the seats. "Just keep making right turns," she suggested.

I wasn't sure if she had intended the double meaning, but since we had no idea where we were, or in which direction to go to find a main road it didn't seem like such a bad plan. It did seem like the roads we were driving on were either logging or mining roads. There didn't seem to be any houses or businesses of any kind and lots of side roads that seemed to go in circles. My innate sense of direction wasn't doing me much good as long as the moon kept disappearing behind the clouds.

The thought that we might run out of gas before ever

actually getting anywhere was beginning to nag at me. Fortunately, we came to a paved road just as the moon popped out from behind a cloud and Andy's suggestion to make right turns did not conflict with my sense that that was somehow back the way we'd come the day before.

But even then, the road seemed to go on forever. I could occasionally make out the outline of a house or two along the road, but none of them had any lights on. Which could either mean no one was home or that they'd gone to bed. It seemed like the best thing to do was just keep going. Besides, the sky was beginning to be brighter to the east, indicating there might be a fairly good-sized town up ahead.

Before we reached the town, however, we spotted the blue and red flashing lights of a police cruiser on the side of the road ahead. I could not see what kind of car the police had pulled over until I was almost past, but I wasn't surprised to see that it was Angel's Pontiac. I made a quick executive decision and pulled off the road in front of the Pontiac.

"You guys stay in the van," I said, opening the door.

As I walked toward the police cruiser I could see Willie and Angel silhouetted in the cruiser headlights and a lone officer standing a few feet back from the driver's door of the Pontiac.

"Get back in your car, Mister!" the policeman yelled at me, taking a step back and putting his right hand on the butt of his service revolver.

I stopped. "I need to talk to you about these two guys," I said, squinting into the headlights of the cruiser. I was careful not to make any sudden moves.

"We can talk about 'em in your car," the officer said warily.

I stood my ground. "That might be too late. I don't know if they're armed or not, but I have good reason to believe they might be. I can tell you this much—they've both been wounded."

"How do you know that?" The cop was not sure whether to trust me or not.

"Because I was the one who wounded them—with a bow and arrow."

Now the cop really had a dilemma. I was talking about weapons, but did not seem to have any—particularly a bow and arrow.

"I don't know if you heard about it or not," I went on, "But one of them is wanted for shooting a man and woman in Jacksonville with a bow and arrow three or four weeks ago. They're calling him the Robin Hood marauder. The other one is a rapist that kidnapped a little girl in Lake City, Florida." I really felt like I was babbling now, but I couldn't seem to stop.

Plus, the cop seemed to be wavering.

"I think you should ask the driver to step out of the car. You'll see that he's been wounded like I said—"

Suddenly the officer thought that might be a good idea. "Okay," he said finally. "I'll do just that. But you stay right where you are. You move and I start shooting."

Seemed like a fair deal to me.

The officer made Angel put both of his hands through the car window and open the door from the outside. In the mean time Willie was to keep his hands in plain sight on the dashboard.

"He's lying, officer," Angel declared as he carried out the policeman's orders. "I'm not this Robin Hood guy ... he is!"

The biggest thing that worried me was that Willie

might jump out of the car and start running, but even if he did he wasn't likely to get away for very long. And that posed no danger for Jamal and the girls.

The minute the officer saw the bloodstains on Angel's shirt he slammed him up against the car, kicked his legs apart and cuffed him. He patted Angel up and down and then ordered Willie to scoot across the seat and climb out the driver's door. Within a few minutes both men were cuffed and placed in the back of the police cruiser.

"Now what's this all about?" the officer asked, joining me with his back to the light from the cruiser's headlights.

"It's a pretty damned long story," I told him. "I've got a van full of very tired, very hungry people—these guys kidnapped us back in Montgomery on Thanksgiving Day."

The cop stared at me for a very long time, apparently trying to decide if his leg was being pulled.

"I should also tell you," I went on, nodding toward the van "that the van belongs to the black one. His name is William McPherson and his grandmother is one of the people in the van."

I still felt like I was babbling but I could see the officer was beginning to get the picture.

"Let me get on the radio," he said finally. "We'll get some help out here and get you folks a ride into town. We'll tow both of these vehicles."

"Sounds like a winner to me," I informed him jubilantly.

"You can wait in the van," the officer continued. "I'll walk you back."

He escorted me back to the van, flashed his light around inside to satisfy himself that I wasn't pulling his leg.

"You folks just wait here," he ordered. "I'll go make that radio call."

It wasn't until the officer's footsteps on the gravel had faded as he walked back to his squad car and another car went past that I first noticed the road sign in front of the van and burst out laughing.

"What in the dickens is so all-fired funny?" Lynn demanded when I was able to stop laughing enough for her to get my attention.

"That sign," I burst into another round of guffaws. "I just fed that police officer a whole line of crap about how Angel shot a couple people in Jacksonville with his trusty little bow and arrow—that they're calling him the *Robin Hood marauder!*"

"So?"

"So," I said, realizing that without another passing car's headlights she couldn't even read the sign. "Look!" I flipped on the headlights for her.

It was her turn to laugh.

The sign read: Jacksonville City Limits

"What—" Jamal and Julie murmured, looking at us like we'd both lost our minds, then to one another for some sort of explanation.

I figured it was time to let them in on the joke. "You guys heard that story in the news about the Robin Hood marauder, right?" I waited for some nodding heads before continuing. Since Andy already knew the full story she had what can only be described as a "shit eating" grin on her face. Ruby too, but more dignified. "Well," I continued when I got their puzzled nods. "The woman in the news is my ex-wife—and guess who was wielding the bow! You can see by the sign that we're almost in Jacksonville—but it sure as hell ain't Jacksonville, Florida. I think we must still be in Alabama."

"You're right, Russell," Ruby confirmed. "It is Jacksonville, Alabama."

"So I've come full circle," I snickered, starting to laugh again.

"I thought it was a private joke at first," Andy said between cackles. "But now I see its not … not unless you're Willie's buddy Angel! Boy is the joke ever on him—"

That set us all off again.

Actually, I realized, it wasn't really that funny. Most of the laughter had been the kind of hysteria that pops to the surface once you realize you've gotten through a life and death situation. It was like being strapped to a rocket sled that smashed through the sound barrier. While you're being buffeted around at 700 mph plus you hold everything in check. Once the ride is over, you just collapse in relief.

The odd thing was at that point in time I knew next to nothing about Willie's buddy Angel—other than the fact that he'd made it obvious that he was willing to go to any length to help Willie defend his freedom, even if that meant multiple murders. So, obviously, I would not be loosing any sleep if the police chose to believe me. To be honest, considering the conditions under which I'd seen Angel, it did seem odd. I couldn't tell you much about him other than the fact he was Hispanic and about the same size and build as Willie. No way in hell would I ever be able to pick him out of a lineup—unless it really was in hell.

Chapter 40

Twenty minutes later a convoy of black and white State Patrol cars from Jacksonville and two tow trucks with flashing lights and sirens came roaring onto the scene, made multiple U-turns at an intersection behind us and came roaring to a stop. The noise of the sirens died away, but not the flashing lights.

"You folks can come with me," an officer told us through the van window.

I started to open the door, debating whether to open the door for Lynn and let the others fend for themselves, or do it the other way round. Before I could decide or exit the van Jamal tapped me on the shoulder.

"What about the gun?" he asked. His face looked like he'd just fallen off the top of a ladder and realized that gravity still worked.

"Oh, geez," I had completely forgotten about that. "Where is it?"

"Here," Jamal pulled the gun partway out of his belt.

"Just leave it," I decided, having sudden visions of Jamal being shot as he tried to turn the firearm over to the police. "Put the safety on and throw it on the floor. They'll find it when they go through the van."

Jamal was almost white with relief.

Lynn, Ruby and I rode in one squad car, Jamal and

the girls in another. The ride to the Jacksonville police station only took a few minutes. The station seemed to be on a side street just off the main square of what was apparently a small college town. No wonder Ruby knew about it. Judging by the length of the drive we'd only been a few miles outside of the city.

I got to be the spokesperson when we arrived at the station. I wasn't positive about the time, but I was pretty sure it was almost midnight and I was starving. I figured Lynn and the others were just as hungry as I was and I was not in the mood for a lot of questions.

"You say one of these guys is a rapist?" the interviewing officer asked.

"That's right. He kidnapped a young girl in Lake City, Florida a few weeks back."

The black officer stared at me blankly for a moment. "Kidnapping is not the same thing as rape—" he began. His name was Brody

I cut him off. "Kidnapper then!"

"How do you know he kidnapped her?"

I was beginning to get angry. "Because I rescued her! That doesn't even matter anyway. Those two guys kidnapped all six of us back in Montgomery on Thanksgiving day … so just lock 'em up and throw away the key."

"I was just trying to get at the facts—" Officer Brody became slightly less truculent.

"I'm sorry, Officer Brody," I apologized. "We're all tired and hungry—"

Brody melted a little.

"We haven't eaten since Thanksgiving evening," I went on. "All we really know for certain is that William

McPherson probably raped at least one girl and may have accidentally killed her, and that he kidnapped another young girl that he was apparently planning to rape. He brought us up here from Montgomery at gunpoint and locked us in some sort of demolition storage shed someplace out in the woods near an abandoned open pit mine of some sort. I'm pretty sure he intended to kill us."

"What about the other guy?"

I shrugged. "All I can tell you is that he's Willie's buddy. I think his name is Angel something and he seemed very willing to do to us whatever Willie wanted."

The questioning went on for another twenty minutes, mostly covering the same ground over and over again, before Brody suggested we might go around the corner to get something to eat. "I'll come get you later and give you a ride to a motel," he concluded with a grin.

...

The walk to the nearest restaurant was hardly even a hundred feet. The place was called Nick's Famous Pizza and claimed to have the best pizza and steak in town. That wouldn't have mattered. I was, as the saying goes, *ready to eat the back end out of a bear*. For once I didn't even care if the place was sit down or not.

It was more than an hour later before Brody came to get us. He had apparently commandeered a van some place that was big enough to hold all of us. He drove us to a motel and informed us that he would be back in the morning to pick us up to finish the questioning and help us get home.

The motel turned out to be another tense moment. The clerk was very reluctant to rent three rooms to a guy with a mixed entourage of companions, none of which had any luggage, and who could only offer a cut-in-half credit card as payment. I'd had to use what little cash Jamal and I had to pay for the food. Where Lynn and the girls' purses were was anybody's guess. The fact that we had been delivered by a policeman didn't help either. I figured we'd have a similar problem renting a car the next day.

But at that point I didn't really care.

When Lynn and I were finally snuggled in bed twenty minutes later, we were both too wound up to sleep.

"Do you think they'll really believe Angel is the Robin Hood Marauder?" Lynn asked, tracing her fingers absently along my biceps.

"I have a feeling that will be the least of Angel's worries."

"You think—"

I nodded. "I think he was way to willing to go along with Willie's plans. This wasn't his first outing, believe me. And I'll tell you something else."

"What's that?"

"You have a lot of reasons to be damned proud of your girls, that's what. They came through this like real troupers."

Lynn was quiet for a moment. "You think we'll make it back in time for Andy's appointment?"

"Does it matter? We can always reschedule."

Lynn didn't reply. She had that far away look that mothers some times get when they start wondering about how many ways they went wrong in raising their children. It was one of those exercises in futility.

"I can tell you something else," I continued.

"What's that?" Lynn murmured drowsily.

"Andy's father is probably going to look like Prince Charming to her after spending all this time with Willie and his buddy Angel."

"Hmm," Lynn moaned.

I was going to say something else but suddenly realized she wouldn't hear me if I did. She was starting to snore peacefully.

I let her sleep. I had some thinking to do myself. Maybe I had been a little too hard on God. I certainly wouldn't want to change places with Willie or Angel. Perhaps blaming the Robin Hood marauder things on Angel was a silly thing to do. There was a real good chance that it wasn't going to work anyway. And I was suddenly remembering that I'd gotten mad and told Brody I was the one that had rescued Wendy—and that was just the same as confessing that I was the Robin Hood guy. But I was still hoping the whole deal would fall through the cracks and I'd be off the hook. Maybe God had put me through this whole ordeal just so I could get hooked up with Lynn.

I went to sleep then and started dreaming about the very real woman, with two lovely daughters, sleeping beside me.

. . .

Brody picked us up at 10:00 O'clock the next morning and dropped up off at the station. "Y'all can go ahead and eat and come over later to finish the questioning."

We were a little surprised, but didn't argue. Since none of us were very hungry because we'd eaten so late the night before and the thought of pizza for breakfast wasn't so appealing, we went to the Java Jolt next door to Nick's and ordered coffee and pastries. I have to say it really hit the spot.

"Why don't you guys just stay here for awhile," I suggested. "It's better than sitting around in the police station and I can always come and get you if the police want to ask you any questions. Oh, yeah … and I'll see if I can find out what happened to your purses. We might just need them to get home.

"I'm coming with you," Lynn informed me. It was not a question.

The questions didn't take very long, mostly a reiteration of what we'd gone over the night before.

"Can I asked a question?" I said when Brody indicated he was satisfied with our story. I was glad Lynn was along because he seemed to accept her confirmation of what I told him as the genuine gospel.

"Fire away," Brody said, yawning.

I imagined he hadn't gotten much sleep either. "Did you get this Angel character identified? I have a feeling he was already wanted by the police."

Brody nodded. "Oh, yeah … we got his ass nailed but good. We got a couple of "*all points*" on him. Wouldn't matter though. Besides kidnapping y'all," he said with a wink, "We got his ass on that Robin Hood marauder thing—"

Chapter 41

I have to admit Officer Brody's wink gave me quite a bit to think about as we made arrangements to get back to Montgomery. The police found the ladies' purses in a plastic bag in the trunk of Angel's car. I wasn't exactly sure how Willie had managed that and had actually thought they might still be back in Ruby's house. Obviously I had not been paying close enough attention back then. Anyway, Lynn produced a credit card that wasn't cut in half and we were able to rent a car to drive back to Montgomery.

I flew home to Minnesota from Montgomery. I could have driven back to Lake City with Lynn but that would have meant an even greater delay in getting the wheels of "selling the office" in motion. And I was fortunate enough to be able to talk Sam Turner into managing my office for the up-coming tax season. The one thing I had learned from the events that had followed my foray into the realm of mischief and mayhem in Jacksonville was that life was too short and fleeting to spend it doing something you really didn't like, just because you could.

I also signed the divorce papers and put my house on the market.

At first, Willie and Angel took their rightful place in the Alabama prison system awaiting trial on six counts of kidnapping and the results of on-going investigations into their past. Willie confessed to burying Sheniqqua's body in an abandoned coal-mine up somewhere along the Coosa River west of Anniston all those years ago. Unfortunately, the Department of Interior had since dumped so much money into removing safety hazards around abandoned mines that the odds that the body would ever be found were about a zillion to one. Its seems there was difficulty in even figuring out exactly where to look after all that time. And without a body—

Willie also tried to claim that Sheniqqua was his only victim to suffer such a tragic end—that any of the other girls he might have molested must have liked it because they hadn't came forward to complain that he knew of. In a way, we all truly hoped for Ruby's sake that Willie was telling the truth, but we all had serious doubts. We were also hoping the number of young girls who would have to grow up struggling with their sexual identity the way Wendy from Lake City might because of what Willie had done to her wouldn't be a very substantial number. But again, we all had serious doubts

It was bad enough that Ruby's Charles would never be honored in his rightful place as one of the Tuskegee Airmen. Equally tragic that Ruby's only son had become a victim of the racial tensions of the times. None of us ever know exactly what kind of hand life is going to deal us, but Ruby certainly deserved better.

She also deserved better than having to deal with the fact that her only grandson was willing to consider killing her to save his butt.

"How could you do such a thing, William?" Ruby asked him when Lynn and I took her up to see him at the Donaldson Correctional Facility near Bessemer about an hour and a half north of Montgomery after he was sentenced.

"I couldn't Gram," Willie told her mercifully. "That's why I drove way into Georgia to pick up Angel."

"Ain't no different," Ruby told him.

"I know, Gram," Willie muttered, hanging his head in shame.

"How'd you ever hook up with that guy in the first place?" I demanded, a little bugged by the situation. *Surely it couldn't be as simple as that old saw: Birds of a feather flock together!* It couldn't be quite that simplistic.

"We met in a police lineup when I was picked as a suspect in a homicide," Willie admitted. "Afterwards, in the holding cell, Angel told me he knew I wasn't the one they were after because he was—but that he somehow knew I was just like him somehow. Then he started bragging about all the young boys he did—"

"Don't even tell me what that means," Ruby said in disgust.

It was a little hard to comprehend. What kind of world do we live in where young men like Angel and Willie seek solace from each other by bragging about their sadistic, animal behavior? There were no easy answers.

But maybe there is a weird kind of justice.

"It doesn't matter now, anyway," William added as an afterthought.

"What do you mean?" Lynn asked, picking up on something in his tone.

William kind of chuckled. "Didn't you hear? Angel got knifed and almost died—"

We all stared at him waiting for the rest of the story to see if we should cheer or not.

"He got sent to the Georgia State Prison at Reidsville … over by Savannah cause he was wanted for some things in Georgia. Anyway, he hardly got settled in when some guy knifed him for messing with his buddy—"

"How did you find that out?" I asked with a smile.

Willie smiled back. "We have our ways … you know, prison grapevine—"

"What was so danged funny?" Lynn asked on our way back to Montgomery.

"What d'ya mean?" I said, checking the rear view mirror to see if Ruby was listening.

"You know … when you asked Willie how he found out about Angel—"

"It was because of what I learn on the Internet," I told her, satisfied that Ruby had dozed off. "It seems the Georgia prison system has something called PREA—"

"What the devil is that?" Lynn demanded.

I smiled. "Nothing much … the letters stand for Prison Rape Elimination Act. When you think about that and what probably happened to Angel … well, it's pretty darned hard not to bust right out laughing."

Lynn did not disagree with me.

…

I also talked Lynn into giving up her job—for the same reasons that I put the tax business up for sale. She wasn't hard to convince. She was just one of millions of women who, unlike Ruby, had had to give up their careers to raise their family.

"If you want to work," I told her, "you need to go back to school and get qualified for something you really wanted to do. Why don't you talk to the girls about it?"

We spend a lot of our weekends with Jamal and the girls. During the week Lynn and I spend a fair amount of time on the Internet—mostly trying to track down Sheniqqua's family to give them closure and to see if we can find Willie's mother. We both agree it might be nice to do what we can about tracking down missing children, but we're both afraid of becoming emotionally burned out if we spend too much time doing that.

Andrea is still going to counseling sessions twice a week but it seems like they might not be necessary much longer. Mostly now, she claims she's just trying to come to terms with the prospect of facing her father and telling him what a jerk he was and that he needs to get his butt in for some counseling as well. Lynn suspects there's a good chance that he behaved the way he did because he might have been molested by his own father. Apparently Steve's mother was a real mouse of a woman until Steve's father died. The mother changed so dramatically after that that Lynn figured there had to be something creepy and unhealthy going on.

Besides that, I decided, there is an awful lot to learn about the South—and you generally don't need a snow shovel to do it.

Epilogue

At Christmas we all went to Disney World and tried to act like normal fun-loving tourists. For me, that was still a major adjustment. Lynn and I haven't talked seriously about marriage yet, but I'm pretty sure that's something that will happen at some point down the road. The news media has given the Robin Hood marauder thing a rest since the police consider the case solved. They're not sure about Angel's motivation but figure with him motivation isn't all that big a deal. I'm not about to argue with them on that.

Some time in January we got word from Ruby that William had written to let her know that Jose Angel Rodriquez Ramirez had succumbed to his knife wounds and the state was not going to have to bother to bring him to trial. He had died like the animal he was. Apparently no one showed up to claim the body.

Shortly after Valentine's Day, Andy announced that she thought she had herself a boyfriend, but that she wasn't quite sure. His name was Allen and he was a senior. They had gone out at least half a dozen times, but they hadn't kissed yet.

I told her jokingly that she didn't have to be prudish about it.

"I'm not," she assured me, kissing me quickly on her

favorite spot in the middle of my forehead. "We'll get there when the time is right. Wait and see."

I am willing to wait, and I am also hoping I have the honor of giving her away.

P. S.

Oh yes, I almost forgot. My divorce from Maria went through fine after I signed the papers. I didn't send her a Christmas card and even though I am now living in Florida among the moss covered oaks and palm trees, odds are real good that I will probably never see her again or ever let her know that I'm practically living next door.

Author's Notes

Sometimes the line between truth and fiction can be sort of hazy. An invented piece of fiction can have the ring of truth, and the real truth can sounds like a bald-faced lie. Russell Martin, one of my grandfathers, is a good example of this. The truth is that some time before I knew my grandfather, the ball joints at the top of his femurs came out of his hip sockets and he was forced to spend the rest of his life seven inches shorter and could only walk with the aid of crutches. True, in my grandfather's day medicine wasn't what it is today. But even so, the truth my grandfather lived with during his final years must have seemed like a cruel lie, especially for him.

I tell you this because my practice as a writer of fiction is to take small kernels of truth and adjust them until I have a believable story that has the ring of universal truth—something writers like to call poetic license. The formula is very simple. Take a few facts, sprinkle liberally with poetic license (lies) and *kah-ching*—you've got a story and, unfortunately, a possible lawsuit on your hands. I therefore feel not only morally obligated but compelled (in the interest of self-preservation) to point out the important kernels of truth in my story … to separate the wheat from the chaff, the truth from the lies.

The section of the story involving Kathleen Henson, Evelyn Mattson, and Lt. Leonard Kramer is loosely based on a real event—the crash of an AT-6 trainer flown by one Marjorie Laverne Davis near Walnut, Mississippi on October 16, 1944. In real life a fellow trainee, Hallie Stiles, took Marjorie's body back to Englewood, California for burial. Lt. Leonard Gonye was their flight leader. But that is the sum total of what I know about these people. Every thing else in these scenes, other than the basic facts of the crash, is pure *poetic license* for the purposes of my story. Of course, I could have altered the circumstances around the crash and the incident would have still worked for my story, but then the reading public would never be made aware of the heroic sacrifices so many of these people made for our country during World War II. I sincerely hope that my approach brings some of these people the honor they richly deserve.

Loosing Marjorie Davis had to be a traumatic experience for Hallie Stiles and Lt. Goyne. Death never sits lightly. I know when my father's sister Edna was killed in a farming accident in the summer of either 1944 or 1945 and I had to ride in the back of our 1935 Plymouth over a dusty farm road with Edna, it left a very lasting impression. As my wife's late father liked to put it: "When you're dead … you're dead a long time.

It also occurred to me during the writing of this part of the book that I might have actually met someone who might have personally known some of these WASPs. During part of 1958 and 1959 while stationed at Fort Knox, Kentucky, I joined the base flying club to take flying lesson. For my sixth hour of instruction I had a women instructor that I had never flown with before. The thing that made her so memorable was that she didn't bother to ask me anything about my previous flying experience before we took off. She simply said, "Go." It had been several months since my previous lesson and I got confused as we started down the runway. For those unfamiliar with the mechanics of single engine Piper Cubs, the propeller spinning in one direction causes the plane to veer to the right. The fledgling pilot must learn to correct with rudder to keep the plane taxiing straight down the runway. If you correct in the wrong way the right wing of the plane will go down and the left one up. When the right wing hits the ground the plane will flip over. Fortunately, training planes have dual controls and my lady instructor was able to cut the power before I suffered that embarrassment.

Tuskegee Air Cadet, Charles McPherson is pure invention and was in no way intended to slur the memory of the many fine men who became known as the Tuskegee Airmen. I salute you guys. Unfortunately, the racial tensions of the times were not an invention. Lynching black men just because they were black is one of the many cruel and unjust embarrassments of our history.

So too is the frightening frequency of sexual incidents in our society involving the rape and murder of young people. Why I chose such a chilling subject for my first novel, aside from selling a zillion books and getting very rich (tongue in cheek), isn't exactly clear to me. To tell the truth, I simply started writing and that's what came out—one thing led to another.

In case you're wondering why I didn't just choose one incident and write a true crime book, it's because I believe a broader more general overall approach could be more effective. In other words, I don't believe these monsters really want to be monsters—that something went drastically wrong in their lives. What can we do as a society to prevent a potential monster from ever getting started in the first place?

I should also tell you that William and Angel are not based on actual real rapists, just archetypes. And, in no way did I ever intend to imply that blacks and Hispanics are any more inclined toward rape and murder than whites. The intended point was that the economic circumstances impacting both blacks and Hispanics might cause an increased incidence of rape and rape related murder among those races in the same way it impacts gang violence.

Ruby's house on E. Washington Street does not exist and never did because I invented Ruby. The Pilgrims Rest Baptist Church however is very real and I apologize to the congregation for dragging them into the fray. Any similarities between characters in this book and actual congregation members named Ruby or Sadie is purely coincidental.

The fact is, although they now seem real to me, none of the characters in my novel are based on real people that need protection by way of disclosure except for the three people associated with Marjorie Davis' unfortunate crash. None that is, except the owners of a couple of very real restaurants.

One of the more pleasant duties of a writer can be checking out the various eating places you send your characters to. My approach to writing the first draft of the novel was to use Internet map software to find restaurants that my characters could visit. The fun thing about that approach is that the only way to make that approach really work is to actually go to the restaurants, sample the fair, and take notes on the décor and other pertinent information. And hopefully that comes under the heading of a tax-deductible vacation—just kidding IRS.

At any rate, that's what my wife and I did and it was a very enjoyable experience. According to Brian Tucker, owner of Tucker's Fine Dining in Lake City, Florida, Al Capone did stay there because the Blanche Hotel was on the major highway between Chicago and Miami. He didn't explain why Governor Cone stayed there. Anyway, the restaurant is on the ground floor behind the hotel lobby just as I described and the food there is absolutely excellent. I did not meet the owner of Martin's in Montgomery, but based on the number of awards hanging on the wall and my personal taste-test the food there is definitely worth any effort to look the place up. Dimitri Polizos' Capitol Grill in Montgomery, Alabama is well worth that effort as well. Dimitri was very nice and was kind enough to let me take his picture holding the framed cover of a November issue of Matha Stewart's magazine *Living* containing a review of the Capitol Grill.

Unfortunately, I did not get the chance to try the fair in Nana's Country Café in Courtland, Alabama. According to Nana's husband on the phone, the café was closed in January because changing the highway so it went around Courtland had too great an impact on the restaurant's business. That happens to a lot of fine restaurants in many small towns all across the country and is one of the prices we pay for progress.

I would also like to tell you that I did try to keep the

explicit sex to a minimum and not gratuitous. Writers are forever warned not to use cliches when writing, but there is one that seems so appropriate in this situation it's hard not to use it. I mean of course, the one that says "you can't make an omelet without breaking eggs." It's pretty hard to talk about rape and rapists without some mention of the sexual things that motivate them.

I would also like to say a few words about coincidence. Tracking William down in this story involves a lot of coincidence and some would say it could never happen that way. Maybe not, but if you think back over your own life you might find certain parts of it have a lot to do with coincidence. I know mine certainly has.

Finally, here's some food for thought: Is it right to impose a requirement that men who have been convicted of sexual crimes register with local authorities after they have served their jail time? After all, if you steal a loaf of bread and spend some time in jail for it, we don't expect you to be labeled as a criminal for the rest of your life? Do we rightly require this registration to protect the community or are we just sticking our head in the sand because we are afraid and don't really know how to salvage these men? Like I said—food for thought.

P. S: Don't come to my house looking for answers to tax questions.